LARRY BEINHART IS THE WINNER OF

Edgar Award

Three Edgar Nominations

Grand Prix de Literature Policier

Gold Dagger

Barry Nomination

Fulbright

New York Times Notable Book of the Year

PRAISE FOR LARRY BEINHART

"The man can really write."
—*NY Times*

"John Grisham meets Jon Stewart."
—*Rolling Stone*

"A tour de force of subversive wit."
—*New Yorker*

"The most important piece of political fiction of the 21ˢᵗ Century."
—*Democratic Talk Radio*

"The Best Fiction in Years."
—*Freemantle Herald (Australia)*

"Funny, ingenious and outrageous."
—*LA Times*

SALVATION BOULEVARD

ALSO BY LARRY BEINHART

Fog Facts

The Librarian

Wag the Dog

No One Rides for Free

You Get What You Pay For

Foreign Exchange

How to Write a Mystery

Wag the Dog

The basis for the film with Robert DeNiro and Dustin Hoffman

Selected by *Capital* (the German version of *Forbes*)
as one of The Top 1,000 Books of the Last 1,000 Years

Selected by Tempe, Arizona,
as one of The Great Books of the 20th Century

Selected by the *Wall Street Journal*
as one of The Five Best Books on Public Relations

SALVATION BOULEVARD

BY
LARRY BEINHART

NATION
BOOKS

NEW YORK
WWW.NATIONBOOKS.ORG

Nation Books is a co-publishing venture of the Nation Institute and the Perseus Books Group.

Books published by Nation Books are available at special discounts for bulk purchases in the United States by corporations, institutions, and other organizations. For more information, please contact the Special Markets Department at Perseus Books Group, 2300 Chestnut Street, Suite 200, Philadelphia, PA 19103, or call (800) 810-4145, ext. 5000, or e-mail special.markets@perseusbooks.com.

Designed by Linda Harper

Library of Congress Cataloging-in-Publication Data
Beinhart, Larry.
Salvation Boulevard / by Larry Beinhart.
   P. cm.
 ISBN 978–1–56858–411–9
 I. Title.
PS3552.E425S25 2008
813'.54—dc22

2008007049

10 9 8 7 6 5 4 3 2 1

To my family:
My father and mother, who taught me to think,
My wife, who inspires me and holds me to the highest standards,
My children, who taught me that there are far deeper currents
than mere thought.

1

Ahmad looked like hell.

He also looked like a kid. I knew he was twenty-one. But if he'd been cleaned up and had civilian clothes on, and I saw him in the hallways at my daughter's high school, I could've believed he was sixteen, seventeen years old.

That was what Manny wanted me to see. Manny had a cause. And for some reason, he wanted me to join up. I didn't understand why. It was unnecessary. Pay me; I do my job. Causes are dangerous; everyone knows that.

Right now, the kid was in an orange jumpsuit, his wrists and ankles manacled, connected by a chain that connected to another chain that wrapped around his waist. He had prison-issue slippers on his feet. He was scared, as scared as I've ever seen anyone. And he'd been hurt. He had bruising on the right side of his face, and he had trouble moving, and when Manny reached out to shake his manacled hand, he flinched.

"Easy son, easy," I said, soft and slow, talking halfway between the way you talk to a person and a wild animal you're trying to coax to your side.

He looked at me, his eyes dark as the night and wet as the rain. He couldn't help himself; the tears started to flow. It happens that way, if you've been brutalized enough: the first gentle words you hear, the tears start to flow.

"Come on," I said and put my hand on his arm to lead him to the yellow plastic chair. They'd provided us with three chairs, no table. They'd even taken Manny's pens away and given him a felt tip for making notes. Pencils were too dangerous. This was not normal. Usually there was a table—bring your own pen, tape recorder, pads.

The CO that brought him in was Leander Peale. He was mostly called Lee, sometimes Leap or Leapy. He worked prisoner escort a lot, and both Manny and I knew him. He was born-again. Saved him from a life of crank before he lost all his teeth. He still rode a bike and had a "Born to Lose" tat beneath his uniform. He used to have an imp with an enlarged penis that said "Satan's Spawn," but he'd spent some serious dollars having it lasered off. He was an okay guy. Not an asshole. He knew that we all have to live together; we all have our jobs.

In addition to Lee, in his CO uniform, there were two suits. They didn't introduce themselves. Manny asked, "Who are you?"

The older one, a homely man with twenty-year-old pits of teen acne still marking his face and thin straw hair, muttered, "Homeland Security," from between thin, grudging lips. But who knows what that means. When I put my hand on Ahmad's arm, he and his younger partner, an iron pumper, thick in the chest, both hunched like they were ready to pounce if the kid went berserk or I tried to spring him.

"Back off," Manny said dismissively.

Ahmad dropped to his knees and put his hands on my leg. He hugged my thigh and wept. "Save me, please save me from these people."

That was too much for the Homeland Security guys to accept. No crying, no touching, no accusations. So they moved. They were coming for him. Manny got between us and them. He looked at them with the authority of a man who sues people for a living and wins.

"They are beating me," Ahmad said, both hands now on my thigh, holding on like I was a life raft, looking up at me like I was the key to the kingdom of heaven. "They stick things in my ass. I am innocent. Tell my mother, please tell my mother, I'm innocent. Don't let them beat me anymore. Please."

Manny looked at Lee.

"Not me," Lee said. We have to parse these things. He didn't say it never happened. He didn't even say, "He was resisitin'," like he would have if some other COs had been overzealous. In the circumstances, it was as good as jumping on a pine box, pointing a long-boned forefinger, and screaming, "Yes, they did that to him!"

"Alright, this is over," the older of the two said.

Manny flipped open his cell phone and took the guy's picture. Then his partner, then one of Ahmad holding my knee and sobbing like a boy who'd just been raped.

"He's lying," the older one said. "He's lying. They train them to say that. And weep and cry."

"He had to be questioned. What if he was planning more murders? What if it was part of a plot? What about that?"

"Tell me your names," Manny said. He's got lots of voices. This one sounded like George Patton on a bad day. "I want names and numbers. Give me some badge numbers."

"We don't answer to you."

"Why don't we all back off, guys," Lee said.

"Back way the hell off," Manny said. "I want to talk to my client. I want the privacy to which he and I are entitled. And I want your assurances this room is not wired. And believe me, if I have any cause to do so, I will see to it that I ask you again under oath. Now, let me talk to my client."

"Come on," I said, trying to lift the kid up. He didn't want to let go. "Come on, you have to sit down and tell us what's going on."

2

Islamic warriors martyr themselves in order to kill infidels.

There's a born-again Christian ruling the West who says he gets his orders from God and he's running a Crusade. It might as well be the twelfth century.

The corpse in this book should be God.

But He lives.

The words belonged to the dead man. His name was Nathaniel MacLeod. He was a professor of philosophy at the University of the Southwest, the largest institution of higher learning in the state, the largest between Texas and California, for that matter.

A bullet had gone through his head. It had entered his right temple and exited near the nexus of the left temporal, parietal, and frontal bones.

The words, which became, in effect, his final words, were on the opening page of a manuscript found in front of him, leaning against his computer screen, the foot of the page stopped by the keyboard.

This is a great mystery.

Contrary to popular wisdom, it's relatively easy to disprove the existence of God. At least of a meaningful, beneficent God.

Furthermore, we have, during recent decades, accumulated enough new knowledge of the universe, and more particularly of ourselves, to understand why we believe. And why it is so important to us, important enough to kill over.

A gun had been found on the floor beside the chair, where it would naturally have fallen from his right hand if he had shot himself. It was a relatively rare and unusual gun, and it was owned by MacLeod. The stippling and powder burns around the entry wound indicated that the barrel had been held against his head when the shot was fired.

In short, it looked like a self-inflicted wound, and when he was first found, the police called it a suicide.

A dead white man is not quite as exciting as a missing white girl, but it's big enough. Especially an educated, upper-middle-class white man, not a piece of white trash shot up in a raid on a meth lab. It got a lot of local and regional coverage. The news shows brought in all sorts of commentators to puff out the story: psychologists, suicide counselors, student counselors, spokespersons from the university. Because of the God-and-atheism angle, they brought in religious figures too. Pastor Paul Plowright, who runs the biggest church in the state, got the most air time.

"Is anyone surprised," Pastor Plowright asked the anchor of WSVX's six o'clock news, "that an atheist committed suicide?

"The despair an atheist must feel is unimaginable to a believer. The emptiness, the hollowness inside. And, of course, atheists have no moral center. To them everything is relative, anything is allowed, so why not commit suicide? They don't understand that life is sacred. Theirs is a culture of death; ours is a culture of life."

The anchor asked him, "What about his statement that it's easy to disprove the existence of God?"

Pastor Plowright smiled gently. Viewers could see he was restraining his contempt out of respect for the dead. "Unbelievers have been saying that for thousands of years. And they convince no one."

"What about this book of his?"

"Bob, how can you disprove something that exists?"

Plowright was far less restrained in his Sunday sermon and in his television and radio broadcasts. The manuscript, he said, was proof positive that there is a war against Christianity. The front lines are at our so-called great universities. The academic elites are Satan's storm troopers.

The student newspaper, the USW *Clarion Call*, said MacLeod had been very popular with his students, that he'd been politically active, especially in the search for peace in the Middle East and most recently in the fight against the privatization of the state-owned university's $5.3 billion endowment fund.

It also published the rest of that first page, including this:

Morality is always the red flag of believers. If we remove God, they exclaim, everyone immediately dives into a drug-addled orgy of degeneracy, excess, and criminal irresponsibility, and the world goes to hell in a handbasket.

That's not true, on the face of it.

There have been numerous societies throughout history—as there still are today—without a monotheistic god, and some with no gods at all, and they have been quite as moral and orderly as Jewish, Christian, and Islamic states. Nor is there any correlation within a given society between the fervency of belief and moral conduct.

Actually, a clear look at morality is the strongest argument against God.

It was as if there were a debate going on between a dead man and a live one.

They themselves would have called it something more than a debate, a battle for souls.

It's natural to assume that a living man has all the advantages over a dead man. But this certainly hasn't been the case since the invention of the written word. Nathaniel MacLeod hadn't done very well against the Bible, a book far older than his own, its authors long dead. How would Pastor Paul Plowright fare against Professor MacLeod's pages?

Absolutely, the opening round went to Plowright.

But then the police suddenly announced that MacLeod's death had not been a suicide. It had been a murder. A suspect had been arrested.

3

Manny was the Goldfarb of Grantham, Glume, Wattly, and Goldfarb, one of the three biggest law offices in the city. The largest was owned by a New York firm, with branches in Los Angeles, Houston, and Washington, D.C. GGW&G was said to be the most profitable. They rolled over billable hours like an electric meter counting watts. Most of their work was corporate. Manny did crime because he had a taste for it.

"So, who do you have?" I asked.

"Ahmad Nazami," he said.

"Manny," I said, "you're not normally the saint of lost causes."

"Do you have a problem working on it?"

"Why should I?"

"I know you're a member of Plowright's cathedral, and he's been on a tear about it, and sometimes people get funny around religion and God."

"Manny, Sunday I give to God, Saturday I give to my wife, five days a week, I belong to Mr. Green."

"That's what I wanted to hear," he said.

"Is what I hear in the news true?" I asked him.

"Is what you hear in the news ever true? Come on, it's been wake-up time for ten years now. Whaddaya mean 'is what I hear in the news true?'"

"I mean I hear it's a slam dunk for the prosecution. That the suspect confessed. I also hear that he's a foreign kid, no money, some kind of Islamist, that it's a terrorist thing, won't even happen in court, national security and all that, he's going to be whisked away to one of those tribunals."

Manny slammed his fist down on the desk. He was wearing a shirt that cost $300, $350. A $150 tie, wide and straight, pimp my neck. The jacket of his $2,400 suit hung over the back of his chair. The view out his window made it the priciest real estate in the city. Manny loved money, and Manny made money. But here he was, slamming his fist down on the desk so hard his coffee mug took a little hop and clack. "Not if I can fuckin' help it."

The way he looked at me, I was afraid that he was going to ask me to cut my rate or even work for nothing. Grantham, Glume, Wattly, and Goldfarb was one of the places that I always walked into happy because it was one of the few law firms where, pardon the expression, they never tried to Jew me down. "This isn't some pro bono thing?" I asked. The problem was that if Manny asked me to cut my rate or throw him a freebie, I would. He was a good client, and you have to do extras for a good client, like your favorite breakfast place gives you free refills. But on top of that, because we were friends.

"You know what, Carl, it wouldn't hurt you to work for the good once in a while. Wouldn't hurt me either. It wouldn't hurt at all."

"Pro bono, Manny?" I asked in disbelief.

He turned his back on me and gimped over to the window. He tries to cover it up with his clothes and a lift in one shoe, but his left leg is crooked, skinny, scarred, and shorter than the right. He looked out on the river and the city that had grown along its banks, every year growing richer and growing faster.

Whatever he saw there, he said, "You gotta believe in something."

"Yes," I said neutrally. Maybe he was going to spin some argument about giving back. About tithing, in a secular way.

"A man has a *right* to confront his accusers." He said it fiercely, like a losing lawyer in front of a hanging judge. "He has a *right* to see the evidence on which he is charged. He has a *right* to a trial. A *right* to a defense."

"He's a terrorist," I said, shrugging it off. "A Muslim terrorist. He blew a guy away."

"Get the fuck out of here!" he snapped.

"Fine," I said, rising.

"Wait," he said.

"What's going on, Manny?"

"You always think it can't happen here, right? Alright, maybe they do it in Afghanistan, Iraq: there's a sweep, they pick up Ali and Abdul, and they throw 'em in Abu Ghraib. Or grab some guy, funny name and mustache at the border, and put him on a plane to Syria.

"The kid's an American. As American as my parents were, damn it. His parents sent him over here nine, ten years ago, escaping the ayatollahs and the Pasdaran. He's over here on his own, trying hard. Learned to speak English like he was born here. Applied for citizenship and just got it a few months ago. He's at the university on a hardship scholarship. Plus, he works. He's an okay student. So what are we doing here? Tribunals? Secret trials? Come on, Carl, is there anything you believe in?"

"Yes, Manny, there are things I believe in. I believe in God Almighty, that Jesus Christ is my personal savior, and in truth, justice, and the American way. But you're not being real clear about what you're doing and what you want, which is unlike you. You're a lawyer, Mr. Goldfarb, one of the best, and usually you're very, very good at saying exactly what you mean."

"Alright, Carl, here's what I'm saying. First of all, there's money."

"All you had to do was say so."

"Second of all," he said, holding up his hand, telling me to wait, "there's pressure. You're right, they want to take this kid away and disappear him. Take him to Guantánamo or rendition him or something. There's big pressure. So, I gotta ask you, are you prepared to stand up to it?" He pointed an accusing finger at me and said in quotes, "'Working to free terrorists!' 'Working against America!'—whatever the hell they're going to say. They'll even say 'traitor!'"

"As long as they don't call me a Liberal," I said, trying to lighten this up.

"Well, they might," Manny said. "They might do more."

"You don't make it sound real attractive."

"I promise you this at least: if you get charged with anything, this firm will defend you. At no cost to you. You have my word on it."

"Now you're scaring me. Maybe I should take a pass."

"Carl, wait."

"What?"

"Meet the kid. Talk to him. Tell me what you think. Will you do that?"

"Sure, alright. When?"

"Now. Come out to the prison with me."

I nodded.

He took the fancy suit jacket off the back of his chair and slipped it on. It was a beautiful piece of tailoring.

"I got a question for you," I said. A capital crime, a slam dunk, an Arab killing an American—before it was done this would be a seven-figure defense bill. "Who's putting up the big bucks for his defense?"

"You know what, Carl," he said, charging past me with his funny swinging gait and leading the way out to the long, carpeted hall, "we're gonna have fun with this one. They're gonna throw everything they have at it. It'll be a dog fight—there'll be press conferences, demonstrations, and death threats. It's gonna be a blast."

4

So, there we were, up at the state penitentiary. I got Ahmad settled down enough to speak coherently so Manny could interview him. "Yes, yes, of course, I knew Professor MacLeod. I took a class from him," Ahmad said. "Nate was a good guy."

"Nate? You were on a first name basis?"

"Yes, I am, we are, we all are, with most of the professors, except maybe in the large lecture classes."

"So, how close were you with him?"

"He was a professor," Ahmad said, trying hard to be normal about it. "He was the kind who liked to talk to his students. He was accessible."

"You ever talk with him privately?"

"I don't know, maybe, maybe once or twice. In his office."

"About what?"

"Course material. Stuff from his classes."

"What was he teaching?"

"Philosophy and Religion 342."

"Did the things he said upset you?"

"I didn't kill him. I didn't, I didn't," he started to cry again. Not the kind of crying you can carry on a conversation through, taste the salt of your own tears as they roll down from your eyes to your mouth, that sometimes you break free of to laugh. These were tears of despair, of a nightmare that had neither cause nor hope.

"Of course not," I said, taking over the questioning from Manny, who looked relieved. Then I repeated, "Of course not," with even more reassurance.

"You believe me?" the boy said. He didn't have that air of trying out a story, then slyly watching his listeners as if they were a focus group, like some defendants do. His question was about me and whether he dared to hope.

I have a stock answer, which is that it doesn't matter if I believe or not. I'm a professional, and I'll do my best either way. Saves me from having to worry about troublesome things like guilt or innocence. Nobody wants to free a guilty man or fry an innocent one. Saves me from lying, from making a judgment that I will later discover to be wrong. Besides, they're hardly ever innocent. I have a stock answer, but this time I didn't use it. This time I said, "I believe you." I didn't know if I did or I didn't, but it seemed I had to say so if we were going to get anywhere.

"I didn't do it," he said.

"I know," I said, digging myself in deeper, "I know. But you know what we have to talk about, your confession."

"I had to. They made me."

"How? How'd they make you?"

"They said . . . they said, they were going to send me to Egypt, and no one would know where I was. I would never see my family, I would never come back, and they would tor . . . tor . . . torture me."

"Egypt? Why Egypt?"

"I don't know," he said. "I'm not Egyptian. I'm not even Arab; I'm Persian."

"Iranian, I thought."

"Iran, Persia, yes, the same place. My family likes to say Persia. They are proud to be Persians. They're not sure about Iran."

"Who? Who made you do this?"

"I don't know. I mean, I don't know their names."

"Their faces, would you recognize them?"

"No," he said.

Lee said, "Hey," like knocking to ask permission to enter hearing range. He had a paper cup of something for the kid to drink. I said, "Yeah, thanks, Lee, bring it over." The two suits were hovering in the background, in the shadows.

Ahmad shrank back as the CO approached. "It's alright," I said. "He's just got something for you to drink." Then I said to Lee, "I'll take it," holding my hand out, and Lee gave me the cup. It was dark, Coke, Pepsi, some kind of cola. I passed it to Ahmad. His chains only let his hands move about six inches from his waist, so I had to hand it to him low. To drink it, he had to hunch over and double himself up.

Manny stood up and thanked Lee with deep sincerity, offering his hand to shake. Lee took it, and money passed from Manny's hand to his. "I don't want any more shit to happen to him."

"Not on my watch," Lee said. And maybe it wouldn't. But the silent half of his answer was that he couldn't answer for the other sixteen hours in the day. Or the fifteen minutes he was on a coffee break.

It was almost impossible for Ahmad to drink with his shackles on. The angles don't work. No matter how you hold the cup on the tips of your fingers, fold yourself double and bend your neck like a goose, your face is down, and you can't pour up. "Let me help you," I said and took the cup from him. He nodded with gratitude and straightened in his chair. I held it to his lips and let him sip.

"What's going on here?" Manny asked Lee.

"He's a dangerous man," Lee said. "A terrorist." And he turned away and left us alone.

"So, tell me the story, from the beginning," I said to Ahmad.

5

Sometime between midnight and dawn—maybe it was three, four in the morning—he wasn't sure—they came for him. Ahmad rented a room in a private house, off campus. He was in a deep sleep.

Someone slapped his head. He opened his eyes, and a flashlight was shining in his face. It seemed very bright, so bright he blinked and tried to turn away. When he turned, he saw a gun. Ahmad tried to raise his hands. "Put 'em behind you, put 'em behind you." He was blinded by the light and couldn't see the man speaking behind the gun.

He didn't understand and said, "What? What? Huh?"

"Your hands, put your fuckin' hands behind you."

The other man—maybe there were just two, maybe more, but at least two—hit him on the forearm with the gun. A short, sharp stroke, and it hurt like hell. He still had the bruise. Manny took a picture of it with his cell phone.

"Put your fuckin' hands behind you." It wasn't loud, half a whisper, but it was commanding, demanding, certain.

So he did. He pushed himself up into a sitting position and put his hands behind his back.

"Turn around. Stand up and turn around. Keep your hands behind you."

The light stayed in his face while he rose. He wanted to shield his face with his hand, but he didn't dare. As soon as he was up and his back was turned, someone grabbed his hands and put PlastiCuffs on his wrists. Then he heard a tearing sound and a moment later realized it was duct tape, and it was slapped across his mouth, and he was afraid he wouldn't be able to breathe, and he began to panic and tried to struggle, but he was rapped with something hard on the back of his head, and it hurt so much that he fell forward onto the bed. Two of them grabbed him. They grabbed him and yanked him up, and when he was up, one of them let go, and the other put a bag over his head and everything went dark. Even cuffed and with his mouth taped, he hadn't felt so helpless, totally helpless, as he did then, after he'd been hooded.

Ahmad slept in his underwear—a pair of boxer shorts and a tank top. That was all he had on when they marched him out. Nobody said a word as they went. They just shoved him along, and he had no choice but to comply, not knowing what he might step on or bang into in his blindness. He was more than just being coerced by them. In his need to be guided, he was dependent on them.

A car was waiting, a full-sized SUV, judging from the height of it when they shoved him in. Nobody said a word the whole time.

Then they drove. He didn't know how long—a half-hour, forty-five minutes, a hundred hours. He tried to calm the panic every time it rose up, to make himself breathe through his nose every time the fear got so great it felt like he would choke on it. Not a word was said by them—except when he tried, through the tape, to make some kind of noise. Then he'd get a slap and a command to shut up.

They put him, he claimed, on a plane.

They told him to get out of the car. They walked him across greasy blacktop—he could feel it with bare feet—and walked him up a narrow set of metal steps. They put him in an airplane seat and even fastened his seat belt for him, his hands still lashed behind his back, chafing, his shoulders starting to hurt from the position. The seat felt cold and plasticlike.

Then he heard the noise of the jets coming on and felt the plane begin to taxi. It stopped, vibrating in place. Then it began to accelerate, which he could feel, and it rose up into the air, tilting him back into his seat, making him feel more bewildered and terrified by the minute.

When they leveled off, rough hands came and tried to pull his underwear off. Why would anyone want to do that? To do sexual things to him? What was going on? He tried to struggle. To keep them on. Someone slapped him on the head. Then someone punched him, hard, in the stomach. He was completely unprepared, and the fist sank deep. There was pain and shock. He thought he was going to vomit.

The punch stopped him from struggling, and he allowed the hands to take his underwear off. Then he felt someone touching his genitals. Such a thing had never happened to him before, an unseen stranger touching his penis and testicles. He was sure it was a man. This was not a time or place for women. Ahmad was not some sheepherding Afghani who would be distraught to have a woman see him naked—he was an American, comfortable with himself, his body, with regular sex and everybody doing the humpity-hump on BET. But for a man to be doing this to him was a special invasion, a humiliation.

But they didn't want sex, whoever it was doing this. No. He felt something cold and hard touch him, pinch him down there. Little clips.

Then the pain came.

Huge, bizarre, tearing pain, right from his own penis, sending spasms and explosions of agony.

Once. Twice. Three times.

Then there was a respite. Someone reached up under the hood, grabbed the tape, and ripped it off his mouth. He gulped in air, sobbing for it, but that sucked the hood into his mouth. He spit it out. "Why? Why? Why? What are you doing?"

The answer came back, "Why did you kill him?"

"Who? Who? I didn't kill anyone."

They connected the wire, and the pain came back.

Sobbing, catching his breath, writhing when it stopped, he asked, "Why? Why? Please, please stop."

The answer came back, "Why? Why? Tell us why you killed him."

He denied doing it. He asked them, pleaded with them, to tell him what they were talking about. As soon as he did that, the pain came.

It went back and forth like that, but eventually they began letting him know the answers they wanted, that he had killed Nathaniel MacLeod, professor of philosophy and religion.

Why? Why would he kill him?

They began to feed him the answers to that too, and he began to agree, bit by bit—anything to stop the electrical shock coming up his penis. At some point, he urinated all over his seat. He realized that the seat had a plastic cover on it. Memory is a funny thing. It's not a filing cabinet with facts slipped in as they arrive. A memory is created every time we remember. So the moments blur and get shuffled around. Maybe he realized that later, maybe at the moment he pissed, when it puddled beneath him, hot and wet, and stayed there, cooling off, stinking and itching. He didn't know.

"Alright, alright, you want me to say I killed him. I will say it. Okay. I killed him. I killed him . . . Why? Tell me again, why?"

"He was a fuckin' atheist, that's why."

"Okay, I killed him because . . ."

"No, you dumb fuck," a different voice said. "Apostate, he was an apostate."

"Apostate, atheist, who gives a fuck."

"It's different."

"Okay, because he was an atheist apostate," the first interrogator said, annoyed at being corrected. "Alright?"

"Yeah, that's fine."

"That's why, sure," Ahmad said. "Please stop."

"Fine," the interrogator said. "You're going to have to write it down and sign it."

"But it's not true."

"Listen to me." The second guy, the one who said it was "apostate," not "atheist," was speaking, sounding friendly, even kind, playing the good cop. "Listen to me, Ahmad. We're flying east. We can keep on going, and we'll bring you to Egypt. Turn you over to the Egyptian secret service. Compared to them, we're sweethearts. We're like your mother and father. You understand? Once we give you to them, you'll disappear. Your mother and father, they'll never hear from you, never know where you went. Write it down, sign it, the plane turns around and brings you home. Home, Ahmad. Just write and sign."

So he signed.

6

We didn't say a word until we were all the way out, out of the interview room, out of the main prison building with its great central tower and the five cell blocks radiating out from it, then out past the great wall that ringed the whole compound, cameras posted everywhere on slow swivels, watching, watching, watching, and like all the other walls, topped with spirals of razor wire.

The big gates swung shut behind us. We were wrapped in Manny's Mercedes Benz S600, the one with twelve cylinders and Nappa leather upholstery, the one that costs $140,000, and moving away from the place before we spoke.

"He sounds convincing," I said.

"Yes, he does," Manny said emphatically. Manny believed.

"I had a job like this once," I said.

"You did?"

"A woman, said she was abducted by aliens."

"Come on."

"She sounded totally convincing," I said. "Completely sincere. As convincing as Ahmad does."

"What'd she want from you?"

"She wanted me to find evidence, show it to her husband."

"So he'd believe her?"

"She'd disappeared for four days. He thought she'd run off with some guy. She said no, she'd been abducted in a space ship."

"So what'd you do?"

"I got her details, where she was when it happened, where they returned her to. Then checked her credit cards. Found where she stopped for gas, bought some food. Went, asked questions, asked if anyone had seen the flying saucer, showed her picture, asked if anyone had seen her. They hadn't seen the saucer, but they'd seen her. And the guy she met. Found the motel, nice place, out in the desert, private cabins, pool. Even found a chamber maid who overheard them going at it."

"So what did you do?"

"I wrote it up, sat her down, and told her what I'd found."

"What'd she say?"

"She screamed at me. Called me a liar. She accused me of being part of the conspiracy, the cover-up."

"The point is, she was lying?"

"I don't know," I said. "She didn't convince me that she'd had sex with aliens instead of an aluminum-siding salesman. But she convinced me that she believed it."

We got on the interstate. Manny took it up to eighty-five and put the car on cruise control. It felt quieter and more rock solid than a normal car doing fifty-five. Money can do great things.

"I believe him," Manny said.

"Alright."

"We have to prepare to go to trial."

"You don't think they'll take a plea?"

"*I* won't take a plea," he said, emphatic and final.

"They got a confession," I said. "Who knows what else."

"The confession was coerced."

"That's what he says."

"They'll kill him inside. Aside from the usual, someone'll kill him."

21

The main gangs in our facilities, like in the rest of the West and Southwest, are Nuestra Familia, the Black Guerillas, the Mexican Mafia, the Aryan Brotherhood, and the Nazi Low Riders. No memberships available to Iranian Americans. He'd be sold into slavery, turned into a girl. Then one day, someone would kill him to show how patriotic they were.

"As part of the plea, you might ask for super-max," I said. "Or even protective custody."

Our new super-max is one person per cell, Plexiglas fronts on the cells, cameras looking in, and the prisoners are in their cells twenty-three hours a day. For their own protection, or for any other reason, they can be in twenty-four hours a day.

"Someone'll get him," Manny said.

It was true. There would always be a moment. A trip to the infirmary. In the library. On the way to a family visit. Or to see his lawyer.

"You need gas?" I asked.

"If I need gas, the thing tells me. It says, 'Manny,' and then it says, 'I need some petrol, please.'"

"Does it really do that?"

"With a German accent," Manny said. "Somewhere between the guy who does the commercials and Arnold Schwarzenegger."

"So let's get a cup of coffee," I said.

"You really want a coffee?" he asked.

"There's a Barnes & Noble off the next exit. They have lattés and all that stuff. How about that?"

"Lattés? You're gonna drink a latté? Rush Limbaugh will disown you."

"You know what's hard to do?"

"What?"

"It's hard to know if you're being followed on a freeway. Straight line, everybody zooming along, you got your cruise control on, steady at eighty-five. The guy behind us, he's steady at eighty-five. So are thirty, forty other cars."

"One of them's following us?"

"It's worth the price of a cup of coffee," I said, "even an overpriced latté, to find out."

"Next exit?"

"Yeah."

"How far is it?"

"Mile, mile and a half."

Manny smiled and put his foot down. I didn't hear a thing, didn't feel a tremor or a shake as the speedometer rolled up to 140 miles per hour. "Terrorists send messages," he said thoughtfully, gesturing with his right hand, as if doing 140 didn't require special attention. "9/11 was a message. Suicide bombings, they're messages. If this was a terrorist killing, where's the message?"

"Maybe the manuscript," I said.

"How so?"

"The manuscript that they found with him, maybe it wasn't just there by accident, maybe someone made sure it was there, a way of saying that this is what happens to people who say, 'God is dead.' Killed him for being an atheist."

"Apostate," Manny said.

"What's the difference?"

"Atheist is when you don't believe there is a God. An apostate is someone who joins a religion and then quits it, renounces it."

A Ford Explorer had broken out of the pack and was trying to keep up. I hoped their teeth were rattling and the guy with his hands on the wheel had sweaty palms. We were almost at the exit ramp.

"In Islam, once you join, if you quit, that calls for the death penalty." Manny turned the wheel and whipped from the fast lane across to middle and slow lanes to the off ramp while he spoke. When we hit the ramp, he took the car down to eighty, maybe seventy-five. The light at the bottom of the ramp had gone yellow. By the time we reached it, it had turned red. Manny accelerated, shot through, and made a left-hand turn. You could tell, he was one of those people who thought that life had granted them immunity.

"You really want the coffee?" he asked me.

"Sure."

He pulled into the parking lot in front of the big bookstore. "My treat," he said.

"Thanks."

"Well, it bills to the client."

"Of course," I said, getting out. I pushed the door closed behind me. The thunk was rich and satisfying. You don't pop for $140K if it doesn't have that thunk. When he stepped out, I asked over the roof of the car, "And that is? I mean, who's paying?"

"Hezbollah," he said.

"Don't even joke like that."

"You think they're listening as well as following?"

"At some point, yeah." I said.

"Ostensibly the family," he said. The car locked itself as we walked away from it. "It's hard for them to get money out of their country. So I think they're getting help from an Iranian-American friendship association. Lot of very rich Iranians here. They don't want to start being targeted. So, who was that following us?"

"Manny, making terrorist jokes these days is like making bomb jokes at the airport."

"Oh, come on."

"If we're going to fuck with these people," I said, "don't make jokes. You'll hear them being played back to you." I saw the Explorer driving slowly, out on the road, like the people inside were looking for something. "There they are."

Manny looked at the blue Ford. It had a government-issue look to it. What Ahmad had told us was just not possible. It wasn't possible. So why were we being followed?

"The guy gets shot, in his office, on campus," Manny said. "Somebody finds the body. They call campus security? Or 911? Even if they call 911, who gets the call? The police or the campus cops?"

The Explorer went past.

"So, the campus cops are the first on the scene," Manny went on. "They write up a report. Then the cops come, and they write up a report, another one. I want you to get those reports for me."

"Discovery," I said. "File your regular discovery motions."

"They'll say 'terrorist,' 'national security,' and they may get a rollover judge who's been shitting his pants since 9/11, or who hates defense attorneys anyway, or who worships the 'order' part of 'law and order' and is annoyed by the 'law' part, and believe me, I know several like that, and the police reports stay buried.

"Even if we get a good judge, they're gonna try. Our DA is not Jack McCoy. When he went to law school, he figured ethics was an elective and took the course in getting TV face time instead."

7

Hello, God. Hello, Jesus. It's good to be with you again.

I know you're with me all the time. I know that, but, you know what I mean, to take some special time.

This cathedral, Cathedral of the Third Millennium, is an awe-inspiring place. It has a cantilevered roof, with no visible support, and it's so high that it feels like the canopy of the sky, the canopy of heaven itself. And way up above, there are 1,250 small, quartz halogen fixtures whose bulbs refract the light and seem to twinkle with shards of color. Not full colors, like Christmas lights, but tints that hide in the white, sometimes there and sometimes not, the kind of colors that the stars themselves display so that you stare at them and ask, Is that one blue? Is that one red?

It's good to take some special time to be with you in a special place.

I was raised lackadaisical Methodist. Mother made us go to church. My father, my half-brother, and I all wore jackets and ties and pants with creases and polished shoes and tried to stay awake. If we couldn't manage that, we tried not to snore.

That's about all there was to it for me.

In my late teens my life spun gradually out of control, and as an adult it spun wider and wider, and I lost my first wife and the family I had with her, and I couldn't find any brakes to put on myself, so it went wider and wilder, and then I lost my second wife and I was on my way to losing my life, I was lying on the bottom, sitting in the gutter, the taste of failures coming up into my mouth like the taste of bile when the vomit rises, a flavor I'd tasted far too often, and someone said to me, a fellow police officer, that was when I was on the job, though on suspension and scheduled for a hearing that would likely have me fired, and Alan Stephens said come to church with me and he brought me to the Cathedral of the Third Millennium and for some reason I did and found myself in tears, real tears and then I went down that aisle and Pastor Paul Plowright put his hands on me, he put one hand on my shoulder and one on my forehead, and I felt the jolt go through me, and I gave myself to Jesus.

The spinning stopped. There was a center. There was order, and I was able to walk away from the alcohol and the whoring and the car crashes and a variety of other excesses that fill the verses of the songs they sing at twelve-step meetings throughout the land. The word went to the hearing board that I'd been saved, and they gave me a pass.

That was six years ago. Four years ago, I met my wife, Gwen, my third, current, and final wife, here at CTM.

She can be daring and has a great sense of adventure, but my first two wives would find her worldviews, especially her views on marriage and a woman's place, to be like putting on a burka and a chador. But there is so much peace in our home. So much order between us. So much comfort in our lives. We made a home that was a suitable place to raise a child, and I was able to get sole custody of Angie, the child of my second marriage, when her mother went to prison because it was genuinely the best thing for our daughter. It would not have been so without Jesus Christ, without the church that brought me to Him, and without the wife that He sent unto me.

Going to church is like going home, going to a picnic with your old friends, getting hugged and loved, and being reminded that there are people, lots of people, who have the same kinds of troubles that you do and who have found the same solution, Jesus Christ. That puts us all on the same team.

And when church is full, that's over sixty-four hundred of us.

That and being uplifted in song and giving your soul a chance to rev its engine all the way up, screaming and crying if you want. Make no mistake, it's a high, a high that doesn't leave you crashing, dirt in your mouth, shame smeared all over the memories you wish the morning light could wash away. A high that lingers and keeps you balanced and sane through the strains of the week to come.

A lot of military and law-enforcement people are members of the church. You can tell who they are just by looking at them.

The people in the service, mostly from the air force base seven miles down the road, are fit, upright, and have short hair. The state police are similar, but their hair is shorter, and they're angrier. The cops from the city and the various towns look like they were once in the service, but now they only work out once or twice a week, if that, and they eat donuts. The correction officers look like they were headed for a life on the other side of the bars but then somehow took a right turn and now are trying to look like they're cops.

Leander Peale was there with his wife and several other Christian COs. We made eye contact and traded smiles of fellowship. I saw Jeremiah Hobson, who was once my lieutenant when I was on the job, living for the city. Now he runs security for CTM, which is more than just the church but a whole empire of enterprises. He was wearing an expensive suit, tailored to hide his extra weight. Alan Stephens and I hugged each other on the way in. Since he brought me here the first time, I owe him my life.

A lot of my job is about contacts like them. It's part of what make me good at what I do and why I make a decent living from it.

"There are one point two billion Muslims," Paul Plowright, our pastor, said, standing up in front of the thousands, microphones and cameras recording him too, and he was as comfortable as your neighbor sipping an ice tea at a backyard barbecue.

He spoke as a man of reason; he spoke of facts. "And the vast majority of them, I am sure, I am sure, are good people. Yes, they are.

"It's only a tiny minority who believe in jihad, violent jihad.

"It's just that pesky minority.

"I don't know how small that minority is. Some people say it's just ten percent. Some say five percent. Some say it is as little as one percent. Just one percent."

"Just one percent," Pastor Plowright mused. "There are those who want to make you think you should not be concerned. Just one percent. There are those who would like you to think you have no cause for worry. Just one percent.

"Astonishing, isn't it, when the math is so easy to do. Why don't they do the math? Why don't they? What is one percent of one billion two hundred million? What is it?

"Why, it's one million two hundred thousand.

"Oh, that's a relief! Just one million two hundred thousand jihadists."

That got a huge response, led by the military guys and their families. Someone was acknowledging the size and power of the enemy they faced, understanding their job, what they were up against. They laughed and said, "Oh yeah! Oh yeah!" They clapped and whistled and chanted, "Hoo-ah! Hoo-ah!"

"That's all. A mere trifle," Plowright said, getting laughter and more applause.

"Willing to hijack airplanes and fly them into buildings full of civilians," he went on. Not funny now. Starting to preach it. "One million two hundred thousand willing to strap dynamite around their waists and get on a bus, a city bus, in the holy city of Jerusalem, in the land of the Bible, a city bus, filled with women going to the market, with children going to their lessons, a city bus, right in the middle of the day and ignite that dynamite, there in the holy city of Jerusalem.

"There are those who will tell you, it's just one percent, so why worry.

"There are those who will tell you that they are mostly over there, that we have our Homeland Security and we have our high alerts and we have the greatest military in the world. . . Hallelujah . . . ."

And the choir—the Angels they're called; Gwen used to sing with them—more dimly lit than the pastor so that you could forget they were there, now said, "Hallelujah," behind him in their heavenly voices, and their voices, though soft, were carried on the speakers throughout the Cathedral of the Third Millennium, and their voices came from all around and filled the room. If you were up among the clouds, weightless, those voices would waft you even higher.

But Plowright didn't need his Angels for emphasis. The congregation hoo-ahed, they clapped, they hollered, "Hallelujah."

"And we're taking the fight to the enemy. Hallelujah."

"Hallelujah," the Angels sang while the congregation roared, six thousand voices or more, in praise of the crusade to defend us all.

"But . . . , " Plowright said, calling a halt to the noise, "but they are not just over there. Oh no. Oh no.

"We find that once again, that they are here. That they are among us. There's the one billion two hundred million—then there's that one percent—one million, two hundred thousand, and out of that more than a million—there is one, there is one, right here!

"One crazed jihadist, Ahmad Nazami, who pretended to be some sort of refugee, who pretended to accept America's hospitality, America's amazingly generous hospitality, who took advantage of that hospitality to pick up a gun and murder a man because that man dared to disagree with his mad version of religion.

"How many more were on his list?

"How many were on Ahmad Nazami's list? Who was next?"

"Well, I too disagree with his religion," Pastor Plowright said. "Does that mean I'm next on his jihad hit list?"

"You disagree with his religion," he said to us.

And we agreed. "Jesus," many of us cried. "We belong to Jesus."

"We have the Bible right here. It's the word of God. I have read this book from cover to cover many times. So have many of you, so if I missed something here, feel free to correct me. But as I recall, nowhere does Jesus say, 'Oh, by the way, although I am the Son of God, I didn't get my gospel right.

"'So wait awhile, six hundred years or so, and then an illiterate Arab is going to come out of the desert to do a *rewrite.*' An Arab, by the way, who married a woman old enough to be his mother, married her for her money.

"Then he married at least fifteen other women.

"One of those marriages was to a six-year-old girl, and it was consummated when she was nine years old. Nine years.

"Do you think that God would send a child molester—we are speaking of a major-league pedophile—to come and redo the scriptures? What kind of religion worships a pedophile?

"Mohammed is a prophet that only the ACLU could love."

Laughter, applause, and amens!

"Let me tell you what Jesus did say. He said, 'I am the way and the truth.'" That got many more amens. "Not *a* way and *a* truth. *The* way and *the* truth, the one and only way and the one and only truth."

"Hallelujah," the chorus sang.

"So, am I next on his list?" he asked, then pointed out to us in the congregation. "What about you? And you? And you?" And into the camera. If you were watching at home, he pointed at you through your TV. "And you?"

"We are in a *war,*" he declared. "Our enemy has no hesitation to kill. No hesitation at all. Our enemy is barbaric and violent. This is not a war *between* civilizations. It is the war *for* civilization.

"I call upon you all to uphold the faith and the gun. This is a war we must win!

"There is no middle ground. Compromise is appeasement, and appeasement is death. Giving aid and comfort to the enemy is treason."

He didn't point at me or call out my name. But I felt as if he was talking directly to me.

I felt as if he was talking *about* me.

Walking out afterward, I felt like eyes were all over me.

The criminal justice business is a small world. Anyone in it knew who Manny Goldfarb was, and he would have been hated as thoroughly as the ACLU itself, except that he made so much money. Doing it for money made it right. I can't say exactly how or why, but that was the fact. Doing it for ideals made it suspect and twisted, subversive and evil, part of the plot against America and the War against Christianity.

A lot of them knew that Manny was defending Nazami, and quite a few would have known I was Manny's number one investigator, something I'm normally proud of, as he has the hot cases and the deep pockets.

But now, it was as if Plowright had hung a scarlet A around my neck, one that stood for ACLU, for Ahmad, for apostate and atheist, friend of the Antichrist.

Jeremiah Hobson gave me one of those cold, don't-fuck-up looks that high school football coaches practice in front of the mirror. He used it a lot when he was running my squad in narcotics.

Alan clapped his hand on my shoulder. He didn't say anything— nobody actually said anything. Maybe I was being paranoid. Alan's expression said, Good luck. Do what you gotta do.

Manny was my number one individual client, but the Christian community that connected through the Cathedral of the Third Millennium, as a group, gave me more business than he did. So I was trying to figure out how to keep everyone smiling, drop the case, and have Manny understand.

Then Leander Peale came up to me, the CO who'd brought Nazami to us. He gave me the kind of smile a hard man with a lot of hard biker miles beneath him has. An inexpensive flipper covered the loss of three teeth on his upper right. He came up close, his idea of discretion, the tobacco smell coming off of him, ashtray sharp, and said, "You gotta do something for that kid."

"I gotta?"

"If that kid kil't mor'n a roach, I'll draw you milk from a bull's tits."

"And you know that?" I asked.

"Carl, I walked C"—that was C block, not the worst, but bad enough—"seven years. Worked the hoo' d'ow'"—midnight to morning, the hoot owl shift. "You know they cry. They call you over, hunk' by the grate and whisper tales. Done the mainline three, and the row two"—that was central block and death row. "Heard every line of shit, every con, hustle, prayer, conversion, the born-agains, Nation of Islam, Black Israelites . . . . Makes you a judge a character, Carl, seeing what I seen.

"That Persia kid, he di'n't do the crime, and you know he can't do the time.

"A'other thing, those Homeland Security guys, there's something ain't right. I don't know what, but they give me the feelin' like some guy pissed on my leg, then tol' me it was rainin'."

"Who are they?" I asked. "Do you know who they are?"

"That's part of the strange. They got no names."

8

Alan Stephens was still on the job. He was someone I could reach out to, ask for a favor and trust too. It was the Tonto and Lone Ranger thing. He saved me, so you'd think I owed him, but he's never asked for a thing, and he keeps offering me his hand.

It was best not to see him at his office in the police building downtown. So I caught up with him at the Bible study group he runs for men in law enforcement. There's talk of making it *people* in law enforcement and letting women in, but right now the thinking is to let them start their own group, women in law enforcement, a separate-but-equal thing.

"As men in law enforcement," Alan said in his introductory statement, "we may well find ourselves in that terrible situation where we have to take someone else's life. Maybe in self-defense or to protect someone else. Sometimes we may unintentionally cause someone's death. We've all known car chases that resulted in a death—to one of our own, to the person running away, or most upsetting of all, to an innocent bystander.

"As Christians, we are fortunate to have God's Word, his Holy Book, to guide us. The Bible is very clear—make no mistake about this—killing is not wrong. Especially if you kill in defense of what is right. Then you're doing God's work, and it is righteous.

"Let's cut to the chase. We've all heard the Sixth Commandment quoted as 'Thou shalt not kill.'

"That's wrong. It's a bad translation. It really, truly is . . . what it should be—and I will show you the Hebrew and the best dictionaries—what it should be—and in some Bibles you will see it the correct way—it should be, 'Thou shalt not murder.' That's what God carved into the stone with his fiery finger, and it is what God meant.

"Murder is the wrongful and intentional taking of a life.

"Murder is wrong. And, in fact, God decrees the death penalty for murder. That is obviously the intentional taking of a life, but it is righteous and God approves, in fact God *commands*, the righteous taking of life.

"Why does God support the death penalty? For the very same reasons that we believe in it. Deuteronomy 19:20, 'And those which remain shall hear, and fear, and shall henceforth commit no more any such evil among you.'

"The strange thing, and the thing that may trouble many of us in law enforcement, is that every time we have an execution, or possible execution, there are ministers out marching against the death penalty to save the murderer.

"Think about this. What does Satan want? He wants to convince people that there are no consequences for their actions. So that they will feel *free*—free to murder, to fornicate, to commit adultery. Free to do anything because there are no consequences. God's law is that there are consequences, that there is punishment, even for his chosen people, should they commit error.

"So why would a so-called reverend take up Satan's work? Or fail to realize that he is taking up Satan's work? Satan uses his own good-intentioned weakness to seduce him to try to seduce us.

"How can that that happen? you may wonder. Lack of Bible study. Even preachers and pastors, and certainly priests—Catholics don't actually read the Bible—you know that, don't you?"

"Anyway," Alan said, coming back to the point, "God *wants* judges and police and soldiers here on earth. To keep earthly order, to keep His order, to protect the innocent, to protect His nations, His beloved followers, and He is not a fool, and neither was Jesus Christ a fool. They understand we live here in real life, with real problems, so they gave us this book with real solutions.

"So if you see a crank fiend, and he is holding up a roadside attraction, and there is danger to yourself or to civilians, you should not be afraid to terminate his existence on the spot, if that is what's necessary. You are doing God's work. Don't harm yourself with guilt afterward. You are doing God's work.

"If you see a terrorist, and he is plotting to go to the university and bomb it because it is critical of Islam, do not hesitate to use any means necessary to stop him and save innocent life.

"And our work here today is to see that this is written down for us in scripture. Because, in something so serious as taking a life, we need to know we're on the right side."

For the next forty or fifty minutes, we talked about Numbers 35:17–19, which ordains the death penalty; Matthew 5:17–18 and Luke 16:187, in which Jesus is very clear that he is here to enforce the old law; Exodus 2:11–12, in which Moses slew an Egyptian who was smiting a Hebrew, the sort of thing a cop can easily be called upon to do; and First Samuel 17:1–51, the story of David and Goliath, in which David, with God's help and God's blessing, killed someone who was threatening God's people.

Afterward, when we broke for coffee but most of the guys rushed off to work, I found a moment to be alone with Alan.

"I'm kinda stuck here," I said. "GGW&G, they're my best client. I said I would take the job, and I don't like to go back on my word."

He nodded. He could understand that, even agree with it. A man's word is supposed to mean something.

"Also, I'm not supposed to start judging their clients for them. 'Don't call me unless you have a case I approve of'—I say that, they won't call me for anything."

"You're gonna lose a lot of friends," he said.

"I got that," I said.

"And a lot of business," he said.

"I have a plan," I said. "Maybe not much of one, but it's the best I can think of so far. What I want to try to do is get Goldfarb a good start, get him enough to go on, enough that I can cut the case loose, and we both feel good about it."

"What do you need?"

"Police reports," I said.

"I'll tell you right now, I can't get you anything on Nazami. That's wrapped up tighter than shrink wrap."

"No, the original report, back when they thought it was a suicide."

"Maybe I could find that."

"And the university, the campus police must've made a report."

"You figure that'll get you off the hook?"

"That, plus interview a couple of witnesses, maybe find some alternate suspects he can throw at the jury."

"I'll see what I can find," he said.

"Thank you."

9

Nathaniel MacLeod's widow, Teresa, said, "You should really talk to his girlfriend."

She said it more cheerfully than you expect a wife to refer to a late husband's girlfriend. I wasn't sure, but it felt like there were tight coils of tension beneath the surface.

"His girlfriend? What's her name?"

"Um, Emma? Emmy? . . . short for something else? I'm sorry, I'm really not sure, mostly he liked to call her his 'own special angel.'"

Teresa was slender, about forty. She wore no makeup, or so little that my eye couldn't pick up on it. Her hair was styled, spiky and short, and it made her look a little bit dramatic. There were fine spider lines around her eyes, and you could see where the lines that would someday appear above her upper lip would be.

Her full name was listed in the university course catalog as Teresa Mansfield-Pellita, which I took to be her maiden name. She had a PhD and was an assistant professor of geography. She taught urban commercial geography, business and environmental geography, and introduction to feminist geography.

The house was relatively small, built in a southwestern style and done up that way inside too. What you call mission furniture, or something like it, sparse with lots of wood showing. A rug with the colors of desert sand.

"Aside from that," she said. "I don't know what else I can tell you." It was dismissive, conversation ending, putting up defenses, yet something in her tone said the opposite, but suggesting, somehow, that there were secret doors, hidden here and there along the walls.

There were several photographic prints on the wall and two small paintings. To keep the interview alive, and maybe find one of those openings, I walked over for a closer look at the most striking of the photos, a desolate landscape, glossy black stones in the foreground leading to a field of sand, dark gray mixed with brown, with an orange-red river of fire running through the center and off into the distance.

"A volcano?" I asked. "Lava flowing?"

"No," she said. "It's a river."

"Oh. The photographer manipulated the color," I said, guessing.

"That's the color, the real color. It's waste. It's the runoff from a nickel mine, and that's what it did to the river and the land."

On the opposite wall there was a set of five photographs framed together on a single panel. All had been taken from the same high angle, looking down at a McDonald's. I said, "May I?" and went to look at those more closely. The series went from morning through night. Each was a multiple exposure over a fifteen-minute period, the aperture set so that the cumulative shots of the restaurant combined to make it seem solid and bright, the way a McDonald's always does. But the figures that passed in front of it had only been given a fractional exposure, so they appeared like specters, dim and semitransparent. The dusk and night shots were even more dramatic, full of bursts of light from passing cars, their headlights leaving washes on the building and illuminating some of the people, as if they were flash attachments that let you catch ghosts on film.

She followed me, and from close behind me she said, "It's from one of my studies."

"Did you shoot it?" I asked.

"No. I had it done. The hottest application of geography these days, so there's grant money for it, is commercial traffic patterns. But the photos turned out to have their own aesthetic."

I turned toward her as she spoke. Her gaze was on me, and our eyes met.

There was a whistling noise from the kitchen.

"Would you like some tea?" she asked. "Green tea or some other kind? Or water? Or a drink?"

"Tea would be fine, and I'll have whatever kind you're having."

"Green tea," she said. "It purifies the blood."

"You think that's true?" I asked as she moved toward the kitchen.

"There was a study," she said. "It proved that if you're a Japanese fisherperson and you drink six cups a day, you'll live longer than a fisherperson who only drinks one cup a day."

I followed her and, when she went in, watched her from the doorway as she busied herself. She took out a Japanese tea set, glazed the color of iron, the pot with flat sides and curved edges, the cups without handles. Her gestures were neat and tidy. Precise and very concentrated.

She was working very hard at being in control and self-possessed, at making everything seem casual and normal.

But it was taking so much focus to do so—first on the pot, then on finding the tin with tea leaves, then opening it—that she blocked out the sound and had even forgotten that it was the whistle that had summoned her until it rose in volume and pitch to a shriek that pierced right through her wall of concentration. Then she yelled, "Dammit! Dammit all!" and threw the tea set to the tiled floor, where it smashed and shattered.

She grabbed the kettle by the handle, yanked it off the burner, and put it on the one behind, banging it down. I was afraid she was going to scorch herself on the flame or splatter herself with the boiling water. I reached over and turned off the range.

"Damn, damn, damn, and fuck and fucking hell, and all of it," she said, kicking at the bits and pieces of cups and teapot on the floor. Then she stood still, standing in front of me, looking helpless and lost, her arms held at her sides. Her mouth was tight, and she was holding back the tears.

"I'm sorry," I said, automatically taking a step toward her.

"Are you?" she asked.

"Yes, I'm sorry for your . . . pain," I said.

We were less than two feet apart. She was looking up at me, into my eyes. So many things were going on inside her.

There was a connection.

It gets tricky. As an investigator, like when I was a cop, I wander in and out of people's lives. I meet women at vulnerable moments, or merely at moments when I'm an unexpected presence, and they don't have their standard controls over their emotional and sexual impulses up and in place. If I tune into that, communication opens up. Back in the day, I would fall into those waters, way past any excuses that it helped with the job, taking advantage, sometimes doing damage. Now, I don't want that kind of trouble, but I do want information, so I let the doors open, knock gently to get them to open, but if it's a bedroom door, I remember that I'm just there to look, from the entrance way, not to go in and participate.

I found myself reaching toward her to put a reassuring hand on her shoulder.

At the moment that I touched her, the feeling in the air drew all together and flowed out of her shoulder and up my arm and back down again. Her tension—one kind of tension, at any rate—released with a slight sigh, and I felt her almost imperceptibly soften and move toward me.

I dropped my hand. There was more there than I had anticipated or understood, and I froze, feeling awkward. Teresa kept her eyes on mine, her face tilted up, the emotions she was feeling as visible as clouds drifting across the sky: now one, then another and another, some far apart, some so close they overlapped in their passing.

I'm not sure which of us moved, or if both of us did, but our bodies were touching. Then our lips touched. Just a touch.

"I'm married," I stuttered, moving back. Immediately after I heard the sound of my own voice, I worried that I was presuming too much, that maybe what I thought I saw in those drifting clouds was the devil's whispers in my own mind. I know that he's always around, waiting for my return.

"I saw the ring," she said calmly, the connections closing down and her emotions going back behind the hiding place of the face that's proper to wear in public.

"I didn't mean to imply that you . . . "

She shook her head, that she wasn't offended and maybe that she wasn't denying that my defensive reaction had cause. "I'm . . . in something of a state . . . , " she said in her own confusion, ". . . emotionally. I didn't mean to embarrass you."

"No," I said. "Your husband just died."

We hadn't moved. We were still so close that with the slightest gesture we could fall into each other, arms around each other, body pressed against body, and her hands, like mine, seemed poised at her sides as if they knew where they wanted to go but didn't know how to get there.

"We better . . . , " I said, stepping back, "um . . . sweep this up. I'll help you."

I bent down and started picking up the pieces, the bigger ones. I still had to ask her questions. I threw ceramic chunks in the trash and retreated back to the living room. I sat and busied myself with my notes but wrote down nothing about how her eyes looked gazing into mine or her lips had been full and moist.

Teresa and Nate had been married five years. Her first, his second. They'd been separated for six months. It was, she claimed, by mutual and satisfactory agreement. Her attitude declaimed that she was a very modern woman who knew that such things happened, and she could cope very well.

I had only seen pictures of Nathaniel MacLeod as a corpse. Dying had not made him happy. Living, apparently had. Alive, he had thrived in front of the camera. He was smiling, exuberant, clowning, involved. He talked, he hosted barbecues, he hiked, waved, and liked to put an arm around one person or both arms around two, three, or four people. He had a big mustache, most of his hair, and a fair-sized belly on a large frame.

"Was he always happy?" I asked.

"Nobody is always happy," she said, cool and adult, then added, with feeling, "but he was alive."

"But lately, being separated and all, was he happy?"

"Oh yes, happier than ever."

"Oh?" I said.

"Listen, I met Nate eighteen years ago. We had a brief thing. It was fun, but we both moved on. No hard feelings. Then I came out here. The geography department is growing. There are a lot of issues in the Southwest: rapid development, suburban sprawl, water usage, the border.

"He was already here and we ran into each other, and bam, it was off to bed. We were pretty fabulous. Better even than when we were younger. I'd learned a lot, a *lot*, in the intervening years . . . but it was great." That was all said in a very straight and informative way, as if she were simply trying to explain their relationship. But even in her circles, however liberal and liberated they were, those were not the sort of things a woman says to a man unless she has reasons to want him to know how sexual she can be. "And we loved each other. One of us mentioned marriage, I don't remember who, and then it was like . . . like Kinky Friedman running for governor of Texas: 'How hard can it be?' and 'Why the hell not?'"

"It was good," she said, "but, you know, maybe good's not enough. It wasn't . . . fate. And we didn't have children. Frankly, it's hard to tell the difference between married, living together, or boyfriend and girlfriend if you don't have children. It's just an agreement."

"But to do what?" she asked.

She had taken out a second teapot, a more pedestrian one, simple and round with a smooth fiestaware glaze, a southwestern green. The leaves had been steeping while we spoke, and now she decided it had been long enough and poured out cups for each of us.

"If we'd had children . . . , " she said. "But we didn't, and things can only burn at white heat for a few years. Even with tricks and toys and . . . exploring the boundaries, like everyone does nowadays. Then the stupid things that don't matter eventually begin to matter. I like tennis. He liked hiking and long, long bike trips. He liked to bait dinner guests and get them into arguments, and he was very sharp, very quick, and he could decimate them. But it embarrassed me. And it got confusing. If I slept with someone, was it because I really wanted to, or was I being competitive? What if I felt emotional? What if he did? And all of that."

I sipped at the hot tea. Of course the marriage had failed. I could hear the sermon in my ears: this is what atheistic, secular humanism led to. Where had the sacred gone? Without it, there was nothing. She was explaining it all quite clearly, but she was unable to hear what she herself was saying.

"So, it was over," she said.

"He moved out?"

"Yes. He got an apartment."

"Listen, I've been divorced," I said. "A couple of times. And I have to tell you, it was difficult. Lot of anger. Lot of depression, confusion. I felt lost."

"No," she said. "Our marriage wasn't like clinging onto a life preserver. I mean, I had lunch with him, two days before . . . before he died.

"He was so happy. He'd just finished his book. He was really excited about it. He said that with the jihadists on one side and the Republican Party as the party of the Christian God on the other side, the world was ready to hear something that explained the madness. People were ready to hear what he had to say. He even thought he could get a popular publisher, not just a university press."

"I'm going to . . . I want to see to it that it's published," she said. "I want to do that for him. He had good ideas. They deserve to be heard."

"Maybe he got turned down. Maybe he couldn't get a publisher."

"No, it was too soon. I don't think he'd even sent it out yet," she said. "Plus, he had that new girlfriend. He was having a good time. He was *not* suicidal. Not at all. That's why I raised such a fuss. I demanded an independent investigation. The university even agreed to hire an outside expert, an independent crime scene analyst. CSI, like on TV. They were just doing it to placate me, but it was going to be done. He was not suicidal."

All free and open and happy, happy, happy.

I didn't buy it. I never had an ex tell me about her new love unless she wanted to hurt me. Or pick a fight, which is the same thing. Nor did I ever find an ex eager for me to say how, after our bed had grown cold and old and stale, I'd found someone who would make it bubbly, fresh, and fun. Maybe that's why she was coming on to me so strong. To get some of herself back, to show she could still compete, even on a campus of new, young treats, eagerly testing out how it was to be away from home. "Really?" I said, "so he told you he had a new girlfriend?"

"He didn't actually say it that way."

"Oh."

"He was talking about a girl in one of his classes. His own special angel who was 'so bright,' she understood 'how philosophy makes the real difference in peoples' lives.' All that gushing about understanding each other's *ideas*. It's the mating call of people who read."

10

"I don't think you should work for a terrorist," my wife said.

Gwen didn't yell but it sort of blurted out of her, like she'd been sitting on it all day, or for several days, and it had grown and now it was pecking its way out of its shell, poking its head out and cheeping.

"It's my job," I said.

"Not to work for terrorists," she said. Cheep-cheep.

"No, my job is to take investigative assignments from attorneys or sometimes other people, and sometimes they're bad people. Many times they're bad people, but that's not my call. My call is to do the job, find the facts, and let other people act on them."

"I think it's wrong. We're all at risk here."

"Look," I said jovially, I hoped, "I'm the hunter gatherer, you're the cave keeper. That's how God organized it. So, you don't tell me not to hunt the big bison, and I don't tell you how to keep the home. We have our places, and knowing them and keeping them is what keeps us happy." That was practically verbatim from the couples counseling we'd had from the Ministry of the Third Millennium before we'd gotten married—and heard repeated in a hundred sermons and at Christian couples workshops. And it had worked. It was something Gwen believed and that I had learned to believe, and it worked. We were happy.

"This is bigger than us," she said. "This is not just a clash of civilizations. It's a war for civilization."

I got angry. The talker inside me was ready to say to her, 'Oh, you better not start this shit now. There's a woman right across town who wants to jump my bones in ways you've never even dreamed of, wants to rock me and roll me all night long. Don't pull this shit now.' Then I realized it was the devil talking. The devil finding a wedge— anger, dissatisfaction, lust, any weakness.

"God made the man the head of the family," I said.

"He didn't say you didn't have to listen to me," she snapped back.

"Listen to you?" Did she mean obey her?

"I meant, didn't have to listen to my concerns, to my thoughts."

"I guess not, but not now, alright?"

"When, Carl?"

"I don't know when. I've been working all day, a long day. It was a twelve-, thirteen-hour day and traffic was terrible . . . I don't have to make excuses. I don't want to make excuses. It's my call, and I don't want to talk about this."

"Why not?"

"Because it's my business, and I said so, and I'm in charge." All damn day, you go out and play it the best you can and question yourself: Did I do it right? Did I do it the best way possible. And your employers question you: Could you get more? Why did it cost so much? And the people you're trying to ask questions of, they don't want to answer; they challenge your right to know, and people hold back records and tell tall tales. So when you go home, you don't want to answer more questions. You want peace, refuge, support, solace. And to give the same in return.

Gwen was both hurt and furious. She froze there. I wasn't sure if she was going to get her gun or start to cry. Then her eyes welled up.

Which made me angry. A woman's weapon. I was supposed to feel guilty for saying what I'm supposed to say, what the Bible says, that I'm in charge? I was supposed to feel bad because I didn't want to talk about what she wanted to talk about when she wanted it? Anger—anger was the devil's trick. There is righteous anger, and there is a place for it. But anger between husband and wife, that's one of the devil's tools to work against God's way.

I took a deep breath. I said, "Let's pray together."

"Yes, of course," Gwen said.

"I will pray to control my anger," I said.

"I will pray to find ways to . . . talk to you without defying you."

The thing about prayer is that just by making the decision to do it, you're more than halfway there.

11

"That's a nice plant," Esther Rabinowitz, the philosophy department secretary said.

"Glad you like it."

"So, why'd you bring me a plant?" She looked to be of retirement age or a few years past it, but alert and feisty. "What do you want?"

"I came by yesterday, and you were out and I looked around and thought, this office could use a plant."

"You're right. I had a plant. But it died."

"They do that."

"People do it too," she said.

"Yes, they do."

"We say things like that here in the philosophy department, even the secretary. We're deep here."

"I believe you are."

"But you do want something, don't you?"

"That's true too."

"That's what we're all about, here in the philosophy department: truth!"

"Is that the department motto?"

"No, but it should be, don't you think? I think the department should have a motto. And maybe more parties. They need to recruit. It's a dying business, philosophy."

"I didn't know that."

"So, what do you want, young man?"

"I want to take you to lunch."

"Me? I'm more than a quarter-century older than you. I know that anything goes nowadays, but this is more than I expected."

"Mrs. Rabinowitz, I don't know that I could keep up with you."

"I bet you could. But meantime, what do you really want?"

"To take you to lunch."

"Uh-huh."

"And talk to you about the department."

"You mean about poor Nathaniel."

"Yes."

"You a reporter?"

"No. No, I'm not."

"Who are you then?"

"I'm an investigator," I said. "I'm working for Ahmad Nazami's defense."

"Show me. You got ID?"

"Yes. I do," I said and showed her my PI license.

"Okay, what's your name again? Carl?"

"Yes. Carl."

"You can take me to lunch, and you can call me Esther. It was nice, bringing me the plant. Nathaniel always used to bring me chocolates. For my birthday. He always got the date wrong, but he always brought them. Really, really good ones. You could put on five pounds just holding the box."

"Nate was my favorite," she said over a bowl of pea soup.

"Why's that?"

"At least you could understand him. These others . . . listen, do you know philosophy?" She was spooning the chunks of ham out of the bowl.

"Are you doing that because you're kosher?"

"Nah, I'm a vegetarian."

50

"Oh," I said.

"But not a religious one. I don't mind a little meat should touch my food, infuse it with flavor. Thomas Jefferson was like that. I just do it for my health. I want to live forever. I have grandchildren. You want to see pictures?"

"Of course," I said.

She took a packet of photos out of her pocket book. "My daughter-in-law, an angel, e-mails me pictures every day." I accepted them and made the appropriate cooing sounds of admiration. "I print them out myself," she explained. "Sometimes I Photoshop them, improve them a little."

"How adorable," I said. "So, tell me about Nate."

"Oh, oh, oh, poor Nathaniel. What a nice man. So much fun. We used to laugh. Who would want to kill such a man. Hah! As if I didn't know."

"Like who?"

"Don't be so quick Mr. Investigator, Carl. I use it as a turn of phrase. In the circumstances, I shouldn't."

"What about Ahmad?"

"Ahmad? Kill somebody? Why do you think I'm sitting here talking to you? If I thought it was Ahmad, I would say, Go away. Leave me alone. They got the killer."

"Not Ahmad, then?"

"No. No, he and Nate were friends. Oh, how they used to argue."

"They argued? But you said they were friends."

"Oh, goyim. What are you, Irish?"

"No."

"My late husband was Irish. Nice man. But his idea of an argument was to step outside and start punching someone. Argue, like philosophers. For them, that's like the joy of sex. For most of them. But there are some, they get so serious . . . factions, worse than Trotskyites. You don't know philosophy, do you?"

"No."

"Nobody does. I'll give you a quick overview from the perspective of the departmental secretary and a grandmother who had a very fine education herself at the City College of New York, back when it was one of the best schools in the country, almost as hard to get into as your Ivy League schools. And it was free. We all think we've come so far, but when I was growing up, an education, a fine college education, was free.

"Anyway, there are two main groups. They call themselves continental and analytic. Are you ready? You might want to take notes. This is going to be on the test.

"'Analytic philosophers want to say only what they can be absolutely, logically certain about. As a result, there's practically nothing left for them to talk about. Definitely not anything important. The continental style, by contrast, is unconstrained by logic, science, common sense, or even experience. It produces work that seems like nonsense to outsiders. Because it is.' I'm quoting. That's Nathaniel's quick and handy definition.

"You can see, with people who take themselves seriously—and why shouldn't they; their livelihood depends on it—he could make them very, very angry."

"So, were they angry?"

"Oh, yes."

"Who in particular?"

"You want me to name names?"

"Well . . . "

"I don't name names . . . but if you were to go talk to everybody in the department and ask if they liked Nathaniel, and they all said yes, they loved him, they adored him, they were his best friends, they would all be lying, except for maybe two of them. All right, three. And, if I were you, I would start at the top."

"The top?"

"The chairman. And if he pretends to be nice, that quote I gave you, just toss it into the conversation. Ho, boy."

"The one about . . . " I tried to look at my notes.

"Analytic philosophy . . . can't talk about anything. That one."

"What about students? Was he close with or did he have problems with any of his students?"

"Close with. Oh sure. There was a whole gang of them. Talk, talk, talk. Especially if you wanted to get God off your back, Nathaniel was the go-to guy."

"Why would anyone want to get God off their back?"

She heard more edge in my tone than I intended. "Are you a Christian?" she asked.

"Would that bother you? I mean, most of the people in this country are Christians."

"You know what I mean. Are you one of those megachurch, born-again Christians? You know, save the fetuses, kill the foreigners."

"Yes, I'm afraid I am."

"Oy, I put my foot in it."

"Look, I'm a Christian working for a Jewish lawyer who's working for an Islamic kid to find out who really killed the atheist. It's America, right?"

"Yes, that's America. That's America the way it should be. Please God, we should keep it that way."

I asked her if she could name some of the other students who were close to Ahmad or Nathaniel or both. She rattled off several of them. I wrote them down. Then I asked if she thought Nate was ever intimate with any of his students.

"Only grad students," she said. "Undergraduates, it's against the rules." She said it like that was just fine, like it made him an upstanding citizen of the university community.

"And his wife didn't mind?"

"Oh, that one," she snorted.

"What does that mean?"

"She was too much of an intellectual and feminist to admit that she ever got jealous. At least, that's what I think. So instead, she tried to outdo him. Go after his friends and anyone he was close to."

"Men and women?"

She shrugged. "I'm not an eyewitness."

I looked down at my notes, at the list of students close to Nate. "I heard," I said to her, "that there was an Emma or Emily, someone with an em sound in their name, who was part of the group or close to Nate? But she's not on your list."

"No," she said.

"Oh."

"Wait. Not em. It's en."

"That's a name?"

"An initial, N."

"What's it stand for?"

"I don't know."

"Isn't she registered for his course or something?"

"I think she was auditing the course."

"Shouldn't there be some kind of record?"

"Of course there should be. And she should have been paying too. But I don't think she was. I think it was an unofficial audit. And if a professor unofficially approves an unofficial auditor, then we ignore it."

"So there was a girl called 'N.'—we don't actually know her name, first or last—taking his course, one of his courses?"

"Yes, I think. Just the one. Religion and Philosophy 342."

"The same as Ahmad?"

"Yes."

"So, he should know her?"

"More than know her, I should think," Esther said. "The few times I saw them together, the way he was looking at her . . . . "

"So he liked her, and she liked Nate, is that it?"

"Oh dear, what have I said?"

12

Troopers were lined up in front of the courthouse. They wore helmets and shields and had their game faces on. The city had their SWAT teams deployed, plus regular officers guarding the flanks of the building and plainclothes people in the crowd. There were camera crews from the three network affiliates and two of the independents, plus national crews from CNN, Fox News, and Al-Jazeera.

The troopers were trying to keep the different camps of demonstrators separated. One side wanted a regular trial, in the state court, open to the public. Most of them were visibly liberal types, from the university, the Unitarian Church, and the bookstores. On another day, they'd be lined up to see the new Michael Moore movie or rallying to save a failing health food store. Their signs read, "No Torture," "No Gitmos Here," "Fight the Fascists."

We have some Muslims around. I expected to see at least a few of them out there, but there were none. Keeping their heads down.

The other side was mostly clean-cut types, the kind of people who also showed up at pro-life demonstrations, with a sprinkling of long-haired country music patriots. Their signs read, "Save Civilization, Send Him to Gitmo," "Stop Islamo-Facism," "The War We Have to Win," and "First, Kill All the Lawyers."

The two sides snarled at each other and hurled epithets.

The first physical incident was an attack on the Al-Jazeera news team. A group charged them and grabbed the camera, which they smashed on the ground. They piled on top of the cameraman, and someone tried to shove the broken parts of the camera into his mouth, screaming "Eat this, you rag-head animal. Eat this!" He suffered a concussion, a torn lip, and a broken tooth. And half of his ear was either torn or bitten off. They also attacked the reporter, grabbing him by his tie and his jacket. He was very lucky. It was a clip-on tie, and it came right off. The reporter pulled himself free of his jacket and scrambled along the sidewalk to safety behind the troopers.

Things were settling down when Manny and I drove up in his Mercedes. Suddenly things came flying from the crowd, fruit and stones and who knows what—bam, splat, bam—they hit the hood and the roof.

"The motherfuckers! My car, my beautiful car!"

Clang. Sploosh. Bam. Eggs, apples, and tomatoes along with the rocks. We're a modern city. Our streets are paved. There are no loose stones lying about on River Street between Fourth and Fifth. Nor is there a handy farmer's market. The crowd had come with supplies. This had been preplanned.

The police didn't seem to be doing anything about it. Bop, thwop, crack!

"Motherfucking police aren't doing anything about it," Manny yelled.

We seemed to be safe inside the vehicle. But I wouldn't want to be the one getting the bill from the body shop. Almost every panel was taking a hit. The damage was certain to be in five figures. And no matter how good the body shop that did the repairs would be, Manny's baby would never be a virgin again. She would be tarnished forever, and Manny was practically in tears.

"It's just a car," I said inanely.

"Just a car? Just a car? Do you want a lecture on German engineering? Do you want a lecture on what one hundred and forty thousand dollars looks like when it's pure and unsullied? Do you? Do you?"

Blotz! An egg hit the window and smeared itself all over the glass. "Come on, Manny, let's pull out of here and go around the side."

"No, no, fuck this." He pulled up to the curb. "Fuck this, and fuck them all."

"Manny, don't. It's dangerous out there."

He wasn't listening. He flung the door open, and he jumped out and stood facing the crowd as if the stones were just drizzling rain. He smiled at them. An apple and a tomato whizzed by, then a rock cracked one of his windows, and he didn't flinch. Like I said, Manny was one of those guys who figured life had granted him immunity.

I couldn't stay huddled inside, damn him. So I jumped out and ran around to protect him. I got between him and the rock throwers and said, "Come on," and tried to drag him toward the courthouse. He pushed me away and tried to climb up on the hood of the Mercedes, but his bad leg wasn't working.

"Help me," he yelled.

"Let's get out of here before we get hurt."

"Carl, get me up."

I'd seen his leg once. I had to bring him some papers, and I caught up with him at his golf club. He was in the locker room changing.

He'd been shot up in Vietnam. There were scars from about mid-thigh to ankle. Some from the original shrapnel, the rest from the operations afterward. The upper and lower parts were not in a straight line, and there was a slight extra angle beneath his knee. He saw me looking and said, "What the hell, I'm lucky they didn't amputate. They wanted to, but I said I'm a lawyer, and if you cut that off, I'll sue."

It looked like it still hurt and would die ten years before the rest of him did.

I gave him a boost onto the hood. Then he put his hands on my head and shoulders so he could shove himself up into standing position.

When he was upright, he yelled at the crowd, "I stand here before you . . . . " Then he turned to the cameras. "I stand here before you not to defend a terrorist. I am not here to defend a terrorist. I'm here to defend you."

A couple of stones and some fruit came out of the crowd. He watched them come, bracing himself in case something hit him, but they missed, and he watched them go by.

"This is America. If this were an Islamo-Fascist state, I couldn't be here. If this were Nazi Europe, I couldn't be here. If this were still King George's colony, I couldn't be here. But this is America, and I have to be here." Things had stopped flying, and the crowd was even growing quiet.

"If lawyers stop showing up to defend even the indefensible, to make sure we've got the right man, then it's not America anymore," he said. "I'm not upset about you being here. I'm glad you're here. I want to thank you for being here. Thank you, thank you all, for being here to witness the fact that just as no man is above the law, no man is beneath it."

He was done, and he reached for me and said, "Help me down."

I did, and we walked past the troopers. The crowd on one side applauded him, and the crowd that had tried to stone him was silent. He smiled all the way up the courthouse steps. At the top, I looked back, and from that height, I could see all of their faces. There was Gwen, among those who had thrown the stones.

I stepped through the doors a moment after Manny. He dropped his smile like he was dropping an empty bottle in the trash, and he said, "What fucking bullshit."

"What do you mean?"

"Do you remember September 30, 2006? Do you, Carl?"

"Can't say that I do."

"It was the day that our president signed the Military Commissions Act of 2006 into law, a bill that overturned the Constitution. Right down to its socks and underwear. Call somebody a terrorist, even an American citizen, like Ahmad Nazami, and he can, under the law, be taken off the streets or out of his own bedroom, like Ahmad was, and hauled off to a secret place.

"They can do it to people who don't have Arab names too. They can do it to you"—he poked me in the chest—"with your 'we were here even before the English' Dutch name. They can do it to me. And that same fucking law says that we don't have the right to come into this court and challenge it. You don't even get a chance to say, Hey you got the wrong guy. You were supposed to arrest Manfred Goldfarb, not Emmanuel Goldfarb. Let alone have a trial and make them prove I actually did something."

"So, come on, my friend." He put his arm around my shoulder and said, "Let us do our best, just in case these are the last days of the Republic."

Arraignments are simple.

The judge reads the charges to the defendant. He asks the defendant if he has a lawyer. If he needs one and can't afford it, they assign one. Then he asks for a plea. The attorney answers guilty, not guilty, or, very infrequently, nolo contendere, no contest.

Then the judge sets a court date for sentencing if the plea is guilty, for trial if it is not guilty.

Judicial appointments in our state are for life. So our chief judge, the Honorable Darren Spoon, in his wisdom, uses the arraignment court as a place to put judges like Frederick Olsen Watkins, who is a drunk.

Watkins naturally does not think of himself as a drunk, or even as someone with a drinking problem, because he never has a drink before noon. As a result, there are two Watkins: the morning one and the afternoon one. The morning one is rather irritable, even cranky. He wants attorneys to speak softly but very clearly. He wants things to move briskly. And he utters his own statements with a cottonmouth sound and drinks constantly from a glass of water, which, in the morning, actually is water and nothing but water. We know this because many people have bet on it over the years and so, intermittently, the pitcher is taken during the lunch recess and tested in front of witnesses.

After lunch is, of course, a different matter, and entirely unpredictable. Courthouse legend has it that if he has two drinks, he's friendly and affable; if he has three, he's somewhat emotional; coming back from four drinks, the emotions grow larger, verging on the operatic; if he has five drinks, he's asleep by three.

It was the afternoon, and we had Watkins.

We also had the DA's most aggressive assistant, if not his best, Danny DeStefano. Tightly muscled and tightly wound, he bounced on the balls of his feet, convincing juries that he was working hard, hard, hard to personally rid their streets of crime and protect them, and the faster they decided to put this creep away, the faster he could get to the next one, thank you, ladies and gentlemen of the jury and madam forewoman.

Danny had company—another lawyer who looked vaguely familiar from years ago. If memory served, he'd been in private practice but not particularly distinguished. I would have guessed that he was a new hire from the DA's office, but he looked too old and was being way too self-important.

Prisoners are almost always transported with shackles on. Nothing personal. It's safer that way. They're taken to a holding cell, and their shackles are removed before they're brought in front of the judge.

But Ahmad had not been given that courtesy. He came in with all his chains on. He had to do the humble shuffle, moving his feet no more than six inches at a time. His chains rattled softly with each step or gesture.

They had done something else, something I had never seen before. They'd put black-out goggles on him. He was effectively blind.

He was guarded by four sheriffs with automatic rifles, one of whom had to hold him by the arm to guide him.

Watkins looked up like he was seeing a dreaded apparition. And he wasn't the only one.

"Who's this?" he asked, sounding bewildered, which was peculiar since everyone in the state knew who was in his courtroom that afternoon.

DeStefano stood up and said, "That's Ahmad Nazami."

The man with DeStefano stood up too and said, "I'm from the Justice Department."

Watkins turned his head toward the prosecutor's table with a heavy, ponderous motion, as if his thick, gray, swept-back hair held the weight of a centurion's iron helmet, and said, "That's federal, isn't it?"

"Yes, sir. I'm representing Homeland Security."

"This is a state court," the judge said.

"Yes, sir. I'm aware of that."

"So, sit down," the judge said.

"Your Honor," DeStefano said.

"Yes, Mr. DeStefano. It's always good to see *you*. What brings you to our courtroom today?"

"This prisoner, Ahmad Nazami. We would like to remand him to federal custody."

Manny was on his feet. "Objection!"

"My, my, my. Emmanuel Goldfarb *and* ADA Daniel DeStefano in my court together. And so . . . operatic. Tell me, Mr. Goldfarb, to what do you object?"

"My client—"

"This man?" He looked at Ahmad, who was moving his head around the way blind people do. There was snot dripping from his nose, and he couldn't wipe it, so he was making sniffling noises as he tried to suck it back in.

"Yes, sir."

"I thought so, though we haven't been properly introduced yet."

"He's charged with an ordinary state crime, and he belongs in this court and should be tried in this court's jurisdiction. I cite—"

"Don't cite." The judge turned to his clerk. "What's he charged with?"

His clerk indicated with as subtle a gesture as was possible in the circumstances that Watkins had the list of defendants and charges directly in front of him.

"Oh . . . murder. Murder's not federal. We do that right here at home. Yes, indeed."

"Your Honor," DeStefano said.

"Yes?"

"This was a terrorist act."

"Ohhh." Something between a moan and a sob escaped from Ahmad.

Watkins looked at him as if he were seeing him for the first time.

"What's that on his face? Is there something wrong with his eyes?"

"Your Honor," DeStefano began.

"Why is this man in chains? In my courtroom?"

"He's a dangerous terrorist, Your Honor," DeStefano said. The armed deputies stood straighter, looked more alert, and held their rifles as if they were ready to spring into action.

"He's crying," Watkins said.

"It's a trick. They train them to do that."

"Unshackle this man. And take that thing off his eyes."

"He's dangerous," DeStefano said.

"This is a criminal court," Watkins said. "We have dangerous people here all the time. That's what we do. But are we afraid? No, we are not. Unshackle this man. And take the thing off his face. And you people with the guns"—the judge waved the backs of both his hands at them, brushing them away—"back, back. Let's all be able to breathe."

"Thank you," Ahmad said, his head turning as he tried to figure out which direction the judge had spoken from. "Thank you, sir. Thank you."

"Don't call me 'sir,'" the judge said. "Call me 'Your Honor.'"

"Yes, Your Honor, sir."

"And get those things off his face."

One of the deputies moved to follow the judge's order, and in the first moment, as the goggles came off, you could see how disoriented Ahmad had been beneath them. The enforced blindness had edged him over so that he stood on the border where ordered life blurs into chaos.

As soon as sight returned and he was able to place himself in the geography of the room—to find the judge, find Manny, find me, to see who his guards were and the familiar furniture and arrangements of a courtroom—his posture changed, and his attitude changed. Even his face took on more definition, and he became more himself.

The deputy who had removed the goggles handed them off, then knelt down and unlocked the chains from around the boy's ankles. Normally the prisoner, whoever it is, takes some amount of pleasure from the brief reversal, at least of physical positions, with law enforcement servile at their feet. But not Ahmad. He was polite and grateful. He knew that if he said it with words, he might break down, so expressed his thanks with a nod.

"You're not going to go berserk and attack the court, are you son?"

"No sir," he said, looking at the judge, doing his best to keep control. "Your . . . "

"I mean, Your Honor, sir, no."

"You hear that, Mr. DeStefano?"

As Ahmad's hands came free, he reached up to wipe his nose. One of the guards got upset at seeing him wipe his snot with the back of his hand and with the annoyed look of a parent took out a handkerchief. For a moment, it looked as if he were going to wipe Ahmad's nose for him, but then he realized that the boy's hands were now free, and he simply gave it to him. Ahmad was so overwhelmed by the kindness that he looked like he was going to kiss the guard's hand. It occurred to me that this was the key to interrogations. Not the beatings or torture but the moments of kindness. If they had the sense to build on this, and Nazami was actually a terrorist, this guy with the handkerchief could pull everything out of him he could possibly know. But that much gratitude was more than the guard could stand, and he said, "Suck it up, kid. Suck it up."

Watkins turned to the defendant. "Now, Mr. Nazami, are you alright? Good," he continued, not waiting for the answer. "Let's take a look at the charge against you."

"Your Honor," DeStefano said, "we wish to release the defendant into federal custody."

"You wish to drop these charges? You have a murder here." Then he added, almost as an aside, "Mr. Nazami, you're charged with murder in the second degree."

"He's an enemy combatant."

"Objection," Manny said.

"Really," Watkins said to DeStefano. "You picked him up in Adwar Province, did you?"

"No, he committed his crime here."

"We've been invaded?"

"Yes, we have, Your Honor. I think Your Honor remembers 9/11, for one."

"Was he involved in that?" the judge asked with genuine interest.

"No, Your Honor."

"What did he do?"

"He shot a philosophy professor at the university."

"Surely that didn't terrorize anyone."

"He did it because he didn't like the professor's beliefs, because he's an Islamo-Fascist who believes apostates must die!"

Manny said, "Objection."

DeStefano said, "We have a confession. He confessed to that."

"Objection," Manny said. "The confession is not in evidence. The confession was obtained through coercion. The confession . . . "

"Spare me," the judge said. "This is a simple arraignment. Do you want to dismiss the charges, Mr. DeStefano? If so, I'll release the defendant."

"I object," Manny said.

"The defense objects?"

"Yes."

"To the charges being dropped?"

"To a remand to federal custody. This is a state crime. If the defendant is charged in a state court, he will be tried with all the normal protections that a citizen is entitled to under the Constitution. If you release him, he will be taken away. He will not be able to have the attorney of his choice. He will not be able to confront his accusers. His testimony can be coerced."

"Objection," DeStefano said. "This is an enemy combatant."

"Mr. DeStefano, you are giving me a headache. If I have this right, the defense is begging me to try the defendant for murder, and the DA's office wants me to dismiss the charges."

"Not dismiss. Just remand. But the charges remain."

"This is a simple arraignment court," Watkins said, giving up. "How does your client plead, Mr. Goldfarb."

"Not guilty, Your Honor."

"Fine," the judge said. "Let's set a date for trial."

Dinner that night was strange.

When I came home, our daughter, Angie, was full of excitement. "Daddy, Daddy, you're on TV."

She had Tivoed the news, and sure enough, there was the Mercedes being pelted with eggs, fruit, and stones. Then, there I was. I helped Manny climb up on the hood, stood there in front of him like I was his bodyguard, then helped him down and walked into the courthouse with him.

Gwen didn't say much about it. I didn't say anything about seeing her in the crowd. It was as if Angie's happiness had lifted us past our differences. That family well-being and Angie's joy were more important than a political issue, which, after all, was outside, something far away.

The next evening Angie came home distraught. There was also a call from the school. She'd been in a fight. Her first ever. Our first ever bad call from school. It was over me. Kids were saying I was helping terrorists, that I was a traitor, that I was working against the United States and against God. She had finally gotten angry, and there had been a physical confrontation. For one of the very few times in our marriage, Gwen took an 'I told you so' position. Worse, she did it silently.

13

It was both one of the sweetest and one of the saddest things I've ever seen. I caught up with Manny at the end of the day at Julian Irvine Elementary School auditorium.

"Sorry," he whispered when I sat down next to him. "These things always run late."

A seven-year-old boy was on stage with a drum set. Recorded music was playing, and he was banging away along with it. He was good. He had perfect timing and could play several complicated riffs. A teacher was standing by him, and Manny's wife, Susan, was over by the podium. She's a special ed teacher.

Like I said, the kid was good, but when the recorded music stopped, he didn't. He went on banging away with just as much fervor and concentration. The woman who was there with him touched him gently to get him to stop, but he didn't until she slid the sticks out of his hands. Then she led him over to Susan, who announced his name and said he was getting the award for best musician in his class and gave him a little statuette with a trumpeter on it.

The other kids and the parents in the room all applauded. Some of the kids had to be directed how to applaud, others not to do it too much, and others when to stop. Each of them had something wrong, was blind, retarded, autistic, in a wheelchair with multiple sclerosis. And all the people in that room—except me, who was just passing through—were shouldering their burdens and helping to prepare these kids for lives of indignity, humiliation, and pain.

Manny leaned over and said to me, "I couldn't find a little drummer. Best I could do."

"He seems happy with it."

"Come on. We can talk in the hall. Nobody'll miss me."

We left as quietly as we could. When the doors closed behind me, I said, "So you get the trophies for them?"

"Yeah, yeah. The way you work with special ed kids is with a lot of rewards. For every little bit of progress, a reward. Susan makes some great progress. I couldn't do it. I don't have the patience. Or the love. She does, and I try to support her. Whadda we got?"

"There's only three mosques in the area, plus one at the university. I went to them all. Ahmad went to one, the one down in Wolvern. It's mostly Pakistanis and Bengalis there, starting to push out the Mexicans.

"I spoke to the imam. He said Ahmad was only there a few times. Far from being a fanatical jihadist, our boy was regarded as dangerously liberal. He said something about white raisins, Ahmad did, to the imam, who was furious about it. I tried to get him to explain, but he kept going ballistic."

"Ah, the white raisins," Manny said.

"You know them? What are they, Iraqi rappers?"

"You want me to explain it?"

"Yes, please. He wouldn't. Or couldn't."

"Muslims believe that God had the archangel Gabriel speak to Mohammed. Then, because he was 'the perfect man,' he got it perfectly right, and he went home and recited what he'd heard to his followers, who remembered it perfectly, then recited it to the scribes, who wrote it down, perfectly. God, Gabriel, Mohammed, immediate followers, secretaries, Koran. That's why you study Arabic to study the Koran, so that you don't pick up mistakes with translations, 'cause you have it there, perfectly in the original. The problem is, it's almost certainly not true."

"Of course it's not true. The Bible is the word of God," I said.

Manny gave me a look.

"Yeah, well, it is," I said.

"You want to hear this?"

"Sure."

"There's a second problem. In Mohammed's day, there were only seventeen letters in written Arabic, all for consonants, and some had to do double duty, and none for vowels. Imagine it in English. If you wanted to write 'cat,' all you could write would be 'c' and 't' and readers would have to figure out from the context if it was actually cat, cut, cot, coat, cite, or city. Later on, more letters were added to the language and then to the Koran. Still, it is regarded as the direct word, God to Gabriel to Mohammed to the Koran.

"This is so serious that it is forbidden in Islam to study the Koran in an external way, to question when it was actually written or by whom or to test it against other historical information and say that the original letters, a few of which have multiple uses, with different vowels could have different meanings."

"What you mean, it's forbidden?"

"I mean you can be sentenced to death for it."

"Are you serious?"

"Yes. And you know that the Islamic suicide bombers believe that by being martyrs, they will automatically go to heaven."

"And they'll be met by a dozen virgins," I said.

"Seventy-two," Manny corrected me.

"That's a lot of virgins."

"Well, you have eternity to get through them," Manny said. "Anyway, one Arabic scholar said that the original text didn't mean 'virgins.' If you change the vowels, which aren't in the text, you get 'white raisins,' and, he said, that's what was really intended."

"White raisins?"

"Arabia was desert country. Their idea of paradise was a garden, with water and fruit trees. White raisins were a great delicacy."

"Not as much as virgins."

The doors opened, and the kids started coming out with their parents and teachers. Each of them was holding some kind of trophy or an award or wearing a big medal around their neck. They were showing them off, holding them up, examining them.

"This is good, very good," Manny said to me. "It shows that Ahmad was challenging Islam himself, the exact reason that he had supposedly killed MacLeod."

"Actually, this imam—it's the Capital City Islamic Center by the way—the imam said something about Ahmad having an evil professor who put him up to asking evil questions. He was really pissed about it."

"Excellent. Can we get him to testify?"

"Sure, I don't think it's a problem."

"By the way, I've got a check for you," he said, reaching into his pocket. "Keep us current on your bills."

"That's fast," I said.

Susan came out, and we both stood up. She took my hand, said my name, and kissed me on the cheek. If she weren't Manny's wife and I weren't Gwen's husband, I would have melted on the spot.

"That's great, what you're doing here," I said to her.

"I wanted to thank you," she said. "For taking this case with Manny. He may not say so, but he really thinks the world of you and your work, but I'll say so, and I'm grateful that he has you on this one."

14

The police gathered in the dark. It was a joint operation. City and state police. The plan was to be in place before dawn. Due to a flat tire on the bomb-disposal vehicle and the late arrival of one of the news crews, they got started a little late. But still, they arrived at the mosque on Geronimo Street just before dawn. They deployed silently—or as silently as people with cars, guns, radios, batons, cameras, ropes, rappelling gear, and a battering ram can.

The snipers got up on the rooftops on the three sides that had any sorts of entrances or exits. The main contingent got into hidden positions on Julia, one block south of Geronimo, to await the signal. A second, somewhat smaller group went around the back to Wolvern Row. They had the battering ram, and the plan was that they would burst in while the people inside were preoccupied with the main troop out front.

As they were moving into position, about ten minutes later than planned, a big, fat, red sun came up over the flat lands to the east. It was the sort of sun that said, Here comes a bright and beautiful day. Come and watch me in my glory.

Just then a voice screamed out in Arabic.

The police took it to be a warning—an alert. Rather than wait to be attacked or for the defenders inside to barricade themselves and ready their arms, the cops sprang into action. The team at the rear, on Wolvern, got its battering ram and smashed in the back door. The drivers of the fifteen cars assigned to the front put their pedals to the metal and rushed into position, slewing and squealing as they braked. Officers with their flak jackets on and their weapons drawn leapt out and took cover behind their vehicles.

Still, the shouting from the mosque continued.

A captain with a bullhorn yelled back, "Come out. Come out with your hands up! Throw down your weapons, and come out with your hands up!"

The voice in the mosque shouted back. It sounded like defiance.

Meantime, there was noise from the back. A shot. It sounded like a shot. Then more shots. So the police in front began firing too.

Still the yelling continued.

The crying voice from the mosque, as later confirmed by the news tapes, had started by saying, *Allah u Akbar, Allah u Akbar. Ash-hadu al-la Ilaha ill Allah, Ash-hadu al-la Ilaha ill Allah,* then continued, *Ash-hadu anna Muhammadan Rasulullaah, Ash-hadu anna Muhammadan Rasulullaah.*

That translates as, "God is great. God is great. I bear witness that there is no God but Allah. I bear witness that there is no God but Allah," then "I bear witness that Mohammed is Allah's messenger," also repeated twice, as were the rest of the phrases. "Hasten to the prayer. Hasten to real success. God is great." Then there is a final phrase, recited once: "None is worthy of worship but Allah."

It was the *adhan*, the call to prayer, that's issued five times a day. It is supposed to be shouted from a tower by the *muadhdhin*, written "muezzin" in English. If it had been a person doing it, perhaps he would have stopped. But this mosque, as many do, used a recorded voice, so it went on and on, through the assault, through the captain yelling with the bullhorn, through the firing.

There were fifteen people inside. Five were injured. A twelve-year-old boy was rushed to intensive care. The imam was killed. Two police officers were hurt. One was grazed by a bullet. One broke an ankle leaping out of his car.

Two guns were found in the mosque, both legal and registered to the caretaker. Various publications were found, mostly in Arabic, some of which were described by the police as Islamo-Fascist texts, though nobody on our local force can read or understand Arabic. Otherwise, they might have recognized the muezzin's cry of the most familiar phrase in that language, one of the most familiar in the world, *Allah u Akbar*, God is great.

They also found a copy of *The Anarchist Cookbook*, an American publication from 1970 and *The Anarchist Handbook*, published in 1985. Both have instructions on how to make homemade bombs and homemade weapons. One of the arrestees claimed the police had planted them.

The governor, the mayor, the chief of police, the chief of detectives, the superintendent of the state police, and the head of their counterterrorist division all had to be at the press conference. When that happens, there's always a fight about the location. The standard solution is to hold it outdoors in Municipal Square, as close to dead center as it's possible to be, between the State House and City Hall.

The Capital City Islamic Center, they told us, was a radical mosque. It catered to the Sunni sect. The details of the investigation that had led to the raid had to remain secret as revealing methods and techniques might jeopardize other ongoing and future investigations and make us less safe.

They also announced that Ahmad Nazami had been a member.

The imam, who could have testified that Ahmad had been much more the wiseass college kid who asked embarrassing questions about the faith than a fanatical follower of Islam, was dead.

"How can you defend that man?" my daughter asked me at dinner. We make it a point for the family to eat together. That makes families work.

"I'm not really defending. I'm investigating," I said. "I get the facts, good or bad, and then I hand them over to Manny Goldfarb. Manny's a defense lawyer, it's true. He brings the facts into court, and then a judge and a jury decide who's guilty and who's not."

"But don't people who are guilty get off sometimes?"

"Yes."

"Don't we have all kinds of strange rules created by activist judges and the ACLU that keep lots of bad people out of jail and make it almost impossible for the police to do their jobs?"

"Some people say so," I said. "Where'd you hear all this?"

"It was in school today. They had a special session. It was to tell us not to be frightened or upset."

"About what?"

"About them finding the terrorist cells, right here, with their bomb-making equipment and explosives."

"They didn't exactly find terrorist cells."

"Yes, they did. They showed us. In school. The tapes on the news. I saw it. There was a big raid. The Islamo-Fascist terrorists," she said, obviously reciting back what she'd been told in school, "fought back, and the police had to shoot their way in. One of them even shot a cop! And they arrested a whole bunch of them. But we don't know that we got them all. Even the ones we did get, who knows if they'll get punished or even locked up. If the ACLU has their way, they'll all get get-out-of-jail-free cards and be back on the streets doing it again."

"I think you should slow down," I said.

"That's exactly right," Gwen said. "I saw it on the TV too."

"They raided a mosque. That's a Muslim church," I said.

"I know that, Dad. Obviously, I know that."

"Yes, we all know that," my wife said.

"What I'm trying to say is that we don't know if this is the way the police say it is or another Waco."

I could see that I had drawn a blank. Angie was too young to remember Waco.

Before I could explain, Gwen asked, "Why would the police lie? This isn't Nicaragua." In her early twenties, she'd spent a year with a Cathedral of the Third Millennium mission in Puerto Cabazas, helping the poor and seeking converts. There had been a lot of violence and corruption around them. She'd sailed through, never flinching, certain that Jesus, like a force field, and her blue passport, like a shield, would protect her. "This is America. They have no reason to lie."

The snap answer—of course they lie, and for all sorts of reasons—sat behind my teeth, ready to be spit out like a bitter stone.

I looked from Angie to Gwen and back again, Gwen so certain and Angie so accepting, and wondered if I should say it. Welcome to the real world.

Back when I was on the job, we'd get frustrated over some perp who we were certain was dirty. Morally certain. Unable to put our hands on the dirt, we'd find some dirt to put on the man.

If someone had asked, what if it's the wrong guy, though no one ever did ask, we would have said, one out of thousand, maybe, but isn't it worth it if it means nine hundred ninety-nine bad guys were put away. Besides, the types of people we went after, if we got them for something they didn't do, they'd done something else, so it didn't matter. Justice was served. Case closed. They were wrong; we were right.

That's part of why I'm Manny Goldfarb's favorite investigator. I can tell when the cops are stretching, massaging the evidence, spinning their testimony, inventing informants, even planting evidence. I can figure out how they're doing it because there's no new way. We all do it the same old way.

Also, I still have friends.

Also, I know where many of the bodies are buried. After all, I was in narcotics.

I can only thank Jesus. I know Jesus was watching out for me because He came for me just in time. In order to get right with the Lord and live right, I knew I had to get out of narcotics.

It happened during the first year of the bounties.

As part of the War on Drugs, the federal government was giving a lot of grants to local police forces. The city had to come up with matching funds, twenty-five percent to the federal seventy-five percent. The city didn't want to raise taxes or take the money from somewhere else. They decided to go into the confiscation business, seizing the assets of drug dealers. It was sort a free perpetual money machine. Every dollar it created was turned into four by the feds. The mayor, the council, the taxpayers—everybody loved it.

To get more money, they needed more busts.

To get more busts, they decided to imitate another federal program, one that paid informants ten percent of whatever was confiscated.

Confiscation falls outside the normal rules of criminal law. It loosened things up a lot and also created new types of informants. They didn't have to have the kind of knowledge that would justify a warrant and that could later be questioned by an ACLU-type defense attorney and lead to a search being thrown out by an activist judge. In other words, they didn't have to be criminals, creeps, and coconspirators.

The informant could be a neighbor who noticed too many people coming and going. A car dealer who sold a BMW for cash. A bank clerk who noticed suspicious transactions. If they fingered someone and it led to a drug arrest, the city could seize both money and property, and the informant got ten percent of the value. Even if the criminal charges didn't stand up, the seizures usually remained.

In order to get a warrant, there has to be due cause. One of the simplest ways to establish due cause is to find someone to say, "I saw," "I heard," or "I have knowledge of" something criminal. It's very easy to make up a fake informant.

The first time a fake informant and our bounty program came together was, I think, fortuitous.

Xavier Garcia, who owned a body shop on Division Street between Sixty-fourth and Santiago Boulevard, was dealing on the side. There wasn't enough information for a warrant, so we made up an informant. The bust went down, and we found an ounce of cocaine. The city attorney was aggressive and went after everything that Garcia had: the shop, the plot it was on, the equipment, his personal cars, and his home. The value of the seizures was $328,000. That meant that $32,800 was due to the person whose information had led to the bust.

Except no such person existed. The check was ready, but we couldn't say that we'd made it up, sworn falsely, and committed perjury.

We could have claimed that the informant had died or gone to Mexico or disappeared. But everyone agreed it was a shame to let that money go to waste.

So, we recruited one of our regular informants to come in and sign for it and tossed him a few hundred dollars.

None of that bothered me. Though it should have. But whoring around and my second wife whoring around and her doing speed and me drinking and no one being responsible enough about our daughter and getting very casual about violence, all of that bothered me. Frightened me, and I was spilling my guts to Alan Stephens one lunch hour in a bar, my mind sloshing around in beer and bourbon, at noon, and he said come with me and made me get in a car and he drove and drove, out past the city limits, to where a great modern cathedral sat on a ridge dominating the whole horizon and there was a big rainstorm coming down from the mountains, you could see it moving like a dense black wall, bolts of lightning coming off its face hither and yon, and he drove up to the Cathedral and dragged me out of the car, every breath that came out of me spewing fumes that would burn if you held up a match in front of my mouth, and he dragged me down that long, long aisle to where Pastor Paul Plowright was preaching in front of a choir that was singing and where the lights were shining and at that very moment he was calling people to come down, to give it up for Jesus, to be saved, and my legs carried me forward as if my body knew already what my mind was yet to learn and I went right up to him, the smell of me preceding my arrival, so he knew full well that he was dealing with a reprobate and drunk, reeling through the afternoon, and he smiled at me, kindness in his eyes, no condemnation, no criticism, not even revulsion, a greeting on his lips, and he put his hands upon me and Jesus came through him and I fell backward. And I was saved.

A few days later, I put in a transfer to get out of narcotics. I was not there when the money was distributed. It was clear that Jesus was looking out for me, that He had sent Alan to come and get me, and He got me just in time.

That was not the end.

For the crew I'd left behind, it was just the beginning. When you drop your bucket down the well and it comes up filled with gold, you keep going back to the well. After all, Christmas is coming. Your wife wants to remodel the kitchen. Your son is dreaming about a $2,800 Mongoose jump bike. Did you know that, with 403 horsepower and 417 pounds of torque, an Escalade is "a personal empowerment zone?" Your girlfriend wants to go to Costa Rica. You want to go to Aspen. All that's needed is an arrest—a righteous arrest, no doubt, of a bad guy—a confiscation, a minor polite fiction, and a check is written, and your dreams can come true.

The arrest rate went up. The city made money. The department made money and was able to maintain its federal grants. The A Team was living large. Everyone was happy.

I know all this because my ex-partner, Rafe Halderson, tried to talk me into coming back. So I could share in the bonanza. Rafe was driving a new Vette by then. He was buying turquoise jewelry as an investment. "I can even afford a divorce," he said.

Instead of being a side effect—call it collateral profit—of legitimate police work, arrests became the means, and money became the end.

They did it too many times, to too many people. One of the fake informants got caught with serious weight by the feds. He asked for a deal, and he offered them a city cop.

Rafe Halderson.

Rafe called me. He was like a kid. He wanted to take it all back. He wanted another chance. He wanted to say how he'd always meant well. They wanted him to rat out all his friends. That didn't worry me very much because I was out before money touched my hands. "I don't know of any other answer," I told him, "than Jesus Christ. Maybe it's time to give yourself to the Lord, put yourself in His hands. He'll see you through, and nobody else will."

He asked, "Won't *you* see me through?"

"How?" I asked him. "How can I see you through? I can't be there in the dock with you. If you go to prison, I can't be there in the cell with you, through the nights, the regret, the fear. But He can. He can be with you everywhere and all the time."

"I don't know, Carl. I don't know."

"Give yourself to Him," I said. "He'll take your hand. He'll walk beside you. Somehow, together, you'll get through all this. Then, there will be a day when this is over, you've paid the price, and you'll be able to say, 'Thank you, Lord, for getting me through the dark times, through the valley of the shadow.'"

That's what I said to him. What else could I say?

When he hung up the phone, Rafe ate his gun.

It was selfish and awful of me, but I thanked Jesus for coming and rescuing me. Could've been me, could've been me. I quit the police force soon after that.

All that was in me. All I had to do was open my teeth, and it would pour forth from between my lips, like serpents and worms out of a corpse, a display to my wife and darling daughter of the corruptions within and without.

We want her to grow up right. And safe. To do so, she needs to re-spect authority. To believe that her parents and her pastor and her teachers and her leaders are all good people doing the right thing with our interests at heart, so she should obey and be a good girl.

If I tell her these things, will it all fly apart? Then what will she hold onto?

In the silence of my hesitation, Gwen's verdict and the official version were accepted as gospel, and we'd moved on.

"I have a question," my daughter said. "The lawyer you're working for is a Jew, isn't he?"

"Yes."

"How come Jews are always working with the ACLU to get people like that out of jail. You'd think they'd know better, what with Israel fighting the Arabs and everything."

That night I longed for a drink. But, of course, I didn't have one.

Ahmad Nazami was a job for me, not a cause.

A college professor was dead. An adulterer. A man who likely slept with his students. Of adult age, perhaps, but still. A nonbeliever. I still didn't understand how that could be. Even when I was lost, I still knew there was a God, somewhere. I just didn't know how to let Him into my life to help me.

When I got into bed, I reached for Gwen and began to kiss her.

"I didn't want to say this in front of Angie," she said.

"What?"

"Somebody called today."

"Who? What do you mean somebody?"

"I don't know, some man. He said to tell you not to work for terrorists, or you'd get it too."

"Get what?"

"You know. I mean . . . "

"What?"

"It was a threat. A death threat."

"He didn't threaten you, did he?"

"No. No, you."

"Look, anytime something gets on TV, people get weird. They come out of the woodwork. Gwen, back when I was a cop and actually busting people, I was always getting threats. It was all noise and bluster."

"They called here."

"I'm listed. I was on TV. We can change the phone number. Would that make you feel better?"

"I don't know, maybe."

"Look, we can't go changing our lives because some idiot calls us up and tells us not to do something. If someone called and said, if you keep going to church, the Muslims will get you, would you stop?"

"That's different. That's my faith."

"Alright. If someone called up and said, Don't wear blue dresses anymore. We're attacking people in blue dresses."

"We're not talking about dresses."

"Come here. Let me kiss you. Come on. It's going to be all right. Nobody is going to attack me."

I kissed her. She kissed me back. She wasn't thrilled. I tried various forms of touching to arouse her. When Gwen gets excited, she can be very, very enthused. But this time, she merely acceded to my touch. She went through the motions as a dutiful wife. I went through the motions thinking that the motions would work, that they would open the doors for sexual healing to work its wonders. They did not.

Having sex with a woman who doesn't truly want to, or only half wants to, or wants to for reasons that are not sexual is strange. But men do it. Or at least, I will do it. The penis has its own needs and sets its own tone, and once it's up and running, it's hard to take it away from where it's gone and say, let's go out to the garage and fix electrical appliances instead. Rather, the penis takes some sort of charge and leads the rest of the body and mind along with it, saying play with her breasts and her buttocks, no matter what she thinks about it—you know I like that. And if she's not responding in your favorite way, it says how 'bout that Teresa. I bet she would. Why don't you imagine how hot and frantic she would be, and what are all those things she'd learned in the intervening years that made her pretty fabulous, that woman with a saint's name who's so eager to play. She'd be whispering hot somethings in your ear. You know she would, urging you on, telling you how big and good you are.

Get the hell out of my mind, Teresa. Get out. I know the games you're playing. Planting seeds that promise to blossom in that garden where the orchids are made of flesh.

I am not going to ruin my marriage, my life, my daughter for you, Teresa.

How about, if you have to drop Teresa, my erectile consciousness said, why not think of some of the women you used to know, when you were a wild young stud, and then it started coming up with their names.

So I ejaculated to get it over with.

15

I scrolled down through the caller list on the telephone until I saw a number that I didn't recognize. I noted the time. Then I went to the bedroom and asked Gwen what time the threatening call had come. She told me. Yes, that was the one.

I put the phone number in a search engine. It popped up a name, Tod Timley, and an address. I put the address in Map Quest and got directions directly to his house. I took a look at the neighborhood on Google Earth. The geography of our lives at the touch of a button. So convenient. So few places left to hide. I went back into the bedroom and began to get dressed.

Gwen asked, "What are you doing?"

"Making sure he never calls again."

Tod drove a ten-year-old Chevy Malibu. It was maroon. He lived in a small ranch-style house in the Castle Creek development.

The house was big enough for a single man or a couple without kids, but not much more. From the streetlights and a little help from the moon, it looked well kept and recently painted. It was off-white with a blue door. The lawn had been mowed and the edges trimmed. There were no unusual shrubs or desert plants. Tod was a neat person but not very imaginative. According to the most recent information available on the net, he was divorced and lived alone. There were many things I didn't know: if he had an alarm system, if he had a gun, if he was trained in the martial arts, if he sat up all night in a rocker with a shotgun on his lap waiting for *them* to come.

So I parked out front. I wore a beige jacket, a white shirt, a tie with an emblem on it, and a western hat so I had a law-enforcement look. I carried a big flashlight that added to the effect and would serve as a weapon too. I walked calmly up to his door and knocked with the knocker, a cast iron fist that hung from a hinge at the wrist. Then I saw the buzzer, and I rang that too. Like I had a right, a duty, to bang at the doors of strangers after midnight.

I waited. I saw a light go on, the glow leaking around the edges of his front windows. I buzzed again.

"Hold your horses," he said.

He came to the door in a bathrobe and peered out the peephole. I figured he'd seen me on TV, so I had the hat pulled down low to obscure my face, held up my wallet flipped open to an official looking ID in my left hand and the flashlight in my right, turned on and pointed at him.

"Who're you? What do you want?"

"Sh'r'ff department," I said. "Had a r'port of prowlers."

"Not from me."

"Could I come in an' talk to you a moment, sir? Security of the neighborhood."

"It's late."

"Could be important. Home invasions lately 'round here."

"Well, I guess."

He unlatched his chain, undid two locks, then opened the door. I saw him there, pale, skinny, hairy legs sticking out below a plaid robe that had been washed a year longer than it should have been. I didn't see a gun in his hands. I shoved the door hard, knocking him back. Went at him fast, kicking the door shut behind me. I stomped on his instep. He grunted and bent toward it. I hit him on the back of his head with the flashlight. He gasped and fell to his knees, his hands reaching up to his head, to the black pain there that had knocked him down and taken the fight out of him, if he'd had any in the first place. I tapped the flashlight on the back of his knuckles, not too hard, not so hard that I broke anything, but hard enough to hurt. Then I kicked him in the side to roll him over.

"You called my house. You threatened my wife," I said.

"I didn't," he said.

"I checked the phone records," I said. "You did."

"I didn't do anything bad," he said.

I drew my foot back to kick him. He put his hand out to block it. So I picked my foot up and stamped on his wrist instead.

He moaned. It had to have hurt.

"You called my house, didn't you? Didn't you?"

"I called, but I didn't threaten."

"Admit it."

"Don't hurt me."

"You do it again," I said, giving his knee a tap with the flashlight, "and I'll make it so you can't walk, and I'll bust up your fingers so you can't even dial the phone. Do you understand me."

"Yes."

"Fine," I said.

"I didn't threaten. I was just trying to explain," he whined. "I know you're a good Christian . . . and if I explained, I knew you wouldn't, wouldn't work for those people . . . I know you," he said.

"What do you mean, you know me?"

"From church," he said.

I turned on a lamp. Yes, I did know him. I'd seen him at Cathedral of the Third Millennium. Like I said, it seats 6,450. Thousands of people come. I didn't know him, but I'd seen him.

"It's us against them," he said, still lying on the floor, half curled up, holding one hand over the other so it wouldn't hurt. "It's us against them, and I know you're with us. I know you are."

"Listen to me, Tod. You stay away, far, far away, from me or mine."

"I will," he said. "I promise."

16

"MacLeod's wife," I said to Manny, "They're recently separated. She claims it was all very happy and good-natured. But almost the first words out of her mouth were, 'Why don't you talk to his girlfriend?' She's forty, forty-something, attractive, but still, women that age get very unhappy about competing with twenty-somethings."

"You don't like her?" Manny said. "What she do? Come on to you?"

I didn't say anything.

"Carl, you're practically blushing. You didn't . . . "

"No. I didn't."

"No, you didn't. If you'd slept with her, you wouldn't feed her to me as a suspect. You're too much the gentleman and too self-aware. But if she came on to you . . . . Did she know you were married? . . . Uh-huh. You're a funny guy, Carl. But you're good. You really think she could have killed her husband?"

"I don't know. I really don't know. But more cause, more opportunity than our guy."

"Fair enough," he said.

I was wishing I could say, here's the person who really did it, here's the proof, so I could walk away. For the sake of my daughter, my wife, my marriage, and, for that matter, my own well-being. I had acted like a thug. Effective maybe, but not who I wanted to be. Self-righteous, sure, but was that good?

"The department secretary," I said, continuing with my report. "Nice woman, one of your tribe. Said there's a lot of bad blood in the department. I figured how much bad blood could there be over . . ." I had to look at my notes, ". . . analytic versus continental philosophy. But then I talked to the chairman of the department, Arthur Webster-Woad. That's a hyphenate, and 'woad' is an archaic form for woods, or a forest, something like that. Very old family, he explained, from the very old country. He started out with 'Professor MacLeod was much loved and will be much missed,' but then I threw a quote or two about analytic philosophy at him, and he went absolutely livid in a very icy way."

"You threw a quote about analytic philosophy at him?"

"Yes, Emmanuel, I did."

"And what was that?"

"Something to the effect of, 'By abandoning the rough, practical empiricism of science for the illusion of logic as an absolute, it had cut its moorings to reality and become as archaic as theology.'"

"You said that?"

"Yes, I did. I admit that I had to rehearse it, and I'm not entirely sure what it means, but it pushed his buttons. I thought, if he had a gun, he would've shot me on the spot."

"Really?"

"The thing is, it's something that MacLeod said. He could push Webster-Woad's buttons big time. I mean, even dead, he can still push the guy's buttons. A couple of the other professors too. Big quarrels going on over there."

"Enough to make one of them a suspect?"

"You could make him blow up on the stand, I think."

We were on the way to the courthouse for a pretrial hearing, riding in Manny's Caddy, a rental CTS, while the Mercedes was in the shop. That was one of his things—come ride with me, talk over lunch, meet me at the elementary school, the golf club. It never felt like, I'm such a busy man, you have to catch me when you can. It was more like he needed to fill the spaces, leave no room for emptiness.

"You said MacLeod had a girlfriend?" he asked.

"Ahh, the mystery woman. 'N.' Just an initial. That's what MacLeod called her. It might have stood for Nina. One student I spoke to said her name was Nina, but when this other student said, 'Hey, Nina,' Nina didn't respond. Then she suddenly did, like she, oops, remembered.

"No last name at all. Was apparently auditing P&R 342, same class as Ahmad. But not registered, not paying. No records. Her and MacLeod were very excited by each other, especially lately.

"We need to talk to Ahmad about her, someplace where we don't think the microphones are on. Seems like he had at least a silent crush on her. I've got half a dozen people saying he used to shuffle and hmmm whenever she was around. Meanwhile, she hung on MacLeod's every word, so maybe we have a classic triangle."

"Find her," Manny said.

We were at the courthouse. There was a crowd, not as big or rowdy as the last time but more media. Manny put on the left turn signal and went into the lot across the street.

"I'd like to," I said. "It would help if you could get me in to see Ahmad again. All I've got is blond, medium height, medium weight, twenty-two, three, four, pretty, but not spectacularly so, dressed modestly, not expensively. No special jewelry or tattoos or marks. Maybe she wore a silver cross on a gold chain. Maybe not." Yeah, I thought, that's the ticket. Find the girl. Then maybe I can gracefully back out.

He turned off the engine. We got out. He gave the attendant a wave and didn't bother with taking a ticket. They knew him. He hit the Caddy with his palm. "What do you think?"

"Plush enough," I said, "but it's not the C600."

"It sure isn't. The damn insurance company doesn't want to pay. You believe that? It's the war, riots, and insurrection clause. Was that a riot? That was not a riot. Uh-uh, it was an act of vandalism. Um-hmm, preplanned vandalism. If they were rioting, they would have attacked everything. But they did not. They only attacked one thing, my one hundred forty-three thousand dollar C600. They're gonna pay.

"Come on," he said and walked out into the street, dodging traffic. His leg was working well.

When we got to the other side, his face lit up. "The Rapture," he said. "I bet insurance companies won't pay up after the Rapture." The police had barricades up and were keeping a corridor clear so you could walk on the sidewalk and get up the steps into the courthouse.

"You don't believe in the Rapture, Manny."

"Of course I don't. But lots of people do. Your guy, Plowright, he preaches the Rapture. We could get rich, a niche market, umbrella policies for the Rapture. Collect the premiums but never have to pay. 'Cause the Rapture is never going to happen.

"Don't get insulted, Carl. Okay? Worst case scenario, the Rapture actually happens. You get whisked up 'cause you're a good Christian, and you're safely out of it. I'm not worried about paying off because, what the hell, with earthquakes, nuclear war, and the Antichrist ruling the UN, who's gonna care about an insurance company stiffing a few people. What do you think?"

Manny's cell phone rang, and he pulled it out of his pocket.

Tod Timley stepped out of the crowd, around one of the barricades. He was wearing a windbreaker. His skin seemed very pale. His eyes were bright. His hand came out of his pocket with a snub-nosed thirty-eight. I said, "No, no, Tod, don't."

He didn't seem to hear me. He wasn't looking at me. He paid me no attention at all. He shot Manny two times before the police opened fire and gunned him down.

17

I caught Manny as he started to fall. He looked at me with confusion. Then some sort of vast regret and sadness passed across his face. Such a sense of loss. Not fear or pain, but loss, a whole landscape, a vista of it.

People were yelling. Lights were pointing; cameras and the people attached to them were gathering around. I could distinguish the police calling for EMS. Manny held onto me.

"Susan," he said.

"Take it easy. You're gonna be alright."

"Susan."

"I'll get her. She'll meet us at the hospital. Hold on."

A cop was trying to push me aside, to get to Manny, to administer to his wound. He'd been shot in the stomach and chest. Blood was flowing out of him. His hand clutched my arm. "Promise me," he said.

"Take it easy. Let the—"

"The medics?"

"They're coming," I said.

He nodded, drifting off. But his hand held on. Then his eyes snapped back to attention, and he fixed his gaze on mine. "You find out who did it."

"We saw. The cops shot him. He's dead."

"Not him, Carl. You got to save Nazami. There's a wrong being done."

"Yes, I'll—"

"Don't bullshit me, Carl. You swear, swear now."

"I promise."

"On your word, your Bible, whatever the hell, you do this for me. You find out who really killed MacLeod, and you save that kid. You swear. Do you swear?"

"Yeah, Manny, I'll do it."

"By all that's holy, you swear?"

"By all that's holy."

The cops pulled me away. There was a lot of shouting—"let 'em through, let 'em through"—and EMS arrived. They put on pressure bandages and carried him away on a stretcher. Manny's cell phone was lying on the pavement. I picked it up to bring to him.

18

"It's the problem of evil," said the rabbi. "At moments like these, we always return to the problem of evil."

We were in Temple Emanu-El, the oldest Jewish house of worship in the state.

We were there for the funeral of Emmanuel Goldfarb.

Manny made it to the hospital. He lived long enough for Susan to arrive and even to say good-bye. "That, at least, was a mitzvah," said the Jewish doctor who told me that Manny was dead.

Death from old age we accept as the course of things. Death by disease gives people time to get used to it, even to see it as a relief and a release, not only for the dying but for the family and the people burdened with the person's care. Violent death interrupts our expectations. Expectations are important to us. The sun will rise in the morning. I will sleep tonight. The sun will be there again tomorrow. So will Gwen and my daughter and the church and its pastor and my friend Manny. But he's not. You see what I mean: the whole fabric of expectation and certainty is torn. If Manny's life can be snuffed out—with a crack like a snapping twig—then perhaps the sun won't rise tomorrow.

But I have the Lord. Who assures me that I am in His hands and that I have life eternal in His mercy. Simply for believing in Him. For giving myself to Him.

Manny, according to all that I am told, will not have life eternal. He will not be there to greet me at the gate, to take my case, should I need the help, to get the incriminating evidence tossed and the exculpatory in, to cite the precedents of other sinners who have gone to heaven, and if that fails, to plead mitigation.

That troubles me.

I know that it should not. After all, the gospel was there for him to take. It's offered all the time. God reaches out. Jesus reaches out. It is for that very reason that we are called upon to evangelize. To bring the good news that there is salvation, that no one need burn in hell for eternity. Here it is. Take it. It's easy. Take it before it's too late. If someone doesn't, whose fault is that?

Still, it troubles me.

If I start on my fingers, then go to my toes, then start using the pages of the Good Book as marks for my count, I will make it to Leviticus before I run out of people I know personally who have taken the Lord into their hearts and will, presumably, be crowding the heavenly subdivisions, whom I like a whole lot less than Manny. Quite a few who deserve it less, if you count deeds and goodwill and good cheer in the face of adversity, instead of just counting that one thing, giving yourself to the Lord.

"How is it that there is evil in the world?" asked the rabbi. "It's a question that everyone asks when tragedy strikes. It is a question that we, as Jews, may ask more than most. It is a question that does not have easy answers."

Manny was well liked, well known, and very well connected. The funeral was a who's who of power and money in the city and state. One of our senators was there, the chancellor of the university, the mayor, the governor. A couple of Goldwaters had come over from Arizona; a few generations back they were Goldwassers and Jewish.

Jorge Guzman de Vaca was there.

He's the Gulf Cartel's front man in our state. If you're not up on your Mexican gangs, the Gulf Cartel is the one out of Michoacán recently in the news for cutting off the heads of their rivals in the gang called Los Valencia.

Jorge has been trying to do the Corleone saga in one generation. He has a host of legitimate businesses. All that cash looking for a home. He contributes to charities and political campaigns; he's on the board of the Mexican American Friendship Association and United Catholic Charities, to name two.

Jeremiah Hobson was also there, to my surprise. He was our lieutenant when we were trying to take Jorge down and always failing. I don't know what Hobson knew or didn't know. There was a sergeant between Hobson and the grunts. Jerry always reminded me of the three monkeys—see no evil, hear no evil, speak no evil—except that he peeked, he listened, and he whispered.

When it all went bad, everyone wondered how far it would go. Hobson was just two steps up the food chain. Then Rafe ate his gun, and it all stopped right there. They called it one rotten apple, and Rafe was too dead to say any different.

Hobson made captain. He quit with his twenty and moved on to Cathedral of the Third Millennium as chief of security. It's a pretty big job with all their businesses, broadcasting, schools, real estate, outreach programs, and missions. In those days, he was Jerry. Now it's Jeremiah.

The Cathedral of the Third Millennium is a vast open door to the future. Temple Emanu-El is a treasure box holding the past.

It's much smaller, of course. It was built soon after the Civil War, which by southwestern standards is old. Outside, it has the look of a Spanish mission—this was once Mexico—except, of course, there's a Star of David instead of a cross. The land was given to the new European Jews, mostly Germans, by Don Efren de Carvajal y de la Leon, who was said to have been a crypto-Jew.

Crypto-Jews were the descendents of the Jews who became New Christians during the Spanish Inquisition but remained Jewish in secret. Sometimes, it was such a secret that it was secret even from themselves. They would call themselves Catholic, go to Catholic churches, and take Mass, but the family would have an unexplained tradition of lighting candles on Friday night. Others were taught by their parents not to worship the Trinity but only the one God Himself, without quite saying why.

They are also called Marranos. Rita Moreno and Fidel Castro both have such ancestors.

The stained glass windows had deep colors like gemstones and depicted Old Testament scenes. There's not a Christ, or a cross, or a saint to be seen, but there's Moses and the Commandments, there's the escape from bondage, there's Abraham and his son, and there's Noah, the ark, and the flood.

Two new windows near the front, predominantly in blues and grays, were memorials to the Holocaust.

"The sun is shining outside," said the rabbi. "We live in the land of milk and honey. Not *Eretz Yisrael*, but a land of milk and honey that is rich beyond all of history's imagination.

"Yet, there is violence. One man picks up a gun and ends another man's life, leaving a widow, leaving family, leaving friends, creating grief, creating pain.

"Stranger still, the man with the gun believed he was doing right. Emmanuel Goldfarb, at the same time, believed that the things that he was doing, which provoked such rage, were the right things to do. Out of all this righteousness, came great wrong.

"These are questions we have had to ask through all our history. We began to think, naïvely, that they would begin to fade away. That differences of belief would be settled through reasoned discourse, and when they could not be, they could cohabit in a land of milk and honey and tolerance.

"We were wrong. These are questions that have become more urgent."

"I watch television," the rabbi said. "And I check out the competition."

That got a laugh.

"A lot of these other religions, they have answers. Here, I'm afraid, you just get questions. What can I tell you, we're Jews."

Another laugh.

"There are mysteries. I believe. I believe there is God above, somewhere, who made us and watches over us and is telling us what is right and wrong. Yet, I also believe that when people believe in dogma, it leads to violence and death, like the tragedy before us, here, today."

So, too, did I believe that I was doing the right thing, protecting my family and punishing the wicked, when I kicked the shit out of Tod Timley. But I had, without intent, without thinking of it, sent his fear and anger in a new direction. Yes, I had probably increased it too, driven him from threat into action.

I didn't need a rabbi to make me realize that. As Tod Timley stepped out of the crowd, in his cheap blue windbreaker, before he raised the gun, I knew and said to myself, my God, what have I done?

The rabbi listed Manny's achievements, his associations, his contributions, how he did pro bono work, how he raised money for the UJA, Planned Parenthood, and the ACLU. The last two would have gotten him hung at Cathedral of the Third Millennium.

"One day," the rabbi said, "when Manny was telling me lawyer jokes—they were his favorite—I asked him about the law and about his profession and how he, himself, felt about it. He admitted that the law, like most things in the world today, ends up serving the rich and the powerful. It protects them; it plays tricks for them. Sometimes it does wrong; sometimes it does right.

"But then he said this, and I say, let this be his epitaph. 'As a Jew, we must hold the law sacred, not merely in the old way, because we claim to be the people of the law, but because we understand that it is the law, and only the law, that stands between us and destruction.'"

19

There was nothing so formal as a receiving line. But the widow stood in the lobby while they loaded the casket into the hearse and organized the cars, and a thicket of black suits surrounded her, saying their condolences. There were red ties and blue and gold. There were shiny leather shoes and the bald spots of serious men, and on their way to the widow, a word or two about an opportunity, a connection, and after they left her, another about a deal, a contribution, support, quid pro quo. There were women with handbags and handkerchiefs, and a lot of dabbing at eyes.

I suddenly found myself next to Jorge Guzman.

He held out his hand and asked, "How are you, Carl?" in a calm, conversational tone. He wore a sober suit. He could have been a cousin in the investment-counseling business. "I'll miss him."

"Yeah, me too," I said.

"I mean personally. Manny was *muy hombre*, or like his people say, a *mensch*. The legal thing too, of course."

"Of course," I said.

"He was good," Jorge said, shaking his head ruefully.

"He was my friend," I said.

"You have no idea how rare that is," he said. "Not you having friends—I'm sure you have many." There was always a certain care in the way Jorge spoke, as if he was controlling his accent or making sure he didn't say anything he wouldn't want to have played on tape in open court. "I meant good lawyers. Most people don't know because they only have a lawyer a couple of times in their lives, usually when they close on their house, or maybe when one of their kids gets into a little bit of trouble, so they don't know how it's supposed to go. But let me tell you, you do a lot of business with lawyers and you find out how bad most of them are. They file papers late, they don't read the depositions, they don't listen, and they don't know the law. It's not like on TV, my friend. You know anybody as good as Manny?"

"Not offhand," I said.

Hobson was staring at us.

"I have got to find somebody. You think of someone really, really good, like him, you let me know."

"Sure," I said.

"How about you? Manny was an important client to you. Are you going to be able to make that up?"

"I'll have to go out and hustle," I said.

"You ever do business investigations?" he asked.

"Sure," I said. "Usually I work through lawyers, but sure."

"Why don't you give me a call," he said. He took a card out of his pocket and tucked it into the outside breast pocket of my jacket.

I suddenly got annoyed. Maybe by the intimacy of the gesture, or maybe because I was going to need some new clients and was afraid of what I might slide into working for the front man of the Gulf Cartel. "Look, Jorge, I always need work. But—look, I don't want to offend anyone—but I remember witnesses disappearing, and juries acting very strange. I'm not a cop anymore, so it's not my business to do anything about it, but I would have a problem being part of certain things, like if I told you a guy was stealing from one of your companies and then found out something happened to him."

"I appreciate so much frankness."

"Oh, you do?"

"Truth is of great value. It's very efficient. Untruths, even polite untruths, waste a lot of time and energy. If I call you, it won't be about something that will distress you." He paused. "I promise," he said with a smile. "In the meantime, I like to think that a friend of my friend," referring to Manny with a tone of respect, "is my friend. If there is ever anything I can do for you, call me."

"What were you talking to that prick about," Jeremiah asked, intercepting me on the way to the widow.

"He's looking for a good lawyer," I said.

Jerry is tall and bland, with the face of a manager, a great test taker and the mind of a Sicilian claims adjuster. He kisses up and kicks down. "Be careful with him," he said, like he thought he was still sitting above me.

"What are you doing here? I wouldn't have thought that . . . "

"That I was friends with your ACLU buddy?"

"Yeah."

"There's an old story or joke about some movie star . . . "

"You're not usually a guy who tells jokes. How come everyone wants to tell jokes at this funeral?"

"Yeah, well, the punch line, or whatever you call it, was that they went to the funeral to make sure he was dead."

"Go fuck yourself, Hobson," I said.

"And while we're on the subject," he said, as if I hadn't said a thing, "let's make sure the Nazami thing is dead too. Let it go, Carl. Give it a decent burial, and let it go quietly."

20

Paul Plowright asked me to come see him.

The city is down on the flatlands by the river. To the north, there's a series of ridges, each higher than the other, until you hit the mountains.

Cathedral of the Third Millennium sits on the first of those heights.

The church itself is a rising wave, optimistic and open. It is anchored to a round office tower to your left as you enter. Like the church, it's mostly glass, but it has wide stripes of white stone facings that suggest columns.

It's always lit. You can see it for miles. The beacon in the desert. The shining city on the hill.

The church has a membership of thirty-eight thousand. It employs about twelve hundred. It takes in over $110 million a year. It produces and distributes radio and television programs; it publishes books, pamphlets, and bibles; it has outreach and missionary programs. It has a prison ministry that is now profitable thanks to federal funding for faith-based initiatives. It develops Christian communities that include schools, which it runs. It has a college.

It has its own exit off the interstate, Exit 31, Salvation Boulevard.

The average church in America has about two hundred members.

That prompts the question, how did Paul Plowright do it? His answer is that God led him to it. He marks out the story of his younger years as Five Revelations. Though he did not recognize them for what they were as they were happening, until the last of them.

The First Revelation:

His father had an insight of his own. He served in the infantry during World War II and came to believe the most important thing in life was a pair of boots that wouldn't raise blisters.

Demobilized, he used his back pay and a bank loan to open Plowright's Better Shoes and Western Boots, with the slogan "We guarantee the fit!" It was downtown, three blocks from the courthouse, until about ten years ago, when real estate skyrocketed and Paul's brother was able to retire by leasing the space to The Gap.

All the kids went to work in the store starting when they were ten years old. Paul, born in 1948, was the oldest of the four. From the first, he was good with customers and was out front while the other kids were stocking shelves and sweeping up.

When he was twelve, his mother took him to Raab's Department Store, down the block, to get his first good suit. Chatting with the salesman, he found out that the man got commissions.

Paul told his father he wanted commissions too!

His father said no. They were a family. All for one and one for all.

Paul had never gone up against his parents. This time he did. Something inside him knew that individuals should reap the rewards, and also pay the consequences, of their individual actions. It would make him work harder—he just knew it would. Not only that, if he sold more shoes, the store would do better, and if the store did better, the whole family profited.

It was a twelve-year-old's intuitive, individual understanding of the difference between free capitalism and collectivism.

There had to be *consequences*.

The Second Revelation:

His father agreed to give it a try. Paul quickly figured out that it was not enough to just work harder. He couldn't force customers to buy. He had to work smarter. He had to watch for those moments when they decided to make a purchase, or decided not to.

His father, who had marched across North Africa and Sicily and up the spine of Italy, was obsessed with practicality. Paul saw that selling was about something else. Customers wanted to *feel* that the shoes made them attractive or special, that they were being 'taken care of,' that the salesman was a friend they could trust, that they were getting 'value for their money' or a 'special bargain.' Whatever that extra thing was, if they weren't sure they were getting it, they hung back, but the minute they were *certain* they were getting it, they bought the shoes.

People craved *certainty*.

The Third Revelation:

Down here, the sixties were still the fifties. The boys had crew cuts and said sir and ma'am. Girls kept their knees together and held out for marriage. When Paul put his hard-earned money into the big adventure of going to an out-of-town college, he was expecting the sort of place where Ronald Reagan was on the football team, wearing a leather helmet and eager to go out and 'win one for the Gipper.'

The University of Wisconsin in Madison did not turn out to be that way.

"I remember this particularly from my second semester," he's said in numerous sermons. "I'd taken Psych 101, and now I was taking a course called 'Deviant Psychology.'

"Everything that the 'science of the mind' had defined as deviant — drug abuse, promiscuity, nymphomania, homosexuality, threesomes, foursomes, and free-sex communes, abortion, women having children out of wedlock and proud of it, defiance of authority, hatred of parents, the public use of foul language, shoplifting, stealing, drug dealing, political unrest, political violence, burning buildings, race mixing, deviant subcultures—was happening right outside the classroom window. Sometimes in the classroom! And it wasn't being condemned; it was being encouraged, cheered on, celebrated!

"They put up posters of Mao Tse Tung, a Communist, atheist, mass murderer, of Che Guevera, who'd helped enslave the people of Cuba. They made a hero out of Eldridge Cleaver, a rapist, who boasted of practicing on black women before he started attacking white women. His partner, Huey Newton, a convicted killer. Their idols were Jimmy Hendrix and Jim Morrison, self-destructive drug abusers. Like little Jane Fondas, they cheered the Viet Cong for killing Americans in the jungle.

"It was worse than wrong. It was tragic. It was a betrayal."

He'd always known that America had enemies. His father had gone off to fight the Nazis. We were locked in a death struggle with the Soviet empire. He was certain of the valor of the American fighting man. He knew we could never be defeated on the battlefield.

But these new things did trouble him.

The third revelation was that the thing we had to fear was *the enemy within*.

The Fourth Revelation:

After a year back home, working, he decided that he was not going to let the radicals and hippies, the atheists and Communists, the drug addicts and sexual deviants stop him from making something of himself. He went back to college. This time to USW. He majored in business. He liked it because it was about responsibility, rewards, and consequences. He minored in psychology but felt there was something wrong with the whole field.

Then he went to the University of Chicago to get an MBA in marketing.

At the university's world-famous school of economics, founded by John D. Rockefeller, they were reviving classical free market economics. It was a time of intense intellectual excitement, so much so that it was visceral, even missionary.

By contrast, there was an experiment in neosocialism right across the street from the university—vast public-housing projects where anyone could see firsthand the tragic results of the welfare state.

The inhabitants hadn't worked for their apartments and had no stake in them. So they broke the elevators and the windows, urinated and defecated in the hallways.

The young men joined youth gangs and dealt drugs. The young girls freely gave their virtue away. There were no consequences. They could get an abortion or get welfare money.

Families just disappeared. Nobody worked.

As Plowright saw it, under the guise of "helping the poor Negroes," the liberals destroyed them.

What he had understood in an individual way as a boy shoe salesman, he now understood as a social issue. The lesson was clear. If there are no consequences, responsibility disappears.

When responsibility disappears, civilization collapses.

The Fifth Revelation:

It was graduation day.

As he sat and waited to go up and receive his diploma, he suddenly saw that it was God who connected it all.

God had selected this new land, and He had given it freedom and democracy so that mankind would have an opportunity to make a fresh start.

Satan was determined to fight back. He was subtle, subtle as a serpent. He invented things like welfare that looked like they were helping poor people but actually destroyed them. He worked through so-called great thinkers, like Freud, who said morality was just repression, so adultery and homosexuality and even children having sex was downright healthy! Paul realized in a flash that "psychology" didn't work to really explain people because it didn't have God in it.

Then, the student sitting beside him nudged him. It was time for Paul to get up.

As he was walking toward the stage, he heard a voice.

It asked, "What are you going to do with this fine education? Will you serve something greater?"

He said, "I will serve you, Lord."

The room became radiant. Paul felt His power and His love.

He kept going forward, unaware that he was doing so, not knowing how, his legs on puppet strings, until he found himself at the podium, the dean of the business school saying his name—he saw the man's lips move but couldn't hear him—and holding out the rolled parchment with the ribbon around it. And he was moved by that same master who had guided him there, not just his feet in those few minutes, but unseen through all the steps of his life, to brush past the dean and up to the microphone.

Then and there, impromptu and uninvited—very much uninvited— he gave his first sermon.

"The Lord is calling us to serve America," he said, "against godless communism and the insidious destruction of morality and strength by the welfare state. Let us keep this country strong and great. Let us serve the Lord. For whatever we give to him, he will give back to us tenfold by His power and His bounty!"

21

SOUTHWEST MAGAZINE
YOUR BEST GUIDE TO AMERICA'S BEST REGION

*Path to Power: The Bible-Guided
Rise of Paul Plowright*

Like movie stars and rock stars, each of the leading televangelists has a distinct style. Joel Osteen is a high-powered motivational speaker in a slick, silk suit. Pat Robertson is God's own senator. Jimmy Swaggart preaches the way his cousin Jerry Lee Lewis plays rock 'n' roll.

Paul Plowright, in person and in the pulpit, projects the presence of a CEO of a major corporation—the type of businessman who gets tapped by a president to be secretary of defense.

What he offers his congregation, above all, is certainty.

His picture was on the cover.

His blue eyes looked straight out from his round face. Age had put a lot of white in his blonde hair, making it the color of a palomino's mane, and he wore it just a little bit long, his one physical vanity.

He explained to the reporter that as an assistant pastor to inner-city churches in Detroit and Baltimore, and then in suburban Houston, he watched the country's geography change. "Real Americans were driven from the cities. By real Americans, I mean the people who believe in God and the flag, who make a commitment to their families, who take responsibility for themselves." And, the magazine reported proudly, they moved especially to the Southwest. Which is why he came home to start his own church. He brought modern business methods and technology to his ministry, did market research, and developed a diversified product line and multiple revenue streams.

The occasion for the story was the last major election cycle. The governor's mansion, a senate seat, and both houses of the legislature were all up for grabs. The races were intense, bitter, and sometimes vicious. Campaign spending reached new highs. Negative campaigning reached new lows.

Everyone agreed that the outcome hung on the evangelical vote.

At the inaugural, Paul Plowright stood on the podium. He carried his own family Bible with him. When the time came, he passed it forward to the chief judge, and the governor elect placed his hand upon it as he took his oath of office.

22

The entire top floor of the tower was Plowright's.

Part of it was an apartment, a circle within the circle, set off center, with windows facing north. It had a view that overlooked the college, then past it to the far peaks.

That left a large crescent, wrapping around the south side from east to west, as office space. His private elevator arrived directly inside, in the center. The public elevator, the one that I came up in, arrived in a small lobby created by a wall that chopped off the eastern tip of the arc.

Paul Plowright was there waiting for me, holding the office door open.

He was smiling and friendly.

So, what did he want?

He clasped my hand. Paul's handshake is not some perfunctory up and down, quick as a nod. It is an embrace. It is also an act of domination, a friendly, paternal one, but still a way of establishing that he is setting the pace and the mood. "Welcome, Carl, my good friend. It's been too long since we've had a moment to spend together. I regret that. Too much to do," he added by way of explanation.

The outer wall is a vast sweep of glass. The inner wall is faced with polished granite, hung with a gallery of photographs of Paul in the company of the important and powerful. One of the larger ones showed him with the governor at the inaugural.

The first third of his office is furnished like a living room, with a couch, armchairs, and a coffee table, all arranged for comfortable viewing of a sixty-one-inch LCD flat-screen TV.

His desk is further down, sitting grandly in the center. Past that, there's an area that looks like an ordinary office: two secretaries' desks, tall filing cabinets, a copy machine, and the rest. None of his assistants were there. I was being treated to a completely private interview.

He asked after Gwen and Angie. I asked after his wife, Shirley.

"Off to Washington, then on a tour of military bases, leading prayer vigils." She travels a lot these days, practically a roving ambassador for the church. "We have to support the troops. The liberals and the Democrats and the media, they're undermining everything."

With a cordial gesture, he indicated that I should sit on the couch. He settled himself into one of the armchairs. The screen had a live feed from outside that looked up toward where we sat. The sun and sky were reflected in the glass like a living painting. The hi-def made the video more vivid than reality.

"Coffee?" Paul asked. The low table was set for two, with cups and saucers, cream and sugar, small silver stirring spoons, and neatly folded napkins. There was also bottled water and a bowl of fruit. He picked up the thermos carafe. "From downstairs," he said, meaning the Starbucks in the Cathedral's food court. I said that was fine, and he poured.

"I hear you had a run in with Jeremiah yesterday," he said as he passed me the cup and saucer.

"Nothing very important."

"I think of you and Angie and Gwen as part of the church family." He sounded very paternal. Like a loving father-in-law.

Gwen works for CTM five hours a day.

Women with children can only work from eight until two. That's church policy. Family is what it's all about. There is no family if both parents are out rat-racing from seven to seven. When a child comes home from school, one of his or her parents should be there.

During the summer, Gwen also works with the Cathedral's Christian Adventure Camp, getting close to God through white-water rafting and building moral character by trekking through the Sangre de Cristo Mountains in New Mexico.

Angie's been going on those trips since Gwen and I got together.

I nodded. Yes, we're part of the church family.

"I hate discord among my friends," he said. He shook his head. "Jeremiah has a rough tongue. He *will* apologize to you . . . " and before I could say anything, Paul assured me, "Oh, he'll mean it," which he wouldn't. "He may not have liked your lawyer friend, but that's not a reason to be disrespectful, of him or you."

"I appreciate it, but I can deal with Jerry myself."

"I'm sure you can. I don't doubt it for a moment." He leaned forward. "But I don't want you two to 'deal' with each other." He brought a verse to the situation, Matthew 5:23–24. "'If you bring your gift to the altar, and there remember that your brother has something against you, leave your gift there before the altar, and go your way. First be reconciled with your brother.' The answer is always in the Book."

"Like I said, there wasn't that much to it. We can let bygones be bygones."

"Good," he said.

He picked up the remote that was on the table and pressed a button. The view on the screen changed.

We were looking down at Angie's school, Third Millennium Christian Academy. A phys ed class was out on the track. They looked very clean and wholesome.

Their motto is "Decidedly academic, distinctly Christian."

They have real discipline. They don't let the girls come to school with their navels uncovered, pierced and glittering like Salome's, or wearing their pants so low below the curve of their bellies that they have to shave or depilate their pubic hair to keep it from curling over the top, clearly intent on letting everyone know it, so that teenage boys drool and middle-aged teachers get confused.

They don't let the boys come to school as baby gangstas, with their pants below the cracks in their asses, with weed, meth, coke, guns, or knives, or even with attitude.

Lockers and backpacks are always open to adult inspection.

They believe in corporeal punishment. Measured and restrained, but enough to make sure there's respect and obedience to the rules.

All well and good, but he was showing me things I knew. What was he trying to impress on me?

"Schools," he said. "The center of secular power is in the schools. They grab our children in elementary school, and they teach them that the Bible is just another book, that Christianity is no different than Islam or godless Buddhism or witchcraft. They have posters on the wall that say it's good to be gay, but it's illegal to put up the Ten Commandments.

"That's why we built our own schools."

He pressed the remote, and the view changed again to a wider shot. It was five miles to the interstate, and the Cathedral owned all the land in between. The area closest to the highway, spreading out around the schools, had been developed into a full suburban subdivision: single-family homes on quarter-, half-, and full-acre plots, garden apartments, assisted-living quarters, and elder-care housing, all on pleasant curving streets and attractive cul-de-sacs. There's a gas station and a convenience store.

"People want to live close to their schools. So close that their children can walk home. *If it's safe enough.* So we built a community around our schools. We made it safe. And people want to live there."

That was true. If there weren't a four-year waiting list, we'd probably live there too. It would make Gwen and Angie happy. It's overpriced, unless you count the intangibles of living in a Christian community. But the price of any real estate is about intangibles.

"What you see is just the beginning. There will be more schools. A bigger community. And everything that a community needs. Stores, recreational facilities, a bank. As it grows, businesses will locate here. What better resource is there than a real Christian workforce?"

He switched to another camera, one to the north, that looked down on Cathedral College. It's fairly small, with seven hundred students and just five buildings, including two dormitories. It specializes in Bible studies, but also offers BA and BS degrees. It was recently accredited.

"They use the universities," he said, anger slowly seeping into his voice from where it simmered on some back burner, over the steady flame of his sense that we were being betrayed, "to set the agenda of what we're allowed to think. They get to say what science is, what human nature is, what history is, what law is—and then force it on the rest of us.

"The college that you see down there, that's merely the seed." From anger, to hope. He was, indeed, a man out to save the world. Though the question kept nagging, why was he working so hard to recruit a foot soldier like me? "Soon it will blossom into a university, a great university," he said. "With a medical school, based on Christian ethics, and with a law school to develop Christian lawyers to fight the ACLU and the activist judges, lawyers who will fight for the rights of believers and free speech for Christians. We will have computer engineering and software design schools." Then he added with a thin smile, "God has got to be able to make better software than Microsoft."

I laughed at his punch line. "Those are impressive goals," I said.

He looked at me, studying my face, as if to determine if he could trust me. Then he nodded slightly. "This is not yet for publication or even discussion. This is just between us."

"I understand."

"They're not goals. They're plans. Solid, concrete plans that will go into effect very soon. In fact, they're even bigger than what I've already told you." Now we had gotten to something new. He went on, "The only thing I worry about is having good people around me.

"You're very good at what you do. As a husband and a father, as the provider for your family, I'm sure you have ambitions. To turn what you do into a real business, with employees and retainers and long-range contracts. Or you might want to be part of a company, an executive with a serious salary and benefits, so you don't have to worry, month to month, if there's money coming in. Those opportunities are here. Safety and security are essential requirements of a successful community. Great opportunities. I need people like you, Carl."

"Thank you. I'm glad to hear it."

"That's why you don't want to be on the wrong side of this thing."

23

We had come to the crunch that I'd feared.

"Pastor," I said respectfully, "I'm not on anyone's side."

"Do you agree that we're in a War on Terror?" he asked, trying to box me in.

"Yes, of course we are."

"And which side are you on?"

"I'm just in the information business," I said, trying to stay out of the trap. "The prosecutors have the cops. So I work for defense attorneys. That means sometimes I'm working for the bad guys. That's just the way it is. The lawyers present the information. Then a judge and jury sort it out. That's the system." I'd seen the expression on his face any number of times on irritable judges, impatient to overrule an objection they didn't like. So I reached a little higher. "That's the way it's set up in the Constitution."

"'The Constitution is not a suicide pact,'" he snapped back. "Abraham Lincoln, Thomas Jefferson, the Supreme Court, anyone with any sense understands, if we don't survive, there is no Constitution. Survival comes first. This is war time."

"I'm sure that's true," I said. "But look, I've met this kid . . . "

"Kid?"

"Frankly, he seems like a scared college kid, hardly the type . . . "

"Like the British doctors? They were hardly the type to set off car bombs in the middle of crowded airports. That's how they play it. How can you be so damn naïve?" He stood up. "Come here," he said, marching toward the middle of the room.

I followed as he'd demanded. His desk was about eight feet wide, custom cut from some exotic hardwood in a shape that mimicked the inner and outer arcs of the room. There was a flat-screen monitor, keyboard, and a printer on top, along with the books and papers he was currently working with. He picked up two pages that had been marked with yellow highlighter.

"This is from the *Kuwait Times*." Emphasizing the source, he said, "An *Arab* newspaper. About how they indoctrinate children in their madrassas. It quotes from their textbooks and their teacher's manuals.

"They teach them that Islam is the only true religion. All the rest of us are infidels. That Jews are monkeys and Christians are swine. A Muslim's true loyalty, wherever he is, is only to other Muslims, no matter how far from home he is, like right here. And under Islamic law, it's perfectly fine to kill infidels. Also adulterers and slaves. Yes, they believe in slavery. Fathers can kill members of their own family without penalty. Grandfathers too. Those are the savages that we're dealing with.

"For them, the Crusades never ended, and their war on us, *the swine*, will continue until judgment day.

"That's what their *kids* are indoctrinated into."

He shoved the pages at me so I could look for myself. "The truth is," I said, being conciliatory, "that I've been trying to get out of this, almost since I took it on. But Manny was a good client. And I can't say to clients, 'I'll take this case, but not that.'"

"Well"—he figured he had me and calmed down—"then you have a way out," he said, putting his hand on my shoulder. There's power in his touch. I don't know how or where it comes from, but it's there. He lays his hands on people, and they come to Jesus. They throw down their crutches and throw off their sins. "With Mr. Goldfarb's unfortunate death, your business obligation is effectively over." The hand on my shoulder opened with a slight push, as if he had just released me from this new, pernicious bondage, the way he'd once released me from a life of sin.

With a contented nod, he added, "It'll go to some court-appointed attorney. Let him sort it out."

"I don't know about the court-appointed," I said, to let him know it might not go that way, but not mentioning that I had some obligation to Ahmad's new council. "Obviously, he wants the best defense money can buy."

"He doesn't have any money."

"Sure he does," I said. "His family, and then there's a group backing them up, helping them out."

"I think you're misinformed. Goldfarb was doing the case pro bono."

"No," I said, "I asked him and he said, no, he wasn't, that there was plenty of money."

"Feel free to check," Plowright said. "But you'll find that I'm right, and for some reason—who knows why—your 'friend' misinformed you."

There's faith certain, and there's fact certain. Plowright was fact certain. It felt like the world was sliding out from under me.

"Who knows, maybe he had some other interest?" Plowright went on. "Maybe he was really working for the ACLU and was using your good name and good faith as a cover, a front. I happen to know that the ACLU wants this case to explode, to make a mess, to embarrass people, and to make it harder to fight the War on Terror."

Did Manny have a hidden agenda?

"He certainly didn't have your interests at heart when he involved you in defending a terrorist. You can only hurt yourself, which is a large part of why I'm talking to you. Hurt yourself and Gwen and Angie.

"Anyway, let whoever catches it, handle it. Nazami did it, he confessed, and he's going to be convicted. If he's smart, he'll plead."

"I have doubts about the confession," I said, while I tried to think things through. "He said he was coerced. I don't mean yelled at; I mean tortured."

"Yes, I've heard the rumor," he said. "And I was very, very concerned, because if it were true, it would be appalling. So I checked, and it looks like the only thing he was tortured by was guilt. People do have consciences. Even Islamics, I guess. Or maybe he wanted to take credit for it, so his family could be proud of him. He wandered into the Wolvern District precinct, ran into a police detective, and said he wanted to confess to a murder. Which he promptly did. The detective took it down. And put him under arrest."

"Which detective?" I asked, since I still knew a lot people on the force, especially down in Wolvern.

Plowright shrugged that he didn't know, and he went on, "When he said that he was commanded to commit the murder by the Koran, the detective figured it was a terrorism issue and called Homeland Security instead of the DA. Then it came in front of a judge who was drunk, so now it's back in criminal court. Still, leave it alone. It will work out, and justice will be done. Too leniently, I'm sure, but at least they won't get to make a circus out of it." He sounded satisfied.

How had Plowright come to know so much? Things that I hadn't been able to find out? Maybe he was right that Manny had hidden motives. Maybe I was all wrong. I was confused and still stuck.

Maybe he had the answer to the real question. Maybe he could figure it out.

"Pastor," I said, "help me out here. I owe you. I owe you my life, and I want to do whatever you want. But here's the problem. When Manny was dying, when I was holding him and calling for the ambulance and his blood was on my hands"—the moment still haunted me, and I could almost feel the wet heat of it on my palms—"he asked me to promise him that I would do this case. I gave my word. I gave my word to a man on his deathbed."

"That's how Satan works," Plowright said, the anger that simmers deep inside starting to rise up. "He takes advantage of what's good in us. We're tolerant, and we believe in freedom. So what does he do? He gets people like those people at that university down there," he pointed furiously out the window to USW, "to twist freedom around so that we're not free to pray in public places. They churn out books, atheist books, to undermine us. Books that say that the way we respond to religion is mindless button pushing, like the way people respond to pornography.

"Oh, but when it comes to pornography, that's something they love and protect. That's what they want free speech for. So that they can produce endless streams of pornography, their new secret weapon." The lid he kept over his rage at all these things had cracked. It was boiling out of him, faster and faster, with more and more force.

"It comes up right into your life through machines," he pointed at his computer, "that are in everybody's home. A secret plague. Addictive as crack cocaine. Nobody's immune. A poll from ChristiaNet found that fifty percent of Christian men and twenty percent of Christian women are addicted to pornography. It creeps in, destroys families, corrupts children. Sex is God's gift to make marriage joyous, and Satan comes and twists it, twists our people around with it. That's how he does his evil work."

He was sermonizing at full power, and I was his congregation of one. I couldn't tell if it was because he wanted to move me or his passions had risen up and seized control of him. Up this close, instead of in a vast hall among six thousand, was as different as seeing a video of a suspect being subdued on *Cops* and being out there doing it in the street, with the fists and batons, the twisting muscles, the grunting, and the sweat-drenched fear.

"One of . . . one of our counselors came to me just this morning with still another tragic story. About a man who was trying to protect his children, so he went on their computer and checked and saw what they were looking at. And he got hooked."

"We're in a race," he announced. In his passion he was bouncing from one thing to another. Each was said with force and conviction, but they connected in some subterranean place within himself. "A race to save this country, to save civilization. He wants to trip us up. Slow us down. Because he knows we're close to winning. That's what this Nazami thing is about. His servants want to trip us up.

"Satan looks at you, and he sees a man who wants to keep his word." He was perspiring as he does when his preaching grows hot, and his face was shiny. "That's a good thing. Yes, yes, of course it is. So *he* sees that's how he can get to you.

"You were there, at the courthouse, when your so-called friend made his rabble-rousing speech. What was he doing? He was dividing us. You saw your wife on one side, and the liberals on the other, the side that hates America. Out of your goodness, you were tricked into being on the wrong side. Do you see that?"

I didn't answer, but he didn't need me to. He went on, "America is strong. We have the strongest army in the world. We have nuclear weapons. We stay our hand. Our own goodness holds us back. There is no enemy in the world that can defeat America." He stopped and looked at me, directly into my eyes. "Only the enemy within. Just as there is no enemy that can defeat Jesus Christ, except"—he tapped me hard, with a single finger on my chest, near to my heart—"the enemy within."

Then he gathered himself. He took a white handkerchief from his jacket pocket. He wiped the sweat off his face, from his brow on down. When the swipe was done, his regular face, the always composed, in-charge, businesslike CEO, had returned. It was if he were a stage magician, and behind the sweep of the cloth he'd performed some sleight of hand and slipped his mask on.

"You asked me a question," he said in a vastly calmer way, caring, but moral and stern, like an old-fashioned father speaking to a wayward, prodigal son.

"Ask yourself these questions. Are you committed to a promise made under false pretenses? In law? In your heart? Or do you owe your allegiance to the higher good?

"I don't want you to choose what you may think I want. I don't want you to choose what you think is the most profitable thing to do. I don't want you to choose out of fear," he said. Then he proceeded to list his threats. "That you'll lose business, that you'll be ostracized. I don't want you to choose because you're afraid that your choice will harm your relationship with your wife.

"I want you to pray, Carl, about good and evil, because I know Jesus will guide you. And then, do what's right."

24

I was wrapped in a spool of anxiety as I rode down the elevator.

It had been way too much. America, Jesus, God, and Mr. Green were all anxious for me to get off the Nazami case? Too much promise and too much threat. The war between Christianity and the ACLU, my ass. I couldn't say if Plowright believed it all, but I didn't.

Most of all, too much sweat and too much passion.

The ride down was interminable. I felt like the elevator was being lowered by a hand crank.

So, what the hell—hell—was really going on? What could possibly be going on? What could Plowright, or someone in the church, or someone high up that he owed big time have to do with the murder of Nathaniel MacLeod? So that we all had to be sure that Ahmad Nazami hung for it?

Did I want to go up against Plowright? And the Cathedral of the Third Millennium? I liked him. I owed him. He had more money than anyone but Pat Robertson and God Himself. And he was connected to every power base in the state.

What was I going to do?

Why was the elevator so damn slow?

What about Manny? Why had he lied to me? How much had he lied about? Did he have a secret agenda? Was it true that he had lied? I would have to check.

Finally, the elevator trembled to a halt and opened on the fourth floor. Gwen works in book sales. I went to her office, but she wasn't there. I asked after her and a sweet Mexican woman named Alissia, whom I knew slightly, said, "She's with the Angels. They're rehearsing something from when she was one."

"Where? The rehearsal halls or the stage?"

"The stage, I think."

I took the stairs. I had to be moving. I couldn't bear the slow creep inside a container.

I entered the church from one of the side doors.

The Angels have angelic voices. They're mostly white, and there are lots of blonds. They're also young and very pretty, in a very wholesome way, of course.

I walked across the church quietly so as not to disturb anyone. Even with the stop-and-go of rehearsal, the music moved me the way it always does. There's a kind of pure perfection that connects everything in ways I don't understand, and the musical harmony suggests other types of harmony and clearly induces good feelings.

I walked up the stairs on the side of the stage.

Such beautiful young women. To look at them, to look past the music and costumes of chastity, is to be filled with temptation. So much of religion is about seeing them as angels instead of human beasts to be rutted with like the animals of the field.

Gwen was surprised to see me.

I wanted her to be ecstatic to see me or something like that. I wanted to know that she was swept away by me. Once and forever. Because I had a question to ask. As with any tough question, I wanted to know the answer before I asked.

I took her by the arm and led her away from them so that we wouldn't be overheard.

"What is it? Is something wrong? Angie?" she asked.

"No, no. I don't know if anything's wrong."

"Why are you here?"

"I have a question to ask you."

"What's that?"

"If, and I say if, if there were a conflict, between me and the pastor . . ."

"You and Paul?"

"Yeah."

"How could there be?" she said.

"If there were, I need to know, whose side would you be on?" Because if there were, she and Angie might be all that I had left.

"But there couldn't be. Why would you ask such a question?"

"If there were," I said. "I want to know. Would you be on my side?"

"How could that happen? Did you have a fight with him? Did something happen?"

"Nothing's happened," I said. "I just need to know." But, of course, by then, she'd already answered. Plowright preaches all the time that God's plan is for the husband to be the head of the household and for his wife to follow him. That's what makes the world go around and marriages work. The whole thing is about certainty, you see, certainty and order. Now there was uncertainty.

I addressed her silence. "I'm your husband. Would you follow your husband?" All of this urgency was spoken very quietly so as not to disrupt the Angels or expose our private business.

"I can't imagine it happening," she said. And then, she added, "Of course, I would choose my husband. Of course." As if she'd been called on to recite her homework in class and had, after she'd given the wrong answer, abruptly remembered what the textbook said.

How do you live in an uncertain world? Do you accept what someone like Paul Plowright tells you and let go of all your doubts?

Or do you check and check until you achieve certainty. I could only know who everyone was—Manny: friend or liar; Paul Plowright: pastor or criminal; Gwen: true wife or just some woman I was married to; and myself: someone who would take a deal or keep his word, who would quietly desert the field or crash and burn before he quit—I could only know who everyone was by going forward and finding out who killed Nathaniel MacLeod. Not that it had a damn thing to do with him.

I looked up, and Jeremiah Hobson was up in the balcony staring down at me.

25

William Thatcher Grantham III had called me. He was the Grantham in Grantham, Glume, Wattly, and Goldfarb. I assumed that he was calling me to terminate my services. I did not return his call.

Since I had not been notified, I could still act on Nazami's behalf, and for that matter, I could still bill for my time.

It gave me another day. I knew it wouldn't be enough. Not nearly enough. But often this world is a matter of doing the best we can with what is available to us.

Teresa Mansfield-Pellita, Nathaniel MacLeod's widow, had also called.

I returned Teresa's call.

She had news. She was letting me know, as I had asked her to do, that the police had released her husband's office. We could now go in. She had a key. She offered to meet me there. Her voice was smooth and smoky, with hints of this and that. It made me think of very fine whiskey, a reminder that there are places where the winter nights are long, that some things should linger on the tongue as their flavors emerged like memories coaxed out of dreams.

The first thing the devil does when he wants you back is offer you a few small lies that you can tell yourself as you walk yourself over to his side.

I did need to see the crime scene if I was going to continue.

It made perfectly good sense—indeed, it was more convenient—for Teresa to meet me there and let me in. There were many things she would know about her husband's work and his possessions that I couldn't understand without asking someone. In fact, there were many things I wouldn't even know to ask.

Also, the standard rule in federal and most state courts is that for crime scene evidence to be admissible, the examination has be witnessed, and she could be the witness.

Obviously, once she'd let me in, she would need to stay there with me.

That's how good the lies are; they're all true.

If the devil's in a really good mood, he offers, as a free promotional gift, one of his special cloaks made with the insulation of righteousness.

My head was spinning around with the story that Gwen had failed me. Make no mistake, the jabber box in my mind said. That she would even think of siding with Paul Plowright against me was worse than some simple act of sexual infidelity. Of course, I knew perfectly well that had Gwen been loyal in all things except some random sex act, then adultery would have topped my list of all available human betrayals.

The title of her sin wasn't what mattered. What mattered was what matters to children: she did it first! So what I did would be caused by her and cloaked in righteousness. I would be immune from blame.

When I heard Teresa's voice on the phone, an audiotape started rolling through my mind: "pretty fabulous . . . I'd learned a lot, a lot . . . tricks and toys and exploring the boundaries . . . . " And I remembered the way she looked at me and the electricity of our connection.

As we were speaking, I had my to-do list in front of me, and I noticed the name of the other widow on it, Manny's beloved Susan. She was more than beautiful; she was graceful and gracious, which made the thought of despoiling her even more thrilling, and it was as if I'd already had Teresa and was craving the next woman down the line.

Something was slipping inside of me. But I didn't really know what or why.

There'd be lies and deception. It would get bigger and wilder, until I found a way to make it all crash. And it would be Angie who felt the most pain.

So I tried to think of Gwen in all the positive ways. She was lovely and sexy and wanted more adventures than we ever seemed to have time and money for. I conjured her up as I'd last seen her, in front of the Angels, the Third Millennium Choir of Angels, and my imaginary eye drifted to them, and a sniggering voice inside me said, "You know that good girls tanked up on Jesus are wilder than strippers snorting speed."

You either stop. Or you don't.

There is no single act of sex that ever satisfies. No single drink or toke or snort or swallow or shot. When Johnny Cash was old, and both his body and his memories were full of pain, but he was off the pills, some reporter asked him, "If someone offered you a pill that would stop the pain, would you take it?"

And Johnny Cash said, "You mean, just one?"

I told myself that when I met Teresa, I would be all business. I would stay focused. I would concentrate on the job.

"So, do you want to meet me at the office?" Teresa asked when I hadn't replied right away.

I said, "Sure."

She said, "When?"

I said, "How about now."

26

"His book is missing," Teresa said.

All the smoky, sexy flirtation was gone.

She was in Nathaniel's swivel chair, frantic and distraught, and she was taking the office apart. His desk drawers were open. She was pulling out his files, stacking them on the desktop, on the visitor's chair, and on the floor. Just as I came in, with my equipment kit in my hand, she took a set of stuffed manila folders and placed them right on top of the chalk outline that the crime scene techs had made where the gun had been found, oblivious to the idea that she was destroying the integrity of the scene, that if I discovered anything, a court could easily refuse to admit it.

"It was important," she said. "It could be a really important book."

"Okay," I said, thinking I should have told her not to go in before me, not to touch anything until I had set up to record it. But I'd been too busy listening to the imps in my mind.

"Just stop," I said. Maybe it couldn't be a full-scale, technical CSI, but at least I could get a sense of what might have happened and what couldn't have happened. "Give me a chance to see things as close to the way they were as possible. It's already been trampled on by twenty people, but let's not make it worse." She paused for a moment and looked at me, close to tears. Though whether of grief or frustration or what, I didn't know.

She said, "I was wrong. I underestimated him. He was always talking about writing an important book. A book that would matter to people.

"You know what my attitude was, my secret attitude? It was, you're in the *philosophy department*. Of the *University of the Southwest*." Her tone made it clear that she meant them as labels of derision, as if nothing that mattered had come out of a philosophy department for a hundred years. And if, by chance, it did, it had better come from a name-brand school—Harvard, Yale, Stanford, Berkeley—where the coastal elites reside. Not from our state university, huge and ambitious as the system might be. Now she felt guilty about it.

But her voice of mockery conveyed too much, too concisely; it was too practiced and came too easily for me to believe that it represented some private inner voice or that she'd kept her contempt to herself. She'd said it out loud, and said it just like that, and said it plenty of times to her late husband.

If it had been me, and I had the sort of ambitions that she claimed he did, I would have hated her for it—and said so. Or, if I'd kept silent and endured it, I would have hated myself, and something inside would have shrunk and dried and withered away. The great world mocks us, we in the Christian community—I know that—as backward and unsophisticated. But we at least try to understand men and women as we really are. And we don't let political correctness force us to lie to ourselves about our own nature. Women want love, but men, above all, want respect. And you can find that in the Bible: Ephesians 5:33.

Something of what I'd thought must have showed in my face.

"I'm sorry," she said, not like she meant it but was annoyed that someone was being critical of her and she might have to admit to being truly wrong. Then she said, "I am sorry," with a sigh and sadness, and meaning it. "All this time . . . since . . . I was thinking that I should get the book published. It would help give his life some meaning. So I was eager to come here, because I thought I could accomplish something, do something, find the book and . . . see to it. But it's gone."

I knelt down to pick up the papers she'd put on the floor. "What are these? Where did they come from?"

"Student papers," she said. "I don't know, from in the desk."

"I'm going to put them back," I said, gathering them. She didn't care.

"We have to find the book. I want you to help me find the book."

"But first," I said, "let me look at the room and try to understand what happened here."

"You don't believe me, do you, that the book was important?" When I didn't answer, she said, "The way I didn't believe him. Do you know anything about it?"

"Just the bit they found that was in the news. He said it was easy to disprove God, right?" Something I found doubtful. More than doubtful. Annoying and arrogant. That's what it was, arrogant.

"That wasn't the point. He said you have to start with one proposition or the other, that God exists or doesn't. If you say He does, that's a dead end. The dead end the world is stuck in now. But if you start with us, with humanity, and ask why we believe, especially in something that doesn't exist, then you can go somewhere."

"I don't want to argue about this," I said. "Let me get down to business, alright?"

"You're not listening," she said.

"Yes, I am," I said, irritated with her. Angry, because she was attacking my faith. "You're looking for a manuscript. Right? And you can't find it. Right? So stop looking for *paper*," I said, as sarcastic as she'd been earlier, "and look on the *computer*. Nobody keeps things on paper anymore."

"I'm not stupid," she snapped back. "Of course, I looked on the computer. That's what I'm trying to fucking tell you. It's erased. It's gone."

"What do you mean erased?"

"I mean erased."

"A lot of stuff can be recovered," I said.

"No, no, no," she said. "Oh, no. Not this time. Somebody wanted his material gone. They deleted all his files, and then started duplicating his iTunes, over and over. There's ten copies of *Love and Theft* on there. They didn't just delete; they wrote over everything so it couldn't be recovered."

"*Love and Theft?*"

"He was a Dylan fan. He had everything. Now there are ten copies of everything Dylan ever did on there."

"All right, so maybe the book is gone. But let's get down to business. Let's try to figure out who killed him and why."

"Don't you see?" she said. "The book is why. They killed him for the book."

"I don't buy it," I said. "I know why people kill. They kill for money, dope, sex, and because they're drunk or stoked, not over . . . "

"Religion? Did you miss 9/11?"

"Well, then you're saying it points back to Nazami, and we're right back where we started."

"Why a Muslim? Were you absent the day they taught the Crusades in high school? Did you miss that we're in a war against Islamic fascism, and we killed two hundred or four hundred or six hundred thousand in Iraq? Come out of your box. People kill for *ideas*. Do you remember Vietnam? World War II? All those wars all over the place during the Cold War? People kill each other over *ideas*."

27

"Sit over there," I said. There was a couch across the room, opposite the desk. The wall above it was covered in bookshelves, except for a sort of display area in the center.

"Why?" she asked. "Did I get to you? Did I make you think? Do you know of someone who would kill over ideas? Remember, you just had a Christian nut kill Emmanuel Goldfarb because he was defending the wrong person in court."

She definitely knew how to push buttons, and she was stomping on mine. "Just shut up for a minute," I barked at her. "Go sit on the couch. I want to do my damn job."

She planted herself more solidly in the chair.

I stepped closer to her, reached out, and took her hands to pull her up. Her hands were smooth and dry and warm, and the contact between us was instant and complete and completely unexpected. I pulled to make her stand. She rose easily, ready, it seemed, to come wherever I wanted to take her as long as I had my hands on her. There was a moment there when we froze, looking at each other, holding hands. She was holding mine quite as much as I was holding hers.

Then I let go with one hand, gestured across the room, and said, "Please."

We both let go, and she went across to the couch. I watched her walk. She knew that. She was a woman. When she sat, she curled her legs up under her, limber as a little girl.

I turned away from her and sat in the office chair. Here I am, I said to myself, where Nathaniel MacLeod used to sit, where he was sitting when he was shot. The entry door was directly to my right. Certainly, if the door opened, he would have known it.

Behind me, to my left, there was a window, a good-sized window. It let in a lot of light but didn't glare on the screen.

I looked directly to my left, at the wall beside me. I saw a photo of Nathaniel with Jimmy Carter. They both had saws and hard hats and were building Habitat for Humanity houses.

When Nathaniel was shot, the gun had been held to his right temple. Blood, scalp, some hair, brains, and bits of bone had splattered against the wall. The splatter pattern was outlined in chalk. Nobody had cleaned it up, and it had dried there. Carter had a splat of blood and something grayer right by his chin. Nathaniel's image had taken some of his own blood. Over to the side of the photo was the hole they made digging the bullet out of the wall. It had a chalk ring around it.

Now that it was quiet and Teresa and I had stopped going at each other, I could smell the stale odors of dried death and decay.

I wanted to put my hand to my own temple, holding something, a book, anything, and then drop my hand and release the substitute object. But it seemed too graphic an act to perform in front of his widow. Still, I raised my right hand slightly, then let it fall, and looked down. The chalk mark that marked where the gun had been found was not directly below. It was about eighteen inches to the right. Alright, maybe his hand hadn't fallen straight down; maybe the recoil had pushed it out and away. But no, the Webley-Fosberry is a strange gun. I'd never heard of one, so I'd looked it up. It's an automatic revolver with a complex mechanism that uses the force of the recoil to turn the barrel to the next cylinder, making it smooth and steady, and in its day, it was a favorite of target shooters. Still, it was possible that he'd flung his arm out. People do all sorts of things at the point of trauma and death.

If someone had set it up as a suicide, they'd done a fairly good job. I didn't see any reason to doubt it.

So why had the story changed? Had Ahmad Nazami really walked into a police station and confessed? We were taking the position that he hadn't. And we were accepting, at least for the moment, his wild story of kidnapping and torture.

The missing manuscript and the erased computer? Could that be the reason? As far as I knew, nobody had discovered that until an hour ago, when Teresa came in for the first time. When it was discovered, could it be included in a tale of suicide? Sure. If he killed himself in despair. What do writers despair about? Their work. So, logically, he could have destroyed his work as well as himself.

Somebody had staged the suicide.

Then changed their mind? Then gone and organized a kidnapping and used at least two thugs, plus a jet and a pilot. Why? What had gone wrong with the first story?

Why kill MacLeod in the first place? Over a book? By a professor?

More questions than answers.

I turned around. There was a display area centered in the bookshelves over the couch.

"That's where the gun was?" I asked Teresa. She nodded. "It's an unusual gun," I said. "Why did he have it, and why on display?"

"Nathaniel wrote some mysteries." She pointed to them, set up around where the revolver had been. Three paperbacks were on display, the covers facing outward. I got up and went close enough to read the covers.

"He used to have more copies," Teresa said. "Three or four of each. I know, I set up his nice little display for him."

There was only one of each. Their titles were *Strangled by Ivy*, *Leaded Glass*, and *Downfall of a Don*, all with the image of something deadly—a gun, a dagger, and a bloody bludgeon—over some academic scene.

"Campus mysteries," she said. "One horrible person gets killed; ten people all have motives. An amateur sleuth, a philosophy professor, of course, solves them. His girlfriend at the time—this was twenty years ago—bought him the gun. It's the gun that killed Sam Spade's partner in the *Maltese Falcon*—not *the* gun, the type of gun."

"He kept it loaded?"

"Yes," she said.

"Let's walk this through," I said. "Would you go sit at the desk." She did, and I went to the door. "So, he's sitting at his desk. It's about two in the morning. Maybe three. What is he doing here, that time of the night? Was that usual?"

"No, not when we were together."

"Was he an insomniac? Work all night? Have a deadline?"

"No. But . . . oh, maybe to meet the girlfriend."

"Why here? You two weren't living together anymore. Home is always more comfortable and private. Anyway, he's here, at three in the morning. Someone comes to the door. It's locked? Unlocked?"

"I don't know," she said.

"When I came, it was unlocked. I just opened it and walked right in."

"Yes, of course, unlocked. He hated doors that locked automatically. He was always locking himself out if they did."

I stepped over to the door. "So, I come in and . . . " I walked toward her in Nathaniel's chair. "I take the manuscript? Except for the first page? And then I erase the computer with all your life's work on it, your e-mails, phone numbers, everything . . . and you let me. Is that likely? A backup, there had to be backup."

"An external hard drive," she said. "It's gone. It sat right here." She pointed at the back of the desk.

"A person comes in," I said, "and goes to the gun." I took the few steps toward the other side of the room and reached for it, suiting my actions to my words. "Knows it's loaded. Takes it down. All this time,

Nathaniel sits politely at his desk. Doesn't yell or call 911 or fight back. Then the person tells him to sit still, and he comes up, right here." I came up behind her and put my fingertip near her temple, not actually touching her, yet still she shivered. "And he shoots him."

"Or she," Teresa said.

"Right, or she," I said.

"He would let a woman in," Teresa said, "and sit there while she got the gun. Because men don't know enough to be afraid of women." She turned and reached up and, wrapping her fingers around my outstretched index finger, turned it away from her. "A man, he would, I don't know, argue, get upset." She still held onto me. "But a woman, he might laugh at her. Then she might shoot him"—she squeezed hard and spoke with anger—"just for laughing at her."

It was as if she was telling me how she had done it. And why. If it had stayed a suicide, a fake suicide, I would have figured her for it, but it didn't account for all that happened with, and to, Nazami. Maybe Nazami was a nut job all the way and had made it up. Maybe two separate things had happened. Put in the possibles and spin them on a spindle and see what lines up in the slot machine. I said, "He would let you."

"Yes, he would," she said, her hot, dry hand loosening and tightening in a slow rhythm on my finger.

"And if you put the gun to his head, he wouldn't be afraid, would he?"

"Not really, no."

"You'd had fights, lots of fights," I said. I was certain they had. She'd shown me she knew how to push the buttons that lead to domestic madness.

"No," she said.

"You don't have to lie," I said with kindness, as if I thought that was just fine.

"No?"

"Not to me," I said. "You had fights."

"Yes, we did."

"You loved him, and he hurt you."

"Yes, you bastard." Angry at him, angry at me, blending both of us together.

"You used to fight. Who hit who? You hit him, or he beat you?"

"He . . . "

"Not you?"

"No," she said, but she didn't even mean to be convincing.

"Not ever?" We were falling into the rhythm of Q&A. It was taking on a life of its own, with its own cadence, a ballad of love and anger, and all three of us dancing to it, she and I and the dead man too.

"Sometimes." It was coming out of her beat by beat. "Yes, sometimes," like the beating of her heart. "I hit him. I hit him a lot of times, but I couldn't hurt him." She twisted my finger and tried to bend it. "Like I can't hurt you. It's not fair, you know, not fair at all that you can hurt me, and I can't hurt you."

"But I don't want to hurt you," I said.

"Yes, yes, you do," she said, holding on to my hand and standing up, pressing against me. "You want to, you want to. I feel it every time I see you. I felt it just talking to you on the telephone."

"So, you were angry at him?"

"Yes," she answered, her mouth coming up to mine.

"And when he laughed," I said and put my hand in her hair to pull her far enough back so that I could see the expression in her face and read her eyes, "you shot him?"

"Me, shoot him? I wish. I just wanted him to get mad enough to pay attention to me. Mad enough to put his fingers in my hair and pull it, like you're doing . . . pull harder . . . harder . . . hurt me . . . then throw me down on the couch and fuck me."

28

"You have a beautiful home," I said to Susan.

She looked around with a wan smile, then gave a slight shrug of regret and indifference. "I'm going to sell it."

"That's a shame," I said.

"No, not really. It's way too big for one."

"Still . . . "

"And I wouldn't want to live in it without Manny."

The Jews have a custom called sitting shiva. *Shiv'ah* means seven in Hebrew. The seven first-degree relatives—husband or wife, mother, father, brother, sister, son, and daughter—are to sit in the house for seven days to mourn the dead. A candle is lit and must be kept burning for the duration. Other relations and friends can come and visit.

"I brought a cake," I said, holding the box out to her.

"Thank you," she said, taking it. Her hands were so lovely.

"I was told it's the custom to bring food. I didn't know what to bring."

She smiled. A beautiful smile, on the verge of laughter.

"What?"

"I just had a vision of you bringing a casserole."

"Should I have?" I asked, feeling awkward.

"No," she said sweetly. We were standing in the foyer. "Come in, come in," she said, leading me into the living room. There were several people there, and food, and a candle burning.

There was an old man with Manny's face, most of his hair gone, the skin over his skull gone thin and tight. His eyes were red and filled with loss.

Susan made the introductions. It was Manny's father, Abraham. The woman sitting next to him, nearly his age, her hair soft and white, was Manny's mother, Betty. He had no brothers or sisters.

The others were neighbors and the wife of a lawyer in Manny's office.

"You knew my Manny," Abraham said.

"Yes. We worked together."

"Carl was Manny's investigator," Susan said.

"Oh, yes," the old man said, nodding. "He liked you."

"Yeah, I liked him too," I said.

Susan asked me if I wanted something to drink—coffee, water, something stronger. I said coffee, and she took the cake and went into the kitchen.

"You were with him, weren't you? That time when he got up on his car and spoke. You helped him up. I saw the video. And you stood in front of him, so the rocks wouldn't hurt him. You were a friend, a good friend." Abraham tried to smile, but tears welled in his eyes. "He was a wonderful son. He didn't just make money; he believed in things too. All of this, this is nothing," he gestured at the multi-million-dollar home.

His wife reached over and held his hand.

"And you were with him when he was shot. Yes, that was you."

"Yes, I was."

"I saw. You tried to stop that man. I saw. I played that video over and over."

"You shouldn't, Abe," his wife said. "Someone made a Tivo of it. He should stop watching it. To see our own son murdered. Shot like that. Some kind of barbarian, he must be."

"You know what is the greatest tragedy in the world?" Abraham leaned forward. He grasped my hands and stared into my eyes. "For a parent to outlive his child." He began to weep. "May heaven spare

you such pain. May heaven spare you. My Manny, how I loved him."
He released me and sat back, his weeping face bare and open to the
world.

Susan came in, all proper and neat, carrying the cake on a platter,
a few slices already cut, a cake cutter on the platter beside them, my
cup of coffee in her other hand. She quickly and quietly put both on
the table, then went down on her knees beside the grief-stricken pa-
triarch. She took a napkin from the table and wiped the tears that he
was too bereft to pay attention to. She seemed especially beautiful in
the comfort and love she was offering. It looked like a scene from the
Bible storybooks we give the children in which the illustrator makes
the good daughter as radiant as a saint.

"Abe," she said, "Manny had a good life. He did. He died fighting
for what he believed in."

"Thank you," he said to her absently. Then he said it again, "Thank
you," with attention. "Yes, to die fighting for what you believe. That is
something. Thank you. You must keep reminding me."

"Yes, father," she said.

I reached over and took the coffee to hide my tears. There was a
miniature pitcher of cream and a bowl with sugar cubes and small
silver tongs on the table. But I wanted it hot and bitter on my tongue
to distract me from the real pain.

After a while, Manny's father calmed down, and Susan patted him
and rose up. I wanted to say something to him too. "He was a good
man," was the best I could manage.

The old man nodded and said, "Yes." Manny's mother said,
"Thank you," and I was afraid she would break into tears like he had
a few moments before. I was going to add that I would miss him, but
it wouldn't be nearly as much as they would. My feelings were so
small beside theirs, so I said nothing more.

"Have something," Susan said.

It gave me the opportunity to say, "I need to talk to you for a
minute, if that's okay?"

"Of course." She excused herself to the others, and I followed her into what had been Manny's home office. He had a lovely old desk on which sat a large, flat computer screen. He had shelves and shelves full of books, enough to make him some sort of kindred spirit to Nathaniel MacLeod. He had a leather armchair with a matching leather footstool and a couch that didn't match. It felt rich but not ostentatious or off-putting. It was comfortable. The whole house was comfortable. It would be a shame to sell it, but that's the way of the world.

"What is it, Carl?"

I sighed. "Manny told me . . . see, I asked him, was this case pro bono. And he said no. But now I hear that it was. Do you know?"

"It was."

"Why would he lie to me about it?"

"He was upset that he did."

"He was?"

"Yes. When you asked him . . . he really wanted you to take the case and work with him, but you caught him by surprise, and he felt that you would feel more comfortable if it was just a job, not a cause. But also, he didn't want to ask you to, or even put you in a position where you felt you should, work for less or for nothing."

"Why not?"

"Partly his politics," she said. "I mean, look at this place. Manny made a lot of money. Off of crooks and corporations and who knows what. So, if he wanted to work for nothing, fine, but he felt it was wrong for someone like you to work for nothing."

"Yeah, 'cause I'm a . . . "

"Oh, Carl, you have to know Manny didn't disrespect you. Manny never respected money."

"You could have fooled me."

"He loved it," she said and laughed fondly. "He loved it, but he didn't respect it. He was sort of amazed. And he just hoped that he wouldn't come to depend on it. And he certainly didn't think that he was better because he had it, or that people who didn't were less. Anyway, once he said it, he couldn't figure out how to unsay it."

"Why me? There's lots of others out there."

"He said you were a stubborn Dutchman."

"Thanks," I said.

"That once you started, you wouldn't stop. You wouldn't be bought or intimidated."

"Why was this so important to him?"

"Maybe because of all the money. He needed to do something for a cause. To make up for it, to make it worth something."

I nodded. That made sense to me.

"He's counting on you to finish it," she said. "To make sure his life was worth something."

"Oh shit," I said and sat down, head in hand. I wanted to quit this job so badly. So damn badly.

"What's wrong?" she asked and put her hand on my shoulder. I looked up at her. It was as if the room were exploding with light. I don't know what to call it—lust, infatuation, possibilities, sin, a road over the mountains to a place I'd never been. She looked back at me in the brightness, and all of it went through her mind too: the permutations, confusions, complications, the inappropriateness, the betrayals, the sheer wrongness of it, and the shining light.

"Oh dear," she said in a very mild tone and withdrew her hand. "Oh dear."

"Well," I said. "Well, I better go."

"I understand. Did you find out what you needed to know?"

29

The Angels sang.

Our hearts were lifted. People rose in their seats. They clapped. They sang. They swayed and danced. They embraced their neighbors. They hugged complete strangers. There was ecstasy on their faces.

I had my own two angels, one on either side of me. My heart was filled with love. And with certainty. My daughter, my wife, my family. This was what I needed. This was what I wanted.

Paul Plowright, up on the stage, began to speak. He said, "I want to talk to the parents. And to the grandparents. And to those of you are thinking of becoming parents.

"My heart goes out to you because it is so hard.

"Why does it feel like you're all alone? All you're trying to do is raise your children to obey the Ten Commandments, and it feels like the world is against you, the whole world."

The people around us were listening, listening intently, as was I, because he was right.

"You're not paranoid," he said. "You're not crazy. You're not bad parents. It feels that way because it is that way."

Yes it is. And that was the response of thousands of others around me. They spoke their agreement out loud. They clapped, cheered, and said, "Amen." It felt good to me to be among like-minded people.

"They go to school, and their teacher tells them—their teacher is *required* to tell them—that the Bible is *just* a book, like any other book. That the Bible is no better than some Communist tirade. One that says religion is the opium of the people just because our faith makes us feel good.

"I admit—I *celebrate*—the fact that our faith can make us happy, that Jesus can bring us ecstasy and sooth our pain, that prayer comforts us in times of grief and gives us strength in times of trouble. But the reason is because His way is the Truth. It does not mean that religion is a drug that turns us into fools and sheep.

"Then, after school, your son or your daughter goes over to visit Joey or Janey across the street. Nice kids, nice parents. But they haven't put adult controls on the Internet. In five minutes, they are watching sex acts that we didn't even know existed when we were growing up. A lot of us still don't. And don't want to know. But our children know, and they have seen them and children learn by imitation."

He stopped and sighed, then changed his tone and rhythm. "You know what," he said flatly and dryly, "you've heard this all before. I've said it all before. I said it and said it until I got tired of hearing myself say it.

"So I did what I always do when I have a problem. I got on my knees, and I prayed. I said, 'Jesus, what about all of these temptations and seductions and perversions.'

"And Jesus said to me, 'Paul, I'm tired of hearing you complain all the time.'"

We all laughed at that. It was just so human. And real.

"I tried to say, 'Lord, I'm not complaining, but these are terrible times.'

"Jesus said, 'I don't want my people to be whiners and bellyachers. That's not what Christians are. Get up off your bottom and do something.'" That was an applause line, a big one.

"Well, I admit, I was a little taken aback. I said, 'But Lord, look at all we've done. Look at this big cathedral. Look at the schools. Look at the TV and radio. The this and the that and the other and . . . and," Plowright sighed, "Jesus said, 'Well, Paul, if you think you've done enough, then maybe you've done enough.'

"I could feel he was about to leave me—not that He ever leaves anyone, but you know what I mean—and I said, 'Wait a minute, Lord. I'm sorry. I'm being a little slow here, but I am a mere mortal, and sometimes I don't get it.' It seemed to me that he nodded. 'It's not enough, is it?' I said. I realized that as long as there's more to be done, it's not enough. Whatever we have accomplished, if there is more that could be accomplished, it's not enough.

"He looked at me with love and kindness, and I felt that he was pleased that I had understood something.

"'You want me to do more, Lord, don't you,' I said. Then I asked, 'Tell me, Lord, what do you want me to do?'

"He just looked at me. And I understood. He gives us so much. He gives us faith and love and strength and community, but at some point, it's up to us. It's up to us to do some thinking, to do the work."

The Angels began to hum behind him, not an identifiable tune but gently rhythmic and uplifting.

"So I prayed some more because I didn't know what to do. But I knew that Jesus would guide me. I prayed until my knees were sore. Until my back was sore. Until I thought I couldn't pray anymore.

"Then I saw what He wanted me to see.

"Jesus gave me a vision. It was a shining city on the hill. And its name was the *City* of the Third Millennium. Not Third Millennium Cathedral, or Enterprises, or Third Millennium Estates. A city, the City of God."

His face shone, and he spoke, as every once in a while he does, like a man who has truly seen a vision and is certain of it and is now sharing it.

"Our own city," he said, "with a great university. Greater than the ultraliberal, radical, anti-Christian university over there." He pointed in the direction of the University of the Southwest.

"So when our children grow up, they can have higher education without being seduced by an atheistic professor into moral relativism, forced to endorse the homosexual agenda in the name of diversity, taught anti-Americanism in the name of multiculturalism. You truly do not have to be an anti-American, homosexual atheist in order to learn engineering, computers, medicine, or law.

"It will have a medical school. With a teaching hospital. A law school, and from it, our own law firms. With high-technology research labs. God's own Silicon Valley. You have to know that God can make better software than Microsoft."

When you have a good one-liner, you use it more than once. It got a good response.

"I know what many of you are thinking. Oh, Pastor Plowright, that sounds great, but such things cost millions, tens of millions, even *hundreds of millions of dollars*, even *billions* of dollars.

"Yes, they do. Of course, they do.

"You may be expecting me to say, 'Oh, let's pray. Let God provide.' You may think that I'm going to remind you of God's law about tithing, that when you fail to give God's one-tenth to Him, He says that you are robbing Him.

"I'm not going to say any of that. What I'm going to say is that God has provided us with sources of funding.

"Yes, he has.

"I am not yet at liberty to say where and how. But in the coming weeks and months, I will reveal it to you as the money comes on line.

"The dream will become reality. I invite you to join us in it. If you don't already live here, think about living in the City of the Third Millennium. If you're a builder or an entrepreneur or a business-man, think about bringing your business to God's own city. We'll need shops and supermarkets, restaurants, health clubs, and recreational facilities.

"And auto repair. Wouldn't you like to have your car fixed by a mechanic who actually believes thou shalt not steal?"

That got a big laugh.

"Banks and financial institutions that will invest in Christian enterprises. We will have our own mall . . . with a dress code."

There were cheers for that.

"This will no longer be a cathedral. This will be a city with a cathedral at the center. A city built around love and obedience to the Lord. We will be 'the light of the world. A city that is built on a hill cannot be hid.'"

So this was what he'd been talking about. Yes, there would be opportunity here. More than opportunity, a way to genuinely bring Christianity into how we all work and live, every day, in every way. I stood and applauded along with the five or six thousand others. We were one. We were a movement. We were going to get things done.

The Angels stepped forward and began to sing "There Is a City on the Hill."

The cameras focused on them and projected their faces onto the giant screens so we could watch them exalted by the music. I put my arms around my own special angels.

Own special angels, own special angel, ownspecialangel, *my own special angel*—that's how Nathaniel MacLeod had described the mystery girl. The girl with no name. The girl who had to make a secret of going to a class where atheism was taught and then was "seduced by an atheistic professor."

That was the connection. One of Plowright's Angels had become one of MacLeod's angels. Why was I so instantly certain of it? I searched the faces, wondering. It would be about more than leaving the choir. More than turning in faith for secularism. There were rumors, but I normally dismissed them because there are always rumors about powerful men and young women.

Who was she? Plowright's own little angel? Who had become MacLeod's own little angel? Which one was she?

On the way out, after services, Jerry Hobson waved a greeting to me. He gestured to me to come over. I excused myself from Angie and Gwen and crossed the lobby to him.

Jerry said, "Have you seen these disposable camcorders?" displaying one. "Under two hundred bucks. You can pick one up at the drug store, shoot what you need, and download it to your computer."

"Yeah," I said.

"Pretty good picture, too. Look at this. Come on, look at it." He pushed a button and the video played on the small viewfinder screen.

I was looking at the side of a building at USW. Then the camera zoomed in. The autoiris worked very well and adjusted to the light inside the room.

My face was in profile, small but recognizable. And there was Teresa, and she was pressing her body up against me. You couldn't see it because the window frame cut us off below the waist, but you could figure our groins were tight together. Then she tilted her lips up toward mine, asking to be kissed.

Then my hand came up and grabbed her hair and pulled her face away from mine. But that didn't make it look less sexual; it made it look more sexual.

"You can practically read her lips," Jerry said, leaning close to me and whispering in my ear. "Fuck me," he said, managing to speak in falsetto, slobber, and keep in synch with Teresa saying the words.

I threw her down. Toward the couch that was outside of the frame created by the window. Then I walked toward her, and I too disappeared.

"They're real fuckable lips, aren't they, Carl boy," he said, still in my ear, and I was unable to push him away, a small blackmail for the bigger one to follow. "Bet you banged that bitch up good. You gonna save some for Jeremiah? Pass her around, like the good old days." He moved back a little bit so I could see his face, and we could stare each other in the eye. "When I tell you to stay the fuck away from something, stay the fuck away. Or I will crush you. I will crucify you, you sad little trailer park sheep, and when I'm done with you, I'll do your wife and daughter too. Do you understand me? You don't even have to talk. Just nod your big, square head up and down if you understand."

Then he smiled, like we were having a normal after-church conversation. "See," he said, taking my hand and shaking it, "aren't you lucky. You got a message, and a warning. Christ's mercy instead of the Lord's wrath."

As he finished, Gwen and Angie came over.

"What are you boys talking about?" Gwen asked.

"Just business," Jerry said.

"Yeah," I said.

"We were talking about the Nazami thing. Carl's going to drop it. I told him that we here at CTM respect that and care about him, so we're gonna find him some extra business to pick up the slack."

"Oh, that's wonderful," Gwen said.

30

Gwen has very light freckles on her breasts, and her nipples are the color of strawberries. Her eyes are blue. Not the intense blue you see when you look to the north with the sun shining toward it; they're the light blue of southern skies.

I kissed each freckle with reverence and fascination and growing arousal, working my way toward placing my teeth on the engorged tips.

Sunday afternoon. Angie was at her church group. Gwen was very happy with my decision. She was rewarding me for doing what she wanted with a good fuck. What an ugly, angry thought that was.

She began to stroke my arms and shoulders, and one of her hands found one of mine and brought it to her mouth, kissed it, then teased at it with her tongue and sucking lips.

The phone rang and rang, but we adamantly ignored it.

I tried to reconsider. Let us say, instead, she was no longer tense and worried and so was free to open up. I didn't want my wife to fuck me as a reward for being a good boy. I wanted her to want me out of her own love for me, out of her own desires, for the sanctity of our marriage. That's what I wanted. I made my way down her belly and she bit my hand with a sound that mixed a sigh, a whimper, and an inclination to moan. As she spread her thighs, she said, "Let my beloved come into his garden and eat his pleasant fruits," from the

Song of Solomon, and when I did she giggled. There are moments when it's sexier to quote the Bible than just yell "eat my pussy, eat my pussy," though Gwen can do both.

I do love her, and I know she loves me, and I let my anger slide away in our sensuality.

The phone rang again. We let it be. No one should call on Sunday afternoon when Angie's at church group.

Just before Gwen took me in her mouth, she said, "The roof of my mouth like the best wine for my beloved, that goeth down sweetly." I'm not as biblically literate as she, so I just said explicit and obscene things to her, and she seemed to like that just fine.

Afterward, as we lay on our backs, my arm under her, I said, "I have to say I'm sorry. For the other day."

"Why?" she said, too adrift for serious conversations.

"I threw something at you, and when you didn't react fast enough, the way I wanted, I got angry with you."

"It's alright," she said, rolling over and kissing my chest, her hand going down to my cock, using her fingernails to toy with it.

The phone rang again.

When I answered, Teresa said, "I have to see you."

I said, "I have to tell you, I'm not doing the case anymore." My nervous system was firing sparks. I hoped it didn't show in my voice or my body, and I prayed that Gwen didn't pick up the extension.

"I thought you were going to help me. I thought you were going to help me get the book."

"Listen to me, I can't," I said.

"Now you're hurting me," she said, pouty and suggestive.

"And besides, it's Sunday," I said, a good, businesslike statement.

"Oh, right," she said. "Time to get your fix. Marx thought it was just a metaphor when he said 'Religion is the opium of the people.' It's not, you know. It affects your mind chemically, and a very versatile drug it is. It can make us happy, bring us ecstasy, sooth our pain, comfort us in times of grief, and give us strength in times of trouble—which is all wonderful. But like any drug, it can turn us into fools and sheep."

"What? What did you say?" It was almost word for word, phrase for phrase, what Plowright had said in his sermon a few hours ago.

"If Marx had been alive today, he might have said, religion is the Prozac of the people, the LSD of the mystics, the valium of the agitated."

"Are those your ideas, or . . ." Was she reciting MacLeodisms? And if she was, did it mean that Plowright had taken his material from the same source? I've heard our pastor a lot over the years. The rhythm and rhyme of today's sermon had followed a familiar tune. But some of the lyrics had been different, like he'd sampled someone else's song.

"What do you mean?"

"Is that something you said, or something from your husband's book?"

"Well, the point is that we have to remember that thinking, emotion, and brain chemistry are not actually separate entities," she nattered on. "They're different aspects of the same event. We respond chemically to ideas and symbols. Pornography uses words and images to create chemical responses so powerful it can be addictive. Religion can work the same way."

"Is that from the book too?" I asked. Were the words in her mouth and in Paul Plowright's both echoes from the same original source, Nathaniel MacLeod?

"It might be in the book. It's almost certainly in the book. He said it often enough," Teresa said. "It's one of his standard memes."

"And he said it that way?"

"Probably. I'm sure I picked it up from him. When can I see you?"

"I told you, I'm dropping the case."

"Please, Carl. Please," she said, like she liked to beg.

"If you have to call me," I said coldly, "call me at the office, nine to five, Monday to Friday."

"Yes, of course. I understand. You can't talk now."

When I hung up, Gwen asked, "Who was that?"

"Mrs. MacLeod," I said.

"And what did she want?"

"Her husband's book," I said. "Seems to have gone missing, and she wants me to find it. She thinks she can sell it."

"What's she like?"

"Upset, like you would expect."

Which was not at all what Gwen wanted to know.

"Attractive?" she asked.

"I don't know," I said.

"What's her hair like? What color are her eyes?"

"Her hair?" I said, like that was a weird question.

"Tell me anyway."

"Well," I said, like I had to think about it, "it's kind of spiky and short." But long enough to get my fingers in it and hold her and pull it until it hurt—not a lot, of course, just enough.

"You mean the campus feminist lesbian look."

"You could call it that."

"Thin or fat?"

"She's thin."

"Thinner than me?"

"Gwen, I was just trying to tell her, I'm not working on this thing anymore."

"Is she?"

I knew better than to say yes. Teresa was naturally slender, small breasted, and angular, with wires of nervous energy darting around in her. Gwen was born to be both rounder and more solid. I answered sideways. "She's older than you. Older than me for that matter."

"Good," she said.

"What's this about? You're not usually like this."

"I don't like women who call you at home on Sunday afternoon."

"Me neither," I said.

She came up to me. All she had on was the shirt I'd worn to church and nothing beneath it. Her breasts moved suggestively underneath it, her nipples clearly defined. It parted with each step, revealing her trimmed blonde bush.

"Come back to bed," she said. "I'm going to show you I can love you better than any half-lesbian university witch."

"I never . . . , " I began.

"I know that. But just in case you think about it, I want you to know you have better at home."

It was very good sex. Loud and long and sweaty and noisy and enthusiastic. Either out of uncontrollable enthusiasm or to mark her territory, she put bloody etchings down my back.

But I wasn't all there. I was in my head. Paul Plowright had virtually quoted Nathaniel MacLeod. Not just generally, but several times and close enough that if it was a school paper, you could make a case for plagiarism.

That could only be possible if he'd read the book. But how could he have read the book unless he had the book? And how could he have the book—an unpublished, undistributed book, of which there were no known copies—unless he had taken the book? Taken it the night Nathaniel MacLeod was murdered.

That was what I was thinking as my wife's thighs were around me, and she was kissing me and scarring me and loving me, as I was inside her, sliding in her tight, hungry heat, as she moaned and spasmed and told me how much she loved me.

31

"I'll tell you why God was born in the desert," Manny once said to me.

We were driving down a two-lane road from nowhere, headed home. Nowhere that time had been a small town in the Chihauhuan desert, near the border, population 628, plus a couple of hundred illegals.

Its main business was smuggling. A sad Mexican American had killed his common-law wife. He had enough coyote pesos to afford Goldfarb for the defense. Boredom, rage, some adultery, drugs, whiskey, hard words, some small violence, harder words, then she threw a pot and then he hit her with a fist, so drunk he let his rage have full rein, and she went back into the old iron stove and never rose again. Not all his tears and sorrow could erase a single line.

We were driving through the night, the desert night, dark except for our headlights and a crescent moon behind a veil of high lacy cirrus. Manny pulled over to relieve himself. When he turned off the ignition and the headlights went dark, an extra ten million desert stars suddenly revealed themselves.

I got out and joined him.

The air was cool and clean. We stood there for awhile after we were done—I don't know for how long, just standing there in all the quiet—when Manny said, "God was born in the desert."

"That's what they say."

"But they don't tell you why," he said. "I'll tell you why.

"The forests—the jungles too, but I know the forests better—are never quiet. Cicadas and frogs, wind and water, even the trees make noise; they groan when they bend, snap when some part of them breaks. At first, you dismiss it as the noises of 'things,' lesser things, things without consciousness or souls. I mean, that is, if you're a modern person, like you or me.

"Then something cries out, and nothing but a human could make a cry like that. But you know there are no other humans around you. Then there's some other sound, and you realize it has meaning, like our voices have meaning, that it's coming from fear or hunger or it's part of a conversation of a family or a pack, some kind of community.

"You listen more, and raccoon couples grumble at each other, and squirrels chatter at each other like any squabbling family when they wake up in the morning. Crows, crows have all sort of business to attend to. Bear cubs play. Adult bears are mysterious; they appear, but their bodies are so black that they eat up the light, and they take one step and disappear, like a magic trick.

"Then at some point, maybe, you notice what the trees are doing. They split open rocks. You'll see one that's been blown over, its root system torn out of the earth, and yet, it's still growing. It's still fighting for life, and it comes to you that something that fights that hard to live is most probably conscious. Its consciousness may be something that is beyond your understanding, but you can see that, in its own way, it's fighting as hard to live as you ever will.

"So you begin to see the spirits within all these things, just as you think of the soul in yourself and in other people. The winds seem to have a spirit too, and the water, and the earth itself.

"If they have a spirit within, then they have souls, and then they must have their own gods. You see what I mean?

"Then you walk into the desert and, suddenly, you're alone. Perhaps not a desert like this, which still has plants and all sorts of creatures, but the true desert, the sand dune desert.

"Then, there is just you and it. And all of it, instead of being populated by hundreds of spirits, all as busy as squirrels, is one

152

great immensity. So we come to imagine, or to have the insight, or to have the vision, something, to see God as One. One God and alone."

"Well, He is," I said.

"I agree with you," he said lightly, meaning that wasn't the point anyway. "That's what I was raised in. That's what I believe. But it is strange," he said, "that man had to come to the desert to find Him."

Maybe that's why, when my prayers failed, I decided to walk into the desert.

When Gwen left to pick up Angie, I prayed.

Pastor Paul Plowright told me, "I want you to pray, Carl, because I know Jesus will guide you. And then, do what's right." Gwen always tells me, "Ask Jesus." What the heck, I always say it too.

There was no answer. So I prayed harder. Not so hard, perhaps, as Paul Plowright, wearing out my back and knees, but hard as I knew how to do. But there was no answer.

When Gwen came home with Angie, I put on as normal a face as I could, but I could not rest content.

So, after dinner and after I made sure that Angie had done all her homework for Monday, I picked up my cell phone and called our home phone. I answered it. I said hello, then yes and uh-huh, and this and that, and took a pen and paper and wrote some nonsense down. When Gwen asked me who had called, I said, "Jerry Hobson. There's some runaway, and he asked me if I could try to track her before she totally disappears. The thing is, I have to go now."

"See that?" Gwen said. "They're already trying to help, just like they said."

I felt like shit for lying. I felt like an idiot for having told a lie that could so easily be discovered. But I needed to go, and somehow it never occurred to me that the truth would have sufficed.

For miles and miles around, the lights from the Cathedral of the Third Millennium obscure the full glory of the night sky.

So I drove south, toward the border, toward Mexico, looking for the dark.

South and then west and then south again. The roads got smaller and smaller, until it seemed I had gone deep enough in to begin on foot. I left my watch and my cell phone in the car. I took a small compass, matches, and a knife with me.

Fear came and went and came again, like puffs of wind. Would I get lost? Get hurt? Snakes? Smugglers? Like puffs of wind. Pain, small pains, came and went, came again, and worked themselves out. I heard the noises of the desert night. The scuttling of small animals and lizards. The cry of some bird. But mostly there was silence except for the noise of my own feet and my breathing.

The thoughts went around and around, the same ones, over and over. Sometimes I would get to ride one, and it would take me to a conclusion, a certain and absolute conclusion, but when it came to that stopping place, all the thoughts I'd put behind me would be waiting for me there, and the conclusion would dissolve and become indecision and conflict all over again.

Loneliness came and solitude, and the sky began to grow ever larger.

"See what I mean?" Manny asked.

I saw him out of the corner of my eye on my right. I knew the words he'd spoken, but I wasn't sure that I'd heard them as sounds in my ears. I didn't turn and look too closely because I figured he would disappear.

"I didn't expect to meet you out here," I said.

"Where else?"

"I meant I didn't expect you to turn up at all."

"Did you expect anyone to turn up?"

"No. Not really. Well, maybe. I don't know. But if someone did show up, I didn't think it would be you."

Manny said, "You got a problem, don't you?"

"You here to enforce my promise?" I asked and kept on walking. He stayed with me, keeping the same distance, a few feet to my right and just a bit behind.

"I can't do that," he said. "That's up to you, but you know that."

"Can I ask you a question?" I finally said. "I have to ask, are you real?"

"What do you think?"

"Thanks," I said ruefully. "Well, if you're real, I gotta ask you because it's been on my mind, did you make it to heaven?"

"And why shouldn't I?" he asked, knowing perfectly well why I was asking but forcing me to be out in the open about it.

"The Jew thing," I said. "It's supposed to be that you have to accept Jesus Christ to get into heaven, and, Manny, I got to tell you, that bothered me." As I spoke, I turned toward him and looked straight at him, and he disappeared. Not with a pop, or a poof, or a whoosh. He simply wasn't there.

I kept on walking.

Sometimes I was tired. Different pains came, and then they went away. The stars were glorious. The ground was difficult, broken, full of rocks and pebbles. I seemed to have as many thoughts as there were stars. And like the stars, they were scattered and unconnected and without any pattern that I could discern.

And where did Jesus stand in all of it? And why wouldn't he tell me?

Walking. Feet hurt. Knees hurt. I got a pain in my side. Just keep walking. The legions walked their way across the empire from Spain to Persia. Jesus walked. He walked into the desert. He went into the desert for forty days and forty nights, and there the devil appeared to him and tempted him.

Where was the devil? What would he tempt me to do? He was silent. I was a soul not worth the stealing.

I got very tired. It was cold, and I shivered and thought I should have brought more, a pack with a blanket, some water and food. The fears hit harder; no longer vagrant puffs of wind, they were angry gusts, throwing sand in my face and chills down my neck.

Then, all by itself, the walking got easier; I got my second wind. The pains fell away and the thoughts did too. The stars got brighter and their colors more unique and particular. From time to time, I saw high up jets and heard the growl of low-flying prop planes. The desert began to speak to me in scuttles and whispers, a distant rattle.

In all that glory, the pure air, the sharp, white moon, the vast swath of the Milky Way, the vastly uncountable stars, I began to find despair. Not what I expected from it, but despair it was. There were no answers. Anything I did would be wrong. Fragments of things I knew of science, from the Discovery Channel and Nova, began to flit through my mind, that ninety-seven percent of the universe is actually dark matter and dark energy, dark because no light can escape from it, dark because it is unknowable, unimaginable to human minds, not unknowable and unimaginable as the glory of God, the essence of God, the mind of God is unknowable but as an indifferent, uncaring bleakness. So alien that it cannot even be aware enough of us to know that it does not care about us.

So much more satisfying, the way they teach it to Angie, a world of perfect design, all balanced, put together, like a fine Swiss watch, but infinitely more complex, infinitely finer, by an infinitely greater designer so that each piece miraculously fits with all the others, and if you pulled out any one, all the rest would collapse, like pulling the keystone from an arch.

But this was not that clockwork sky, the one with a heaven in which God resides.

This was the blackness with random fires. Every fire with a time to die. Cosmic time would come to each, and it would explode or implode, then disappear. No eternity for them or for me, no heaven, no hell, and so how could it matter who killed the atheist? How could it matter if the Muslim disappeared into the maw of our gangland state prisons to become a bought-and-sold fuck toy and die of AIDS or from a shank? What did it matter if my friend the Jew had died for nothing?

There were no answers. There was nothing.

I was tired. Empty. Nothing. Nothing.

I turned around and began to head back. "I'm sorry," I said to Manny, but not really, just saying it out loud. "I can't do it."

It was done. It was over. There was nothing left but the long, long trek back. Everything was the same as when I started, but bleaker and bitter as the taste of dust. My aching feet took their steps, one after the other, just one step at a time.

He didn't just appear. I felt him arriving. He was moving alongside me for awhile before he spoke. "He that hath wife and children hath given hostages to fortune; for they are impediments to great enterprises, either of virtue or mischief." He sounded understanding about it, even forgiving.

"Is that Proverbs?"

"Francis Bacon," he said. "He was a great man. He helped invent science. He formulated the idea that we should start with observations of the natural world, then make up hypotheses about what it meant, and then come up with experiments to test them. He thought it should be done step by step, in small doses. Before we get to the grand conclusion."

32

Cathedral of the Third Millennium's telecasts are very slick, multi-camera operations with split screens, effects, lots of shots of the congregation, and, of course, our beautiful Angels. Nowadays, they're available on the net. I downloaded several, some old, some new, searched for close-ups of the girls, grabbed individual frames, to create a homemade mug book, then burned it onto a DVD.

I drove over to USW, walked into the philosophy department offices, and said, "Hi, Esther."

She looked at me with anger and suspicion, and asked, as though it were an accusation, "Why are you here?"

"I wanted to see if you could look at some pictures."

"No. Go away."

"Wait a minute, what's the matter?"

"Your people destroyed his book. That's where it starts. That's where it always starts."

"What do you know about his book?"

"Teresa told me. She called to see if there was a copy here."

"Is there?"

"No, and it was an important book. Your people thought so, enough to destroy it."

"Why do you say my people?"

"Who else?"

"How do we know?" I said, trying to be reasonable. "We don't know what was in the book."

"I know."

"How?"

"I read it."

"How? When?"

"He used to give me pieces to read for him, as a regular person, not an academic."

"But you don't have copies?"

"No. I would mark them up, whatever I didn't understand or didn't like, and give them back."

"Why do you think my people would destroy it?"

"Because it explained what religion, your kind of religion, really is. A false answer to the greatest human need. And your people won't stand for that."

"Look, I don't know why MacLeod hated religion—"

"He didn't hate it. He wanted to understand, to bring it into balance. He wanted to do something to stop the madness before it's too late."

"What madness?"

"This insane, worldwide religious war you people are trying to have. What are you going to do, kill everybody who believes different than you? Nathaniel understood you can't kill faith. Look at us Jews. You would think after five thousand years of people killing us we would say, 'Enough already. Look, I'm wearing a cross. Leave me alone.' But we don't. As long as there's faith, people will be willing to die for it. And whenever people of faith have power, they'll kill for it. All you can do is try to balance it with sanity and humanity. And the way you do that is by understanding that a religious war is like killing someone over who has the better imaginary friend."

"That's not what we want to do," I protested.

"I've listened to your Pastor Plowright. He wants to make this a Christian nation. When that happens, do I become a second-class citizen in my own country?"

"Come on. No. We have nothing against the Jews," I said. How could she think that way? "CTM is a big supporter of Israel."

"Oh, just the Muslims then. They'll be the second-class citizens. And the Hindus and the atheists. We've seen this before. England expels the Jews. The Italians invent the ghetto. The Russians send the Cossacks. Hitler creates the Final Solution. And it always starts with the burning of the books."

"Look, wait a minute. I can't argue all that with you. Let's start somewhere else. Do you want to know who really killed Nathaniel MacLeod?"

"You bet I do," she said fiercely.

"Alright then. I do too," I said, figuring to get a point of agreement and then build on it.

"And you're a liar," she said with contempt. "I guess that comes with the territory."

"Why . . ."

"Teresa told me you're off the case. So what are you really doing, Mr. Investigator? Trying to clean up the details, make sure nobody finds the truth."

"Esther, you know Teresa," I said, trying to calm her down. She'd already told me that she didn't have the highest opinion of Nathaniel's widow. "She has her own agendas. She called me at home, on a Sunday afternoon, three times, and my wife was looking at me like 'who's that?' So I told Teresa I wasn't working on the case. At least not for her. Am I right about Teresa?" I got a grudging look of agreement. "Can you understand why I would say that to her?"

"Maybe," she said grudgingly.

Having opened the door a little bit, I thought I'd try to deal with the rest. I said, "And I think you're wrong about, 'us.' I know those people. They're good people, people who want to do good."

"Of course, they're good people. Everybody wants to think they're good. You can't get thousands of people to do evil unless you first convince them it's a good thing. Do you think the 9/11 bombers thought they were doing evil? No, they thought they were doing good. Your people scare me because they're so damn sure they're doing good."

"Esther, let's bring it back to Nathaniel. Are you going to find out who killed him? Are you equipped to do that?"

"That's for the police to do."

"They have their suspect. He's been arraigned. They're done."

"But now Teresa can go to them," she said. "With the new evidence, about the book, and they'll . . . "

"Don't kid yourself. Some detective has signed off on Nazami's confession. And he's not going to admit he's wrong. The whole department, the whole system, is invested in that cop being right. They're done."

"The university?" I went on. "A murder on campus, the quicker it's over, the quicker it's forgotten. No one cares. So, you know what? If you care about Nathaniel, I'm all you got."

"Why do you care?" she asked.

The best way to question someone is by playing good cop, bad cop. Everyone's seen it a million times on TV, but it works like a charm. There were plenty of bad cops in the room, five thousand years worth of them. I had to separate myself from them and become the good cop.

What made them bad? Certainty, righteousness and certainty. Just like in the interrogation room.

The way you reach out is by offering the person a piece of yourself so they'll think you'll understand. And Esther was right. I'd hardly ever met a suspect who didn't want to think of themselves as good, and being understood allowed them that.

What could I offer that would make me the good cop? Doubt, doubt and confusion.

I sat down. I said, "I don't know. I've been thinking and thinking about why, and I could give you a whole list of reasons, but the truth is I don't know."

"Truth is," I went on, "I have a whole list of reasons why I shouldn't do this, why I should quit. I tried to. But I found myself going to my office and putting together some pictures. Voting with my feet. And here I am, in your office, trying to get you to pick one out . . . and really, if you won't help, I'll start asking questions around campus and find someone who will."

"And if it turns out that it is your people who did this? What then?"

I shrugged. "Then it goes where it goes. If you'll look at the pictures, we'll find out if there's a link between 'my people,' and MacLeod."

"And you're not afraid of that? It doesn't bother you?"

"Yeah, it bothers me. It bothers me a lot. More than can I say."

"Alright, show me the pictures."

I gave her the DVD. She put it in her computer. It whirled around for a couple of seconds, then the pictures came up, and she began to click through them. Along about the fifth, she said, "They all look so alike," and added, "That must be how your pastor likes them."

She looked to me for a reaction. I didn't give her much of one, though maybe she was right.

She peered at each one doubtfully, like she really couldn't see much difference, and I began to wonder how good a witness she was. Suddenly she stopped and said, "That's her. And there, there's the little cross she wore. I thought I remembered that."

"You're sure?" I asked her.

"Absolutely, no question. Who is she? What's her name?"

"I don't know yet." I said. "That's the next step."

"Find out. Find out the truth," she said urgently.

"Let me ask you something," I said. "Before you said religion is a false answer to the greatest human need. What did you mean?"

"Nathaniel said that our greatest need is to understand what the world means in relation to ourselves. It's ahead of all the others because if we can't figure what food is, what's up and down, or what sex is, we'll eat dirt, walk off cliffs, and try to do it with trees.

"We come to a point where there are no answers. Why are we here? Why do we die? Things like that. The real answers—'I don't know,' 'it's just accident,' 'the universe doesn't care; it'll get along just fine without us'—don't answer the question, which is, what does it mean in relation to me, me, me? That causes us pain. That's how our needs work. They push with pain, and when they're satisfied, we feel good.

"But if there is no answer, what do you do with the pain? If a false answer kills the pain, you'll take it, like any other pain killer. And it will feel good. So good we can't ever give it up."

"And that's from MacLeod?"

"Yes, that's what he said."

"And did he offer something better?"

"He tried. I liked it. You might not. Find the book, and you can read it for yourself."

33

Understanding that I had made a decision made me feel almost euphoric. It could turn out to be the wrong decision, even a disastrous one. But that didn't seem to matter.

Nathaniel MacLeod and his number one disciple, Esther Rabinowitz, might have explained it as brain chemistry. They might have said that a state of indecision creates chemicals that make us uncomfortable in order to push us into choosing, and then, when the choice is made, those chemicals go away, that pain goes away, and it's replaced by a chemical reward. Everybody with their own internal dope dealer.

Interesting theory. Whether it was right or not, when I sat down to dinner with Gwen and Angie, I looked at them and was filled with love. When we said grace, I felt the grace of God's love and of having a family, and I felt gratitude for being together and having food and a home.

"We have to spend more time together," I said to Angie out of the closeness I felt.

"Okay," she said.

"What'll we do?" I asked.

"I don't know," my daughter said in a kind of awkward but pleased way. What do you do with your dad?

"Help you with your homework, with school projects maybe?"

She didn't look exactly thrilled about that. "Well, Mom helps me a lot," she said. "And I'm doing pretty well anyway."

"Yeah," I said. I never liked it when my parents, all four different ones, tried to help me with school. Which wasn't very often and just turned into them telling me what I was doing wrong. Or them getting frustrated because they understood the material even less than I did.

"We could play basketball together," I said.

The two of them looked at me as if I'd said the lamest thing in history. My only excuse was that she used to like basketball, and we did play together sometimes, but that had faded fast with the arrival of puberty. Now she was a cheerleader. Something I didn't know how to do.

"Alright, alright, alright," I said.

"And where are you going to find the time?" Gwen said.

"It's important," I said. "I'll find the time."

"And work?"

Our mortgage, health insurance—which is huge—car payments, Angie's school fees—in spite of the discount we get because Gwen works at CTM—the phones, the cable TV, the credit cards, my business expenses, tithing, and all the secular taxes—it goes on and on. We make it, but I have to put in a lot of hours to make it.

"Hey," I said, "you want to come to work with me sometime?"

"Yeah, cool," Angie said.

"Do you think that's actually a good idea?" Gwen asked.

"Come on, Gwen, you know that what I do isn't what's on TV. I mostly look things up, deliver papers, interview witnesses, maybe find people."

Angie looked disappointed. She wanted it be exciting, of course.

"She'd be in the way."

"We could try it some time and if didn't work, then . . ." I shrugged. We'd drop it. "But it might be fun."

"Yeah, Mom," Angie said.

"Fine," Gwen said. "If it's what you two want. But you'll be careful?"

"Of course," I said. I would never take her out if I thought anything remotely dangerous would happen. Then I said to Angie, "The next day you're off school, and I'm working, you'll come with me. Alright?"

"Yes, Dad," she said to me with a smile that made me melt.

"And besides," I said to Gwen. "You do more than your fair share. I should do more."

"You do fine," she said, but I could see that she was pleased.

We had pie and whipped cream for dessert.

I'd printed out the captured image of MacLeod's "little angel." I couldn't go up to CTM and start asking, who's this girl? In the circumstance, there was no one up there I could trust. But I could trust Gwen, who worked with the choir regularly and knew them all and most of the gossip.

After we did the dishes, and while Angie was in her room doing her homework, I showed the picture to Gwen and asked, "Can you tell me who this is? I think she's in the choir."

"Nicole Chandler," she said instantly, with a tone of annoyance.

"You don't like her?"

It was nothing that serious. "She missed her last four rehearsals and the last two services. Without a call, or a by your leave. Just didn't show up. It's inconsiderate."

"Do you know much about her?"

"Not a lot."

"Could you do me a favor? Get her address and phone and such for me. Even ask around if anything's up with her."

"Is she the runaway?"

"No. But she might have something to do with it. But she might not. And if I start asking around, people will immediately make more of it than maybe they should. I don't want that to happen. For a bunch of reasons. So don't say anything to anyone. Just, you know, 'What's up with Nicole? Is she ever going to show up for rehearsals?' Just casual, normal, alright?"

"Of course. I can do that. I've been dying to play PI with you. But I have to take Angie for her checkup tomorrow."

"Oh, let me do it. I have to go downtown anyway. It's practically on the way. I can drop her off, take care of my business, and then pick her up. Give me a chance to spend time with her."

"That's a good idea. I'm glad you want to do that."

"Me too," I said.

"What do you have to do downtown?"

"William Thatcher Grantham III of Grantham, Glume, Wattly, and Goldfarb called to inform me that my services are no longer needed. I mean on the Nazami thing. It was Manny's case, and they're dropping it. I have to give them my final bill. I figured it would be better to, you know, drop by, remind them that I'm friendly and useful. They pay top dollar."

"But you're done working on it?"

"I don't have a client," I said.

"What if his new lawyer wants you to keep on it?"

"He's gonna get a court-appointed," I said with a shrug. We don't have public defenders here. The court appoints from a pool of lawyers willing to work for $35 an hour, $45 an hour in court. The quality of their work is related to the rate of compensation. People who know defense lawyers just from TV and books—super clever, fully strategic, with knowledge of the law, doing research and calling experts—have no idea of what the realities are. Most of those guys handle a case the way a cook at McDonald's assembles your order, except if you asked them to hold the onions, they'd screw it up.

If your life depends on it, rob a liquor store so you can pay a good lawyer.

Indigent defendants are entitled to a defense. To do that adequately, if the facts are at all in question, means they are entitled to an investigator too. In recognition of that reality, the state will pay for one. The state has set our compensation rate at $10 an hour. You can do better working at a Cumberland Farms convenience store. At least that comes with benefits, sick days, unemployment insurance, and worker's comp.

There are some old guys who have full pensions from something else and do a decent job. But I can't afford government wages. With one exception: working as a licensed crime scene investigator, which I am. That comes under the expert witness category, and the rate is $125 an hour. And that's just fine. But that wasn't what was at issue in the Nazami case.

"I mean, even if I were willing to work on it, who would pay me?" I asked. An excellent point. Who was going to pay me? "So that's it. Kid meets with his new lawyer, five, ten minutes maybe. Lawyer calls the DA. They make the deal. And it's all over. It's gone and we can all forget about it."

34

I was headed down the interstate with Angie beside me.

I asked her who her favorite friends were in school. She named them, and I asked her what they were like. Her best friend, Cynthia, had started getting into trouble, challenging the teachers about biblical things. Her latest offense was passing around a list of the sex stories in the Bible. How Abraham passed off his wife as his sister and let other men marry her—twice! And the one about Lot and his daughters. My daughter couldn't bring herself to say more than that since the story is that each of them, in turn, got their father drunk and then went and had sex with him and even got pregnant by him.

"And she even said," Angie was letting me in on something shocking, "that marriage in the Bible is not between one man and one woman. It's between one man and as many as he can get."

"Well," I said. "Well. Hmmm. Is she in a lot of trouble for that?"

"Yea-ahhh."

"Making her parents crazy, is she?"

"Yea-ahhh."

"Any other signs of rebellion in the ranks?" I asked.

"Dress code," she said, nodding wisely, as if to say, what can you expect from adolescent girls?

"Um," I said.

Then she said, "Thanks, Dad."

"For what?"

"Saying you would take me with you to work."

"Hey, I'm looking forward to it," I said. "But you may find it boring."

"That's okay."

We were close enough, and the moment was relaxed enough, that I decided to talk about something difficult that had been on my mind. "Your, um, mother . . . Jeanette."

"She's not my mother. Gwen's my mother."

"Yeah, well, you're lucky I guess. You sort of get to choose your mother."

"I choose Gwen."

"That's fine. And I agree with that."

"Good," she said, her mouth set with unarguable certainty.

"But Jeanette's going to get out in less than a year. And she will want to see you."

"I don't care."

"Look, she's got her problems, and we all know what they are, but she does love you."

"No, she doesn't."

"Of course she does," I said.

"If you love someone, you don't do things like that, so that you'll be sent away from them. You do things so you can stay together. It was her fault that she left us. And I'm happier now."

"Hmm," I said.

She looked away, unhappily, out the window. So I just looked straight ahead, concentrating on driving.

It was like that for awhile. Then I thought I heard her say, "So let's get a cup of coffee."

I was startled. Angie doesn't drink coffee. "You really want a coffee?" I asked.

"Huh? What?" she said.

"Did you . . . oh, never mind," I said, puzzled. I checked the radio. It was off.

My mind was playing tricks on me. Then I heard myself saying, inside my head, "There's a Barnes & Noble off the next exit. They have lattés and all that stuff. How about that?" I answered myself, reflexively, "No there isn't," because there wasn't one off of that exit. "It's hard to know if you're being followed on a freeway," was the next line, and I realized my mind had drifted off into the memory of my ride with Manny, leaving the fortress of stone, "Straight line, everybody zooming along."

It had to have been my subconscious cuing, because when I looked purposefully in my rearview mirror, I saw that there was a dark blue Ford Explorer about eight cars back. It's a pretty common car. No reason to assume that it was the same as the one that had followed us then.

But I thought I better find out.

I checked. Angie had her seat belt on. Angie always has her seat belt on. She's good in that way, as well as many others. "I'm gonna pull off this next exit here," I said.

"Okay, sure," she said.

I had my cruise control set on seventy-six miles per hour, as a lot of the drivers did. I accelerated some, not like Manny could've in the monster Mercedes, but enough to see if they pulled out of the seventy-six-mile-per-hour club too.

"She can't take me back, can she?" Angie asked abruptly.

"No, baby, she can't," I said. But I knew better. If Jeanette found a sugar daddy with a pile of money for lawyers, or a gung ho woman's group to back her, and she fought for her "natural mother's rights," it would be a hell of a battle. And an expensive one. If CTM turned against me, especially Jerry Hobson with his nasty, blackmailing, evidence-planting tricks, it would be one we could certainly lose. I was almost glad that I had another problem on my hands to distract me.

I wanted to make an abrupt move and cross directly from the inside lane to the exit ramp, forcing them to show their hand. Or not, and turn out to be just another couple of guys on their way to the mall in their SUV. I kept an eye on my side and rearview mirrors, and at the last moment, I yanked the wheel and cut off a gray Toyota Tundra—the driver leaned on his horn and gave me the finger—cut in tight behind a dented Hyundai sedan, and then steered hard onto the exit ramp, my tires complaining and threatening to cut loose as we went into the curve.

"Don't ever drive like this," I said to Angie.

But she was shrieking, "Dad, what are you doing?"

"Hang on, baby," I said, trying to slow down without provoking a skid.

There was a light at the end of the ramp. It was red. I pushed down on the brakes hard enough to come to a semistop. I looked back toward the start of the ramp. The Explorer was charging into it, way too fast for normal driving.

The motherfuckers were after me. With Angie there.

35

"Dad, Dad, what are you doing?" Angie said.

I was overreacting, being cowboy stupid, with Angie in the car. I could have found out that we were being followed without the drama. So what if someone was following me? What would they find out? That I was taking my daughter to a doctor's office and dropping in at a big downtown law firm?

"You want an ice cream?" I asked, like I'd pulled off with a reason. It was pretty thin, but she said, "Sure."

I looked around. It was one of those nowhere exits for development that would surely come. Probably built because someone politically connected owned the surrounding acres. But so far, it didn't even have a gas station and convenience store. There were some signs up, one to an industrial area—refineries we could see in the distance—and I knew that there was a development a couple of miles behind, but I didn't want to double back. If we'd kept going toward the city, the next exit would've been eight miles ahead, Kavanaugh Golf Club Estates, a very expensive subdivision built around one of our more exclusive golf clubs, with the river running through it. If the road in front of us stayed roughly parallel with the highway, that's where we'd end up, and there was a high-end mall with a Hagen Daz and a Godiva Chocolates and other nice places for treats, so I turned left.

The Explorer was almost up to us, and when we turned, it followed.

The road started veering to the west, away from the main road, into the choppy scrubland, clumps of salt grass and scattered ephedra in the stony, sandy soil.

"Do you know where you're going?" Angie asked.

"I'm kinda guessing," I said.

"Mmm," she said.

"Mmm, yourself."

A mile later, the Explorer still behind me, the paving ended, and we were on a sandy track. The area is full of them. Lots and lots of nothing in front of us, and more nothing on either side of us, and Angie asked, "Are you lost?"

"Well, yeah, sort of," I said. "Don't tell Mom."

"I won't."

I glanced up in the rearview, thinking that maybe I should turn around. The Explorer was no longer hanging back and keeping a tail. It was coming up fast, very fast. In a moment it was practically on my bumper, and then it pulled to the left, like it was going to pass me. I wondered what they were up to, if they would flag me down or cut me off.

As it came up alongside, I looked over, and the passenger-side window was sliding down. I saw one of the two guys that I'd seen in the prison when we'd met with Ahmad. The one with thin hair and acne pits. He was looking back at me. And then I saw the gun come up. I reflexively reached out for Angie and shoved her down and stomped my foot on the brake at the same time. They zoomed past.

I turned hard right, off the road, into the scrub and the sand. I was hoping to circle back onto the road and run the other way, back where we'd come from. Could I outrun them? In Manny's car, sure, but in my seven-year-old Cherokee? Who knew what they had under the hood.

We were bouncing like mad over the bumpy ground, and I was wondering what the hell I should do. I've been a cop. I know the worst thing in the world is to run from cops. It makes them excited and scared, and worst of all, righteous. "He ran" opens the door to just about anything. But if what Ahmad said was true, and what Manny said was true, they could just grab me and say I was aiding and abetting terrorists or some damn thing, and they could take me away, and I would never even get my one phone call. Besides, they hadn't identified themselves as police. They'd identified themselves as someone who wanted to shoot me. "Jesus," I prayed silently, "please protect us. I have my daughter with me."

I unclipped my key ring from the ignition key. "Angie," I ordered, "unhook your belt." She had to think I was nuts, bouncing over the dirt and rocks like we were, and she didn't move. "Do it! Do it now!"

"Yes, Daddy," she said.

"Take these." I thrust the keys at her. "The one that looks like a bicycle lock. Crawl in back, open the tool box. Come on, go! Go!"

"Okay," she said, taking the keys. She didn't sound frightened. Kind of excited even.

I concentrated on the driving, trying to get some distance without wrecking us or flipping. At least they weren't gaining.

"You there? You there?"

"Yes."

"Tell me when it's open."

Time passed—three, four, five, ten heartbeats. "Got it."

"There's a vest in there. Put on the vest."

The bastards were getting up close. I shoved the pedal down. We accelerated way too fast and got airborne. I heard a "Whoa!" from the back, while I was yelling "Hang on!" We came down with a thud and almost bottomed out. I was grateful not to hear anything break underneath.

Their suspension was no better than mine, and I could see that they almost lost it. The ground was getting rougher, small hillocks up ahead and a dry riverbed.

"There's a handgun and a shotgun in there. Get them both. Get them up here, but stay low. Crawl, baby, crawl. Put the back seat down so you stay flat . . . . Are you doing that?"

"Yes. I'm doing it as fast as I can."

"Don't hurry. Do it slow and careful. We're gonna come out of this."

"I know that," she said. "I'm with you, Dad," expressing full faith and trust, beyond reason.

I heard the seat go down. A moment later, my shotgun appeared between the two front seats. It's a Remington 870, the barrel cut down to fourteen inches by a smith up in Nebraska, which required a whole ton of paperwork, but it was legal. I took it with my right hand and set it on the seat. Then I reached back as she handed me my handgun, a Heckler & Koch USP compact .45. It only takes eight in the magazine, but they're big ones.

Now I was armed. What was my next move?

"Angie, get down on the floor. Between the seats."

"I want to see," she said.

"Get the fuck down," I yelled at her.

She gasped, but got down.

"Sorry," I said. I never swear at her, or even in front of her.

"That's okay," she said.

I needed to put some distance between us—so that I'd have a moment, even half a moment, to do something. How? If I tried to turn, that would put my side to them as the distance was closing, and they could get a shot off. They hadn't shot so far. No point, bouncing the way both of us were. There was some professionalism there. Not necessarily a good thing for me.

I needed a moment in which I could get turned around so I would be facing them. Preferably with something between them and me.

There was the dry riverbed almost right in front of me. I veered left toward it. I dove into it. The ground was smoother in there, and I was able to pick up the pace.

The Explorer did the same and followed me in. Dust billowed up behind me. That was good. It had to be blinding them, maybe even slowing them down. The river's track got deeper and shallower and then deeper again. When we were in a deep spot, lots of fine earth kicking up into a cloud behind me, I turned hard right and went up the bank. As I came over the edge, we got airborne again. This was going to cost me hundreds of dollars in shocks and who knows what and was taking a year off the Cherokee's life, and it was already a year too old.

We came down hard. I turned right, sliding and skidding, and hit the brakes. As we slid to a stop, I flung open the door, grabbed both guns, and jumped out. I got lucky. Buried in the dust cloud, they'd missed my turn, and they had to put on the brakes and make their turn after my spot.

When they came up out of the riverbed, I was leaning over the hood of my SUV, facing them, the bulk of the Jeep between us and the Remington pointed straight at them.

I fired. The gun roared like thunder. The sound rolled in waves out across the scrub in every direction. The Explorer hit a bump as I fired. It rose up so that my shot missed their front windshield, but I took out a headlight and peppered the grill. I pumped and put another round in the chamber and fired again. They were starting to turn. I got the side window and saw it shatter. I put the shotgun down on the hood and picked up the HK. I stood—there was little chance of them getting a decent shot off, careening around like they were—and held it two-handed, steady and calm, just like they taught us to at the academy, following the target for a tracking shot. I thought I put it right through the busted side window, but I couldn't tell if I hit anyone.

They were turning away. I shot off three more rounds, hoping to hit something. If not either of them, then the gas tank or a tire. But I didn't hit anything except the body of the vehicle, if that.

I cursed myself. I'd had my chance and I'd blown it.

Now they could do what I'd done. Get some distance. Get out with their vehicle between us. Maybe with rifles. Who knew what they had. Once they were on foot, they could get good, steady shots off. They could circle around and come at me from two sides. Or one could pin me down from in front, while the other got around behind me.

What had I done to my little girl?

36

God was with us.

They drove off. Maybe one was hurt. Or dead. Maybe they just didn't have the stomach for a firefight. Whatever the reason, they were going. If they stopped to set up an ambush, I would know it because their vehicle was kicking up a dust cloud that was visible for half a mile.

I opened the back door, asking Angie, who was lying on the floor, "Are you alright?"

"I'm okay," she said.

"You can get up. They're gone."

She gathered herself up and stepped out of the car.

"You're sure you're alright?" I asked.

She nodded. And looked perfectly fine. She looked at me with a small kind of smile, then said, "And, Dad . . ."

"What?"

"I won't tell Mom."

I started to laugh. It wasn't that funny, but the laughter came up from in the middle of my chest. I tried to hold it in because, after all, this had been *serious*. But I couldn't. Then her smile burst into full bloom, and she started laughing and giggling too. We laughed harder and harder. I laughed so hard that I had to lean against the car and hold my stomach. Angie was laughing just as hard, tears coming into her eyes. The laughter kept coming and coming until I made it stop just so I could breathe.

I put my arms around her and held her close. "I love you, Angie," I said. "I love you so, so much."

"I know," she said. "I know you do."

There we were with my arms around her completely, holding her as close as I could, with her arms around me, her head against my chest. We were like that for awhile when she said, "Dad, that was awesome. That was totally awesome."

"You peeked," I said. Then I said sternly, "I told you to stay on the floor. You could have been killed. Angie . . . "

"I'm sorry," she said. "But it was totally awesome."

"Alright," I said. "And I won't tell Mom."

37

Inside Kavanaugh Golf Club Estates, which is a gated community with very high security and its own patrols, there's a large home— almost a compound because it has two cottages—with its own walls, its own gate, high-tech surveillance cameras on all corners, and its own security team.

It belongs to Jorge Guzman de Vaca.

I'd come to make a deal with the devil.

I needed something desperately: safe haven for my daughter. And I couldn't trust any of the saints.

Such deals are the stuff of legend. All the stories are the same. The human wants some material thing; the devil wants his soul. Make no mistake, I'd trade anything for my daughter's life. But the contest would be to see if I could negotiate a better deal. Then both of us would watch out, because as the stories tell, there's always a twist in the contract's tail.

After we'd gotten into the estates and then past Guzman's own security, he came to the door himself, and, holding it open, he said, "Carl, my friend, welcome. Please come in. Wonderful surprise, you coming to see me. And who is this young lady?"

Angie was completely wide-eyed. More agog at the mansion and the man than she'd been in the chase and the gunfight.

"My daughter, Angie," I said.

"Welcome to my house," he said to her and offered his hand. "My name is Jorge. And if there is anything you would like, please, it would be my pleasure. Come in, come in," he said, leading the way. The house was Spanish—Mexican—in the grand style. He led us through the high-ceilinged foyer into the living room. That was higher still—two stories high with a balustraded balcony that ran around three sides. I guessed that the bedrooms were up there. The fourth wall was mostly glass with arches and columns. A second set of columns and arches outside created a covered walkway that kept the sun from shining directly into the house. The windows looked out onto courtyard with a pool and an artificial waterfall, land-scaped—just like the front of the house was—with flowering desert plants and lush, trailing bougainvillea.

"I need to talk to you," I said.

He understood that I meant not in front of Angie. He smiled and said, "Give me a moment." He went over to Angie and told her, "Look around if you like. In these cabinets here," he opened them, "there is an immense collection of music CDs. Maybe you will see things you like. I will be right back. Sit anywhere. Do what you like."

When Jorge was gone, Angie came close to me and said, "What is this place?"

"He's a man I know," I said, trying to figure out how to explain it all and failing as she looked at me, waiting for the rest.

Fortunately, Jorge returned. He was with an older woman, maybe twenty, twenty-five years older than he himself was. Her clothes were expensive and dignified, a thin gold chain and gold cross around her neck, and the glitter of a diamond in each ear. "Carl, I would like you to meet my mother, Luisa."

"How do you do," I said.

"Is my pleasure," she said, with the Mexican accent that Jorge had worked so hard to erase in himself. "Welcome to our home."

"And this is his daughter, Angie."

"Hello," Angie said respectfully.

"That's a lovely name," Luisa said. "Is it short of Angelina? Angelique?"

"No, it's just Angie," my daughter said.

"From the song," I said. "The Rolling Stones."

"Oh, Mick Jagger," Luisa said with lively eyes. "I love that song. When I was young, it would make me cry. What a wonderful name," she said to Angie. "Much better than those other ones."

My daughter, who'd been mildly burdened by her name and the explanation that went with it, especially to most of her own generation who had barely a clue about the greatest rock band in the world, was quite taken with this response.

"Why don't you and I go into the kitchen and get you a Coca-Cola or whatever you want, and maybe some food. We have our own cook," she confided. "For when I get lazy."

They walked out together.

"She's very kind," I said to Jorge, though I wondered, as she had raised Jorge and his younger brother, who was a stone cold killer. On the other side of the scale, their youngest brother was a heart surgeon. There were very fat dossiers on Jorge in every law-enforcement agency in the Southwest.

"Yes, thank you. I think so," he said.

He led the way out to the courtyard. As we went through the glass doors, he touched a switch and music began to play from the outdoor speakers. "Ahh," he said with some pleasure when he heard what came on, *Eine Kleine Nachtmusik*." He led me to an elegant cast iron table with matching chairs near the waterfall. It was a lovely effect. Also, the splashing, combined with the piano and strings, would shred any attempt at audio surveillance.

"I need a favor," I said.

"If it is in my power, it is yours."

"I'll get straight to the point," I said. He gave me a nod that said that was good. "Someone tried to kill me half an hour ago. With Angie in the car. I don't know if there are more of them out there, or if they're waiting for me at home. I need a place for her to stay."

"What about yourself?" he asked.

"Yes, I wouldn't want to leave her alone very long. But someplace I could leave her and go out and not be worrying every minute, is it safe?"

"We have the two cottages. One is for staff," he said, by which he meant his bodyguards. There were four of them, two on and two off, twenty-four/seven. That would put an armed guard, and a small fortress, around my daughter.

As for her being safe from him, I also knew from all those dossiers and the thousands of hours of surveillance that his public posture of respecting women was pretty genuine. His sins were all of the venal kind, not the carnal. Unless you counted the mistress that he kept in very respectable style in her own small home at the other end of the estate. They'd been together fifteen years, and she'd be about forty now. On those occasions where he'd been observed straying from her, it was always with adult women. He was a proper and careful man who only committed crimes for profit. Once there was money on the table, of course, there was little that he wouldn't do.

"The other was for my mother, but since my wife passed away, she's moved in here. It has a telephone, cable, whatever you need. For how long do you think this will be? No, no, it doesn't matter. As long as you need."

"Maybe just a few hours, maybe a day, two at the most. If it's more than that, I'll find some other solution."

Again he nodded, agreeably. "We'll get you keys, tell the guards. You can come and go as you please."

"Wait," I said. "I want to be clear about this. I don't want to owe you anything."

He sat back and showed me, with restraint, his other face. His business face. His crime face, if you will. I knew perfectly well that he assumed that if he helped me now, he would own me forever. If that was the deal, I would take my chances out on the street.

"So, I'm going to pay you up front," I said.

He looked skeptical. Very skeptical. And cold as a snake.

"Your cousin, Domingo."

"Yes?" he said.

Domingo was doing mandatory life as a three-time loser. Both Domingo and Jorge knew that he'd been set up. But what they didn't know was how lazy and sloppy the cops had been. Another tidbit from Rafe Halderson in his giggle with glee days, before he took the last, hard fall. What a hoot it had been that they'd done it with ten ounces of mannitol and baking soda and a lab tech who generally found it easier to certify that a seizure was anything the cops said it was rather than bother to cook it and put it through his chemistry set. An independent test would be a Harry Potter magic key that unlocked the fortress of stone. "I don't know the technicalities of how you would do it—" I began.

But he stopped me. He held up his hand and said, "Wait."

"What?"

He sat quietly for a moment.

"If you come to me in friendship, asking my hospitality, I would give you that. With all that it means. You would come under my protection, which is what you want. But that's not what you ask. Because you don't want to incur an unknown obligation. Which is businesslike, and I respect that. But I don't want unknowns either. I need to know what I'm getting into. Who is trying to kill you? And why?"

"I don't really know," I said.

"This man, you don't know him?"

I told Jorge where I'd seen him before. And how a blue Explorer, probably the same car, had followed me and Manny after we'd left the state prison.

"So this has to do with Ahmad Nazami?"

"It seems like it has to, but I don't see how," I said. "It was Manny's case. I was working for Manny. His law firm has dropped it. So I'm not working for anyone, so I should be out of it."

"That's your only connection to these people?"

"All that I know of."

He looked at me coolly and thoughtfully, as if he was certain that there were things I wasn't telling him. The music changed to a piano piece, elegant and soothing. Eventually Jorge said, "So we get back to my original question. Why me?"

"Like I said . . ."

"Carl, you have many friends in the police. You have many friends at that Cathedral of yours, and they are always telling how you are a community and help each other out. And there are many, many *policia* there. In fact, they are like a secret organization inside all the other police. The born-again squads.

"Yet, you don't go to any of them. You come to me." He looked at me and waited for a moment so I could answer if I wanted to. But I didn't. "It has to be because you don't trust them. So this has to do with the police —"

"I told you these guys are supposed to be Homeland Security."

"And," Jorge said, "with people at your church."

He waited again. Finally I said, "It might. But I didn't want to say so because I have nothing to prove it. It might not be true."

He nodded. His expression said that he thought my excuse for not coming clean with him was pretty thin, but he would accept it anyway. He thought some more. "You are afraid one of them might betray you. I see."

"Yes," I said.

"Alright. Now I know. Let us make a deal."

"The thing with Domingo . . . , " I said, beginning to explain it.

"No," he said flatly. With a gesture as negligently dismissive as tossing away a soiled tissue, he added, "He's a gangster." Then he leaned in. "I have a different deal. I have a job for you. For which I will pay you your regular rate. It's a business investigation. I was watching your pastor's TV show on Sunday."

"But aren't you . . ."

"Catholic? Yes. But . . . whatever . . . I was watching. There he was, and he said he was going to build a city. An entire city. Hundreds of millions of dollars, even *billions*, he said, and he said he has the financing.

"Find out about this for me, what the plans are, where the money is coming from."

"What's your interest?"

"Roads, houses, office buildings. I build things. I develop. I invest."

"I'll find out what I can for you, but . . . "

"But what?"

"You may be wasting your time. I don't know if they'll work with you."

"Because I'm Mexican? Or because they think I'm associated with criminals?"

"The whole idea," I said, trying to explain, "is that Plowright wants to build a *Christian* community."

"And?"

"And you're Catholic."

"You have something against Catholics?"

"Wait a minute, no . . . " I had a sense of what Plowright wanted, a feeling for it, though I'd never thought it out in detail. I never thought about it excluding people. It was meant to bring people together, a particular kind of people, so we could support each other and be comfortable, more than comfortable, joyous and enthusiastic in our choices, but yes, it was meant to leave other people out, leave them behind. An earthly, practical, here-and-now version of the Rapture, the good Christians levitating to the City of God, while the unbelievers, infidels, apostates, Muslims, Jews, Catholics, agnostics, and atheists crashed and smashed in the hellish plains below.

"Look," I said, "what you're asking me is to find out what his plan is in terms of what'll work for you, right? So, I'm starting here and now. It's not about you and me. What he has in mind—that's what you want to know, right?—is Christians having their own place without really anyone else. All Christians living there, doing all the business."

"And a Catholic isn't a Christian?"

"In the minds of"—I couldn't bring myself to say "my people" or "my religion"—"a lot of the people up there, a significant number of them, and, I would guess, including Plowright, the answer is no."

"What are we then?"

The things people say among their own, in the routine way that cops use ethnic slurs, often won't bear repeating when we're facing outward. I've heard Catholicism called many things, sometimes as off-hand, casual remarks, and sometimes seriously, to explain how we differ from them. To some of us, Roman papism is a cult masquerading as Christianity, a pagan cult, the apostate megacult, a cult of idolatry, and Rome, as shorthand for that church, is called the Great Whore, mother of harlots and abominations. The pope's chair is called Satan's throne, and there are people who will make the case that the pope—not any particular one, but whoever is there—is the Antichrist.

"I'd say they'd call it a cult. Like Mormons or Jehovahs."

"Is that what you think?" he asked with black-eyed anger. "Is that what you think of the Holy Mother Church?"

"Jorge, this isn't about what I think. It's about whether you can do business with CTM."

"You're right. You are completely right," he said, his anger doing a fast fade, like the filament in a bulb. Just as quickly, he switched over to self-satisfied enthusiasm. "I knew you were the right person for this. So, the real job is to find out what will get those people to overcome their prejudices and do business with this particular 'member of a cult.' Find me the hook, the angle."

"You could go get saved," I said. "That's the easiest way in."

"Are you joking?"

"I'm sixty an hour."

"That's high for a PI."

"That's what I charged Manny because he wanted the best."

"All right," he said. No more bargaining. He would pay for the best. "And on top of that, you find me what I need, a bonus, a big bonus. This could be huge."

He held out his hand. I took it. We shook on it.

Then he put his hand on my shoulder. "Would you like something to eat or to drink, some coffee perhaps. My mother will be very pleased if you have something. I know her. It is already bothering her that you haven't."

"Coffee would be fine."

"You know," he said, "I am still thinking about why you came to me. I think it is not that you fear you will be betrayed but that you already have been. Yes," he suddenly smiled, "you are very lucky, my friend."

A line from an old song whispered through my mind: "a friend of the devil is a friend of mine." I asked, "Why's that?"

"Because I am an expert in treachery," he said with what sounded like the pride we have in having survived old and bitter trials. "I will even tell you," he said, leaning toward me, "who it was who betrayed you."

"Yeah?" I said, trying to sound skeptical, but it came out rasping, like there was desert sand in my throat.

"It's the person who is closest to you. The one you trust the most. It always is."

Gwen. I knew that.

38

Luisa showed us out to her cottage.

It was quite feminine, of course, but not overbearingly so. It was well built and immaculately maintained, with two bedrooms, a bathroom, and its own little kitchen. I couldn't help but contrast it with my own home, built with lower-grade materials, put together with less care, showing wear, and in constant need of small attentions.

When Luisa was gone, I left Angie in the bigger bedroom to watch TV or do whatever she wanted.

Then I went into the smaller one, closed the door, and prayed.

Alone and on my knees. *Ask, and it shall be given you; seek, and you shall find; knock, and it shall be opened unto you. For every one that asketh receiveth; and he that seeketh findeth; and to him that knocketh it shall be opened.* Matthew 7:7–8.

I had asked, and it had been given. I had been seeking, and I had found. Be careful what you ask for. Now, on my knees, I asked what was I to do about it?

"It is hard for thee to kick against the pricks," a voice said. Acts 9:5, if I remembered my Bible study right. But I'd never heard it said quite that way before, with a touch of sarcasm, emphasizing the word "pricks" for the puns in it.

"Will you go away," I said to Manny, who was standing just at the edge of my peripheral vision.

"Now you want a choice, not just any dead Jew?"

"You got me into this mess in the first place. Will you please stop."

"There's something I want to talk to you about," he said in a tone of mild chastisement.

"I'm sorry," I said. "For the way I thought about Susan. I—"

"Don't be ridiculous. Who cares?"

"The Ninth Commandment," I said. Thou shalt not covet thy neighbor's wife.

"This is America," he said. "That would be a thought crime. Didn't we argue once about the Commandments not being the basis of our legal system?"

"Yes," I said. "Now, would you tell me what you want and then leave me alone."

"Alright. It's my cell phone."

"What?"

"You picked it up when I was shot, and you never returned it."

"You came for"—I turned, incredulous, to look at him directly—"that?" And, of course, he was gone.

Yes, I had his damn cell phone. It was still in my car. His cell phone. The day we'd met with Ahmad Nazami, Manny had used it to take pictures of the two men who were supposed to be from Homeland Security.

39

The Internet is an amazing thing.

After I recharged Manny's phone—courtesy of Jorge, who had a drawer full of phones and chargers—I uploaded the pictures onto one of the computers in Jorge's home office, then sent them out by e-mail to a couple of associations of private investigators that I belong to. They sent out an automatic blast to the members, asking if anyone could identify the two men. Within an hour I had their names.

Eduardo Alvarez and Daniel "Beef" Polasky.

From there, I was able to get credit reports, job histories, current and past addresses, and the cars they drove. Both of them lived over in Arizona, about an hour and a half away. Eduardo was married and owned a condo. Polasky was single and rented. And he owned a three-year-old blue Ford Explorer.

Alvarez had been with the DEA until five years ago, then worked for two private security companies. Then he went to Iraq for eighteen months with a private contractor called Custer Battles whose motto is "Turning risk into opportunity." He'd been back a little over a year.

Polasky had been with CBP, Customs and Border Patrol, which is part of Homeland Security, but he left them two years ago. He too went to Iraq, also with Custer Battles, and returned to the land of malls and SUVs at about the same time as Polasky.

Both of them currently worked for a firm called FOB Security, Ltd. The trail stopped there. Its address was a P.O. box address in Delaware, and it had no listed phone number. A funny way to run a business.

Jorge wandered in and out during the process, constantly making and taking phone calls. I didn't realize it—and I hadn't asked for his help—but he was checking his own sources. They had the gossip that colored in the outlines.

Alvarez had worked with the DEA in the Ramparts section of LA, where he'd gotten into the rip-off and resale business. Word was, he had resigned before the rumors snapped around his wrists.

Polasky had been palling around in Brownsville with a group of National Guard and army recruiters who were smuggling drugs. He was the man at the gate and let shipments through. The military types escorted them north and east, using their Federal IDs to keep from being searched. A couple of sergeants and a guardsman had gone down in an FBI sting. Either there was no direct evidence against Polasky and they dropped the charges against him, provided that he quietly resigned, or he earned his hall pass by testifying. Nobody was sure. Since the only folks who went down were Anglo amateurs, the *narcotrafficante* hardcores hadn't cared enough to find out—or do anything about it.

"You going to go after them?" Jorge asked after he told me all that.

"Yeah," I said, and he nodded. "But I haven't figured out how yet. Maybe I can get something on one of them, and turn him."

He made an impatient gesture, then mimicked a scissor with his middle and forefinger—"*Los albondigas*," their balls—then added his tactical opinion in a thoughtful and considered way. "I'd go for the muscle man. He won't want to lose his beauty."

I just looked at him, letting him know that I wasn't about to cut peoples' body parts off.

"I just see that on 24," he said, like he would never do anything like that either.

I put thoughts about Alvarez and Polasky aside for the moment and tried to think of other ways to approach the problem.

There was Gwen.

I was going to have to call her soon. I couldn't just disappear with Angie. But thinking about her twisted me up so much that none of the thoughts would come out straight.

Nicole Chandler.

I started with phone listings. I found two Nicoles and three N. Chandlers. A Web search turned the Ns into Norman, Nyella, and Nixon. The other Nicole was seventy-eight and living in a retirement home. That left Nicole D., who was twenty-three years old, worked at a pharmacy in the mall ten miles down the road from CTM, and lived in an apartment not far from both of them. She drove a Honda. She'd bought it from a used-car dealer and was still making payments.

I called her home. There was no answer, and her phone wouldn't take messages because it was full. I called the CVS where she worked. She wasn't there. I went into a sincere pitch about being her uncle, and her aunt was going into the hospital and wanted to talk to her, but we hadn't been able to reach her for days and days. She'd called in sick a couple of weeks ago and hadn't been there since.

That took it back to Gwen. She knew the girls in the choir and could get the gossip if she wanted to. But I still couldn't unravel how to deal with my wife.

There was the crime scene. I hadn't done it right. I was certain that it could tell me more. Provided it hadn't been cleaned yet. But I'd have to have a client, with a lawyer, to make a formal request to the court.

Or go back to Teresa. She had a right to get in.

Which made me think to call my office, and, yes, Teresa had called. She'd had sense enough, and was careful enough, to at least have left a businesslike message. She wanted to hire me to help recover her husband's missing manuscript.

But if I went to Teresa without getting straight with Gwen first, I'd end up in bed with her. Maybe it would just be sex. Maybe it would be something more. She was quick, clever, and intense, educated, smart, and complex. I doubted she was nurturing, patient, and supportive. She was destructive, dangerous to herself and others.

I shook my head, like a dog trying to shake off the rain.

What I really wanted, what I needed, was to get things right with Gwen. If she had betrayed me, I wanted it to have been a slip of the tongue, an innocent accident. So I could go back to being in my happy home. So I would have a home for Angie. One that would stand up to whatever Jeanette might try to pull when she got out.

Besides, I loved Gwen, and she was my wife.

40

Everything about Gwen had always seemed simple and clear. Now it occurred to me that perhaps I didn't know her as well as I imagined I did.

She was an army brat.

Her father had been a staff sergeant in the Quartermaster Corps, sergeant first class, with an E–8 pay scale by the time he retired. He took orders from above, gave them to those below, and in both cases expected they would be carried out. A mostly practical man, he liked his beer and, when he'd had enough of it, told funny stories about military life and foreign adventures.

Her mother was a complacent woman and ran the house in a well-organized fashion.

They'd done a fair amount of moving around. But the changes in geography were just changes in scenery. The essence always remained the same: a rented house in a suburban neighborhood near lots of other military families, shopping at the PX, a public school, church on Sunday, strict, no-nonsense rules, and no talking back at home.

She'd been a tomboy and treated the army's obstacle course like a playground. She claimed that when she was ten she could have made it through basic training. She was still active and fit. She liked hiking, camping, and rafting. She loved to shoot and was as comfortable around guns as most people are around cars, and she handled them with somewhat more confidence than she did pots and pans.

The first time she had sex was when she was sixteen. She got pregnant at seventeen. The boy was nineteen, a soldier on the base. When she missed her second period and told him, he immediately said he wanted to do the right thing. He loved her, he said, and she felt the same. Her father was less angry than she'd expected. He'd seen it happen enough other times. Her mother seemed sad, at least at first, but didn't scold very much or get hysterical, and when the wedding came a few weeks later, she shed happy tears.

Gwen miscarried in her fifth month.

Then came the first Gulf War. She and her husband decided to try for a baby before he got shipped out. By the time she was certain she'd conceived, he was in Saudi Arabia. She wrote to him, and they were both overjoyed.

Twelve days after he got the news, he was killed. Not in combat. It was one of those strange but horrifying accidents that could have happened anywhere. A Humvee tumbled off a loading ramp and crushed him.

Gwen miscarried again.

She turned to Jesus. He held her in his arms and helped her through the grief. She began to make the church the center of her life.

I met her a few years later. By then, most of the emotional trauma seemed to have healed. She appeared happy, healthy, and athletic. She was wonderfully uncomplicated. No hidden motives, no secret agendas. She was happy with her job, partly because she had no grandiose ambitions or bitter resentments, partly because she was serving a cause, happy to be a foot soldier in the army of the Lord.

The first time we kissed, I knew, too, that she loved sex. We could barely keep our hands off each other. But she wanted to wait until we got married. I did too. It would be a way to commit to a clean, fresh start. Which was something I needed in my life. I'd jumped into beds and backseats too quickly, too often, with too many unwanted consequences.

We talked, from time to time, about having children of our own. It was the only issue that made her uncertain and conflicted. Another miscarriage was the only thing in the world that I'd ever seen her fear.

We left it alone. We had Angie. That was enough for me, and it seemed to be for her too.

Where to catch up with her? I didn't want to go home. If someone was looking for me, it was the obvious place to wait.

It was already too late to intercept her on the way back from work. I thought of calling her and getting her to meet me somewhere. But I might just be setting myself up. Even if I spotted it, it would mean I wouldn't get to talk to her.

It made me angry that I had to plot and plan to speak to my own wife.

In the end, maybe because I'm just not clever enough, I decided to go straight on in.

The least I could do was try some misdirection.

I left a message that I'd be home late. I was going to take Angie out to dinner. Maybe even a movie. Yes, I knew it was a school night, but we were having such a great father-daughter thing that it was worth it. We wouldn't get home until eleven or twelve.

If someone was listening to our phones, or if Gwen was passing on information, that's when they'd expect me. But I planned to get there hours earlier.

They'd be looking for my car. I rented a black Chevy Impala.

I'd left the house in a jacket and tie. So I went to Marshall's and bought black sweatpants and a black sweatshirt with a hood and a pair of running shoes.

I crept into our subdivision just after dark. I did a slow drive by to check for any unfamiliar vehicles or unusual activity. Everything seemed normal.

I went away and made another pass half an hour later. It was still the same, just Gwen's Tercel in the driveway.

It was time. But I didn't want to announce my arrival by rolling up the driveway. There's a 7–11 about three-quarters of a mile away. I parked in the far corner of their lot.

You can't walk through a suburb unless you've got a baby carriage or a dog. But you can jog. I even saw a couple of other runners on my way, including a neighbor, and we exchanged waves. Perfectly natural, no big deal. The XL hoody gave no sign that I was wearing a shoulder holster with my HK .45 underneath.

When I got to the house, I trotted slowly across the lawn like I might have if I were coming home from a normal run. As I passed the windows, I peered in, searching for an extra face or even an extra shadow. I got in close to the house, moved along the side wall, opened the gate to the yard, and went around the rear.

I crept up to the kitchen window and peeked in.

It was dark and empty. There was that TV flicker of light coming through the door to the living room, so I figured she was in there. I put my key in the lock and let myself in as silently as I could. Gwen was watching a cooking show. I could hear the Barefoot Contessa explaining her endive, pear, and Roquefort salad.

I took the HK out of its holster with my right hand. I eased past the living room door, went down the hall, and checked the bedrooms. There was no one there. Looking around Angie's room in the dark, I felt tears welling up in my eyes. I got hold of myself and walked down the dark hallway into the living room.

"Carl, what are you doing?" Gwen asked, looking at me in black sweats with the .45 in my hand.

I stared at her. I didn't know where to begin.

"Angie! Where's Angie?" she asked.

"Safe," I said. "She's safe."

"What's going on?"

I glanced around the room. The drapes were closed. That was good. Nobody could shoot me through the window.

"You tell me," I said.

The Barefoot Contessa was yapping about the Peppermate Pepper-mill, which she was selling for $35. I wanted to shoot the television. I stepped over and hit the power switch.

"Carl, what are you doing?"

I walked slowly around the room until I was behind the high-backed armchair she was sitting on. She twisted to look at me. I could barely look at her. I needed to control my rage. I put my hand on the top of her head and turned it so she was facing forward, un-able to see me.

"You're scaring me, Carl." She didn't sound frightened. Gwen is ridiculously fearless around guns or any kind of physical danger. She meant that she was worried that I was going around the bend.

I took a breath. "What happened today, Gwen?"

"Nothing."

"I don't believe you."

"Nothing happened. Nothing special."

"Nicole Chandler," I said. "Tell me about Nicole Chandler."

"I didn't . . ."

"Didn't what?"

"Didn't find out anything."

"Did you talk to anyone about Nicole Chandler."

"I . . . not really. I didn't get a chance."

"I don't believe you," I said. I couldn't see her face, but I could feel through my fingertips that she was lying.

She didn't say anything.

I said, "You told someone that I was looking for her. Who did you tell?"

Once again, she didn't reply, and I knew she'd set her lips in a tight line, the way she does when she's restraining herself. Or disapproving.

"Are you my wife?" I asked her.

"Yes," she said in a tight, dry, minimal way, nodding slightly.

"Do you love me?" I asked, but before she could answer, I said, "Do you love Angie? Do you care about Angie?"

"Oh, Lord, yes," she said with far more enthusiasm and conviction than she'd displayed about being my wife. "You know I care about Angie. How can you ask that?"

"Alright," I said and took my hand off of her.

She looked up at me as I walked out from behind her and went and sat down on the couch. "I'll tell you about my day," I said. "Then we'll figure out who you are and what we are to each other. I was driving down the interstate. With Angie beside me. I noticed a car that seemed to be following, a car I'd seen before. So I pulled off at the next exit to see what they would do. They followed. I kept driving, and we got out on a dirt road in the middle of nowhere, and they suddenly pulled up alongside, and the guy in the passenger seat pointed a gun at me. I slammed on the brakes and made a turn. They chased me across the desert. We had a gunfight. With Angie there. I managed to drive them off."

"Carl, what have you gotten yourself into? How could you put Angie in danger like that? How could you?" she said, splattering accusations and disapproval like spittle.

"Gwen, don't make me any angrier than I am."

"You're the one sitting there waving a gun around."

"Did you tell someone that I was looking for Nicole Chandler?"

"Why, what does that matter?"

"Who did you tell?" I insisted. "What happened, Gwen?"

"What are *you* up to, Carl?" she spit out. "Why don't you tell me that?"

"What do you mean, what am I up to? How dare you ask me that?"

"How dare I? I ran into Jeremiah—"

"Ah," I said. There it was. But she ignored me.

"I said, 'Thank you very much, for sending Carl that job.' And of course he said, 'What job? I didn't send him anything.' And then I, like an idiot, said, 'You called Sunday night and . . . .' And he's looking at me like, what a stupid woman I am, but then he very politely said, 'I'm sorry, I didn't call him. Perhaps you're mistaken.' But I wasn't. Then I realized who had really called. That woman again. And that's where you went."

"Is that what you told Jerry?"

"And humiliate myself further? Thank you very much, no I didn't."

"Then what happened?" I said, but I was calming down. I could see how it had unfolded, and it was my own damn fault.

She got silent again.

"Talk to me, Gwen," I said. "We can straighten this out. But there are things I have to know."

"He said he was worried about you. That you were going off doing strange things."

"And then you said?"

"He asked if I knew what you were up to. He said he wanted to help, to watch out for you. I said I didn't know. Then he asked me if you were still messing around with that Nazami thing. I said you weren't. That's what you told me. That you were going into the city to hand in your final bill because the law firm had dropped the case. That you were just looking for some missing girl."

"And then?"

"He asked how I knew. I said, well, it had something to do with Nicole Chandler. That you . . . you asked me to find out about her."

"Then what happened?"

"Nothing. That's all. He said he would try to get Paul to speak to you, bring you back to your senses, whatever was going on."

I sat back, the tension leaving my body. It was alright. Gwen hadn't betrayed me, not really. Now it was just . . . the other problems. And if Gwen and I were alright, I would deal with them. "My mistake," I said. "I'm sorry. I should have told you the truth."

"About that woman."

"It's not about that."

"Well, that's what I want to know about."

"She came on to me. I said no."

"And that's it, and she called our house three times."

"What it's about—"

"And where did you go, Sunday night, after we made love?"

"I went out to think."

"To think? And where did this thinking take place?"

"In the desert, down southwest of here. Other side of the city. I had to think things through."

"What things? Us? Her?"

"Nazami," I said.

"You said—"

"I tried," I said. "But it bothered me. I was going to let it go, then during the service, it hit me. The murdered professor, MacLeod, had a girlfriend. Nobody knew her name, but he called her his 'own special angel.' And there were our special angels, bigger than life, up there on the screens. Every once in awhile, I hear rumors about Plowright . . . ."

"Never. He's like a father to them. What he does is sacred. Paul Plowright would never, ever do anything like that."

"So I got some pictures of the angels and showed them to someone on campus, and she said, that's her, that's MacLeod's mystery girl. And then I showed it to you, and you said, that's Nicole Chandler. And dear Nicole is missing. Not just from choir but from her home and her job. And tell me, when did you speak to Jerry?"

"Around eight. I met him on the way in."

"And three hours later, a man I met in Ahmad Nazami's cell, who claimed to be Homeland Security, is trying to kill me."

"It's your own fault. Your own stupid, stubborn fault," she said, sharper and angrier than I've ever heard her. "You're ruining our lives. Pastor told you. Jeremiah, who only wants to help us, told you, and you, you won't listen."

"Shut the hell up," I yelled at her. "Are you my wife? Are you?"

She didn't answer.

"I made a decision here. 'Wives, submit yourselves unto your own husbands as unto the Lord.'"

"And if you're wrong?"

"'For the husband is the head of the wife'"—I went on, continuing to cite Ephesians 5—"'even as Christ is the head of the church. Therefore as the church is subject unto Christ, so let the wives be to their own husbands in *every thing*.'"

"If you defy our pastor, then you are leaving Christ. And you will be lost," she said, defiant and adamant. "A wife does not have to submit to a husband who does not submit to Christ."

"No man can tell me, or you, how to relate to God. It's a personal relationship. That's why we don't have a pope. And Plowright is just a man. And so were the popes in Rome. They cheated and stole and whored and had their bastards, and there's no reason to think that Plowright can't be doing that."

"Never. Paul would never do things like that."

"Well, he's doing something. There's a man going to prison who shouldn't, and there's one man dead, and there could've been two more today, and one of them would have been Angie."

"You've gone crazy, Carl. I don't know if it's that woman or you're drinking again, but you've gone crazy, accusing Paul of murder."

"Paul? Why do you keep calling him Paul," I asked. "How close are you to Paul?"

"How dare you? I'm a wife and a good wife. How dare you? I'm not the one who lied and strayed."

"Alright, if you're my wife and a good one, obey me in this."

"No, no, you are so wrong."

"Gwen," I said in despair, no longer in anger, "you must."

She looked at me in a way that I'd never wanted her to look at me. "You are the one who is defying the ways of the Lord. And you are bringing destruction down upon us."

41

When I got back to Jorge's, I looked in on Angie. She was sleeping peacefully. I went into the other bedroom, drained of everything and grateful for a bed. I kicked my running shoes off and lay down for just a moment, planning to get back up and have a shower before I slept. But I didn't get back up.

There were a lot of dreams. The one I remember is the one where Manny showed up. He said, "It's good to have your daughter safe."

Naturally, I agreed.

"Though you probably shouldn't consider any place around you as safe."

"I feel like I'm stumbling through the darkness," I said. "Like in the desert, but worse. I know there are things happening out there that I need to know about, but they're way in the dark, and I don't have any idea what they are."

"That's what humans do, stumble through the darkness. You have no idea, Carl, how much darkness there is, how much we are blind to. That's why seeing the light is such a precious experience."

"Does it matter if the light is the true light? Can there be a false light?"

"Any light will do," he said gently. "After all, we have to sail on." While I was considering that, he said, "I didn't know all this would happen. Sorry."

"You really didn't know?" I asked, remembering our first conversation about the case and then his rabble-rousing on top of the Mercedes.

"Well, sometimes we don't know what we know."

"Yeah, right," I said.

"I was rereading the transcripts of your conversation with Jorge," he said.

"There are transcripts?"

He gave me one of those "don't be naïve" looks.

"But with the music and the waterfall?" Their noise should have defeated any surveillance.

Another look: of course not from where he was.

"I thought it was interesting that he described himself as an 'expert in treachery.'"

That woke me. If CTM was after me, it might occur to Jorge to offer me up in trade. I got up and went to check on Angie. I wanted to lie down beside her to make sure that I could protect her, but she's not a little girl anymore and that didn't seem right. I went back to my room, took the blanket and a pillow from the bed, got my gun, lay down in the hallway, and slept on the floor in front of her door.

In the morning, I called my half-brother, Arthur. We're not very close. We only lived as brothers for four years or so. He disapproved of me in my wilder years, and even now his mild Methodism disdains what he considers the excesses of the evangelical community. But family is family, and he's a good man. He and his wife, Veronica, agreed to have Angie as their guest, more willingly and happily than I expected. I got online and booked her on the first flight I could get to St. Louis, then called them back, and they said they'd be at the airport to meet her flight.

I explained to Angie that I needed to keep her safe. "What about Mom?" she asked, meaning Gwen, of course.

"She'll be okay," I said.

"I want to call her," she said.

I thought about that. It was all so insane. Like a drunk or an addict, I wouldn't stop. But to what was I a servant? Could it get sorted out in the end? It didn't seem so. But I said, "Yes, of course, you can call her."

Angie smiled. Now it was all alright. I would die for her smiles. But I was on a course that would destroy them.

"But," I said, "you can't tell her where you are."

"Why not?"

"Because . . . . " Because she told the men who tried to kill us where we were. And she might well do so again. Or they might snatch Angie to force me to come to them. "Because . . . , " I said, "you know about wiretaps and all?"

"Of course," she said. What would TV drama be without them.

"Well, the people who came after us might be listening."

"Are they the government?"

"No. I found that out for certain. In fact, you can't tell anyone where you are, not your friends either. I'll just tell the school you're out sick."

"I'm not sick."

"Okay, I'll try to figure out something they'll accept that's not a lie. That you won a trip across America."

I knew a motel with weekly rates that was happy to take cash. I booked a room. It had a view of a parking lot and an expressway.

I snuck back home while Gwen was at work and packed a couple of suitcases. The house was mine. Maybe she'd get half the value, maybe not. Maybe Jesus would touch her heart, and she'd see the light, and we'd live happily ever after. Skepticism was entering my view of the Christian way of life and marriage we'd both sworn to live by. It seemed that the husband wasn't the head of the house after all, just like in any secular humanist, atheistic, falling-apart, modern American family.

After I settled into my box of a room, my clothes neatly stashed in the closet and dresser, I called Teresa.

She was happy to hear from me, though she was upset that I'd taken so long to get back to her.

"Do you want me to find your husband's book for you?" I asked.

"Yes, absolutely," she said.

"Do you understand how expensive an investigation is? For starters, I want to do a real crime scene analysis. Have they cleaned it yet?"

"The office? No. Tomorrow, I think."

"Well, stop them."

"Alright. When will I see you?"

"As a CSI, I get a hundred and fifty an hour. For the rest, sixty an hour. If you hired me through an attorney, he'd be charging you probably two, two fifty, and a hundred. It easily gets up into the thousands. Are you prepared for that?"

"The university," she said. "They were going to pay for the crime scene stuff anyway, and the stolen book, that was on their property, so they're sort of responsible. I'll ask them. I'm sure I can get most of it."

"Fine then. The first thing I'll want to do is go to the scene."

"I'll meet you there," she said.

"No. It's slow, meticulous, boring work. I want to do it without interruptions."

"But I know things. I can help."

"You really want the book?"

"Yes, yes, I do."

"Then let's be professional about this."

I had copies of the original crime scene analysis from back when they thought it was a suicide, before Ahmad Nazami had turned up and supposedly confessed. There were photographs, sketches, and notes. It had been a relatively cursory job. Giving the police the benefit of the doubt, you could say that was because it seemed so cut-and-dried.

Worse, they hadn't come back when the conclusion had changed. Possibly because the integrity of the scene had been largely destroyed by then. All sorts of people had trampled in and out, the body had been removed, and who knows what else had transpired. So anything they found on a second go would face serious challenges in court. Still, they should have.

Since an independent investigation had already been authorized and the money earmarked, Teresa got the go-ahead. A full investigation and a search for the missing book was another matter, requiring an additional appropriation. It was being considered.

This time, I brought a campus security officer to be the witness. I record what I'm doing, as I go, with a voice-activated Dictaphone, and I use a JVC GR-X5 for both video and stills. When we arrived, I announced my name and his, the location, date, and time. I noted that I had been there previously with the widow of the deceased and that she had moved certain items pursuant to the new investigation, the search for the manuscript. Then I videoed the scene.

After that, using the police and campus security photos, I restored the scene as best as I could to how it had been before Teresa had moved things. I wore latex gloves throughout the process. Then I divided the room into quadrants and began a search and an examination.

I began with the desk and the computer and dusted for fingerprints, especially on the keyboard. Both Nathaniel and Teresa had touched the keys, but I was hoping to find a third set that belonged to neither of them. Perhaps Plowright's or Hobson's. No matter how contaminated the crime scene was, there would be no explaining how their prints got on MacLeod's computer. I dusted the screen and the cord that had gone to the backup device.

There were lots of prints.

They would have to be sent to a fingerprint analyst, along with Nathaniel's and Teresa's, for elimination. And Ahmad's. If his were there, it would implicate him. If they weren't, it would tend to be exculpatory. Any that remained would point to someone else.

"We have had," I said into my recorder, "two narratives for this crime. The first was a suicide. There were, and are, a set of facts consistent with that narrative. I am now going to ask Oliver Noble a security officer of the University of the Southwest assigned to me today, to occupy the place of the deceased. Officer Noble, could you sit in this chair please?"

I put the camera on a tripod at the back of the office. I took my gun, removed the clip, then demonstrated for Noble and the camera that the chamber was also empty. I had him hold the gun in his right hand and put the barrel to his temple. I had him hold a piece of yellow cord against his left temple and ran the other end to the bullet hole.

"This is creepy," Oliver said.

"Yeah, sorry," I said, then explained to the camera that the cord illustrated the trajectory. "In addition, according to the original notes, the victim's fingerprints were found on the gun, and there was powder residue on his right hand, all consistent with, and supporting, the theory of suicide."

"Now," I said, rolling up the cord, then walking over to Oliver's right side, "we have a second theory of the crime. That it was a homicide. That a second party fired the gun. The nature of the wound, the stippling around the entry, and the trajectory of the bullet"—I took the gun from Oliver but held it in the same place—"still demonstrate that the gun had to have been fired from here, in this position, against the victim's head."

"However," I said, "how are we to account for the victim's prints on the gun and the residue on his hand. Oliver, with your permission," I said, taking his hand.

"Yeah, sure," he said.

Continuing to narrate each step of the way, I put his hand around the gun and put my hand over his. "Now," I said, "I am going to force Officer Noble's finger to pull the trigger," and I began to squeeze.

"No fucking way, man!" he yelled and flung the gun out of his hand. It clattered across the desk and banged up against the wall. He glared at me, his face full of fury.

I looked at the camera and said, "This is a demonstration of how hard it would be to force someone to fire a gun into their own head. In this case, even though we had thoroughly demonstrated that the gun was unloaded and of no danger, our stand-in reacted with a violent reflex of resistance."

"Wow," Noble said, "very slick. Yeah, nobody would let somebody do that."

He was great. I hoped I would get to use the tape in court someday.

"So what the fuck did happen?" he asked.

Narrative number three.

If you can't get a living man to fire a bullet into his own head, leaving evidence on his hand and on the gun, you have to kill him first, then use his dead hand to fire a second shot. That meant two shots, two bullets, and two bullet holes.

I had Oliver, who was now beginning to enjoy himself a great deal, assume the pose in which MacLeod's corpse had been found. MacLeod had bled profusely. The splatter pattern, what was left of it, and the blood evidence indicated that he had stayed in one place. It wasn't conclusive, but that seemed to be the case.

I put the gun in Oliver's hand, the way I had before, with my hand over his, to determine what range of motion I could get without moving the body.

If I had killed MacLeod by standing beside him and shooting him in the head, then wanted to restage it as a suicide, where would I aim the second shot. My first choice would have been out the window. The bullet goes away, far, far away, and there's no bullet hole. I opened the windows and tried to determine if, by bending MacLeod's arm—Oliver's arm—over his back, I could get a clear shot through the open windows. It seemed exceedingly difficult, and I demonstrated that with the yellow cord again.

An easier, and more likely, direction to shoot would be in the victim's natural range of motion, a cone-shaped space, biased to his right. The door and a blank wall were directly to his right. It was easy to see that there was nothing there.

By raising the victim's arm, however, it would be easily possible to fire into the books on the shelves above the desk. How many times in my life had I heard the story of the soldier who had the Bible his mother gave him in his breast pocket, which stopped the bullet that would have struck his heart? The atheist's books would also have stopped a bullet. Then the perpetrator could have collected the book, or books, along with the bullet itself, removed them, and replaced them with other volumes. There had to be a couple of thousand books in there, and who would know if one, or two, or three were out of place?

Teresa might.

My mind slid easily, and without conscious effort, into fantasies of how that would play out, starting on the couch or leaning on the desk . . . now that Gwen had stopped being my wife in the terms we both understood that to mean.

The aromas of tobacco and burgers and the peculiar way people sweat under a polyester uniform, coming off of Oliver, all two hundred and forty pounds of him, brought me back to what I was there for. A damn good thing I'd come here with him, not her. Much better for my concentration.

Would firing a bullet into a book leave some sort of trace? I didn't know offhand. I would have to get a few and test fire into them. Not Bibles, of course, but secular material.

The most natural shot, given the position of the body, was under the desk. I had Oliver move out of the chair. I set up a small, portable battery lamp to illuminate the area and began to examine the floor underneath, taping my search. There was dirt and dust and a crumbled receipt, which I put in a baggie and marked.

And there they were. Little bits of paper, like confetti, with letters and bits of letters on them. And what looked like, possibly, charred edges. It would have to go to a test lab to be sure.

The killer had put some books on the floor, wrapped MacLeod's dead hand around the gun, and fired into them. Possibly the deceased's own work, the missing copies of his mystery novels. They'd been right beside the gun. It would have been natural to grab them at the same time.

Both sides of the desk had drawers in them. The set on the right ended eight inches from the floor, but the ones on the left only cleared it by about a half-inch, and I couldn't really see underneath them.

I photographed the desktop, disconnected all the lines to the computer, and took everything off that was likely to fall. Then Oliver and I carefully lifted up the desk, which weighed a ton from all the papers in it, and moved it out toward the center of the room.

There, amidst ancient dust and old crumbs, was a shining silver cross.

I was ready to take bets it was Nicole Chandler's cross.

42

I was wearing a sports jacket to cover the gun that I now carried all the time.

When I entered her house, Teresa came to me and kissed me on the cheek. The kiss itself was polite and restrained enough to be a simple greeting, but her body came in closer than was appropriate for someone who wanted to be just a client—and stayed there longer.

I'd set a line of proper conduct between us. It had the effect of putting both of us in that state of aroused awareness that makes every point of contact—the spot where her breast touched my chest, the feel of her thighs on either side of one of mine, and her hand on my arm, placed there so casually in such a normal position for that kind of greeting—electric and hypercharged.

"Let's sit down," I said, breaking the contact, "and I'll tell you where we are."

"I'd like to know that," she said.

When Gwen spoke, her voice was a single tone that delivered just one message. When Teresa spoke, or even looked at me, there were layers upon layers and aromatic hints of distant flavors. Some complimentary, some contradictory.

In this case, there were at least seven varieties of curiosity. A simple one that wanted information about the investigation. A more anxious one about where we stood. That held both a faint, hidden trace of hope and a tight anxiety about being rejected. There was an earthy subtext that was wondering what it would be like to be rutting on the couch. Yet another, less necessary to disguise, about getting the book that she sought, and with all that, a kind of child's eagerness to just hear a story.

I sat in one of her living room chairs and put my attaché case on the floor beside me. She asked me if I would like anything to drink.

"Water," I said. "Or club soda."

I watched her walk away into the kitchen. She was wearing a gray skirt and a lighter gray top, a snug cotton spandex blend, with a white mesh vest over it that played hide-and-seek with her prominent nipples. The skirt hung to just above her knees, reasonably proper, but it clung to her shape so closely that I knew no more than a thong, if anything, could be underneath it. She brought me a bottle of imported sparkling water and a glass with ice in it.

"I'm going to have something stronger," she said and went to a combination liquor cabinet and wine rack in the corner. From there she asked, "Are you sure you won't join me?"

"This is fine."

She came back with a bottle of Old Charter Proprietor's Reserve, a thirteen-year-old bourbon, and a glass for herself. She opened it and poured out two fingers. The aroma of it, sweet, sour, and expensive, reached out to me.

"Tell me," she said, lifting the glass to her mouth and taking a small sip.

"I'm accepting the premise," I said, "that whoever killed your husband also took the book. Though I still don't really understand why.

"I've identified the girl you told me about, though she's not a girl. She's a young woman, twenty-three. Her name is Nicole Chandler. The reason, probably, that he referred to her as his 'own special angel,' is that she was—is—a member of the Choir of Angels at Cathedral of the Third Millennium."

"Your church?"

"Yes. She seems to have disappeared. My next major step will be to try to find her. In the meantime, I did the crime scene investigation."

"What's that like? What do you actually do?" she asked with the kind of eager interest a lot of people react with, as if a TV show had just walked into their home.

"If you like," I said, "I can show you."

"Go back there?"

"No," I said. "I video what I do to create a record. I have it with me. I can show it to you in the camera, or I can play it through your computer where it'll be a whole lot easier to see."

"A Mac's okay?"

"Sure."

"Great. Follow me," she said, taking her drink with her.

One of the two bedrooms had been turned into an office. She was obviously working on a project. There were books and papers spread out on her desk. Several aerial maps, marked up with pale blue and light red highlighter, were tacked to a wall lined with corkboard. There were four paintings on the opposite side. Three of them had that Mexican style, vivid colors, but very flat, as if they came from a world that had just two dimensions. The fourth was a nude of a slender woman, her back to the painter, just a hint of her profile visible, and I guessed that it might be Teresa herself. We played don't ask, don't tell.

It took me a few minutes to hook up her computer to the camera and get into iMovie. When I got it set, I had her sit in her office chair, and I stood beside her to run the camera. I began to take her through it, fast-forwarding past all the dull stuff and explaining what I was doing and why.

I got to the point where I was speaking into the camera about the various versions of the crime, and she asked, "What do you mean by that?"

"The goal of a crime scene analysis is, in a way, to establish a narrative," I said, looking down at her.

"You can't know what actually took place. But you look at the facts you do have and then imagine a story that would explain them," I went on. She looked at me with that rapt attention a good-girl student gives her teacher. "You do that both informally, intuitively as you go, and then formally as you get further along. Once you have that story, it implies that you will find other things consistent with it. And you look for those things. If you don't find what should be there, or you find things inconsistent with your narrative, then you have to revise it. Of course, as you start to develop a theory, it influences what you look for, where you look, and how you look. So, to some degree, you have to fight that tendency and be thorough and methodical, even though your instincts say you're done and you're wasting time. So, you're trying to do both at the same time: create the story, because that's your ultimate goal, and prevent it from blinding you to facts that contradict it." By then she had turned away from me and was looking at the screen, making me think I'd gone on too long and bored her.

"Here, I'll show you," I said and started up the video again. I was fast-forwarding, looking for a good part, when she reached up blindly and took my hand. She pulled it to her face and held it there, and I felt the warm moisture of tears.

I turned her face toward me, and they were rolling down her cheeks. She looked truly bereaved.

"What? What is it?"

"I miss him," she said. "I miss him so much. Oh, you can't know. You sound just like him."

"What do you mean?"

"What you just said." She sort of half-laughed through her tears. "That could have been Nathaniel describing 'how we actually determine what reality is,' and 'the commonsense version of the scientific method.'" She looked away from me, holding my hand to her cheek and crying. "Hold me," she said softly.

There was no sexuality in it this time. Maybe that made it more insidiously seductive, reaching around my defenses, but I put the camera down and awkwardly put an arm around her. She leaned into me and cried, genuinely sobbing. Her other arm went around me, and she held on tight.

Then she stopped, let go, and sat up slightly straighter, not looking at me, and reached for her drink. She took a swallow, not a sip. After it went down, still facing away, she said, "I'm sorry."

"Don't be."

She got up, holding her glass, and walked out of the room into the bathroom. I heard the water run. When she came back, I saw that she'd washed her face, and she gave me a small, nervous, apologetic smile.

All I could say was, "It's okay."

"Show me the rest," she said, and we went through it quickly. When it was done, as I was disconnecting the camera, she stood up and, looking at me, said, "You're very good. You really are."

"Thank you," I said, looking back at her.

She came forward and kissed me, her mouth just slightly open and her lips very soft, and I could smell and taste both her and the bourbon, one almost as enticing as the other. It was quick, and it was over before I had a chance either to stop her or join her.

We sat in the living room. Me in the chair again, her on the couch, legs tucked up, as she liked to do, showing a lot of her thighs.

"Where do we go from here?"

"Like I said, I send the stuff out to the labs. I'll let you know in advance what it'll cost. If it turns out there are unidentified prints, particularly from the computer, I'll try to get the prints of the people I suspect and see if we have a match. This all would be much easier if I were still a cop"—able to have a DA get warrants and threaten people with the power of the state—"but . . . "

I shrugged. I'd find some way. "While that's going on, I'll look for the girl." That was about it, and I sounded like I was done.

"You're wearing a gun," she said, which kept the conversation going. "You weren't before."

"Well, it's . . . . " I felt awkward about it. "Someone came at me."

"You didn't tell me that."

"No."

"Why not?"

Because I didn't want to admit to a stranger, to a woman who wanted to go to bed with me, that my wife had betrayed me. I didn't want to say out loud to this university person, with all her condescending contempt for religion, in particular my kind of born-again, megachurch, evangelical faith, that another pastor, still another one, my own, the one who had brought me to Jesus, was involved with a young woman outside of his marriage and was possibly a murderer. And that he wanted to destroy me because I was stumbling toward the truth. Admitting it to her would be like turning on a light in a room I wanted to keep dark, and with her eyes upon it, I too would have to see it for what it really was.

She'd finished her first drink, and now she reached to pour another, but she paused and tilted the bottle toward me, offering. I declined, but it took a moment.

"It bothers you," she said, figuring at least some of it out, "that these people whom you're so close to, whom you look up to, who tell you what's right and wrong, that they might be involved."

I shrugged, like I didn't care.

Getting nothing out of that and seeing me adjust my body, preparing to get up to leave, she asked, "Can I see your gun?"

"That sounds like a line from an old movie."

She laughed, "Yes. Yes, it does."

"Well," I said.

"Well," she said back. "What you said before. About how you make up a narrative. If you start applying that to some of the other things you think—"

"Like believing," I said, annoyed.

"Yes," she said calmly. "Let's say that God is one of your narratives about this great crime scene we live in."

"Why do you care about what I believe in?"

"Because you might decide to put your faith ahead of—"

"Of what you want," I snapped, cutting her off.

"I was going to say, ahead of the truth."

Would I, if I ever got there?

"So, I was going to say," she went on, "that we have this great mystery. And we made up a narrative. Call it the God story. God did it, did it all. Then we said, 'In fact, he's the answer to all the mysteries.' But the detectives among us, people who think exactly like you do, looked at that story and said, 'All right, let's examine the evidence on the assumption that the story's true,' but they found things that were inconsistent with that story and facts that seemed to require a different story. If that happened to you in an investigation, you wouldn't hesitate to change your theory."

"Like what?" I said, challenging her. But it felt like my mind was in two parts: one was on the surface, up front, certain and sure of my Lord and his word, but another, like some soulless accountant, was running the tallies in a back room, then sending e-mails to headquarters that the numbers weren't adding up.

"Well, let's take the narrative itself. I write. I'm not much of a writer; I just do academic stuff. But if I were God, I would be a perfect writer. So why did we have to have an Old Testament and then a new one. And all the different prophets in between, with the story always changing. Why not write it down, or have it written down, perfectly the first time?"

"Because we weren't ready to understand it. He gave it to us as we were ready. There were whole different periods. They're called dispensations, in case you don't happen to know that."

"You know that doesn't make sense. There's nothing in the New Testament that the people in the Old Testament couldn't've understood."

"God moves in mysterious ways," I said, shaking my head. "We can't pretend to understand the mind of God." Phrases I'd heard and used a thousand times, and they always seemed to answer for all. But speaking them in front of her, I heard them differently. They had the hollow sound of a suspect in the interrogation room who claims he was home alone watching the game on TV and, knowing it sounds too thin, tries to prove it by telling us the score.

"Everything moves in mysterious ways," she said. "I can try to understand you, but you will always be a mystery to me, an interesting and exciting one, but always a mystery. And me to you. We can't understand what an electron is—that's one of Nathaniel's favorite examples—but we make up a narrative about what it might be and then we put it in circumstances where we see if it acts like the thing we made up in our story. The 'mysterious ways' thing is just a dodge to hide from the obvious truth, that the story doesn't make sense. In exactly the same way that the story of Nathaniel's suicide didn't."

"And what am I going to do," I asked, feeling like there were cold winds blowing down from the wilderness, "if I have no God?"

She looked at me caringly, came up off the couch and got on her knees beside me and took my hand. I wondered if this was how Nathaniel MacLeod got up inside Nicole Chandler, a little doubt, a loss of faith, and then, when the proposition came, there was nothing left to say no with, just the lost soul's sigh, "Why not?"

"You'll do what you're doing now. Trying to be a good man. Looking for the truth. You know what's right and wrong inside you, not because your pastor told you what it was."

It sounded so good and so possible. She didn't know how crazy and destructive it could get. Or maybe she did, and that was what she wanted.

She was on her knees beside me, holding my hand. I bent forward and put my lips to hers, slowly and carefully, tasting. And it tasted quite as good as I expected, better even, warmer and more intuitively responsive to each nuance of what I seemed to want than I had imagined.

Then she was up in my lap, her arms around me, and my hand, which had been curious, so very curious for so long, began to stroke the smooth and tender flesh of her thigh. I wanted to take a long, tantalizing time getting where this was going. I left her thigh and trailed my hand, barely making contact, up over her belly to one of her breasts, exploring the shape and tenderness of it. I felt the nipple against my palm, and it grew firmer. I had been touching her lightly, as lightly as I could, but then I took her nipple between my thumb and forefinger and squeezed it hard, with just a touch of the barbarity she craved, and she sighed with recognition.

Then my cell phone rang.

43

It was Gwen.

I said, "Hello."

She said, "I'm sorry. I'm so sorry. I was wrong."

"Oh," I said.

"I want to help. I think I know where Nicole might be."

"Where?"

"In the citadel," she said, meaning the cylindrical office building attached to the Cathedral.

"Why do you think that?" I asked.

"Because," she said.

"Because why?"

"I'll tell you when I see you, alright?" she said, sounding flustered.

"How could I get in there?" I said, not really asking her so much as thinking out loud.

"I know a lot of the security codes," she said. "I'm so sorry. I want to help. You're my husband, and, and I should help."

"Thank you," I said.

"Come home. Will you come home?"

"I better not," I said. "Let me think of some place to meet. Then we'll figure things out. I'll call you."

"When?"

"Tomorrow," I said. "Tomorrow after work."

"But—"
"Do as I say," I said.
"Of course," she said.
I hung up and looked at Teresa.
"I have to go now," I said.

44

I looked down upon Gwen from the top of the atrium, three stories up.

I watched her walk to the specialty coffee shop, the one that roasted its own free trade, organic, kosher beans. I saw her stop and marvel at the prices they charged and compare them mentally with what we pay for Yuban at Wal-Mart. Amazing what you can imagine people are doing from looking at the top of their heads from forty feet in the air.

My cell phone rang. I looked at the caller ID. It was a discount attorney named Dante Mulvaney who worked out of a cubicle in one of the older office buildings downtown, close enough to the courthouse to walk. He shared a reception area and a secretary with four other lawyers with similar cubicles. I very much doubted he'd have any work I wanted.

I shut off the phone. Then I used the prepay cell I'd gotten from Jorge to call Gwen's cell. I asked her where she had parked. I told her to enjoy a latte or a cappuccino or whatever she wanted and then go back to her car. She said, "I don't understand."

I said, "Just do it."

Then I went out to the parking lot and got my rental car. I moved it near to where she had parked. When she came out of the mall, I watched some more. Nobody seemed to be following her. When she got into her car, I called her again. There was a diner about three miles down the road. I told her to go there and, when she got there, to find an empty table near the back. I followed. The route required four or five turns. If anyone was following her or was with her, between the three or four of us, it would turn into a parade.

But as far as I could tell, she was alone. She hadn't set me up. My relief was immense.

It was late for lunch and early for dinner. There were about twenty people there and room for a hundred and twenty. Gwen was at the back, like I had asked her to be, at a round table set in a booth. When she saw me, she waved. Normal enough. She watched me eagerly, but nervously, as I came through the diner.

"Carl," she said, as I slid into the padded bench seat across from her, "come home. Please, come home."

"I want to," I said. "But not yet."

"I miss you. I miss Angie. I can't stand this, Carl."

"We have to get things sorted first," I said.

"Can't you just, I don't know, talk to people, get things settled?"

"Talk to who? Get what settled?"

"With . . . , " she began but stopped, realizing, I expect, the trap of saying the names.

"With Paul Plowright and Jerry Hobson?"

She nodded, but miserably.

"Someone tried to kill me. So, if I settle with them, then they'll stop trying to kill me. Is that what you mean?"

"I can't believe . . . but if you believe it," she said, forcing the words out of herself, "and you say it's so, then I have to . . . to agree." She looked at me hopefully, though not happily.

"You can't have it both ways," I said. "If it was somebody else, then settling with them does nothing. Somebody will still be after me. And Angie—or you—could turn into 'collateral damage.' I can't live with that."

She nodded. I was trying to protect my family. She could understand that. There was no arguing with that, and she reached tentatively across the table for my hand.

I put my hand around hers and held it. I so much wanted us back together.

A waitress came over and smiled at us holding hands. "Here's the menus," she said. "You all call me when you're ready to order, unless you want something right away."

"We're okay."

"I see that. Take your time. I'm here when you want me."

"That was nice," Gwen said when she left.

"Look, Gwen, this is hard for you. It's hard for me too to think this way. That if it is Hobson and Plowright, then they're people who kill people. Or have people killed. Why should I settle with them?"

"They can't be. They just can't be. Not Paul, never. Jeremiah? No . . . I can't . . . I'm sure there's an explanation. Just call them and talk to them."

"They have my number. They can call me."

"I miss Angie," she said. "Both of you, so much."

"You want anything to eat?"

"No, I can't eat."

"A soda? We should probably order something."

"Sure, alright."

I waved at the waitress and ordered a Diet Coke for her, the grilled chicken platter special and coffee for myself. "I missed lunch, running around," I said to Gwen.

She smiled, pleased at the normality of it. "Are you okay?" she asked. "Eating regularly? The place you're staying, is it alright?"

"It's clean. And I'm not starving to death, no. But I miss your cooking."

"I wish I were a better cook. I try."

"You do fine," I said.

Our waitress brought my coffee. I stirred in some cream. "What makes you think Nicole's in the tower?"

"This is terrible, Carl. I don't like to . . . maybe she's not. I don't know."

"Well, tell me what you do know."

"You think she's"—it was hard for her to say it—"she's having a relationship with Paul."

"Yeah."

"Here's what, well, what some of the girls say. His private apartment, that's where . . . the girls say"—she couldn't bear to be the one saying these things and had to put the words off on others—"that's where he . . . goes."

"With his girls."

"I guess," she said, desperately reluctant to acknowledge it. "Yes."

"So there's more than one."

"I don't know. I didn't think about it."

"What do they say? With his girls or with his girlfriend?"

"With 'someone special,'" she said.

"Alright, he goes to his private apartment with someone special. Did anyone say Nicole Chandler was his someone special, his 'own special angel'?"

"One of the other girls in the choir," she said. "When I was asking . . . I did what you wanted . . . I asked if anyone'd seen Nicole or what she was up to, and one of the girls said, in a catty kind of way, 'Oh, Pastor Paul's special angel.' Then she said, 'Maybe he's locked her away in his 'own special heaven.' And I asked, 'What's that mean?' She said, 'The private apartment, so near to God.' I mean, normally, I just refuse to listen to things like that. But . . . but now I did. This is horrible, Carl. I don't like it."

"Me neither."

"Can't you . . . "

"That's not a lot to go on."

"No," she said unhappily. "I know it's not, but I thought . . . I thought if I showed you I was trying to help, you'd come back."

"I want to come back," I said. "I do."

"I'm glad," she said, with the unspoken question—when?—on the end.

"When it's over," I said again. "How can I get in?"

"Do you really want to do that?" she asked. Her tone let me know that she'd still rather I didn't.

"Yes," I said.

"I thought you would," she said.

"Will you help me?"

"Yes," she said reluctantly.

CTM has very good security thanks to Jerry Hobson. Most of the locks are number pads. Gwen is constantly going in and out. I never asked because there was no reason to, but now I did. "You know the codes?"

She gave me a tight little nod.

"Including the one to the private apartment?"

"Yes," she said. "I've brought papers up, and once or twice he said, 'This is private. Put it in my apartment,' and told me the code."

"He trusts you a lot."

"I feel very bad about this."

"Look, if there's nothing wrong, no girl hidden away there, then we've found out he's innocent, and we'll both feel a lot better. But if we don't go, this will fester forever. You'll never be able to believe in him again, not entirely, and things will never be right between us. There'll always be the question. So, if we're going to have a marriage, and if we're going to be members of the CTM community, then we have to get this settled, and I don't know any other way to do it."

"Alright," she said, nodding miserably.

"Good," I said. "Sooner rather than later. Let's do it tonight."

"No, not tonight," she said, sounding frightened. That was natural enough. It was one thing to talk about it, another to face doing it. But it turned out that she had a specific reason. "They're setting a special stage set and display of the City on the Hill with a giant cross—I mean giant for inside—that they plan to build outside, later, and they'll be working late. And you know how those things go. They always take longer than everyone expects. They could be there all night tonight and Saturday too."

"When then?"

"Sunday night would be best. Sunday night it's quiet. But late, midnight. And . . . and you could go in from the college side." The way she stuttered showed that even though she'd agreed, it still wasn't easy for her. "You wouldn't have to go through the Cathedral at all."

"Here's what I need you to do," I said. "Get me the keypad codes to get in, go up the elevator, then into his office and his apartment."

She nodded.

"Gwen, listen. Can you go there tomorrow?"

"I'm supposed to, to help with the choir."

"Good. Walk it through. Not all at once but in pieces. Notice where there are locks. Then make sure you have the codes. I don't want to get in and get halfway and find some stupid door we didn't think of."

She nodded.

"Good," I said. "Then we'll meet up sometime Sunday afternoon. We'll go over it all, and you'll give me the numbers."

"Sunday afternoon," she said, sounding sad and wistful.

"Sunday afternoon," I said, putting my hand over hers and looking her in the eyes. "We're going to get our Sunday afternoons back, baby. We will."

She looked at me, her eyes brimming with tears and with love. "I want that. I want our Sunday afternoons back."

45

Dante Mulvaney had left a message and marked it urgent.

"I caught the Nazami thing," he said when I called him back.

My gut reaction was, Oh, no! Poor Ahmad. Dante's a lifetime member of the "meet 'em and plead 'em" club.

"It's a big case," I said, trying to pump him up. "Make a name for yourself."

"Nah, it's a piece o' shit," Dante said.

"I'm telling you—" I began.

"Don't tell me," he said, like a guy who's upended his piggy bank for bus fare and doesn't want to hear about the express that's just twenty bucks more.

"Well then?" I asked.

"Kid insisted—*insisted*—I bring you."

"Bring me?"

"Yeah, I show the kid gold—I'm talking a pile of shinin' shekels—and he says, no, he has to talk to you first. Whaddaya you two got, a thing goin'?"

"Dante, would you tell me what's going on—in order?"

"Yeah, sure. Caught the case. Lo and behold, DA's office calls me. They got an offer. Man two. For a guy put a gun to another guy's ear and capped him, that's lower than as low as it can go. And all he does is seven to fifteen. Keeps his nose clean, he'll be out in five 'n' a half. What's not to love?"

"Have you seen the state's material yet?"

"Nah, but everybody knows, the kid confessed."

"Have you seen the confession?"

"What? What's to see? I'm gonna overturn a confession? Come on, come on."

"I think the kid's innocent," I said.

"And I think my daughter's a virgin."

"So what happened?"

"So, I schlep all the fuckin' way up the fortress of stone—for just one case," he said, wanting sympathy and commiseration, because the game, when you're getting the state rate of $35 an hour, is to have at least three or four guys to see, give them each fifteen minutes, then bill for full hours, and maybe bill the travel time in multiples too. "I offer him the deal, and he says no. So how about you help me out, run up there, and tell him this thing's golden, and let's wrap it up. Whaddaya say, Carl?"

"Yeah," I said. I didn't think I was interested in convincing Ahmad to take a deal, but I did want to talk to him. "When?"

"No time like the present," Dante said, which I took to be a sign of how little work he had. "Let's put a bow on it and deliver it to the judge."

"You set it up?"

"Yeah," he said, "I'll ding 'em right now."

"Fine," I said. "Call me back, give me the time, and I'll meet you up there."

"Why'n't you swing by. I'll go up with you," he said.

I knew he wanted a free ride and then he'd bill for the mileage. I understood. Every nickel counts. Especially since the price of gas more than doubled this year, and the state won't raise the mileage allowance until the legislature votes on a new budget next January. But I was driving around with one eye in the rearview mirror, and who knew, maybe Mulvaney was setting me up. He'd do it for fifty bucks. Why not? It was more than his hourly rate.

46

Ahmad looked better. A lot better. He had much of his dignity back.

I guessed that a lot of it came from the Koran he held in his hand.

"Thank you for coming to see me," he said.

"I tried earlier," I said.

Dante, a fat man with a brush mustache and sad eyes, was already sweating in the closed, dead air of the prison's interview room, and he looked uncomfortable in his suit. It wasn't a very good suit, but he wore it because he believed that's what lawyers did. His tie was loose, and the top button of his shirt was open. He didn't have much choice about that. He had more neck than it would hold. "Carl here can tell you," he said, eager to be done and on his way, "what a golden deal I got for you. Right, Carl?"

"Have you made any progress with the investigation, Mr. Vanderveer?" Ahmad asked. However tight he held his holy book, he could only squeeze solace out of it. He was reaching out to me for hope.

"Yes, I think I have," I said. He exhaled, releasing the fear that I was there as the bearer of evil tidings. "But I need to ask you some questions."

"Of course," he said politely.

Mulvaney rolled his eyes.

"I see you have a Koran," I said.

"Yes, it helps."

"I thought . . . you being close to MacLeod . . . and I talked to that imam before he was shot, and he gave me the impression that you weren't a particularly good Muslim."

Ahmad smiled. It was the first time I'd seen him smile. It transformed him. Suddenly he was someone who had a life, with laughter and pleasure and memories. "Oh, yes, he was quite upset with me."

"The raisins," I said.

The smile turned into a grin. Then a chuckle. "Yes, the raisins."

"What the fuck are you guys talkin' about?" Mulvaney asked.

"You need to be sure," I said, "that they can't paint you as a fanatical Islamicist."

"I was raised in Islam," he said, the smile fading to something wistful and sad. "The things we have around us when we're children"—it was strange to hear that from someone young enough to be my son—"they're very strong. I can't have my mother and father, my sisters and my cousins . . . the food, any of it . . . but I can have this," he said, gesturing with the book, which had an intricate design and Arabic letters on the cover. "It's funny. I wouldn't have thought of it. It was CO Peale who suggested it."

"Leapy?" I asked, incredulous that Leander Peale, dedicated member of the congregation of the Cathedral of the Third Millennium, had turned someone on to Islam.

"At first, he tried to bring me to Christ."

"That sounds right," I said. And it would have helped his case.

"But . . . . " He shrugged. "Then he said I needed something. To make it through. And also, he told me that if I get released into gen pop, I'll need a group. He thought I could hang with the Black Muslims."

Desperate times.

"The motive is supposed to be that MacLeod was an apostate," I said, which wouldn't work if Ahmad was practically an atheist, but it might fly if he came into court clutching a volume with Arabic squiggles on the front.

"I may need something to hold onto," he said. "But I still have my rational mind."

"Get on with it, get on with it," Mulvaney said, snapping his fingers on both hands.

"Tell me about the girl," I said to Ahmad.

"What girl?"

I took a picture of Nicole Chandler from my pocket and showed it to him.

"Oh, Nina," he said, using the name she'd gone by at USW, and it was clear from his tone and expression that he liked her. Liked her a lot.

"Tell me about her."

"I don't know that much," he said, his features tightening in concentration. "She didn't . . . she wouldn't talk about herself. Only about ideas."

"Tell you what, tell me about her in chronological order—when you first met her, what happened, what happened next."

Ahmad nodded. "She would come to the class . . . . "

The first class she just sat in back, like a stranger in a strange land. That appealed to Ahmad because it was how he felt much of the time. At the same time, she looked like his dream American girl: blonde and clean and pretty, but not so gorgeous as to be one of the unobtainable goddesses.

After class, she hurried off. Not talking to anyone, avoiding even eye contact.

But she came back, and in the third class, things changed.

The subject was the problem of evil: if God is good, all knowing, all powerful, and the creator of all things, how can there be evil in the world? It's a very old question, going back at least to Epicurus, around 300 BC. There is a whole subcategory of theology, called theodicy, that is still attempting to deal with it twenty-three hundred years later.

MacLeod was presenting his own version, which was colorful, and had a little twist at the end.

A man is sitting beside a pool, enjoying his cigar and a mojito. A woman and her child are nearby. A stone falls out of the sky and knocks the woman out. Unattended, the child falls into the pool. It's only three feet deep, so it would be easy for the man to get up and rescue the toddler, but he sits by and watches the child drown. When the woman wakes up, she finds her baby dead. She screams and weeps. She yells at the man smoking his cigar, "Why didn't you save my baby?" The man tells her she should be grateful for this great chance to experience grief and loss. Furthermore, she should love and adore him for giving her that opportunity.

Then MacLeod asked the class if they thought the man's actions were evil. Everyone had to agree that they were, but the metaphor was obvious, and one student spoke up. "That's true for a man," he said, "but not for God. God moves in mysterious ways, and we can't understand the mind of God."

"Fine," MacLeod said. "Let's accept that for the moment.

"Here's the question, the real question. We all agree that the man was evil. How is it that we hold ourselves to a higher moral standard than we hold God?"

Ahmad, who was peeking at the mystery girl, saw that the question had reached in and caught her like a hook. After class, she approached MacLeod and spoke with him.

From then on, she would join their professor after almost every class, sometimes alone, but usually with two, three, or four other students. When they talked about the subject of religion and philosophy, she seemed very involved. Not just in an intellectual way, but in a very emotional way. Her academic background was very spotty. MacLeod constantly said, oh you must read this, you must read that, and soon started bringing her books and essays to read.

But she never talked about her private life. She fended off personal questions and avoided any social involvements. Ahmad had tried, several times, to get her to join him for coffee, a movie, or a campus event. Others did too. "We're going to the concert at Farrel Hall tonight. It's free. Wanna come?" She always said no.

In class, she continued to sit in the back and rarely spoke, as if she felt she didn't really belong there and was afraid of being found out.

I asked him if he thought she and MacLeod had a sexual relationship. He said no very definitely. I said it sounded as if she clung onto his every word. How could he be so certain of it?

One day after class, Ahmad told me, she had approached MacLeod and clearly asked to speak to him alone. Nate excused himself from the other students and went off with her. Ahmad followed them to a campus coffee bar. He sat where he could see them, but not so close that he could hear what they said. Nina, the name he knew Nicole by, seemed distressed, near to tears. And very uncomfortable to be so upset in public.

They got up and left.

Ahmad, curious or jealous or some combination of the two, continued to follow them. They went to MacLeod's office. After they entered and closed the door behind them, he stood outside in the hallway and tried to listen. There was a lot he couldn't hear. Also, when people came by, he had to move away from the door and pretend he was waiting for an appointment. From what he managed to make out, it seemed that she was crying over a man she'd been having a relationship with, who was older and married. Nate had opened her eyes to how wrong it all was, how deluded she'd been. She said some other things, very softly, murmuring, maybe embarrassed.

MacLeod replied, sounding formal and professorial, that she was an adult and could have any kind of relationship that she wanted, but that she could also leave any relationship if she wanted. She was very emotional, and there was a lot about how she used to think it was right and special, even holy, but now she was angry, and she thought it was all lies.

Her voice grew soft, sweet, and murmuring, but too soft for Ahmad to make out any of her words.

Then he was able to hear MacLeod say, fairly clearly, "No, no. You're my special angel, but moving from him to me is the same thing with different labels on it. It's giving your body to show what a good follower you are. You need to figure yourself out a different way."

I didn't necessarily accept Ahmad's assessment that the relationship between Nathaniel and Nicole had remained so chaste. Desire persists; temptation bides its time and waits for an open door. Such things have a way of moving on.

The department chairman, Arthur Webster-Woad, arrived at that point with one of the other professors, and they stopped in the hall, talking about new hires and the squash league. They babbled on forever. Ahmad couldn't keep up his pretense and had to leave.

Every time Ahmad mentioned her, you could tell by his tone of voice that he still dreamed about her. And he didn't even know her real name.

I was excited. Nicole was no longer just a girl who had been in the choir at CTM and audited a philosophy class at USW. She was a young woman having an affair with an older man.

My immediate assumption was that it was Plowright. But maybe it was someone close to him, maybe the money man with the hundreds of millions to invest in the City of God. She was trying to leave him, or had left him, and the church too.

It was an explosive combination.

She might decide to leave in a glorious blaze of scandal. One that would tear Paul Plowright out of his Pulpit of Glory and Wealth and drag him down to the Hall of Shame, one more hypocrite hanging alongside Jimmy Swaggart, Ted Haggard, and Jim Bakker for the secular world to mock.

47

Dante, of course, saw things differently. "See that? He's diggin' himself in deeper. Now there's the confession, plus the apostrophe thing," he said, meaning apostasy. "And now there's a babe. Come on, let's close the deal."

"What do you mean?" Ahmad asked.

"The plea," Dante said. "Time to cop the plea."

Ahmad looked to me. I said to Dante, "You don't understand. You just grabbed the brass ring. This thing, it's gonna be a circus. The state's case is a disaster. They'll be sending in the clowns, and you get to be the ringmaster. When it's over, you'll be the white Johnnie Cochran." Dante looked completely underwhelmed. The extent of his ambition at this point was to get outside and have a smoke. So, I tried to appeal to his sense of financial well-being. "No more taking the state's thirty-five an hour. You'll be billing three hundred fifty, four hundred, maybe even New York prices. The top guys there are billing over a thousand an hour."

"Yeah, well," he said, like I had predicted that a snowstorm would close the Panama Canal. Then he said to Ahmad, "Kid, take the deal."

"Dante," I said, "he didn't do it."

Mulvaney looked at me like that was the stupidest thing I'd said yet. He knew—and I should know—that short of having hundreds of thousands of dollars for a Manny Goldfarb, backed by a team of associates, jury-selection consultants, unlimited money for investigators, and hired experts, once someone was this deep inside the criminal justice system, innocent was no longer one of the options on the table. He said, "The state's payin' me to dispense all my years of wisdom and experience in fifteen minutes. He's already got almost two hours, not countin' the travel. You hear what I'm saying."

"Listen to me," I said. "You don't have to do anything. Give me a week, a couple more likely, and I'll have it all wrapped up for you. Gift wrapped, ribbon on it. All you have to do is walk it into court and unwrap it."

"I told ya."

"Told me what?"

"The deal."

"What about the deal?"

"It's a special, today only."

"You didn't tell me that."

"Yeah, I did."

He hadn't. But it wasn't worth arguing about. "Why?" I asked him.

"How do I know? They didn't say. The DA's mind moves in mysterious ways. Who the fuck cares? It's a one-day offer."

"It's bullshit," I said. Ahmad's eyes went back and forth, watching us play ping-pong with his life.

"So, you want to tell him to bet on you and your gift wrapping?"

"What charge?" I asked him. What would it be if Ahmad didn't take the deal.

"Cap murder."

"They can't do cap murder on this."

"Sure they can. Terrorism."

"How can it be terrorism? I mean, come on."

"He's an A-rab with a funny name. Trust me, a funny name can fuck up your whole life."

"This sucks, Dante," I said.

"It always sucks, Carl. It's never good. Except, like I said, this deal, this deal is golden." He turned to Ahmad, "Golden. Take it. Listen to me, kid. I'm your attorney. I'm appointed because I got experience and wisdom. I know what's what. Just fuckin' take it."

Ahmad looked at me. "Do I have to?" he asked.

"You know what," I said. "If you did it, it's a great deal. If you didn't . . . "

"I didn't. I swear."

"They always do," Dante said.

"It's up to you," I said to Ahmad. "Your lawyer works for you. If you don't want the deal, you say no."

"I'm insisting," Dante said, furious and adamant. "For his own good."

I looked at the court-appointed lawyer, sweating in the clothes that just didn't fit right, a button popping over his belly and his belly hanging over his belt. It was hard to imagine him abusing anything but pork chops, layer cake, and tobacco, but he'd been in rehab two times that I knew of. That's okay—lots of good and capable people have. But Dante couldn't even get his addictions right. Hooked on cocaine the first time and meth the second time, he'd still gained weight. I could find him an eyewitness that saw someone else kill MacLeod, and he would still screw it up.

I looked at Ahmad, a skinny college kid, and tried to imagine him surviving even five years inside, holding up a second-hand Koran as a shield, trying to pass for a Black Muslim.

That prick MacLeod had his hook in me too. What was I going to do, sit by the pool, and say it was God's will that sent Ahmad this porky archetype of ineptitude to be his lawyer and let the boy drown?

"For that matter," I said to Ahmad, doing something I've never done before, something totally unprofessional, "if you don't like your attorney, you can dismiss him."

"No, he can't. Not a court-appointed. You can't go shopping when you're taking charity," Dante said furiously.

"Would you help me find another lawyer, Mr. Vanderveer?" Ahmad asked. His tone was very polite, almost formal, but quietly determined. He had this one small chance to put his destiny back in his own hands, and he wanted to take it.

"I can try," I said, wondering where I would go.

"You cock-sucking son of a bitch," Dante yelled at me. "I bring you in, you're supposed to help me out." This one time, he was completely right. "When I tell the legal fraternity that you steal clients out from under their lawyers, you'll never work in this town again."

"I would appreciate that," Ahmad said.

"I'll try to find someone good."

"Thank you," he said. "I am depending on you. For my life." Neither begging, nor pleading, he made it a simple statement of fact in that polite way he had, standing straight, filled with courage and dignity.

"You back-stabbing prick," Dante said to me. "When he gets the needle, Carl, it's on you. It's all on you."

48

Hello walls.

The loneliness hit me like a stone.

I told myself angrily that I had no right to that much maudlin, country music self-pity. Compare the motel room walls to the walls within walls within walls of Nazami's cell. Plasterboard walls to concrete and bars and a double-thick palisade, curlicues of razor wire, and rifle towers. The annoying sound of a too-loud TV next door, to the cries of rape and hate and the weeping of guilt seeping down penitentiary halls.

Then I realized what the emptiness all around me in the stale air, on the blank TV screen, and in my heart was. Jesus had left me. Or I had left Him.

I needed to talk to someone. I picked up the phone to call Gwen, dialed, then hung up before it rang. It couldn't be that. How could faith fall away so quickly and just be gone on the puzzle of a paradox? A twenty-three-hundred-year-old paradox. Why was there no answer to it?

As if by themselves, my fingers went to the phone and hit redial.

"It's me," I said when she answered.

We both said, "I miss you," at the same time.

"I want to come home," I said.

"Why don't you?"

"I did something . . . I don't know . . . . " I was stumbling, trying to figure out how to explain it to her. "I did something today that I shouldn't have done."

"What?" she asked, guard up. "That woman?"

"No. About Nazami. He got a terrible lawyer, just like I thought, and the lawyer told him to take a deal, and I told him not to."

"Why? Why are you doing this, Carl?"

"I don't know if I understand it myself," I said. "I admit that. Listen . . . . "

I wanted to explain the problem of evil to her. It wouldn't work. It would just circle around to "We can't understand His ways. If you would only talk to Pastor Paul, he could explain it. He could explain everything."

"What?" she said into the silence, caring, I thought, worried about me.

"Do you remember Rafe? Rafe Halderson?"

"You talked about him."

"The night he . . . shot himself, he called me. And he wanted me to help him. I said he should give himself to Jesus."

"Yes, that was the right thing."

"No. Don't you see? He didn't call on Jesus. He called on me. And all I did was pass it on."

"But there's no true answer except Jesus."

"What happens if you call on Jesus, and he doesn't answer?"

"He always answers. You know that, Carl."

I'd been calling on Jesus regularly, constantly, daily, and all I'd got was Manny Goldfarb. I'd enjoyed his visits, but if I had to bet on it, I'd put my money on hallucinations. "This kid," I said, "Ahmad, if he gets the needle, and he's innocent, and he's a Muslim, or an atheist, or whatever, does he go to hell?"

"He can come to Jesus if he wants to."

"Gwen, I love you. I love you a lot, and I think you love me. I believe you love me."

"I do."

"What would happen . . . did you ever doubt, Gwen? Did you ever stop believing?"

"How could I? That's . . . how can you doubt reality?"

"What if I stopped believing? What would happen to us?"

"I would pray for you. I would pray as hard as I could, and I know you would come back."

We had become two strangers living on different planets, using words that were in the same dictionary, but when we picked them up and put them together in sentences, they spoke in foreign tongues. I was angry. Deeply, terribly angry, that she would choose . . . that I couldn't explain without losing her . . . I held my anger . . . I needed her to get into the citadel . . . and I needed her to be there if I ever found my way back. I disliked myself for my weakness and essential dishonesty.

I said, "I love you. I'll see you Sunday."

Then I went out for a beer.

49

The first sip was almost like the first time. I was eleven. Everyone talked about beer, and the TV told me how it was satisfying and refreshing. So I approached my first can with great expectations. I figured it would be like Dr. Pepper, which I considered the height of beverage perfection at that age, but doubled, or maybe squared.

After all that buildup, I was shocked and outraged that it tasted like what I imagined cold piss must taste like. But I got used to it then, and in spite of my long layoff from alcohol, I got used to it again. By the middle of the bottle, I knew I was with an old friend. Kickin' back, chillin', takin' the edge off.

It was an easygoing, friendly place named Donohue & Bazini. Two big rooms. One was just a restaurant doing a family trade. The room I was in had a big square bar in the center, a pool table on one side, and tables around two of the other sides. I'd found myself a spot alone toward the back, just watching how people lived, before I tried to fit myself in.

Teresa had called four times that day. One of those times, the third, I think, she'd left a message. She said she was entitled to know what was going on. Not the personal things but the business things. That if she had hired a lawyer, or real estate agent, or anybody else, she'd want to know what they were doing. That was my

Teresa, always ready with a reasonable reason. We could talk on the phone, she went on, but she'd prefer to speak in person.

During my second beer, I called her back. She didn't answer. I waited for the beep and said, "Sure. Let's do it. Let's hook up. Call me."

I signaled the waitress. When she arrived, she gave me a professional smile. She was barely out of her teens and cute. The evening was young. Indeed, it was happy hour. I decided to imagine it was personal and smiled back, asked her name and where she was from, made some other chit-chat, then ordered a burger and some fries to slow my metabolic rate.

While I was working, slowly and carefully, on my third beer, Manny showed up. Sitting in the chair to my right.

"Want one?" I asked automatically, starting to raise my hand to call the waitress back.

He shook his head. When you're dead, you can't drink beer. I should've realized that right off.

"I don't know how you do it," I said, then corrected myself. "Did it."

"What's that?"

"What it is . . . when you're a cop . . . see, you work for an organization. When you live a Christian life you have a Book . . . ." The table next to me was empty, but one of the people a couple of tables away was starting to look at me funny. Whether Manny was my guardian angel or my hallucination, I figured nobody else could see him, and I wasn't anywhere near drunk enough not to care if people thought I was talking to myself. I fished around in my pocket, surreptitiously, and took out my Bluetooth and stuck it in my ear. A great invention for people having self-on-self conversations in public. Properly equipped, I got back to it. "You have a book and a church and a pastor to guide you. When I was working for you, all I had to do was go out and get the information, then *you* were responsible if they went down."

"You do the best you can," Manny said.

"What kind of answer is that? Is that what you said to yourself? Fuck it. Did the best I could. Poor fuck is doing life without parole, but I did the best I could, so it's all right?"

"I gotta admit, no, it still . . . "

"Come on, Manny, with where you are, you gotta be able to come up with a better answer than that."

"It is better," he said carefully, "than if you didn't do the best you could."

"See, with Nazami, I can't lay it off anymore, not on you, not on get-it-all-wrong Mulvaney, not even on poor old Jesus. It's down to me, Manny. I'm not used to that. I don't like it. Most of all, I don't know if I'm up to it."

People were staring at me. Bluetooth or not.

"Can we take this outside?" I asked.

"Since you're embarrassed to be seen with me," he said, "you get the check. I'll meet you out front."

"You'll be there? You sure?"

He was gone. I threw enough money down on the table to cover the tab, got up, and headed out the door. My feet worked just fine. Didn't bump into a single table. Or a person. Or anything. I could have a few beers. No problemo.

The prick wasn't there. I looked to the left, to the right. Nowhere. I thought about going back in, but they would all think I was weird, so I headed for my rental car, got in, and started it up. When I turned to look around before pulling out, Manny was in the passenger seat.

"People talk to themselves in their cars all the time," he said. "I thought this would be more comfortable for you."

"Is that what I'm doing, talking to myself?"

"What did you want to talk about?"

"You really want to know? You really want to know?"

"Yes, of course."

"Are you in hell, Manny?" He didn't answer. "'Cause if you're in hell, I sent you there. I fucked up, big time, with Timley and . . . and

246

Rafe. I didn't help him. Is he in hell? Could you check that for me? He was a hell of a sinner, Rafe, but he was a good guy. Ahmad, if I fuck that up, him too? I got a problem with that, sending all you people to hell."

"You didn't send me to hell," Manny said.

"'Cause there isn't one, is there?"

He didn't answer, just sat there, looking at me, waiting for me to work things through.

"If there were and you got sent, if Ahmad gets the needle and gets sent, and I die, and I go to heaven, just 'cause I stumbled into a church one day and said, yeah, this is it, that wouldn't be fair. That wouldn't be justice. That would just be flat out fucking wrong."

"Are you sure of that?" he asked me.

"Yeah, I'm sure. I'm flat out positive. Which means, even if it means . . . I'm putting my judgment over God's. This is a mindfuck for me, Manny. I'm having trouble with it."

"I see that," he said.

"What are you playing at, being a psychiatrist? Kicking it back to me? Give me some answers, Manny. Give me some answers."

"No," he said. "But I'll ask you a question. Have you done the best you can?"

"You're right," I said. Eduardo Alvarez and Daniel Polasky were out there. I had their home addresses. Why hadn't I gone after them? Fear? Confusion? Weakness? What was I waiting for? They were less than an hour away. "Yeah," I said, "time to kick ass and take names."

I rolled out of the parking lot and headed for the state line. Manny was gone, so I stopped by a convenience store and picked up a six pack to keep me company on the road.

50

Daniel "Beef" Polasky lived in a spiffy new little California-style development just outside of Davis—two-story townhouses, duplex apartments, a nice-size pool, and a couple of tennis courts.

I called, knocked on his door, looked for his Ford Explorer. He wasn't home.

On the way in, I'd seen the sales and rental office, so I parked in front and ambled in. The twenty-something saleswoman inside was happy to tell me about Rancho Verde Estates and show me around. I told her I was looking to rent, but I didn't know for how long. Her eyes went down to my left hand. She saw the ring and asked if it was just for me. I said I was in the process of moving out and, yes, it was just for me. "Oh, you'll just love it here then," she said, getting extra flirty. "There's a very lively social scene." She wanted to show me the pool. There were five women and three men hanging out, catching rays before the sun went down. One of the women, wearing a string bikini, looked me over, then looked away and began to oil her legs.

The saleswoman gave me a satisfied, "see what I mean" look. Welcome to the land of friendly smiles and hungry eyes. A vision of life after Gwen.

I said, "My friend Danny Polasky told me how much he likes it here. I was going to say hello, but he doesn't seem to be around. You know where I might find him?"

Her smile lost about a hundred watts. She said he was probably at the gym. I asked where that was, and she said it was about five miles down the road.

The place was called For Bodies. It was one story high and had a big glass front. The sun was going down by the time I got there, so the lights inside made it look like a giant display window in a department store that was having a big post-holiday sale on muscles.

I spotted the Explorer. I parked three spaces down, got out, and looked it over. It had been repaired. There was a black panel van with smoked windows sitting next to it, with a guy in the driver's seat, waiting for someone. He looked over to see what I was doing.

I strolled over to the front of the health club. I was feeling good. On just two more beers. When I'd come to Jesus, blinkers had gone over my lusting eyes and chains of restraint had wound around the reckless impulses that beat out of my heart. Now that He'd gone— bye-bye, so long—they were falling away. The loose and easy flow was feeling good.

There was Danny boy, "Beef," on view through the window, doing barbell squats with big plates of iron. He was wearing a loose tank top and tight Lycra shorts to mid-thigh.

He was huge. I hadn't realized how large he was when he was playing Homeland Security in a cheesy suit. Six foot three or four, and a real steroid shooter. Fuck it. There never was a muscle big enough in this world to stop a bullet.

I knocked on the window. He was about fifteen feet away and concentrating on all that iron on his back, working for the testosterone rush. I knocked again. This time he looked. It was probably hard to see out, with the bright lights on inside and dark on the street, so I waved at him. Now that I had his attention, I pointed at him with my forefinger, thumb up, the way a kid does when he's playing gun, and mouthed the sound, "Bam."

Then I stepped away, disappearing from his sight.

I took the HK out of my shoulder holster, made sure the safety was off and there was a round in the chamber, and waited for him to come out. Once we got past the introductions, which would be a little rough, we could discuss impersonating a federal law-enforcement officer. That might loosen things up.

When he didn't come out, I figured I'd push a little harder. I went in. The fellow at the desk, all buffed, but still only half Danny's size, asked for my membership card. I said I was just looking for a friend of mine. That seemed all right with him. But I didn't see the big man anywhere. So I headed back outside.

He'd disappeared. Oh my, what a fun game.

As I made for his SUV, I reached for my HK.

His fist came down on the back of my head like a baseball bat, and I went sprawling to the pavement, my hands barely breaking my fall before my face hit the blacktop. He was on me, over two hundred pounds of him, instantly, both his knees on my back. He grabbed me by the hair, yanked my head back, then wrapped his forearm, thick as a normal human's leg, around my throat and began to choke me. I clawed at him. I twisted and turned, trying to get him off me.

It was no use. I couldn't breathe. The blackness came. I was going to die, but the joke was on him since I now knew that there was no hell.

51

I saw a light. A brief, dim flash in the darkness.

Then the pressure seemed to be gone from my throat. I figured it was just me, that I was drifting off into the dead zone, out past pain and sensation and struggle.

Suddenly, I was gasping and choking and trying to get air. I pushed myself over so I could breathe better. There was another flash of light. I was fighting for air and blinking my eyes, trying to figure out what was happening, all the feet scuffling around alongside of me. There was a pain in my side for a moment, and I realized someone was stepping on me. Three, four, five people? Four. Danny boy was stumbling, no, being dragged, into the van. They were grunting and cursing in Spanglish about his size and weight.

He started to kick and struggle.

Flash. The light again.

It was a stun gun. They'd zapped him. He spasmed. They yanked. His feet disappeared inside. The side door slid sideways from inside and shut with a slam. The black cargo van was already in gear, backing out and rolling away.

I hauled myself up into a sitting position and, once I was there, flopped back against Polasky's Ford for something to lean on. That set off his car alarm—an ouuu-ah, ouuu-ah siren right against my head. I got off his car and stood up, watching the van driving away.

Then I ran to my car, jumped in, and set off to follow them.

I drove like no one should drive unless he has gumball lights on top and a siren screaming. My hands were bloody, my face was scrapped, my neck and back hurt like hell, and I was terrified that if I was stopped, I'd pop the top on the breathalyzer.

When they finally came into view, I slowed down, relaxed, and grabbed another beer to kill the pain.

They drove through the night, taking it easy, mostly about five miles over the limit when the road was clear. I had no idea where we were until we hit US 131, and they turned south, heading into Davis, where there's a crossing into Mexico.

We passed under a sign that said the border was coming. It's a losing proposition, chasing gangsters in Mexico. They cut off people's heads down there. But I knew I would follow them anyway. Feeling depressed about it, I finished my beer.

Then my luck changed. A half a mile before customs and immigration, they turned off 131 into the sprawl of depots and warehouses that serve the border trade.

They made a series of random turns, probably checking for a tail. I pretended to go straight after the third one, then shut off my headlights, backed up, and took the street they'd taken. I saw their taillights as they turned again. When I got to the next corner, they were gone.

I started cruising around. I'm not sure for how long—twenty, thirty minutes, another beer anyway. Up in the northeast portion, which was dotted with empty lots and where many of the buildings looked like they weren't being used, I spotted a black van that I thought might be theirs. I turned and drove past, and as my headlights swept by, I thought I caught a glimpse of someone standing outside, smoking and casually holding an automatic weapon in his other hand. Just a glimpse. I drove on by and kept going two more streets before I turned, turned again, and headed back, lights out, to come around behind the building.

I left my car in the dark, a few hundred yards away from the back of the warehouse and went the rest of the way on foot, using the shadows and the dark for cover.

I made it to the building safely. The back wall was blank as best as I could see. I felt nostalgic for Jesus. If still I believed, I would have prayed, but on the other hand, I would've been sober and probably known better than to be there. Might've called 911 or something sensible like that.

I crept around the corner and started making my way along the side of the building. There were two overflowing dumpsters and lots of litter on the ground: bottles, cans, boxes, crates and old pallets, a busted up office chair, and a still-shiny porcelain urinal. I stepped carefully to avoid kicking a can or breaking a bottle—or tripping and falling on my face. About twenty feet along, I found a door. It would be stupid to try it, because if it opened, I had no idea what it would open on—three guys with guns probably. But I tried it anyway. Luck, not Jesus, just blind luck, was with me; it was locked. What I needed was a window.

There were none. What the hell did they do for air? Vents. Up on the roof. If I had a ladder, I could get up on the roof. If I had a hammer, I could build a ladder. Well, if I put a pallet on top of one of the dumpsters, the one closest to the wall, I could use the pallet for a ladder. If I could do that quietly enough, the guard wouldn't discover me and shoot me. It was, without a doubt, an excellent plan, and I proceeded to put it into effect.

Standing on top of the pallet, which was on top of the dumpster, I was able to reach the top of the roof. I grabbed on and began to haul myself up, my feet scrambling for some extra purchase. My hands were in terrible shape, but sufficient beer kills all sorts of pain. It doesn't make you graceful, but it does kill the pain.

With a jerk, I got myself up to armpit height, flung my arms out lat on the roof and was able to hang that way and catch my breath. I didn't think I could go down without crashing and clanging, so there was nowhere to go but forward. And up ahead, catching the light, were shining aluminum vents, those cylindrical things with spiral cuts that let the heat rise up and have fans inside to help move it along.

Better not to dangle there too long. There wasn't much to grip onto. I clawed and heaved and wiggled until I got my chest and abdomen up. From there it was easy. I just sort of rolled over at an angle, and my legs followed, and I kept rolling, and there I was on the roof.

I could hear voices. One of them sounded like Danny. That was good. It would've been a bitch if I'd crawled up there and all they were doing was smuggling illegals and cocaine. I crept up to the vent.

"Will you give me something, give me something for this? It hurts," Danny said.

"When we're done, got a whole bottle of Percs for you, soon as you tell us everything," someone with a Mexican accent said.

"I'm telling you . . . I'm telling you everything I know," Danny said. Clearly, they'd been at this awhile. "Mostly all we did was keep an eye on the girls."

"Plowright's girls."

"Yeah, like I said. Nobody said they were Plowright's girls, but that was obvious."

"Nicole Chandler, what about her?"

"We watched her a couple of times. All she did was go to church and go to work and go to some class at USW."

"You snatch her?"

"No, man, not us—"

"You and Eduardo?"

"Yeah, me and Eddie, never did nothing to her."

"The other girls?"

"If they got out of line, we straightened 'em out. We've been doing it for about a year now, year and a half. Would you give me one of them now? Just one, man. Come on."

"You come on, Danielito, come on. How'd you straighten 'em out?"

I had to look if I could. I tried lifting the vent up. It wouldn't go. I felt around the base. It was held in place with simple metal screws. I searched in my pocket for some change, looking for a dime, hoping it was thin enough to do the job. I found one and began to work it into the slot of the nearest screw.

"The usual—slap 'em around. If that di'n't work, a little more serious. One of them was stubborn. We spent the night with her, a nice blondie, about C-cups, real ones, none of your gel packs, you know. When we were done, she left the state. Never came back no more. Bye-bye."

"How did you decide who to lean on?"

"We get the word. Jeremiah says, we do. This motherfucker hurts, man. Please."

"Stop whining, *chilito*. Just talk. What about the money? Tell me about the hundreds of millions, *chilito*."

"I don't know anything about that. I don't."

"Then why were you watching Plowright's girls."

"He's the meal ticket, man. He rakes in the big bucks. They're getting rich over there. You ever see Jeremiah's ride? That Hummer? The preacher banging the choirgirls—same old shit—kills the golden goose. At least it's not the choirboys. But hey, that's a Catholic priest thing, right?"

A beat later Danny yelled, then whined, "You don't have to hurt me. Come on."

Meantime, I'd gotten one screw loose and out, and I was starting on the second.

"You only raped the one of them? Is that right? Just one? Tell me rue, or you know what I'm gonna do."

"Come on, man, come on. You got my fingers, man. I'll tell you whatever you want. Two. Alright, two. What do you care how many got porked? It was just Plowright was getting out of control, ou know, with the babes, and Jeremiah said we just hadda keep a id on."

The second screw was easier. Maybe I was just getting better at it. Once I got it loose, I was able to turn it with my fingertips.

"You were up at the prison saying you were Homeland Security. How'd you do that?"

"That was fuckin' amazing," Danny said with some enthusiasm, in spite of whatever he was going through. "Right, we walked in. I mean, Jeremiah took my old ID when I was CPB, right? And he used that to make up this ID that said Homeland Security. Well, fuck, man, nobody knows what a Homeland Security Terrorist Task Force ID looks like, and there's nobody you can check with 'cause it doesn't exist, or I don't think it does, and if it did, they wouldn't answer 'cause it's the War on Terror and they don't have to tell nobody shit. If you want the ID, hey, I'll give it to you, just for one of those Percs, man. This is, like, throbbing."

"If you would tell me about the money, you could have all the pills you want."

"I would tell you if I knew, man. I would. I really would."

The third screw was done. I felt around the base, and that seemed to be all there was. Now, could I lift the vent off without being discovered? I began to gently pull and sort of work it back and forth. It was tight at first, from just sitting there for who knows how long, but then it began to move, and once it started, it came pretty easily. I put it down and bent over to look in.

There was a fan inside, and I couldn't see much through the blades and wire mesh underneath. But I could make out Danny. There was a bright light shining on him. The rest of the place looked pretty dark. He was naked, sitting in a chair. It looked like his feet were tied to it, and there was something around his chest. His big arms were free, but he was clutching his right hand with his left, holding it tight to his chest. A rag, his shirt, was wrapped around his right hand, and it was muddy red, blood soaked.

"What else did you do for Hobson?"

"There was this one other weird thing . . . alright, I'll tell you, I'll tell you. We snatched this haji, and we took him up in a plane—some private jet, maybe Plowright's, but I don't know. I'm just a fuckin' grunt—you know, do this, do that, yes sir, no sir, whatever the fuck you say sir. Yeah, we got 'im up in the plane, wired his dick to a battery, like in sand land, got him to confess to killing some guy, that professor guy, and then we brought him to the prison and said to hold him."

That was it. I'd done it. I had my witness!

52

"Good story," I heard the interrogator say. "I like that story so much, you can have some Percs."

"Thank you, man," Danny said.

I was already on my way. I'd go in and grab him, gun blazing if I had to. Before I went over the edge, I had a moment of good sense. I called 911 and whispered that a man had been kidnapped and was being held in a warehouse. I gave the cross streets. The operator tried to ask more questions, but I hung up, looked over for the pallet and dumpster, found my position, and started to slide over.

I hung from the lip and felt around with my feet for the slats.

I touched them, let go, and tried to fall forward, toward the wall. That was successful, but the slat I was standing on broke, and then I was sliding down on the pallet, trying to cling to the concrete block wall tearing up my hands even more. The pallet skidded out from under me, and I crashed-landed on the dumpster with a huge metallic clang. I stopped there, on my hands and knees again, got my gun out and hoped the police would come before I got killed.

I let myself down off the dumpster, got up against the wall, and edged forward, making my way to the front.

Suddenly, I heard the sound of the warehouse doors opening and the voices of the interrogator and one or two others. They were coming out. I had to move. I jogged toward them, my feet stumbling over trash and blown papers, holding my gun out in front of me.

I got to the corner in time to see two men pile into the back of the van, one of them carrying a bag. A third climbed into the front seat beside the driver. Danny wasn't with them. I ducked down and let them peel out, then rushed into the warehouse.

I smelled it before I saw it. Burning gasoline.

Fire rose from a wide splash across the warehouse floor. The flames lit up the abandoned interior, and the heat came at me in waves. A wall of flame was between me and Danny—my witness, Ahmad Nazami's salvation—and then a new smell came to me, like roasting meat. The building was beginning to burn too, and it would only get worse.

I ran to the side to get around it, or at least through the least of it. Then I charged forward, holding my arm up over my face. I felt like the fire was cooking me, and the fumes were getting in my lungs, and it was hard to breath.

When I got past the worst of the fire into an open place, I stopped and gasped for breath. I looked back and saw that it had spread wider, and flames were beginning to climb up the walls. I turned to my left, looking for Danny.

He sat, unmoving, as the flames danced around the base of his chair, starting to cook his bound feet, as if a sacrilegious modern artist had inserted a naked muscleman into a medieval painting of a Catholic martyr being burnt at the stake.

The wire around his upper body held his trunk upright. His arms dangled, and I now saw that his right hand was missing three fingers. They lay on the floor, already black and charred, burning down to he bones. A long-handled hedge cutter lay in the middle of the fire.

He was covered in blood, and his head had flopped forward. Through the smoke and the waving distortions created by the heat, I ould see the big exit wound on the side of his head. They'd shot him first. The purpose of the fire was to destroy any evidence they'd left behind.

Then I heard sirens. The response to the 911 call. The men who had done it were gone, and all that was left was me and the corpse, trapped behind a wall of flame.

I looked around wildly. I was near the door that I'd tried from the outside. It was shut tight with a dead bolt. I grabbed it and pulled at it, but it wouldn't budge. I took out my HK and used the butt as a hammer, banging at it until it loosened. Then some more to get it all the way clear. I kicked the door open, then stumbled out into the night, gasping for air. I pushed the door closed behind me, leaning on it, sucking for oxygen, trying to push the smoke out of my lungs.

I couldn't see the police cars, but I could see the blue and white and red of their lights rising up into the sky and bouncing off buildings as they came toward me.

53

I made it to my car before the police came around the corner. I knew that when they saw me, they would stop me. I stank of the fire and of gasoline. They'd haul me in, and then it would take about five minutes to book me for arson and murder.

I turned off the dome light, grabbed my last beer, and got out. I was by another warehouse. I sat on the ground, leaning my back against the chain-link fence that surrounded it. Then, regretfully, I poured half the beer over myself.

The cops pulled up while I was drinking the rest. They jumped out of their vehicle to look at my rental and then noticed me. When they came over, I said, "Fuckin' Mexicans took my fuckin' beer. Go get 'em. Get my beer back!"

One of the two leaned down to me. His face wrinkled in disgust at the way I smelled. "What happened to you?"

"Tol' you. Fuckin' Me-ki-kins took my *beer*. You gon' he'p me or not?"

"Come on," his partner said.

"You've had enough anyway," the first one said, turning away. They had more exciting things to do.

After they'd driven off to the fire and the big crime scene, I slunk back to the car, made sure the lights wouldn't come on, and started it up. When I was a few streets away, I turned my headlights back on.

I made it back to the motel. I showered and did my best to clean the cuts and abrasions on my face, hands, and knees. My throat, the back of my head, and my lower back all hurt from the beat down I'd taken from Danny Polasky. May the son of a bitch rest in peace. So I went down to the night clerk, Pratap, a Bengali, like the owner, and asked if he knew any place I could find some painkillers stronger than aspirin. He sold me two generic hydrocodone tablets for $10 apiece and told me he could get me some Oxycontin if I wanted to wait a couple of hours.

I took a half. It had been a long, rough day, the longest and roughest. I expected it would knock me out and put me to sleep. It made me feel better, but I was wide awake. Awake and unbearably alone. So I set out to do what I normally do at the end of a day's work: make notes. Write down what I know and don't know. What I've found out and what I should look for next. I found myself writing something else. Maybe because I was a little bit high.

Once I had a world.

In that world, I had a wife and a child. I had a job that I did well enough to make a living. I belonged to a church. That gave me a community. Mostly of wonderful and supportive people who would help me if I were ever in need. That church had a leader who was eloquent and intelligent and hugely successful, who was making that community larger and stronger. He preached the word of the Lord, who held us all in the palm of His hand. Whose word gave all the answers. Whose love bound all the other loves together. Whose order held everything in place.

Then I took a job. A small contract.

In the course of that job, I discovered that my pastor, the man who had taken on the role of guiding me and people like me, was a hypocrite and a liar who had crimes committed on his behalf. It was not merely that he had girlfriends. I'm a man. I understand sexual temptation. He did more. He had people intimidated, beaten, and raped in order to si lence them. He had a man kidnapped and tortured in order to frame him for murder. A murder that he had, perhaps, committed himself.

A bad man can still say good things.

The Bible itself is full of flawed heroes. Did not Saul plot to kill David? Did not David plot to have Uriah murdered so that he could have Uriah's wife, Bathsheba? Did not Lot lay with his daughters? Did not Saul persecute Christians before he became Paul?

The flaws of a man, any man, all men, do not deny the truth of God. But I am face to face with the truth that a man of faith, of belief, a man of God, is not made good by his faith. Are we to say that he would have been even worse if he had been an unbeliever? That is not sufficient. It can't be demonstrated. I don't think it's true. What then, is the point of all that faith?

As a result of that job, as a result of the way I did something in that job, my friend was killed. He was a Jew. My religion told me that he was going to go to hell. I honestly thought that he was a better man than me. But my religion told me that I would go to heaven and have life eternal. There was something wrong with that. Something unsustainable.

At the same time, I found myself among unbelievers. And hearing the words of unbelievers.

Their words rang true.

If God is who we are told He is, the world would have to be a different place. If the world is the way it is, and there is a God, he must be either indifferent, so indifferent as to mean almost nothing, or perverse and evil.

Or, we have got it all wrong, and we mistake good for evil and evil for good. For if we were to act as God does, to model ourselves on Him, then we would be indifferent to suffering and injustice, we would make the innocent suffer for the sins of the guilty, and we would slaughter without mercy.

Now I am alone.

I took the other half of the hydrocodone. Then I wrote some more.

What is left?

I love my daughter, and I love my wife.

I believe in them. But I don't know what belief is. Yet, I feel it. I know it.

I may lose them too. As a consequence of my own actions. I can't seem to stop what I'm doing. It is as if my actions go forward, and I follow. It is not only God who moves in mysterious ways. So do we all. I am a mystery to myself.

So I move forward. The only hope is that if Gwen can see what I have seen, she may change. Not lose her faith. I don't need her to do that. I wouldn't wish this feeling of emptiness and loss on anyone. But enough that she can understand, and love me, and build our lives out of something else than the lies of hypocrites. That's my goal.

54

"You're hurt," Teresa said, care and worry in her voice—and curiosity.

"I'm all right," I said. I was on the second hydrocodone. Just one a day, that can't be bad. And I had a margarita. So I wasn't feeling much pain, not physically. I reached for the chips. She saw how hard it was for me to use my hand. She took it and turned it palm up. "I'm all right," I said.

She kept her eyes on my mine as she raised my hand. When it was close to her, she bent her head slightly, kissed my palm with a feather touch, then moved her lips lightly across the scars and scabs on my fingers. "Of course, you are," she said, looking back at me, her touch lingering as she let go of my hand. "The other night . . . I mean, the way you walked out, I didn't even know if you were still working on the case."

Saturday night, at Barbarosa, a good Mexican place over on the cheating side of town. That's one of those sentences that can be turned around—it's a good cheating place on the Mexican side of town.

If you get a booth or a back table, you can talk without being over-heard, and it's so dark you have to use the table candles to peer at the menu. A lot of cops go there—and politicians too. Never with their wives. That's understood.

It's at the far end of the Wolvern District, all low-rise commercial buildings, auto body and transmission shops, discount markets in strip malls, showrooms for furniture and TV rentals, a couple of welfare motels, and one upscale motel that seems out of place. It services mostly the same people who go to the restaurant. So nobody wanders into Barbarosa by accident, or from shopping, or because they're visiting cousin Joan.

The restaurant itself is tucked up against the blank curving wall created by the exit ramp off the east end of Colonel Bender Bridge. Parking is in an unpaved lot alongside, or if you're really worried about your car being spotted, there are spaces around the back.

The food is good. The chips come with four different homemade salsas: *molcajete*, mango chipotle, corn and tomatillo, and one made with cilantro and lime. I ordered the grilled sirloin strips with a side of tomatillo salad. Teresa got the red snapper with *napolitos* in cilantro sauce.

I summarized most of what I knew. Leaving out how I knew it. I didn't want anyone to place me at the scene of Polasky's murder.

But what Teresa really wanted to know was what had brought our last night together to an end and, by implication, where we likely stood now. I told her, "That was my *wife* who called. Even though it's Plowright, and she's very close to him, she respects the fact that I'm her husband, understands that enough that she's helping me. She heard a rumor that Nicole Chandler might be up at CTM."

"In the Cathedral."

"No, the other part, the office tower. They call it the citadel. Plowright has a private apartment there."

"The princess in the tower," Teresa said, teasing. "And the knight will ride to rescue her. Is that the plan?"

"No. My *wife*," I said, waving the word like a cross in front of Dracula, "works there, and she'll make it possible for me to get in."

"It sounds dangerous," she said. "I don't want anything more to happen to you."

"It won't," I said.

"And you're going to do this when?"

"Sunday night, tomorrow night, when it's quiet."

"There's something I don't understand," she said.

"What?"

"The other night . . . we seemed close . . . ."

I gave her a look that meant to say, you may have been close, but I wasn't, though that wasn't true. There'd been something between us the moment we met. She felt free to reach for it; I feared what would happen when we got it.

She let it pass and said, "You've made it clear how important your marriage is to you. So for us to be the way we were, there had to have been something wrong between you and your wife."

"No."

"Well, it felt like it. And when she called, you were surprised. And you were surprised she wanted to help you."

"Yeah, I did something stupid. I lied to her."

"Why did you lie to her?"

I told her a short version of what happened, then pointed out, "Because you had called me at home, over and over again, on Sunday, she thought I went to see you."

"I'm sorry," Teresa said. "I didn't mean to cause trouble for you."

"Don't bullshit me," I snapped back at her. "You like trouble." It had been in her voice when she apologized. Sincere on top, but underneath she was deliciously excited by her own mischief and had a hidden feeling of accomplishment. "You knew perfectly well what you were doing."

"No . . . not . . . alright, yes." Caught out, nailed. "I'm sorry," she said, finally near to genuine about it.

I explained the rest, emphasizing again how Gwen had come back around, and we were right as husband and wife again. I left out the part about my losing my faith and my wife not understanding me.

When the food came, the waitress noticed that Teresa's glass was empty and asked if she'd like a refill. She said, "Yes, please," to her fourth margarita.

Mine was nearly finished as well, so I said, "Me too," going on my third.

We began to eat. Teresa said how good it was and complimented me for picking the place. She ate small, neat pieces. Her refill came quickly, and she sipped at it. "Can I ask you something?" she said.

"I have a question for you," I said.

"What?"

"How the hell do you live with no God?"

"Lots of good sex," she said.

"And that's enough? For you?"

"I was teasing," she said. "Flirting."

"What was his answer?"

"His?"

"Nathaniel's. He was the one going around saying there is no God. But there are people who have God, who want Him. Having Him makes them happy. Sometimes it makes them good—it doesn't necessarily make them good, but sometimes it does. And it makes all kinds of other things happen. So, if you take God away, then what do you do? Fuck a lot? Get drunk? Fuck some more? Get stoned? Come on, what the hell do you do? Did he think about that? Or did he just say, I'm going to rob you of what makes your life meaningful, and you can stand there with your dick in your hand wondering where to piss?"

"I'm a little drunk," she said.

Me, too. Once upon a time, my body would barely have noticed just two drinks, but now I was already feeling the glow. Once upon a time, I had a drinking problem. Maybe she had one now. Maybe I'd have one again.

"Can I flirt with you while I talk?"

"Sure."

"How much? Am I allowed to touch you?" she asked, taking my hand again. "Big, strong hand. Hurt hand. Did it feel all better when I kissed it?" This time she kissed with her lips open and wet, her tongue briefly coming out and teasing. I wanted her mouth on my mouth. I wanted her mouth all over my body.

She stopped and said, "You're different than him," talking about Nathaniel. "But like him. 'You don't know what you have until you've lost it.' Maybe that's why . . . . " She smiled and made a gesture from her to me that ended with her caressing my upper arm. "We would make a good couple, the academic and the tough guy."

Then, changing focus, she said, "That was his question. You can't just stop things with reason. Reason says that sex is for having children. If you want four children, you should only have sex four times. But you can't reason desire away." Her fingers walked the words down my arm, back to my hand. "God is an answer to other things we desire," she said. "Can't just reason him away. You have to offer something else instead."

"What? What do you offer?"

"Ourselves. We claim we worship God because He made us, but if we made Him, shouldn't we turn it around."

"Shit," I said. Maybe that was a reflex. I'd heard a hundred sermons against secular humanism as the mock religion of me, me, me, limitless indulgence, no rules, no salvation, nothing higher than our petty, crawling, sinful selves to answer to.

The waitress came with fresh drinks and, after asking, cleared away the dinner plates.

"Do you know the story of the three hundred?" Teresa asked. "The Spartans who stood up against the three hundred thousand, or million, or whatever it was, Persians."

"Yes," I said, irritated because I felt she was talking down to me in her little game of the educated intellectual slumming with the illiterate stud.

"Well, I don't know what you know and what you don't know," she said defensively. "I don't know if you read Herodotus."

"It was a comic book too," I said sarcastically. "Then it was a movie, but the comic was better."

"I'm sorry," she said.

"Whatever."

"The point is that they fought for glory. They knew they were going to die, but they fought for glory. Nathaniel said that kind of glory belongs to each of us because every human being stands at the edge of the abyss, his whole life long, battling to hold back the chaos. To fight that endless war, we created love and honor and glory, rationality and tools and justice and all the rest. We did that. God didn't do it. We know that we're going to die in the end, but still we fight, and that's glorious. That's what we should celebrate, the human struggle against chaos and destruction."

"Does that work for you?" I asked her.

"Nate thought that was the answer because glory was what Nate wanted," she said. "He wanted to answer the big questions. Most people get over that during sophomore year and realize they're just sort of ordinary." She said that last with wistful sadness, a great sadness, like someone looking at a landscape she used to know as a wide and shining lake, the sun glittering off the clear, sustaining water, that had somehow gone dry, the space now empty, the earth barren and cracked.

"Did he? Get to the answers?"

"Put your arm around me. Will you put your arm around me?" she asked.

I did, and she leaned in close into my shoulder.

"So, did he?" I asked again. It felt good to hold her, warm and sexy and comfortable too.

"Yeah, I guess. I don't know. I mean, it depends more on who you are and what you need than on what the answers actually are. Find the book, and you can judge for yourself. Or you can just stay with me, and I'll tell you about it, or what I think is in it, bit by bit, like Scheherazade, for a thousand and one nights." Her hand was on my leg, stroking lightly. My hand was nudging up against the side of her pliant breast. "Personally," she said, "I would take love over glory."

"Is that what you want, love?"

"Umm," she murmured. "You don't know until you've lost it." Then she said, "I have a question."

"Alright."

"Promise you won't get mad at me. It's just a question."

"I'll do my best," I said, drinking with one hand. The other— healed, I'm sure, by her kisses—slid down along her waist and began to explore her hip and thigh.

"I'm happy for you—maybe a little disappointed for myself—that you and your wife are back on solid footing. Really, I am. And I don't want to undermine that. But if I were just a disinterested friend, you know, there are things that would bother me."

"Yeah? Like what?"

"It's like you've been telling me two different things at once," she said slowly. "One story is that you think that as a husband in this Christian marriage—"

"It's not just about being Christian," I said, upset.

She misunderstood the reason for the stress she heard in my voice. "I'm not mocking," she said. "You have this marriage where it's up to you to make the decisions, and she follows, which she does, except for a brief moment caused by your own mistake, and now she's back on the right track. Is that what you said?"

"Yes," I said, "that's about it." And although I was talking about Gwen, I was only really thinking about how smooth Teresa's skin felt through her skirt and how much I liked the shape of her and wondering if I could inch that skirt up and get to the flesh beneath it without being seen in the restaurant.

"I heard another story at the same time."

"What's that?"

"It's your wife's story. Her story is that her faith—this church you belong to and its pastor—comes first. That you're head of the house, sure, but she only has to follow you to the degree that you follow them." She said this thoughtfully, her hand idly tracing patterns on my thigh. "And each time she had a choice, she chose them over you."

"You're a bitch," I said, just stating a fact. My hand tightened on the leg it had been caressing, twisted and squeezed hard, not a rejection, an adjustment in our relationship. "You're not going to drive a wedge between me and my wife."

"Don't be mad," she said. "I'm not driving anything. What you didn't tell me was *why* she would change."

"Yes, I did," I said.

"What?"

"That she thought about it. She had time to think about it."

"You want to believe her, don't you?"

"Yes. And I have reason to," I said, taking my arm from around her. I moved her off my shoulder and turned to face her. "You live in a world without belief, even in people. You like it there. Fine, stay there."

"Carl," she said softly, "Carl . . . I'm trying to—"

"Leave Gwen out of this," I said.

"Carl, here's what we're talking about. You're going to break into—you're not going to just walk in—you're going to break into some huge institution in the middle of the night. Don't they have security there? Cameras? The university does."

CTM has very good security. I could see it in my mind's eye, the cameras over every door, including the service area in back, where I planned to enter. And yes, there were people who watched those images all night long.

She nattered on. "And you're going to do this because you want to believe in your wife."

"Gwen wouldn't—"

"Belief blinds us."

"I know my wife," I said. "You're trying to say she's setting me up."

"How long has your wife belonged to that church?"

"A long time," I said.

"She works there. She socializes there. All her friends are from there. How important is it to her?"

"It's her life," I said. "Aside from Angie and me."

"What if they told her that they just needed to talk to you, to explain. What would she do?"

"I've already dealt with that," I said. "I told her if they wanted to talk to me, they could pick up the phone."

"Her belief makes her blind to what they are. Just like your belief makes you blind to what she is."

Gwen was all I had left, Gwen and Angie, and this bitch was trying to take them away from me. I reached into my pocket, took out my wallet, threw enough money on the table to cover the check, and walked out.

55

She came running out into the parking lot after me.

I ignored her, but she caught up to me and grabbed hold of me by my jacket.

"Wait," she said.

"No," I said, trying to pry her hand loose.

"The men who tried to kill you, they haven't been able to find you, right?"

"No," I said. Polasky's death hadn't ended anything. Alvarez was still out there, as was Jerry Hobson. Probably looking even harder.

"What do you do, if you can't find someone?"

I took her fingers and bent them back off my jacket. It had to hurt. She didn't try to pull away; she didn't complain.

"I was watching TV," she said, blathering away frantically. "I know it's stupid to talk about something you see on TV, but the cops couldn't find someone, so they set up a sting—told the guy he had won the lottery or something, but he had to come in to sign for the money. They can't find you. So they dangled something you want, something you're looking for, that girl. And they used someone you trust to send the message so you would believe it."

There were a few people in the lot, either headed in or back out to their cars. Mostly they ignored us. A certain number of the conversation

274

across the dark, intimate tables at Barbarosa are the kind that end in yelling and tears. But one or two looked on, amused.

"You're a fucking bitch, Teresa. You're prepared to destroy everything good in my life just so you can get laid."

"That's not why I'm saying this."

I let go of her hand and said, "Get a vibrator and leave me alone."

I started walking away from her, around the back, where my car was. She came after me.

"You're a fucking bastard," she said, grabbing hold of me again.

"What, you want me to stop believing in my wife so we can bang each other?" I snarled at her, grabbing her by the wrist and twisting it. She liked the pain, and right then, I liked hurting her.

"I want you. I do want you," she said. "I told you that from the start."

"There was no start. There's nothing." But there we were again, pressing against each other.

"That's not true," she said, her mouth reaching up for me.

The fingers of my other hand found their way into her hair. I pressed my mouth down on hers and kissed her violently. She yielded eagerly, almost sobbing, as our hungry mouths slobbered at each other. The hand that held her wrist didn't let go either, but squeezed and twisted. I was hard and hungry for sex and angry and drunk.

I let go of her wrist and lifted up her skirt. She reached for my zipper and belt and started opening them up.

I turned her around and pushed her face down on the hood of the nearest car. As I shoved her skirt up and pulled her thong down, she arched her back, eager for me.

56

I leaned on top of her, pressing against her, and I spoke into her ear. "Let me tell you something. If I do this, we unleash the chaos."

"Take me," she said.

"Do you want love, or do you just want to be used?"

"Carl, I want you. I want you."

"After this, we'll get drunk a lot, and I'll fuck other women."

"I don't need to own you," she said.

"It'll hurt you because I'll hate you, because there's no going back for me. And you'll try to hurt me back, but you'll lose because you'll love and I'll hate. You understand that?"

"Take me. Just take me," she said, hips moving, seeking.

"It won't take long. Maybe this one fuck is all you get." I wanted to break her. "There's already someone I want more than I want you." I said it to break what was between us, because I didn't have the strength to control myself. "Who I think is better and more beautiful than you. So if I have you, it'll be this one, quick fuck, and then I don't care what I do anymore, and I move on and go after her."

It hurt her as much as I wanted it to. She turned over toward me her skirt all crumpled, the heat and lust crumbling from her face "You're a bastard, a fucking bastard."

57

Clean and sober, Sunday morning I went out in my rental car.

I followed Gwen as she headed toward the Cathedral, then on Route 28, between the Borders and Devontown Mall, I pulled up alongside her, honked my horn, and motioned her over. She went into the mall with me following. I passed her, parked, got out, took my kit with me, locked the car, walked over to her, and opened the passenger-side door.

"Carl, I thought . . . "

"Change of plan," I said, getting in beside her.

She looked at the scrapes and bruising on my face. "What happened to you?"

"Gwen, we have to talk. First, I'm going to ask you, did you get all the codes? Can we get up the elevator, preferably Plowright's private elevator? And into his private apartment?"

"Yuh . . . yes . . . , " she said.

"Good," I said. "If we're going to do it, we'll do it this morning."

"But . . . it's time for church."

"I know that."

"What are you going to . . . "

"CTM has great security," I said. Teresa's motives didn't matter; what she'd said had been the truth. "Cameras almost everywhere.

There's not a hope in hell of sneaking up and breaking in, even if I can open every lock in the building, in the middle of the night. Never happen. But you know what I can do? I can walk in, in the middle of six thousand or so other people. Then I can head for the men's room with a few hundred other guys relieving themselves, and you can head toward the ladies' room, and then we can open that door that says, 'Private, Staff Only,' to the hall that runs backstage. And while Plowright is out there in front of the cameras, we can ride up to his office. Hide in plain sight—that's my best shot, I figure."

"Too many people know you."

I shrugged. "I'll tell you what else I think. I think if I go in there at midnight, Jerry Hobson will be waiting for me. And I expect he will then kill me and dispose of me."

"No, no . . . ."

"No, he won't be there?"

She didn't answer.

"Or no, you don't think he'll kill me?"

She tried to say, 'he wouldn't,' but it didn't quite come out.

"What did he tell you? That they just wanted to meet with me, to pray with me? If you could just get me there, we would all pray together, and it would be alright? That's what they told you, right?"

She shook her head from side to side, but it wasn't even a real denial, and she couldn't look me in the eye, let alone look at me with love and devotion. Finally, she said, "If you think Jerry is going to do something, won't it be even more dangerous now?"

"Not for me. He won't kill me with sixty-five hundred people watching and the cameras rolling. Middle of the night, sure. Just him and me, haul my body out, toss it in the dumpster. Midnight's good for Paul and Jerry, not for me."

"Whatever you say, Carl," she said in the agreeable voice you use with the crazy people you're afraid to argue with.

"And you're coming with me."

"Why? What?"

"Because I love you."

"I don't understand," she said.

"Because I have to know. I have to know if you're really on my side or theirs. Because I won't take things on faith anymore. I don't believe. I need proof. I want you beside me when I try the codes and find out if they're the right ones. When we get up to Plowright's private office, I want you with me when we find out that Nicole Chandler isn't there. And if she is there, then you can hear about whatever the hell is going on, hear the truth about her, her and Paul."

She began to cry.

"Gwen, listen. I know you think I'm wrong, even crazy, but nobody will be happier than me if the evidence shows that I'm wrong. I want to be wrong. I want to believe."

Through her tears, she said, "How can you say . . . say you don't believe?"

"I'll tell you what I do believe," I said. "I believe you would never do anything intentionally to harm me. Or Angie. I believe that, Gwen. I truly do."

She looked at me, nodding her head to say, yes, that was true.

"But I'll tell you something else, and you had better believe this. I'm carrying a gun. If you see Jerry Hobson and you say something to him, if you betray me, Gwen, and they come for me, they won't take me easy. I'll tear the temple down. I will tear the temple down. And if I die doing it, that's alright, because if you betray me, I don't care if I live or die."

58

Once I realized that Teresa was most probably right and decided that the safest thing to do was go in broad daylight, I decided I'd have to try to disguise myself. I looked at myself in the mirror. The abrasions on my face and the purple, blue, and black bruising on my throat gave me the idea of using bandages. I went to an all-night drugstore and cruised the aisles looking for other possibilities. It was a big place that even had a wig section. I bought a cheap black rug that looked exactly like what it was, something for Halloween or for someone doing chemo whose medical plan wouldn't pop for a real hairpiece. Then I got a pair of those big, wraparound plastic sunglasses they give to old people after eye surgery.

While Gwen drove, I put on a big medical dressing that started on the right side of my face and went around my neck and chin all the way to the left side. Then I added the hairpiece and the glasses.

Gwen watched me with sideways glances. When I was done, I turned to look at her and asked, "What do you think?"

She burst out laughing.

The Cathedral of the Third Millennium was thronged. That was obvious when we tried to park. Lots A, B, and C—Acts, Baruch, and Corinthians—were full, and we had to go all the way to Deuteronomy to find a spot.

When she parked, I took off the glasses and the stupid wig for a moment. "Gwen, I'm going to give you a choice. You don't have to do this."

"If you want me . . . "

"Shh," I said. "You need to know how dangerous this is. Jerry Hobson had at least two men whose job it was to keep tabs on Plowright's girlfriends."

Her mouth tightened in disbelief and disapproval that I should be uttering such slanders.

"And not just keep tabs. Intimidate them if he thought they were going to create a scandal. Jerry drives that Hummer, the big one— that's a one-hundred-forty-five-thousand-dollar ride. He wants to make sure the money keeps on coming. They raped at least two of them.

"One of the guys, Danny Polasky, tried to kill me a second time. Almost choked me to death." She was beginning to believe me. I could see it. Maybe because it was specific, with names and the damage to my face and hands and throat.

"Is that what . . . "

"Yes." I said. "Some other men, I don't know who they were, grabbed Polasky. They took him away and tortured him. Then they killed him and torched the place where they did it. It's not just MacLeod and Nicole Chandler. I don't know what it is, but that's two dead." Hearing myself, hearing what I was saying to her, brought me to a complete stop.

"I'm wrong," I said. "I am so wrong. I'm sorry. I got this all backwards and screwed up. 'Cause I'm obsessed or some damn thing. Give me the numbers. Just give them to me. I'm going to do this alone."

"What? Why?"

"I'm listening to myself, and it's crazy, and if something happened to you, I couldn't live with that. I'm gonna do what I gotta do, and you go home and stay safe."

"What?" she said. "And miss church?"

It was a face I hadn't seen for a long time, excited and casually fearless. Her favorite memories, when I'd met her, were about hitchhiking with a girlfriend to Baja when they were sixteen because they wanted to learn to surf—drove her parents ballistic—about getting caught in a blizzard in the New Mexico mountains on a church-group camping trip, and about the year in Nicaragua. It was a face I'd almost forgotten, one that had disappeared during our married years, with being a family, paying for the house and Angie's tuition, putting away money for college, being active in church affairs.

"You don't understand."

"No, Carl, I'm doing this with you. I don't know what you've been told or what you think you've been told, but somehow you've got it wrong. There is no way, no possible way, that Paul Plowright is . . . is doing the things you say. Having people murdered and raped, that's impossible. With seven thousand people around him . . . no, millions, millions of people watch him and know him, and know what a good man he is. The things you're saying are impossible."

"Gwen, I'm sorry you don't believe me. So be it. But it's too dangerous, and I'm going to do it alone."

"It's not dangerous because it can't be true. The only thing that's dangerous is for you to keep thinking the way you're thinking. So I'm going to go with you, and we're going to find out the truth together, before you go around saying these things to anyone else, before you do any more damage than you've already done."

"No."

"If you try to do it by yourself, I'm going to march up there and tell Jeremiah you're here. How are you going to stop me? Take out your gun and shoot me?"

"We'll walk up separately," I told her as we got out of the car. "And stay separate until we meet outside the restrooms and go for the private door. Act like you would normally act if I were away and you had come alone. Smile, normal, all fine. Understand?"

"Yes," she said and started on her way, circling right as I went out to the left.

As I got closer to the Cathedral, there were more and more people. I tried to follow behind groups, not close enough so that anyone spoke to me but near enough to be a tree in their forest.

"Hey, how's it going?" a cheerful voice said from my left. I looked over slowly, like a man half blind and in pain. It was Norton Cantine, a man I knew moderately well. A retired plumber who was very busy in church activities. A nice enough fellow. He looked at me closely, staring even.

Then he asked, "First time?"

I pressed my lips together in a sick man's smile and nodded a silent yes, afraid the sound of my voice would give me away.

"Well, you're in for a treat," he said, enthusiastic as a Bible sales-man. "Might do more for those eyes than any fancy surgeon. Jesus does miracles. Yes, he does."

I nodded eagerly and gave him a big thumbs-up.

"See you inside, friend," he said, slapping me lightly on the back. Fortunately, nice and high, so he was nowhere near my .45.

"Thanks," I croaked in a whisper.

There was sweat in my pits and in my crotch. I smelled like fear.

As I got closer to the entrance, up in Parking Lot Acts, I began glancing into car windows, looking for unlocked cars with the keys left inside. Some people are bound to do that by accident, but a certain number of the congregation do it deliberately to prove to themselves how much better a Christian community is than the regular world outside, where you have to lock everything all the time, and they brag about it to their friends, 'I leave my keys right in the car at CTM. And I drive a Lexus 450h!' with a 'How about that!' expression. I guess they're right. I've never heard of a car be-ing stolen during services.

Well, I was prepared to do it. I had lost my faith, and moral rela-tivism had already crept in.

I made it to the entrance of the Cathedral, wading through a morass of fear and pricked along by adrenaline. Getting inside pushed us all closer together, and I was suddenly near enough to Gwen to see her face and that she too was full of tension and fear. I wanted to pray that she would keep it together. But I had the weird thought that if I prayed, it would draw God's attention to her, make Him aware of what was going on, and He might take the other side. Best to be quiet and try to sneak by Him. I know it's childish to think you can sneak past God, but that's what I felt.

Inside the lobby, there's an information booth to the left. On the right, there are two cloak rooms, one where you can check things with an attendant and one where you can just leave things. Most people use that one, especially, it seems, for baby carriages. I saw one old man leaving a cane, one of those very medical, metal ones with four feet for extra stability.

I waited until he had hobbled off, leaning on a younger man's arm. Then I stole it, adding one more level of infirmity to my disguise. I very much intended to return it before the services were over. Or if I failed to, maybe he would be healed and no longer need it.

As I shuffled forward to the internal doors to the auditorium, I spotted Gwen.

So did Jerry Hobson. He focused on her. Looked all around her to see if I was nearby. Then he headed straight toward her, his cop's eyes checking her out.

I wanted desperately to get close enough to hear. Would he sense something was wrong? If he asked, would she be able to lie to him, to tell him that I would still be coming at midnight, stepping into his trap? Would she want to lie to him? Or did she think I was a dangerous loon and that for the good of God and God's minister, it was best to tell Hobson that I was there in my foolish disguise?

The best I could do was get into a position where, if Gwen looked away from Jerry, she would see me. I circled around with my three-legged hobble.

I could tell that he was trying to hold her gaze. But she didn't want to look at him, which is unlike Gwen. She mostly looks right at people when she speaks. Now, however, her eyes were darting around. Suddenly, they moved across me. When we look for someone or something, we look for what we're used to seeing. The silly wig, the glasses, and the cane were not signals that said Carl to her. Then she remembered. Now that I had her attention, I made a gesture, reaching around behind my back where my gun was. Panic shot over her face.

Jerry caught it, and turned to look for what Gwen might have seen.

I turned to the right, showing him the profile with the big dressing on it, but behind my glasses, I kept looking toward him.

Jerry's gaze jumped back and forth, at me, behind me, and around me, but it was like looking for someone at the mall on Saturday afternoon. You can't actually look for faces; you look for hair color, known items of clothing, a familiar posture or way of walking, signs and symbols.

At last Jerry turned back to Gwen, said something with a fake pleasant attitude, touched her on the upper arm, and turned away. She had not betrayed me.

59

We each headed for the restrooms, then walked casually past them to the door that led to the backstage corridors. I left the cane behind before we went through. Surely someone would spot it, and it would find its way back to its owner.

We made it down the hallway, along the backstage corridors, to Plowright's private elevator without incident.

I looked at my watch. I wanted to be in and out in twenty minutes. Services would last at least an hour and a half. They often went longer.

The elevator was on the ground floor. When Gwen punched in the code, it opened right away. As we rode up, I drew the HK from its holster. "Just a precaution. I don't intend to use it," I said softly and held it low, by my side and a bit behind me, so that anyone who might be up there in the office wouldn't see it, and we could try the talking cure first.

As the door opened, Plowright cried out, "Here it is!" full of fervor and enthusiasm, as if he'd been waiting for us.

Reflexively, I brought the gun up, pushed Gwen behind me, and pointed it out in front of me.

There was music and applause. I realized it was the broadcast of the services down in the Cathedral. I took a long slow breath to still the beating of my heart. Then we began to move slowly into his office. There it was—there he was—on the big LCD TV.

The scene was on a wide shot.

A cross, fourteen feet tall, was just upstage of Plowright. He was pointing to his left at a gigantic display table covered by a cloth. A team of Angels appeared. Choreographed and rehearsed, they gracefully whisked the fabric away to reveal a three-dimensional contour map of the land on which we stood with a model of Plowright's great dream built on top of it, the City on the Hill.

The Cathedral of the Third Millennium was at its center, at the highest point. Roads radiated out in all directions, like spokes, and circled around it in rings. There were all sorts of buildings, small and large, private and commercial.

Miniature lights popped on and illuminated a cross alongside the tower. If it were to scale, the real one would be over two hundred feet high when it was built.

The cross on stage came to life simultaneously. It was made of a multitude of thin neon tubes, and once it stuttered to life, in silvery white, silvery blues, and a fine light gold, it was as vivid as anything Las Vegas could boast of, and it cast a halo of holy-looking light upon both the minister and his model municipality.

"This is it. This is the future. This is seed from which we will grow a truly Christian America!"

The crowd went wild, standing, applauding, calling out, "Amen!"

"The Lord has promised us dominion over the earth, Genesis 1:26–31. The Lord *requires* us to take dominion. Let us do as He commands!

"Our job is to reclaim America for Christ, whatever the cost. As the vice regents of God, we are to exercise godly dominion and influence over our neighborhoods, our schools, our government, our literature and arts, our sport arenas, our entertainment media, our news media, our scientific endeavors—in short, over every aspect and institution of our society."

The applause and the voice grew even louder. Shining, fervent faces filled the screen. There was an upswell of music, and the Angels came forth to sing.

I looked around desperately for the controls and saw a remote sitting on Plowright's desk, rushed for it, heedless of whether anyone was there or not, grabbed it, and hit the mute button. The silence was a great relief.

I reached up, tore off my bandages, and tossed them in a trash bin.

The cameras cut back and forth between audience shots of ecstatic faces as they sang along with the Angels and close-up details of the city to be: miniature office buildings, an expanded airfield with toy planes visible through the doors of model hangers, subdivisions with little trees and green-carpet lawns like a Lionel Trains display, and where the college was now, presently just four modest buildings, there was something much larger, large enough that it could call itself a university. There was a hospital with a Matchbox ambulance parked in front of an awning with a tiny sign that read "Emergency Entrance."

In the silence, I turned away from the mesmerizing screen and looked and listened to determine if anyone was in the offices. Also to better understand the man I was dealing with.

When I'd been here before, Plowright had always been in the room with me, his presence, personable, energetic, visionary, dominating it, giving it a life. And I had looked at it through the eyes of an admirer, the eyes of a disciple. Now it was empty, and my eyes were cold.

Plowright had this whole top floor to himself—and for whatever assistants he wanted around him at any given time. Fortunately, it seemed that all the courtiers were downstairs watching his show. The sweeping arc of his windows gave a lordly view of all his lands. As expensive as the square footage in Manny's downtown office building was, compared to this, it was still a jumped-up version of the basic white-collar shoebox. This was the center of a twenty-first-century fiefdom.

Then there was the circle within the circle, with his personal, private apartment. It would have a view to the north, toward the mountains. The door to that inner sanctum was made of polished wood, thick and heavy. A keypad in a flat rectangle was beside it.

Gwen and I both looked at it, both of us, in different ways and to different degrees, afraid to find out what was behind it.

She looked at me, waiting for me to make the move.

I stepped aside and gestured to Gwen to punch in the code.

60

She was there.

Nicole Chandler, in a blouse and a skirt much like the uniform Angie wears to school. She was holding a Bible in her hands, the big NIV study Bible, 2,936 pages, with twenty thousand study notes, seven pages of full-color timelines from both testaments, sixteen pages of full-color maps, an expanded topical index, and a "Harmony of the Gospel" section.

I turned to glance back at Gwen, as if to say, "See!"

Nicole snapped the Bible shut. I barely saw her out of the corner of my eye as she swung it, two-handed, with all her might, and smashed it on the top of my head. I went down, seeing stars. If the wig hadn't been there like a pad, I think she would have knocked me out cold. As it was, I went down on my hands and knees, head throbbing, trying to figure out what had just happened. I had dropped the gun and didn't know where it was. Nicole tried to rush out past me. But Gwen was coming in after me, coming to my aid, yelling, "What are you doing? Get away from him." They collided, Nicole trying to push past, I think, and Gwen trying to grapple with her, and they got entangled in my legs and fell over, both of them, on top of me. Pushing me flat.

They were fighting like women, clawing and grabbing. Legs, arms, and elbows jabbed into my back. Still dizzy, I put my palms on the floor and pushed upward, trying to get them off me and turn over at the same time. I heaved, and they moved. I turned, and there I was between Nicole's legs. Her short skirt had flipped up, and her kicking legs were spread apart.

She was screeching, "Let me go." She pulled Gwen's hair, and Gwen yowled. I put my eyes back in my head, rolled away, and kicked the door shut before someone heard us. Then I looked around for the gun, figuring I better get to it before either of them did. I saw where it had landed. So did Nicole. She kept yanking at Gwen's hair with one hand and was reaching for the gun with her other. She got to it before I did. The safety was off, there was one in the chamber, and she'd only have to squeeze, and someone would be dead.

I leapt—I tried to leap; it was more like I staggered and fell—on top of her hand holding the HK. I reached blindly, found the barrel, held it tight, and twisted as hard as I could to rip it from her. It came loose before she could fire it. I shoved it away from us and went after her other hand to make her let go of Gwen.

Nicole started yelling at the top of her lungs, "Help, help!"

All of us were rolling around on the floor. I pried Nicole's fingers loose from my wife, then twisted her arm up behind her back. That put me behind her and forced her into a sitting position, her legs out in front of her, her back bent forward from the upward twist against her shoulder joint.

She was still shrieking, so I put my free hand over her mouth. She bit down. I yanked my hand away before she could chomp a piece of flesh off, and she started yelling again. I pulled my wig off and put that over her mouth, hairy side first. "Bite on that, damn you. Bite on that." Which she did and got a mouth full of whatever the fake strands were made of. She started trying to spit the wig out and twist her head away.

Gwen was sitting on the floor. She held her head where Nicole had been tearing at her. There was a big scratch on her face.

"Nicole, come on. Quiet down. I don't want to hurt you," I said, though I was doing exactly that as I pressed her arm up to immobilize her.

Her skirt was up around her waist. Gwen looked at her with disgust. Nicole reached down with her free hand and covered herself, but she didn't really stop struggling.

"We're here to help you," I said. She shook her head as violently as she could, trying to get rid of the wig at the same time. "If I let you go, will you be quiet?" Not getting a response, I pushed her arm up even harder and held her tighter.

She made a muffled noise and tried to nod yes.

I took the wig away from her mouth but kept her arm up behind her back. "Why did you attack me?"

She coughed and gasped and spit the black strands from the wig out of her mouth.

"Why?"

"You're going to kill me," she said bitterly.

"No, we're not," I said, trying to sound reasonable, although my head was throbbing.

"I know who you are," she said. "You're Jeremiah's friends," as if that were proof enough of the reason we were there.

"I'm not," I said. "I'm really not. And I'd like to get out of here, with you, before he shows up or Plowright does."

She panicked. "I won't go," she cried, trying to pull away from me.

I pressed up on her arm again, locking her in place. "Calm down, Nicole. Calm down, and listen. We're not here to hurt you or kill you. We're just trying to find out who killed Nathaniel MacLeod."

"Nate is dead?" she cried out in disbelief and anguish. "Nate is dead?" Her surprise and shock seemed real. All the fight went out of her. I released her. She curled up in a ball and began to weep and moan, crying out, "No, no, please, God, no."

61

"How could you not know?" I asked her.

Her sobbing stopped for a moment, and she spoke like a bitter, sarcastic child. "All I know is what *Pastor*"—she was extra snide when she used his title—"tells me." Then, sniffling, with the tears coming back, pleading, she asked, "What happened?"

"It's been all over the news."

"I don't have a radio, TV, Internet, anything."

"How long have you been here?"

"There's a TV right there," Gwen said, gesturing at a screen across the room.

"How long?" I asked Nicole.

"Since they took me," she said.

"When?" I asked.

"Thursday night," she said. "It was a Thursday night, late, Friday morning."

"Which Friday, last Friday, the one before?"

"Three weeks," she said, making it the night of MacLeod's death. It also meant that she'd been right there, behind the wall, while Pastor Paul was trying to convince me to leave the case alone.

"From where?" I asked. "Where were you when they took you?"

"He was alive. He was alive when they took me out."

"There's a TV right there," Gwen said again insistently. She didn't like Nicole, with her schoolgirl outfit, claiming to be a prisoner in Plowright's private apartment. Sleek and new, the forty-two-inch HD screen, set up to be easily viewed from the king-size bed, looked like a few thousand dollars' worth of evidence that Nicole wasn't being exactly truthful.

"It only plays DVDs," Nicole said.

"Sure," Gwen said with disbelief.

I got up. My head hurt like hell. I felt my scalp. There was no blood, but a bump was rising. I went over to the machine to have a look. There was only one cable, and it went to a DVD player.

"Just Bible movies. We watch Bible movies. And *Left Behind*. Rayford *Steele* and *Buck* Williams," Nicole said, mocking the names of Tim LaHaye's heroes. There was a DVD rack, and I looked. Sure enough, *Left Behind* was there, plus the sequels, *Tribulation Force* and *World at War*. Also *Joseph: King of Dreams*, *Quo Vadis*, *The Ten Commandments*, *The Passion of Christ*, of course, the documentary, *Seven Signs of Christ's Return*, and lots more like them. There were also blank DVDs, the kind that you can burn videos on, in plain plastic cases.

"And lots of porn," Nicole said.

"Liar," Gwen said.

I took one of the unlabeled DVDs from the rack, put it into the player, found the remote on the bedside table, and pushed play. The screen asked me if I wanted to start from the beginning or resume. I resumed. A hard-core scene came on, larger than life. The standard obscenities of dramatized lust chanted from the speakers. I shut it off.

When the sound stopped, Gwen accused the girl, "You brought those here, didn't you?"

Nicole looked at her, full of contempt and disgust, and then looked to me, full of pain. "What happened to him?"

"He was shot," I said.

"Oh, God," she said. "Who . . ."

"Ahmad Nazami has been arrested," I said.

"Ahmad? He wouldn't . . . he's . . . "

"Where were you when you were kidnapped?"

"In, in his office. Nate's office."

"When?"

"It was about, I don't know exactly, about three in the morning."

"Who kidnapped you?"

"I don't believe she was kidnapped," Gwen said.

"Pas-*tor* Paul, *da*-ddy Paul," she said in a mocking, kiddy singsong, and then in her own voice, "and that bastard Jeremiah."

"Can't you see it?" Gwen said, almost yelling at me. "She's a whore. A cheap whore, with her school girl outfit, and her pornos. She seduced him, and now she's making up stories and lies, horrible, horrible lies. It's not true."

Nicole turned on Gwen. "Those are *his*." It came spewing out, full of anger and vituperation. "He comes up from preaching, and he's all full of himself, pumped up from all the loooove he gets and worship from everyone. And the first thing he does, all stinking of sweat from jumping around and preaching the *Worrrd*, is go to his computer, and he looks on the Internet to see what The *Enemy* is doing, what Satan is doing. And he looks at all the *evil, degenerate, secular* porn sites, and he gets a woody, his biggy-wiggy woody, and while he's looking at those videos, he's burning them onto DVDs, and then he brings them in here, and he shows them to me, and I have to say, oh yes, how *evil* it is, but when *we* do it, it's Holy, and I'm his innocent little schoolgirl, and we're in the house of God, so it's sacred, and I have to do whatever's in the pornos, or as close as he can come, since his biggy-wiggy is actually littlely-widdily. And I have to fake all the noises too. You want to hear me! Uh-uh-oooooh . . . " She moaned loudly, then twisted the long, drawn-out syllable into a sneer. "Ooooh!"

"It's a lie, a lie," Gwen yelled. "You claim you're locked in here. How do you know what he does out there? You're a liar. Carl, can't you see it, or are you mesmerized by the sight of what's between that whore's legs too!"

"You don't believe me?" Nicole yelled back at her. She rushed over to the bedside table, pulled open the drawers. With a second cry of "You don't believe me?" she began flinging the contents at us: vibrators, eggs, penis extenders, penis rings, tubes of lube, and more. I'd left the wild side just before the dildo explosion arrived, and there were several items that I'd never seen in person. Pastor Paul Plowright was way ahead of me. "*Christian* sex toys," Nicole called out, "from *Christian* websites." She reeled off their names: "My Beloved Garden, Covenant Spice." A plastic vial with a prescription label, half-filled with blue tabs of Viagra, rolled across the floor to my feet. I picked it up and put it in my pocket.

"How do you know what he does out there?" Gwen yelled at her, pointing toward the offices beyond the wall. "How do you know if you're locked in."

Nicole slowed down and stopped and looked lost and ashamed. "From before."

"Before?" I asked.

"Yes," she said. "When . . . when I thought it was . . . when . . . "

"I told you," Gwen said. "She seduced Paul."

Nicole looked to me, hoping I would be more understanding. "He performed *miracles*," she said. "He was on *TV*. In front of millions of people, and all the girls wanted him."

"If you don't like it, why haven't you left?" Gwen asked. "Why won't you leave with us?"

"Because Jeremiah wants to kill me. He's waiting for me to leave or even try so he can kill me. Pastor Paul thinks he can convert me back. Whenever we're not fucking, we're praying together and watching crap like *Left Behind* to scare me into being a good Christian."

"How do you know that?" Gwen snapped at her. "You can't know that!"

"I know it because they said so."

"Alright," I said, glancing at my watch. We were still safe, but I wanted to calm this down, figure out what was going on, and get moving. "So you were having a"—I wanted to phrase it in the leas confrontational way—"a relationship with Plowright. And then you started to have one with Nathaniel MacLeod?" In spite of what Ahmad told me, that had to be it. What else could it be?

"No," Nicole said adamant about it and sounding surprised by the accusation.

"You weren't lovers?"

"Nate was my *Teacher*," she said, making the word a title, a deep honorific, like Guru or Sensei. And she became miserable again, tears welling in her eyes.

"Your teacher?"

"He led me from the darkness. He made the complex simple. He dispelled the mysteries. He taught me that I had a mind. That I could use it. I read now—books, real books, not Bible stories and adventures in chastity."

"Let me understand this," I said. "You're in MacLeod's office at three in the morning. Your lover, Paul Plowright, and his security officer come and take you away and lock you up here, and it's not about your leaving him for MacLeod?"

"You don't know. You don't know anything. It wasn't about sex. They wanted the e-mails."

"You had e-mails?"

"Yes, Plowright's e-mails. And I was giving them to Nate."

"E-mails between you and him, talking dirty, so MacLeod could launch another sex scandal about another minister and embarrass Christians again? Like that?"

"No," she said, exasperated. "About the money."

62

Nicole still wouldn't leave. I couldn't march her out at the point of a gun. But she was willing to talk. Things came out in bits and pieces and not always coherently. Partly because she was conflicted about her role and her self-image. The presence of Gwen, full of disapproval and distrust, made her even more defensive. Partly because we always lie to ourselves and others about our relationships. But mostly because she'd been assaulted and held prisoner, and the time frames kept snapping back and forth between a romantic then and a traumatic now and the various points in between, colliding and shattering each other into fragments.

This is her story, as best as I could sort it out, sometimes reading between the lines and making connections between the dots that she herself did not make.

Nicole said Plowright seduced her.

Gwen was certain Nicole started it. It sounded like a coconspiracy to me. With an edge toward Plowright. He'd been doing it for awhile and had probably developed a knack for finding willing conquests.

Once it began, Plowright told Nicole she was his chosen one, like Solomon's Sheba and David's Bathsheba. He also said that in the Bible, kings and great men had more than one woman. We now live in an age that doesn't understand that. Because the world is in a particularly dangerous and unstable period, an *unbiblical* time, it i necessary to preach that one man with one woman is God's way for everyone. So, although it was really God's way for it to be different for his chosen leaders, they had to keep their love a secret. One day, that would change, and then they would be able to make their great love public.

He even admitted to her that there might be others. Solomon, after all, had seven hundred wives and three hundred concubines. But she needed to keep in mind that only one of them was named and remembered, only one of them was special. As the Queen of Sheba was to Solomon, so was Nicole to Paul Plowright.

He would summon her when the constraints and burdens of the world would permit it, and she would come unto him. That was the way it was for kings and their consorts. In biblical times, of course.

Was that Plowright's standard story, or had he been particularly smitten with Nicole? I guessed it was choice number one. His marketing and business training made him appreciate the economics of reusing what worked over improvising new tales every time.

Nicole hated Plowright now. Admitting that she had once been an eager participant was shameful and embarrassing and conflicted with her role as the victim. Still, it was clear that she had originally bought into the fantasy.

At one point, Nicole blurted out a story that was clearly intended to embarrass Gwen and tear at her illusions about our pastor's sanctity. It also revealed that the relationship was more than consensual; she had relished and reveled in it.

Plowright liked Nicole to play at being Mary Magdalene, the whore who could tempt even Christ. She would wash his feet, though not with tears as it's difficult to produce enough water that way, then dry them with her hair, which he found an incredibly sensuous experience. Then, like the woman at the Pharisee's house in Luke 7:37, she would anoint his feet. The Bible does not name the brand of the ointment used in olden times. Instead, Paul supplied Happy Penis Massage Cream from Book22, another online Christian sex store, advertised to produce a sensation of warmth and to be edible, which was important because, in a slight reversal of the order of things in Luke, the anointing was to be followed by the kissing.

As often as being the other woman is a great thrill when adultery is new, disenchantment and restlessness are as certain to follow. Nicole was at least smart enough to know that the time Pastor Plowright had spoken of, when they could take their Solomon and Sheba act public, would never come. His image required that he publicly maintain his marriage with the mother of his five children. He could make sure she did a lot of traveling, but he was going to keep her. So, she didn't react by demanding more. Which was fortunate for her, at least in the short term, because if she'd threatened to make a fuss and reveal their affair or gotten herself pregnant, Hobson would have sent Alvarez and Polasky to straighten her out.

However, as the excitement began to wane, she began to see her hero as an actual person with limitations and flaws. The greatest of which was hypocrisy.

Actually, it was something more than that. It was not that he was preaching against adultery while committing adultery, that was practically normal. He was using the Bible to support both. It revealed the Book itself to be full of contradictions, which he could use for whatever he desired, instead of being what she had been taught, the Book of clear truths, direct from God, that said one and the same to everyone.

She figured it would be useless to confront him. Instead, she just sort of wandered off to see if there were other ways to think about all of it. Maybe because he railed against USW all the time, that was where she headed. She would go by the big lecture halls and look at the name of the class on the door, and if it sounded like it was something she might understand, she'd just walk in and listen.

Then she got a catalog and found that there was a course about religion. Nathaniel MacLeod's class. Even though it was a regular class, with just twenty or so students, she was interested enough to take the chance of being caught out. She was lucky, MacLeod was not the sort who took attendance. Though he noticed her, he didn't say anything and let her stay.

It was her first exposure to those sorts of ideas, and she was swept away by them.

She also had a natural inclination toward older men in positions of authority, and she was swept away by Nathaniel too. She became almost an acolyte.

However, she did not make a clean break.

She didn't say it this way, but even though she was the other woman with Plowright, it was as if her relationship with him was her marriage and her relationship with MacLeod was an affair.

As with a marriage, as with my marriage to Gwen, Plowright was not just a single person; he was part of the package that was her life. The Cathedral of the Third Millennium was her social network, her support system, and her habit. Singing in the choir, twice on Sunday and once on Wednesday, plus rehearsals, more than anything except the dull and empty routine of work in the drug store created the shape of her week. It gave her feelings of accomplishment, purpose, and participation, and the music lifted her.

The university was still a strange and threatening place where she felt intimidated. She was not ready to throw it all away and go be a philosophy student.

Nathaniel was really the answer.

It was clear that she was in love with MacLeod—or wanted to be. f he would just take her, he would be the new older man who vould guide her into a new world, a journey she was afraid to take n her own, and show her how to make a new life when she threw way the old one.

But, as I knew from Ahmad, MacLeod had turned her down. Out of ltruism, he said. But maybe it was because he liked women who were lder, better educated, smarter, more sophisticated. Like Teresa. Or 1aybe, after Teresa, he just needed a vacation from women altogether.

Nicole's relationship with Plowright continued. Sometimes she felt ke she was "just a booty call, not the Queen of Sheba." She was starting » say no. He would react by paying her more attention, flattering her, or ying to dazzle her. He succeeded often enough that he kept at it.

Then came the critical day.

It was after choir practice. Plowright came by. He was being particularly nice—a sign that he was particularly eager. He invited her up to the office. She was reluctant. Maybe she didn't want to go; maybe she knew that would get her more attention.

He said he had something special, really spectacular to show her.

When they got there, he turned on the computer and revealed 3D drawings of the city he was planning to build. He said it would have its own university, a real university, just like USW, and she could go there as a full-time student. She could even get a full scholarship if he gave the word. She wouldn't have to sneak around and just audit classes at USW.

It was the first time she had any idea that he'd been keeping tabs on her and knew about her secret life, inoffensive at it was. It creeped her out. Instead of being seduced, she got sullen and pulled away.

His reaction was to try harder. To show her how smart, how totally brilliant and awesome he was. He told her *how* he was going to build the City of God. He said he was going to use the enemy's own money to make it happen.

He was really excited. Nicole described it as 'like when someone has a secret, especially when they're really getting something over on someone else but can't tell anyone, but they want to tell so they can really enjoy it.' Plowright said that he was going to get control of the USW endowment fund. He was going to be able to invest it however he wanted, in secret. He was going to take all that atheist, secular humanist money and use it for the City of the New Millennium. For the glory of Jesus.

The USW endowment was $5 billion.

It was quite a prize. You could build a whole city with it.

Normally, that would have meant nothing to Nicole. Aside from its being an astoundingly huge sum of money.

But it was an issue that concerned Nathaniel.

Currently, the money was controlled by the state's board of regents. They had open meetings, and the accounts were public. The governor had announced he was going to privatize it.

MacLeod was outspoken and passionate in his opposition. Under the privatization plan, the money managers could act in secret and didn't have to report on the specifics of their investments. That meant, according to Nathaniel, they could use it as a personal slush fund to reward themselves, their friends, and their political allies.

He talked about it in class, after class, and he was one of the leaders of a committee that was trying to stop it.

Now Nicole had discovered a whole new dimension to the plan. Something that Nathaniel didn't know, that no one knew—that Plowright was involved and how the money would actually be used. She could barely wait to tell her teacher what she'd found out. This was something that would make her special. Not just in that fond, "my special angel," pat-on-the-head kind of way, but truly special.

She knew that she could find out more by acting stupid and naïve. She laid it on thick. 'Oh that can't be true! How can you do that? I know you're incredibly smart, but I don't believe anyone could do something that brilliant.'

By then, Plowright was going on as he usually did about the evil that comes out of secular, anti-Christian institutions like USW, that teach moral relativism, and he had opened up porn sites to illustrate what he was talking about, while he went on to say how taking their money would be turning evil into good.

Like a tom turkey fanning his feathers, he was far too puffed up with his own display to think about any risk involved in answering her questions. Strutting, he said, "I'll prove it." He opened his e-mail to show off the messages between himself and the governor. Plowright had written to name the company that would control the endowment. The governor had replied, "Thanks for your recommendation. I'm sure they're exactly the right people. I appreciate your support in the last election and look forward to it in the next."

Nicole understood that anything that just came from her, a choir girl having an affair with her married pastor, would be easily mocked and discounted. The e-mails were hard evidence. They were the real prize. She was determined to get them for Nathaniel.

Plowright was fondling her and pressing his erection against her.

If she could distract him before he closed up the computer and get him to take her into the apartment, she could wait until he fell asleep afterwards, then sneak out and get the e-mails. She saw sex in service of a greater good as a heroic act. Had not Esther given herself to the king of Persia and in his bed discovered the plot to kill the Israelites, then brought the news to her uncle, Mordecai, and saved her entire people? Had not the prostitute Rahab harbored Joshua's spies and given them the information that enabled him to take Jericho. It was even said, though not in the Bible itself, that after the battle, Joshua had taken Rahab as his wife. They had children, and through them, Rahab had been in the direct line of the ancestry of Jesus himself. Yes, that was who she would be, Rahab to Nathaniel's Joshua.

"Yes, you are amazingly brilliant," she said to Plowright, yielding to him, pressing back against him. Then he started to reach for the computer. She didn't know his password and had to stop him before he shut it down, so she acted eager and said, "Now. Oh, love me now. I want you."

Afterward, he did fall asleep. The first time she tried to sneak out he woke up. The next time, she waited almost an hour, until he was snoring and seemed out cold, before she slipped out of bed. She went out to the office and clicked on the computer. To her relief, it was still open. The e-mails were still there. She was about to forward them to Nathaniel but then decided she wanted to hand them to him physically, in person, and be there when he got them so that he would know, instantly, who had done this for him. She wanted to be there to receive his love and admiration.

She printed them. As she was taking the pages from the out tray Plowright opened the door from the apartment and saw her.

Nicole grabbed the evidence and ran.

63

She called Nathaniel on her cell phone. She wanted, really, to go to his home, but he told her to meet him at his office, that it was simpler since she knew where it was.

Fifteen minutes after she got there, Plowright arrived with Jerry Hobson.

Hobson had a gun. While he held it on her and Nathaniel, Plowright got his e-mails back.

Nicole tried to snatch them and make a run for it. Hobson grabbed for her with one hand and got her by the hair. Hobson flung her to the ground and put his foot on her neck, holding her there. That's when the chain that held her cross must've broken, but she didn't notice until later.

Hobson gave Plowright the gun and said, "I'll get her out of here. You make sure he doesn't do anything." Then he twisted her arm up behind her back and made her get up. He marched her out, holding his other hand over her mouth so she couldn't yell.

He put her in his car, the big Hummer. Then he put what she called "weird plastic handcuffs" on both her hands and feet. His cell phone rang, and he answered it. He said, "Yeah," listened, then said, "I'll be right there." He put tape over her mouth, made her lie down on the floor, and attached the "plastic things" to the bottom of the seats so she couldn't move. Then he went away. She couldn't say for how long. It seemed long, but she didn't know.

Then he came back with Paul, and they drove away.

"We have to get rid of her," she heard Hobson say.

"No! Oh, no, we can't do that," Plowright said.

"We have to."

"No, I forbid it," Plowright said. "She's been misled. I'll pray with her. I'll bring her back to Jesus."

They smuggled her into the tower and up to the apartment.

Hobson went through the place. He removed the phone, disconnected the TV cable hookup, and took the radio. He got a garbage bag and tossed anything he thought could be used as a weapon into it. He argued with Plowright again about what to do with her while she lay on the bed, arms and legs cuffed, the tape still over her mouth.

Then Plowright came and sat beside her. "I know you were misled," he said. "I understand. I'm going to take off the tape, and I want you to tell Jeremiah that you want to come back to the path of righteousness and that we will pray together."

When he removed the tape, she gulped in deep breaths of air. Then she screamed, "Help! Help!"

"Be quiet!" Plowright yelled at her.

She kept screaming.

"Shut up. No one can hear you."

"Let me go! Let me go now! I won't tell if you let me go now."

"You have to stay," he said implacably.

"I'm not going to stay with you. Not ever!" Then she started screaming again. "Help!"

Plowright gave her one of his righteous looks, showing that he was severely disappointed in her. He got up and walked out of the apartment. She screamed one last time, hoping that when the door opened someone might hear her voice.

Then Jerry took over.

When he was done beating her, or maybe before it ended—she wasn't sure—Plowright came back. She was whimpering and moaning, in more pain than she'd ever felt in her life. Than she'd ever imagined.

Plowright sat beside her once again. He touched her hair gently. She flinched and turned her head away. "It's alright now. I'll protect you. I want to save you, body and soul. In the morning, I'll come back, and we'll pray."

"If you try to escape," Hobson said, "I'll kill you."

"No, no," Plowright said. "We don't want to do that. That won't be necessary, will it, Nicky?"

"No," she said.

She needed clothing. Plowright brought her a set of school uniforms from Third Millennium Christian Academy.

If she got snippy, he would impose corporal punishment, just as they did at the school. If she got defiant, he would threaten to bring Hobson back. She called his bluff. But only once.

So they prayed. Watched inspirational movies and pornographic DVDs. And had sex.

Gwen said, "That's totally unbelievable. You don't have sex and watch pornography with people who beat you up and who you hate."

In her world, where people had control of their lives, that might have been true. If she'd been on the job and met the battered wives, gone to the brothels full of women beaten into sexual slavery, visited the fortress of stone where once-straight men became other men's bitches, she'd have known that people of both sexes who have been hurt and abused and are living under constant threat will engage in sex and perform with apparently great enthusiasm. Whether that's feigned or real, or some combination of the two, is another matter.

There was one more thing. "I always thought Nathaniel would come to rescue me," Nicole said, crying. "Now I know why he didn't."

64

"Nicole," I said as gently as I could, "we have to get out of here, before Paul, or Jerry, shows up."

"I'm scared," she said, sounding it and looking it and unwilling to go.

"She doesn't really want to leave," Gwen said, looking down at the sex toys scattered all over the floor, then over at Nicole.

There was something to that. But Gwen didn't really understand. Gwen had Jesus, big time and for real. And she was innately courageous. She would burn at the stake before she would break.

She didn't understand how prisoners adapt. How people flow into the world around them the way water goes into whatever space is open to it, compromising one day at a time, taking consolation in whatever pleasure or relief they can find. After that, leaving means facing the dreadful knowledge of what you did, of what you became, and knowing you'll never quite believe the excuse that it was just to survive.

Even the strength and consolation of faith was lost to Nicole. It was through Jesus that she had been seduced and abused and imprisoned. It was the men of God who had killed the man she loved.

What awaited her outside this room? Nathaniel, the man who was to be her new salvation, was gone. No one she knew would see her as a Rahab who had opened Jericho to the Israelites; everyone would see her as what Gwen had already called her, Delilah, a whore and traitor who had seduced their Samson in order to worm his secrets out of him and betray him to the Philistines.

I went over to her and put my hand on her shoulder. She jumped back, away from me, onto the bed, and curled up. I went to her, but not too close, and squatted so that I would be at her level, not looming over her. "I won't hurt you," I said. "Please, listen to me. I'd let you stay if I could. I'd leave it up to you. But with what I know now, tomorrow the world is going to know, and then . . . then you won't be safe here anymore. You have to come with us now. I have to get you out of here. Otherwise . . . and I can't let that happen."

She lifted her head and looked at me, then past me at Gwen, then back at me. "I want to . . . , " she began, and I thought she was going to say, "trust you." But then it got lost, and she asked, "How do I know that you haven't just been playing me to get me to go quietly and kill me? How do I know?"

"Oh, please," Gwen said, offended by the idea. "What do you think we are? We're not going to hurt you."

"I don't know what to think of you," Nicole snapped back, "but you've made it damn clear what you think of me."

"Whatever you are," Gwen said patronizingly, "whatever you've done, we wouldn't kill you. We're good people, Christian people."

It was exactly the wrong thing to say. Nicole froze. "Get out! Get out! Leave me be!" she blurted, then began to cry, almost hysterically.

"Nicole, listen to me. You know that Nathaniel wrote a book?"

She nodded yes.

"Plowright and Hobson tried to destroy that book, to erase everything that Nathaniel was, like he never existed. One of the things I was hired to do was find that book. So that Nathaniel will be remembered, so that his life will have meant something."

That got her attention.

"I need you to help me. If you can help me, then you will have done something really special, truly special for him, the most special thing that anyone ever could do."

"Do you think he'll know?" she asked me.

I thought about Manny. Were his appearances real or just my imagination?

She asked, "Do the dead know what we do after they've gone?"

Had Manny known, even before he died, that he could trust me to carry on when he was gone? Was that how the dead know what we do?

"Yes, I think they do. I don't know how, exactly, but I think they do."

"Alright," she said, reaching up to take my hand. Plowright, MacLeod, now me. I was her new guide. "I'll go with you."

65

We stepped cautiously out of the apartment and back into the office. I went first, gun in hand, but it was still quiet and deserted.

Nicole stayed close to me. I was prepared to accept the role she put me in for as long as it took to get her out of there—and maybe up on the witness stand.

Gwen still didn't buy Nicole's story. She was ready to hear Pastor Paul explain it all away, and she would believe him when he did, no matter how far-fetched his stories were. She showed her disapproval by keeping her distance from us.

She made me realize that there were plenty of people out there just like her. In a contest of he said, she said, Plowright would win. I needed hard evidence.

I could see on the screen that Plowright was still down on stage, the model of his City of God beside him. The light from the neon cross created a halo around his head and painted one side of his face with blue, cold silver, and pale gold. The effect of having the sound off, combined with the hyperreality of high-definition video, made the image strangely lurid, like an illustration on a poster from a 1950s movie that screamed warnings about the wages of sin. When the camera cut to a close-up, his face twice life size and his wet lips moving in fervent, unheard speech, I couldn't help thinking of him with Nicole, the toys buzzing and the downloaded videos yelping and moaning away.

He was nowhere near done. There was time.

I went to his computer. When the screen came on, it asked for a password. His birthday? His wife's birthday? His name spelt backward? Something biblical? "What's his favorite passage?" I asked Gwen.

"What are you doing? Shouldn't we go?"

"His favorite passage, what is it?"

"Genesis 1:26," she said.

"Dominion?"

As I began to type it in, I heard a ping.

I looked toward the source of the sound.

A little red light was blinking on the closed-circuit TV monitor over the regular entrance to the office. The screen showed a view of the small lobby on the other side. It made sense that a preacher who liked to watch porn and rub the flesh of his choir girls would want warning bells to go off before someone came in.

The little monitor showed the elevator door in the lobby opening. Jerry Hobson stepped out. Another man in a suit and tie was just behind him.

One more step and his identity was revealed: Jorge Guzman de Vaca.

"Down," I hissed to Gwen. "Hide." I took Nicole's hand and pulled her back toward one of the secretary's desks and down behind it. Gwen froze for a moment, then saw the two men on the screen just as Jerry was opening the door into the office. She scrambled backward and found a spot behind the tall filing cabinets.

"Here we are," I heard Hobson say. "Plenty of privacy. What do you want?"

"I want in on the action," Jorge said.

"That's not going to happen," Jerry said with that casual contempt for civilians that comes so easily to cops. He'd always had it. Especially toward Mexicans.

"My construction companies are some of the best in the state," Jorge said, sounding unfazed and unoffended. "We do it all—housing, offices, roads. I have a company that does financing. Cash looking for a home."

"You mean money laundering," Hobson said, like he disapproved of it.

"These are big things you're doing here," Jorge said, sounding impressed. "Plenty for everybody."

"Nah' for chu, *cholo*," Jerry said, sneering at him with a broadly fake accent.

"I got something you should see," Jorge said, still the pleasant business man working on a sale. "Hey, are you a PC guy or a Mac guy?"

"What are you talking about?"

"I got this promotional video. Did it myself on iMovie. It's so easy, even a grown-up can learn it. You got a DVD player? You want to see this, Jerry."

"*Chingate*, Cheech."

"You need to see this," Jorge said, serious as death. "If you don't see it, you will regret it later, very much regret it."

"Sure I will," Jerry said sarcastically. But he wasn't sure enough to call the bluff; he needed to find out what cards Guzman was holding. "Alright, go ahead."

They were silent for a moment, and there was some moving around. Then I heard Jorge say, "Sound, you need the sound."

"Some idiot hit the mute button," Jerry said and turned the sound back on.

A new voice said, "We're working for Jerry Hobson, this company he's got, but it's him." It was Daniel Polasky.

If they were watching the DVD on the same screen that Plowright's sermon had been on, then their backs were likely turned toward me. I slipped my HK back out of its holster. Then I took the risk of peeking around the edge of the desk.

The two of them were standing three-quarters turned away from me.

Danny "Beef" Polasky was on the screen, naked, tied to the chair, one hand clutching the bloody rag wrapped around the other hand. He was illuminated by a single harsh lamp that threw a dark shadow onto the dingy, cinder block wall behind him. While

I'd been peeking through the vent on the roof, there'd been a camera down there, beyond my angle of vision, looking straight at him.

"What do you do for him?" asked an offscreen interrogator.

"Mostly the girls—we keep an eye on Plowright's girls."

I looked over at Gwen as Polasky spoke about "straightening them out." Reality was tearing pages out of the Bible stories in her mind. She looked devastated.

Nicole clutched my hand when Polasky went on about the rape of the "nice blondie." It could have been her, and she was starting to snivel. I got her attention and put my finger to my lips. She swallowed and tried to control herself.

When I heard the interrogator say, "If you don't tell me the truth, you know what I'm gonna do," I peaked around again. The pruning shears poked into the frame and prodded his crotch. Whoever was holding it had been careful not to appear in front of the camera.

". . . It was just that Plowright was getting out of control, you know, with the babes, and Jeremiah said we just hadda keep a lid on."

That was it for Gwen too. She looked over at me, devastated. I wondered how the hell we were going to get out of there. Would they finish soon and leave?

Jerry said, "Alright, I get it."

But Guzman didn't shut it off, and Danny told the story about kidnapping and torturing Ahmad. There was my evidence. I didn't know what it would do in court, but it should be enough to free Ahmad. I thought maybe I should just try to take them. But then what? Try to march them out of the Cathedral at gunpoint?

There was more. The part that I'd missed when I was trying to get down from the roof.

". . . And that detective, we were supposed to take him out. Jeremiah called us and said, 'Get over here right away. He's going to be headed from his house to the city at around 11 a.m. Wait for him near Exit 28, where he'll get on the interstate, and find someplace to take him out.'"

314

Gwen had just been convicted of her complicity in the attempt to kill me while Angie was by my side, by the dead man's testimony. She began to cry. She was trying to stay silent, and I prayed that she could.

There was silence. I guessed the DVD had stopped.

"So, what I want," Jorge said, "is in."

"Well, maybe I can steer some construction your way."

"No, no, my friend," Jorge said. "I want *in*. Your man is talking about hundreds of millions of dollars—I listened to him on the TV—billions even. I want *in*, like you got in, from the top, the bottom, and the sides."

"That's worthless," Jerry said, trying to dismiss it. "You can't bring that into court."

"Court?" Jorge said. "I don't need no stinking court," using a movie Mexican accent, mocking Jerry. "I'll put this up on YouTube, and all of this, this Cathedral, and all the hundreds of millions of dollars—that's over, and you'll be lucky you get a job as a security guard at Taco Time."

"I'll talk to Paul. I'm sure—"

"Don't *talk* to Paul. You *tell* Paul." Jorge snapped his orders like he had a whip in his hand. "You tell him he has a new partner."

"We'll work something out," Jerry said.

"I'll tell you what we'll work out. I'm your partner."

"Yeah, sure, alright," Jerry said, step by step to surrender.

"There are a couple of details," Jorge said.

"Like what?"

"I understand there's a girl who could cause trouble."

"Maybe," Jerry said.

"We can't have that with this much money at stake."

"I'll tell you what. If you want in so bad, why don't you take care of her," Jerry said.

Nicole was curled up beside me, shaking. I stroked her head, like you would a frightened child or pet, trying to calm her. Gwen looked over at us, and I could tell from the expression on her face that she finally believed that Nicole had been a captive of fear.

"This was your fuckup," Jorge said. "I'm your partner now, and if something you did fucks up my deal, you pay for it. Now, if you can't take care of it, then you can come to me, and you say, 'Jorge, my friend, I am in trouble, and I can't handle things. Will you help me out?'"

Jerry had to be steaming, and soon he'd start twitching like a boiler under pressure.

Jorge kept pushing at him. "And then I will say to you, 'Jerry, of course, I will help you,' and here's what it'll cost. A little bigger piece, points off the top. And there's your friend the Dutchman. He's on to you, and you know why he's on to you, because you and your Pastor Plowright, you're both fuckups, and you practically waved flags in his face and said, 'We did it, so don't investigate.' He's a stubborn prick, and he needs to be stopped. Are you going to do that? Or do you need me to do it? If you need me to, I can—for a few more points off the top."

"Fuck you, Hor-hay," Jerry said, the lid coming off. "You know what, let's take care of it now."

Something was happening, and I wanted to look and see what, but they were no longer watching the DVD and could well be looking straight in my direction when my head popped out alongside the desk. Then I heard Jerry laugh and say, "Relax. It's not for you."

Jorge did not reply, and I thought I heard them moving.

"Time to get rid of the pastor's bitch," Jerry said, like a man deciding to pop a boil.

Nicole made a noise. A moan, a shriek, a squeak of fear.

I knew Jerry would be turning toward the sound, toward me. When he'd said, "Relax. It's not for you," I'd figured he'd taken out a gun. Jerry favored a 9 mm with double-stack magazines. He liked the idea of being able to fire lots of shots.

I rose up into a kneeling position, gun pointing over the top of the desk.

Jerry saw, or sensed, my move and pulled Jorge in front of him, arm around his neck, as a shield.

"Drop it, Jerry. You're done," I said.

"What we got here," Jerry said, "is a Mexican standoff." He laughed, very happy with his joke. But it was true enough. Neither of us was likely to win with the first shot. That meant either of us was equally likely to die with the second.

"Everybody slow down," Jorge said. As the person most likely to die no matter what happened, he became the spokesman for reason. "There's enough money here for everybody to get rich. I think it's time for 'Let's Make a Deal.' What do you say, Carl?"

"I say you wanted to have me killed two seconds ago."

"That's because I thought you wouldn't make a deal. Carl, if there is one thing I know, it is better to be rich and alive in this life than poor and dead in the next one."

When the DVD had stopped, the giant screen had resumed the live feed from the Cathedral. The neon cross still bloomed, the model of the City of God was still front and center, but Plowright had left the stage. He was probably riding in his private elevator already. When he emerged, he would be between us, though not in a direct line, to my left and to Jerry's right. Maybe that would alter the equation.

Gwen had her eyes closed. She was praying. Nicole was crying out loud now.

"Shut that bitch up," Jerry yelled at me.

Plowright's elevator door slid open. Jerry's eyes flicked toward it, but not enough for me to take advantage of the moment.

Our pastor stopped when he saw us with guns drawn and Jorge Guzman held hostage. I'll give him this, he didn't panic. He was used to controlling everyone around him. "What's going on here?" he demanded to know.

"Why don't you put your hands up and step over by them," I said. "You're going down. For the killing of Nathaniel MacLeod, for kidnapping, for torture . . . "

"Carl, Carl, have you gone mad? I would never do anything of the sort."

"I have Nicole Chandler. I *know*. I know it all."

He was taken aback, oh, for a nanosecond. Then he found the answer. "She's a Jezebel. I tried to help her, that poor demented child. She's some sort of sex addict, her mind addled with pornography. It was the atheists, the atheists and secular humanists at the university, who did that to her. I was trying to save her, save her soul, her eternal soul—"

"You shot and killed Nathaniel MacLeod."

"Never. It was Jeremiah."

"Me? You lying fool. We had it all, billions, and you couldn't control yourself," Jerry snapped at him.

"Don't listen to this man. He is a dishonest man. He is a man of violence. Surely you know that. I would never do such a thing. It was him. You missed the sermon, Carl. I am building a City of God. Think of the good we will do, the service to God. We're this close to making the vision real! This close. Don't stop it now!"

"It was under control, under control," Jerry yelled at him. "I leave you alone for two minutes, and you have to shoot him."

"He was an atheist, a militant atheist," Plowright said, preaching to me. "I saw him destroy young minds, seduce them, steal their faith. And he mocked God. He mocked Jesus. He laughed and called Christians deluded fools. You know what he said to me? He said to me, 'Your religion is to faith what pornography is to sex.'"

"You!" Gwen cried as she stepped out from behind the protection of the filing cabinet, "You"—she pointed her finger at Paul Plowright— "have angered the Lord. You have broken his covenant."

"Get back," I said, but she ignored me like I didn't exist.

"Jerry," I yelled. "Keep your gun pointed at me. If it moves a quarter inch in her direction, I'll shoot you. If you even flinch, I'll shoot you, the both of you. I don't care."

Gwen kept walking toward Plowright. Her voice was unnaturally calm and uncannily certain, and she spoke the words that Jesus said. "Is it not written, 'My house shall be called a house of prayer for all the nations'? But you have made it a den of robbers."

Jerry and Jorge looked at her like she was simply crazy.

But Plowright looked shaken, truly shaken. It was as if, instead of Gwen, that loyal, familiar member of his congregation, one of the many insignificant employees from down below, he was seeing an avatar, a sword-carrying angel of righteousness who possessed her and spoke through her, and its voice said, "Jesus went into the temple of God, and cast out all them that sold and bought in the temple, and overthrew the tables of the moneychangers."

"Gwen, get down," I said.

"Be without fear," she said to me. "My savior is my shield."

She turned her gaze on Jerry. "Babylon the great is fallen, is fallen, and is become the habitation of devils and the hold of every foul spirit."

"Don't fuckin' move, Jerry," I yelled.

"Put your gun down, Carl," he yelled back at me, "or she's dead. Do it, Carl. Fuckin' do it."

"Gwen, get down," I called to her.

"He will keep me safe from the hands of this Philistine." The clarion certainty of her words rang true. He would; yes, He would. Unless Jerry shot and a bullet entered her.

"If your gun moves a millimeter, Jerry, you're dead," I called out frantically.

Then Gwen turned on Hobson. With the words that Joshua spoke to the Israelites, she uttered God's curse upon him. "Ye have transgressed the covenant of the Lord. Ye shall perish quickly." The words of the Book have power and tap our primal fears. No man is so rational that when the voice of the prophet calls his name to ride the hell-bound train, he will not waver. And Hobson flinched.

Jorge sensed the hesitation. He seized the moment and launched himself sideways, twisting out of Jerry's grip.

As Guzman went clear, I fired.

The big .45 slug hit Jerry's chest, right over his black heart. I fired again. That one hit him too, even before the impact of the first shot made him stagger back. His arms flew up. Arterial blood spurted from his chest. And then I fired another, a tracking shot, as he fell.

I turned the gun on Jorge. He was reaching for the slim little Beretta that he had on his belt under his suit jacket. He stopped. He pulled the gun out with his finger tips and dropped it. He backed up toward the lobby.

Plowright made a run for his private elevator. He was unarmed. I wasn't going to shoot him. But as I turned to see what he was doing, Jorge lunged toward the door and made it out. I let him go and went for Plowright, but the elevator closed before I could reach him.

We watched on the TV screen as, moments later, Paul Plowright ran out on the stage. He yelled, "There's murder, murder, murder in the house of God. Upstairs. In the citadel. Evil is unleashed. Murder. Stop them. We must save the City of God."

He was waving his hands and pointing, and he struck his hand against the cross. Several of the tubes broke, the glass slashed his hand, and he started to bleed. In frustration and fury, he shoved the cross away, then realized what he was doing and tried to grab it and save it.

Clutching the crumbling cross, he suddenly froze.

He reeled, turning in a circle. He let go of the cross, and it fell across the model, smashing and breaking into thousands of fragments. Plowright put a hand to his head and staggered. His feet caught in the cables, and then he fell.

When he fell, the high-voltage line that was tangled at his ankles was yanked from the ballast box, and it arced. The arc set the cloth drapes around the bottom of the display on fire.

The model city was made of cut foam and plastic, balsa wood, and paint, and the moment a flame touched it, it offered itself up as if fire had always been its true desire. It hissed and it crackled and it sighed, and it seemed that out of the sounds of destruction, there came the mad cackle of John the Revelator, crying out from Chapter 18, "Alas, alas, that great city, that was clothed in fine linen, and purple, and scarlet, and decked with gold, and precious stones, and pearls! For in one hour so great riches is come to naught."

66

So many things must come from that moment. Running off in different directions, crisscrossing each other, as we all work out our own destinies.

Gwen and I had each been in the same place, lived through the same moments, heard the same words, threats, confessions, lies, and pleas.

She had experienced the presence of the Lord. He had held her in the palm of his hand. He had protected her with his sword and shield.

Admittedly, I was a little miffed that she gave Him all the credit and none to me, as if I hadn't kept Jerry in check and finally killed him. As if I were merely an incidental instrument of the Lord, to the degree that I mattered at all. But that's a minor thing.

I loved her more than ever. I was in awe of her faith and the courage it gave her. I envied it.

But I could not share it.

I didn't think that Paul Plowright had erred in spite of his faith. In his sexual misconduct, and even some of what followed from it, he could be seen as a sheep who had strayed. But he had also committed crimes as a direct result of his faith. The same faith that gave him the strength to do great and good things told him to commit deceptions and theft and to engage in coercion and conspiracies, even murder, certain that he was good and righteous and doing the work of the Lord.

It wasn't a matter of finding some other church, maybe one less dogmatic and certain. Or some other pastor, one less powerful and less of a sinner. The lesson of the parable, for me, was that belief, in and of itself, was neither good nor evil. It wasn't even a guide to good and evil. They existed independently of faith, came from a different source and resided in a different place. That struck at the very root of the thing. It couldn't be fixed by trimming branches here and there.

Where would Gwen and I go from there?

If Gwen and I couldn't make it, what would happen to Angie?

Even if we could, then what? I had exposed the leader of our community. I had killed his closest advisor. Rumors were already flying around. No one knew the truth; most of them wouldn't believe it even after they heard it. How could Angie go back to school? How could she go to church in the face of all that?

Did I want her to go to Third Millennium Christian Academy? Or to any other religious school where people like Paul Plowright set the curriculum and taught that the Bible was the inerrant word of God, that obedience came ahead of thinking, that the world was seven thousand years old, and where they were so obsessed with the sins of lust that their moral compasses only and always pointed due south to the genitalia?

67

Homicide is the taking of someone's life by another person. I had committed homicide.

Despite what the Ten Commandments say or how they're translated, homicide is not a crime.

There are a whole variety of circumstances in which it is not a crime. When it is ordered by the state, as in war or an execution. When the police use lethal force, in a reasonable way, carrying out their duties. When it is an accident. Provided that it was not done during the commission of a crime and provided that there was no contributory negligence.

Finally, and most importantly for me, when the killing is done in self-defense or in defense of another.

Facts do not speak for themselves.

As a matter of law and as a practical matter, a district attorney speaks for the facts. He speaks to a grand jury. There are exceptions, and in some states it's different, but in our state he makes a presentation to a grand jury. The person who committed the homicide, which is at that point not yet a crime, may speak to the grand jury and present his version of the facts. The grand jury determines if the homicide is a crime.

In almost every circumstance, the grand jurors decide how the district attorney wants them to decide.

"Your case is a clear case of justifiable homicide," my attorney, Max Hernandez, said.

That was the good news, and my body automatically sighed with relief, though my mind knew there was more coming.

"Provided we accept the facts as you told them to me."

At the very beginning, which seemed like long ago, Manny had told me, "I promise you this at least. If you get charged with anything, this firm will defend you. At no cost to you. You have my word on it." I had called in his marker.

As the flames devoured the model of Paul Plowright's dream, I tracked down William Thatcher Grantham III on his cell phone. He was in the locker room at Kavanaugh Golf Club. It was true that I was no longer working for Grantham, Glume, Wattly, and Goldfarb when I shot Jerry Hobson, but I told him that I had only continued the job because I'd made a promise to Manny.

He listened until I was done. "Manny was my friend," he said.

They assigned Max Hernandez, a relatively new associate. He was a local boy who'd gone to USW, then to Columbia Law. He spent three years with the Manhattan district attorney's office because he liked criminal law. He'd come home because he liked it here better than there, then joined Grantham, Glume, Wattly, and Goldfarb because he liked money too.

While I told him the short version of what I knew, Max had taken notes. He paused thoughtfully, looking at them, then he said, "This is a pretty high-profile shooting. There's going to be pressure to bring charges. If the DA doesn't, then there will be howls of outrage, and the Christian community is a very politically important group. They're not going to want to accept that a couple of their leaders were involved in kidnapping, torture, rape, and murder, which led you to commit justifiable homicide."

"There are witnesses," I said.

"Bear with me here," Max said. "I was an ADA, just like you were a cop, so I know how prosecutors think.

"If I were prosecuting, and I wanted to put you away, here's what I would say.

"You entered into a conspiracy, with your wife and Nicole Chandler to extort money from the Cathedral of the Third Millennium and Paul Plowright in particular.

"You were short of money. I'd pull up your financials and establish that.

"You heard Paul Plowright talking about hundreds of millions of dollars. Wow, that sounded great. You wanted a piece of that.

"Maybe you did hear rumors that Plowright had sexual relationships with some of his congregation. But you didn't even have to hear it. You could have just thought it up yourself. Look what happened to Jimmy Swaggart, Jim Bakker. From millionaires to nobodies overnight. Plowright should be willing to pay a couple of hundred thousand to keep from turning into the next Ted Haggard.

"You found a girl, Nicole Chandler. She had been seduced by a lecherous, old, atheist professor over at Secular U. Under his spell, she came to hate religion and Plowright in particular. You said, Hey, we got a way for you to really get at this guy. Just say you were having sex with him. True or pretend, it doesn't matter. He'll have to pay, big time, and you can have a share.

"Then you decided to really dress it up.

"You made up a DVD that said he was having girls beat up and raped.

"The DVD was there; you were there; it's yours.

"Maybe you staged the scene with Polasky—fake blood, all of that. Maybe you really tortured him. There's a corpse, so we know he's dead. You have the DVD, so you're my number one suspect for that killing too. Why kill him? If you tortured him, the reason is obvious, and so is the arson to cover it up. If you faked it, you killed him because he had second thoughts, or you didn't want to share four ways.

"Daniel Polasky is not available as a witness. Nobody can ask him what happened. Jorge Guzman is not going to come forward and admit that it was his DVD.

"Next stop, you and your wife and Nicole break into Plowright's private offices and private apartment. Yes, you broke in. Just because employees have access to certain parts of an institution doesn't mean they can enter places they're not authorized to go. That's breaking and entering just as much as if a stranger did it.

"You bring a sack of sex toys and dirty DVDs and the torture DVD with you. Your plan is to plant the sex toys and all the rest in Plowright's apartment. Put the DVD in the player, then when he comes up from his sermon, surprise him. Here's the girl. Here's a really embarrassing collection of marital aids and pornography. Here's a video alleging physical assaults and rapes. How about a couple of hundred grand, maybe a million?

"Plowright arrives. But with a surprise: Jerry Hobson. Hobson says that you're blackmailing bastards, and he won't stand for it, pulls his gun to arrest you. He's head of security; that's his job. It's their property, their place of business. You're illegal intruders. He's certainly entitled to restrain you. If you do something threatening, he's entitled to kill you.

"You panic, or go crazy, or whatever, and you pull your gun and shoot him.

"You were there to commit another crime. That makes it felony murder. No need to prove intent. No need to prove that you went there to kill him.

"They can dress it up too. Bad blood between you and Hobson from your days on the force, when you were a corrupt cop and a drunk and he was your supervisor and tried to discipline you.

"You still have your two witnesses. One is your wife, so we discount her supporting statements.

"What about Miss Chandler?

"If I were the ADA, I'd bring her in, scare her with a particularly foul and repulsive interrogation room and whatever other tricks I usually use. Then I'd explain the law to her in regard to felony murder. If murder takes place during the commission of a crime—in this case the breaking and entering and the blackmail—then all the participants in that crime can be charged with murder. Then I would give her a choice: get charged with murder and do seven to ten, or change her story about how she had conspired with you to blackmail Plowright, and in return, she'll do eighteen months, minimum security. Or even just get probation and counseling.

"Now I have a choice.

"Do I want a show trial with lots of TV face time, or do I want you to cop a plea? A trial's always a risk. I could lose. But it's a risk for you too. You could end up with life. So maybe I decide to go with the sure thing. And I have a big bargaining chip. Your wife. If you take the plea, I let her walk. If you go to trial, so does she. You're the kind of guy who would go to prison to protect your wife, aren't you?"

68

Paul Plowright was in a coma.

A blood vessel had broken in his brain. Nobody knew if he would live or die. The longer it took for him to come out, the closer he would be to a vegetable.

All the congregation's prayers were with him, as were those of millions in his viewing audience, in addition to special prayers being led by other preachers and televangelists. If he recovered, they would all take credit for the prayers that produced the miracle. If he ended up like Terry Schiavo, they would pray some more. If he died, nobody would take that as a sign that prayers don't work.

If he woke up, and if the powers that be decided to believe my version of events, then he would be charged with a wide ranging assortment of crimes.

If he then went to trial instead of cutting a deal, holy hell would break loose.

It wasn't just about Plowright. It touched the governor, the city police, the warden at the state penitentiary, the DA's office, and the whole Christian community. And if you have police who can do things in secret, how can you ever be sure there aren't fake cops doing the same things under cover of the same secrecy? Or real cops doing the wrong things with no way to make them accountable?

"What are your goals here?" Max asked me.

"What do you mean?"

"Personally," Max said, "I was a lukewarm Catholic. Now I'm a lukewarm lapsed Catholic. But some of my friends are angry lapsed Catholics, and they cheer every time an altar boy wins a million-dollar lawsuit. Is it important to you to tell the world that they're hypocrites and criminals, that the whole thing is a big lie? Do you want to tear the temple down?"

"You don't understand," I said, frustrated, even angry. No one seemed to understand. Maybe because I didn't really understand it myself. "I was lost," I said. "Then Jesus saved me. Through Paul Plowright. It is not that I believed in him; it's that he believed in me. I was drunk when I went down that aisle. I was worthless. But not to Paul Plowright. To him, I was worth saving."

"I'm not the only one," I said. "And I'm not the last one."

"Maybe it's a lie. All of it. But . . . I don't know how to say this because . . . I guess because I don't understand it. Even though it's not true, it is true. It's false, but it saves people.

"If you take it away, what's going to replace it? Philosophy 101? Prozac?

"And that's not all. Most of the people there, they're good people. They were my friends. You think I want to tear their world down?"

"Fair enough," he said. "Do you want to make money?"

"How so?"

"Go after CTM with a civil suit?"

"I don't know."

"I saw a little glimmer of attention there. Everybody wants money."

"Not like that," I said.

"Well, put the thought in your back pocket. If you decide later, let me know. We'd be happy to handle it, no money down. We take thirty percent of the gross. I think Nicole Chandler wants to sue. Which is good for us because that'll help keep her on the side of the angels, or antiangels, or whatever we are in this one."

"Let's get through this first," I said.

"Do you have a political agenda? Want to tell the truth about corruption and for the perversion of justice to come out?"

"Max, I don't understand how this matters."

"If you did, I'd try to find someone who has it in for the governor or Plowright and offer you up as a star witness in return for immunity for everything, and you could spend several years helping them make cases.

"If you wanted to go after CTM and the whole Christian thing, we would talk about going to trial. Get you on the stand, tell your story, find Plowright's other girls, everything we could get hold of. Every day a new surprise, a new scandal. There's a chance we might not win, but you'd have the bully pulpit."

"Max," I said, "I just want to get out of this clean. I did the right thing. It was justifiable homicide, and I want the record to say so."

"Fine," he said.

He looked at his notes.

"Fine," he said again. "Here's our strategy.

"Of the seven judges this could get assigned to, three are born-again. The others are a Methodist, two Catholics, and a Jew, a devout one as it happens.

"Let's assume the jury pool is the same as the general population. That means eighty percent or more believe in God, seventy-three percent believe in miracles, seventy percent believe Jesus is the Son of God, and sixty percent believe in the Devil. A certain number of jurors will want to serve so they can act in defense of Jesus. They'll be quite happy to lie about that. They may even get coached on how to mask it because, after all, they'll be serving a higher master than the law.

"We do not want to bring your case to trial.

"We want the grand jury to no bill it.

"Which, as we have discussed, means we want the DA to want the grand jury to kick it. Which is easy, if it's what he wants. He brings it you, Gwen, and Nicole as his only witnesses. You tell it like you told it to me, clean and simple; it's clear-cut self-defense.

"We have to convince him that it does him more harm than good to bring you to trial. And that the good things he might be hoping for by putting away the man who shot someone at one of our great religious institutions, he can get somewhere else. Make Hobson the scapegoat or indict Plowright, even though he's in a coma. We'll guide him to that."

"There's one more thing," I said.

"What? I just made a terrific speech, laid out a great strategy. I have it all figured out, and you want to throw in one more thing?"

He was joking, but he wasn't joking.

"Yeah, I do," I said. "Ahmad Nazami. I made a promise to Manny. All this, it was for nothing, including his death, if I don't get Ahmad Nazami out."

69

Ahmad Nazami was still being held. The DA hadn't decided what to do yet.

Once prosecutors have somebody, they hate like hell to let go. When somebody they've convicted years before asks to go back and check the evidence for DNA, you would think, if they were neutral parties interested in justice, they'd say great, if the guy was guilty, we'll have proved it twice; if not, let's get him out and find the right person. But they don't. They fight tooth and nail to prevent the tests from taking place.

The good news was that Max agreed to pick up where Manny left off, pro bono.

He resumed Manny's demand for discovery, which had never been met. He wanted the full police crime report, all lab and ballistics work, and the confession. The confession that the defense had never seen. He wanted the name of the police officer who claimed to have taken it. He also obtained a subpoena for flight records in the area. It was information I had asked for but not received.

After three days of going over what happened, Max said, "There is one thing. Ms. Mansfield-Pellita, Teresa, that's the full name, right?"

"Yeah."

"Have you seen her since?"

"No."

"Spoken with her?"

"No. She called me a couple of times. But I haven't gotten back to her."

"I don't want to be insulting. I think you've been pretty straight with me. In fact, you're kind of a hero to me, but the only thing that doesn't quite ring true is the description of your relationship."

"What do you mean?"

"What do I mean? I mean if you want to maintain that you were never intimate with her, I'll respect that. But from what you say, she's very intense and acts on her emotions. So, my advice is that you get back to her. Talk to her. Make sure you're both on the same page. You know what I mean? That she doesn't feel scorned or abused. I don't mean go have an affair with her. I mean find a nice public place and have a nice quiet talk. Don't suborn perjury—you know I'm opposed to that—but make sure she's not going to make you look like a liar."

70

I spent as much time with Angie as I could. I wanted her to understand. Most communication between a parent and child, in my experience, is about giving orders, then checking up to make sure they're being followed. To do that, parents keep up a front about an orderly world of authority figures and followers. Certainly, in my own case, I had never spent much time telling my daughter my troubles, my thoughts, my doubts.

Now I did. Perhaps because I had wandered from the geometric city of answers into the wilderness of questions. Most of us do end up, at least for a time, in a place where the roads run out and the signs that post the standard directions point the wrong way. She needed to have some idea of how to navigate if she ever found herself there.

Nicole Chandler was a mess.

Sometimes she was withdrawn and completely noncommunicative. Other times she was almost manic. She was dead set on suing, both to get revenge and to make millions and millions of dollars.

Max got her into therapy. It was going to look good for her law suit, but I don't know if it helped. She was calling me all the time. Often in the middle of night, to talk, for company, to soothe and reassure her. The night she'd let me lead her out of Plowright' apartment, she assigned me a role in her mind, and sex was her way of making certain that I would be the person she needed me to be. So, along with all the fear and neediness, or because of it, she was flirty and seductive.

Gwen picked up on it, and it upset her.

Even though Max was urging me to be attentive to Nicole because I seemed to be the only one who could calm her down, and she needed to be in control of herself both for my case and her own lawsuit, I put Gwen first and stopped taking her calls.

Nicole stood that for one day, then swallowed half a bottle of the pills that the therapist had prescribed for her, phoned me again, and announced on the answering machine what she'd done. I called EMS, then rushed to the ER to make sure she was still alive.

It was very manipulative. By responding, I was enabling her. I understood all that. But testimony from a live witness who has been enabled is more convincing than the silence of one who's been tough-loved to death.

Holding her hand was a short-term solution for other people's immediate goals, mine and Max's. Nicole had been betrayed and abused. She blamed herself and Plowright and almost anyone else who came into her mind. Anger, pain, desperation, and sex are a bad combination. She was a danger to herself and others. Mostly to herself. Would she find salvation in time? Through therapy, a support group, medication?

She certainly couldn't turn to Jesus anymore.

Max met with District Attorney Roy Lathrop over drinks at the Cattleman's House.

Lathrop had been in office for ten years, two and a half terms.

They started out with some small talk. The chances of USW's basketball team, the Gila Monsters. Max had played for the Monsters, second string, but he'd played. They weren't all that good then, and, they agreed, they weren't much better now. Who they knew in common. Some local politics. Some national politics, which normally

Max would have stayed away from, but he wanted to tsk-tsk over the spectacle of the U.S. attorney general's having to say, over and over, that he didn't know what was going on in his own department.

Roy said, "Let's cut to the chase. What do you want here? You want a plea? Or what?"

"Since you ask, I want the grand jury to no bill my client."

"I can't . . ."

"Come on, Roy. Three solid witnesses say it was justifiable homicide. And there's nobody to say different. Whoever's presenting would have to work pretty damn hard to overcome that."

Roy nodded, not necessarily agreeing but certainly agreeing to consider it.

"And I want Ahmad Nazami out."

"That's not going to happen in a hurry," Roy said.

"He didn't do it. Plowright and Hobson did it."

"We have a confession," Lathrop said. "People don't confess to something they didn't do. Especially murder."

"They do if they've been tortured. Here are my case notes," Max said, sliding a file across the table. "You can make a case against Plowright and Hobson, and you can make it fairly easily because they did it. If you go to trial with Nazami—and he will not plead, you have my word on that—you will embarrass everybody. This one is bad, and it's out of control. Take a look. See for yourself."

Lathrop opened the file and began to glance through it.

"Roy, we are not out to embarrass anyone," Max said. "Mistakes get made. We're all human. You shouldn't be held responsible for some error one of your assistants made. Like putting evidence that some city cop fixed up in front of a grand jury. Or waltzing into court with a fake U.S. attorney. You don't want to be put in the position where you have to say you weren't even aware of what they were doing."

"Don't try to push me around, Hernandez. I'll make your life hell in this town if you mess with me."

"I'm not trying to push you around. I'm truly not. I'm showing you the facts, which maybe your subordinates have kept from you

I'm trying to put you in a position where you have control over what happens."

"I'll take a look at it."

"That's all I ask," Max said. "And once you do, I expect you'll see it the same way we do. There are a lot of risks here, but there's a lot of potential too. I really am not trying to push you around. One thing I was at USW, I was a team player. Still am."

The next day, around two in the afternoon, Lathrop called Max. He said, "You're on."

71

I called Teresa and invited her to see me at my office two days before the grand jury hearing.

I have a room in an office suite in one of the older places downtown near the courthouse. Just like Dante Mulvaney.

I rent from a small father-and-son law firm that occupies the rest. I have the use of their secretary at no charge for incidentals like sorting the mail or showing someone in, but I pay her by the hour if she does something more substantial.

The secretary, a pleasant woman named Karen, buzzed me and then sent my visitor in.

Teresa closed the door behind her and stood there, both bright eyed and awkward, holding some papers in her hand. I got up. Both of us were standing there. After a long pause, each of us trying to figure out where to begin, let alone where to end, she blurted out, "I just came to tell you, I got an e-mail from a publisher. That's what I called to tell you. He has Nathaniel's manuscript."

"That's great," I said.

"He's actually had it for about a month," she said. "Kind of ironic."

"I guess it is."

"He really likes it. He wants to publish it."

"Even better. Would you like to sit down?"

"No. I just came to . . . the publisher, he's so excited about it, he sent me a mock-up of a cover and a few pages . . . to show you, if you want to see them."

I walked around the desk toward her. It was all there between us, and no matter what, the closer I got, the more electric it felt. She offered the papers, it seemed, just as something to do.

I took them.

"I can just leave them with you . . . computers . . . I can make . . ."

"Let me look," I said, shuffling through the pages, then reading.

The Book of Nathaniel

Introduction

This is a book about the mysteries.

Many of them have been with us for a long time, for at least the length of human memory. What is truth? Is there a God? If there isn't, why do we believe? What is reality, and what is illusion? What are good and evil, morality and ethics, and where do they come from?

And more recently, what is science? What is art? What is emotion? How do our minds actually work? How do we deal with such unsettling new ideas as relativity and uncertainty?

In 1609, everybody knew, and everyone could see, that the Earth was at the center of the world.

Above it there was a series of transparent crystal shells. One held the sun, another the moon, still others the planets. The final one was hung with stars. Each of them was a perfect sphere.

They revolved around the Earth. And they were moved around by angels.

Then Galileo picked up a tool that had recently come into being, the telescope.

He looked up. The mountains of the moon, the spots on the sun, the moons of Jupiter, and the vastness of space between the stars all appeared. The angels did not. Nor did heaven.

It only made sense if the heresy of Copernicus was correct, that the Earth moved around the sun.

It is time to turn the telescope around.

To look at ourselves. The tools to do so are available. They are closer at hand than that early telescope was in the seventeenth century. We only have to pick them up and use them.

When we do so, the mysteries will dissolve.

"We used to argue," she said. "Well, you know that. About doing academic philosophy. That's what they want, I said, because I was concerned for his career. But the publisher really likes it. He compared it to Eric Hoffer."

I looked at her blankly.

"He was . . . oh, never mind. Anyway, they want to publish it. I'll send you one of the first copies."

Actually, I was interested. But I still had a lot of anger in me. About how she—and her husband, from the grave—had messed around with my mind. So, in spite of the fact that the reason to meet with her was to make sure the waters were smooth, I said, with an edge in my voice, "See that? Everyone's prayers get answered."

Her expression showed that she'd taken it as the slap I'd meant it to be. "I'm sorry," I said, instantly apologizing, not just for that, but for all of it. "I am sorry."

"No, no," she said, "I'm the one who should . . . "

"I didn't mean it. I want to see the book."

"Do you?"

"Yeah, maybe there are some answers in it."

"I hope you find what you're looking for," she said.

"You too," I said, meaning it.

"I better go now," she said. "I have a class."

"Teresa . . . "

"Shhh," she said, soft smile and sad eyes. Then she said, "I'll mail you your copy," her eyes becoming mischievous and her smile too, "to the office, not your home."

I held the door open for her as she left.

As she walked out, Gwen came in the front door of the suite. A surprise visit. They walked past each other with polite smiles.

But I watched my wife's eyes. She could have been a cop on foot down in Wolvern on a Saturday night who'd spotted a Mex with prison tats and she gave Teresa the once-over, exactly to see what weapons she had concealed beneath her clothes.

When Gwen reached me, she asked, "Who was that woman?" But it was not a question at all. Not at all.

72

The next day, when I came home from the last rehearsal of my testimony with Max, Gwen was waiting in the living room.

"I've prayed and prayed over this," she said intensely. "Can you come back to Jesus, Carl?"

I sighed. "Do you want me to lie to you?"

"You can lie to me. I believe you have lied to me. Over and over. But that doesn't matter. You can't lie to Him. He sees what's in your heart."

"You believe," I said, "and that's fine with me. I don't, and maybe, I don't know, maybe someday I'll see the light again, but I can't now. I love you, Gwen. I respect what you believe. I'm not going to fight it. I want to reach across it."

"I have prayed for you, Carl," full of fervor for her faith but cold as ice for me. "I really, truly have, but you have to open your heart."

"And close my mind?" I snapped back at her. "Shut off my mind? It's not all heart, not all soul. We have minds too."

"He wants you back. He really does."

Her righteousness made me furious, but I pressed my anger down. "I understand," I said as carefully as I could, breathing slowly, "but it's not something I can do."

"When I testify tomorrow, I'm going to tell the truth," she announced. "I've prayed over it. And He says tell the truth, even if it is about your husband."

"What do you mean? What are you talking about?"

"I'm going to say that we were in no danger at all. That we were in His hands, that He would have protected us."

"Maybe His way of protecting us, protecting you," I barked, "was having a husband who was there to kill the son of a bitch."

"Those things about Paul," she said, deaf to me, shaking her head against my reality, "perhaps he had fallen into sin when that Jezebel seduced him. But Pastor Paul Plowright is a man of God. When he awakes from his sleep, he needs to come back to his church and continue God's work. He will humble himself and apologize and ask God's forgiveness. He doesn't need ours, only His. Then he can continue his good work, His work." Her eyes shone with stubborn certainty.

"What about Hobson and his thugs, intimidating other women and raping them?"

"That's slander and lies, Carl. Can't you see that? Who told us about that? Gangsters. A Mexican gangster with a fake video who was trying to blackmail good people. We can't fall for that."

"This is crazy," I cried out, watching my world fall out from under my feet.

"No, it's you who've gone crazy," she said, announcing her accusations, one by one. "You were seduced by that woman. Not just into sex and the sin of adultery but away from God. You went crazy and became obsessed. You went mad, Carl, but you can come back. Join me now. Pray with me. Accept Him back into your heart. Save yourself."

"Do you understand what will happen if you tell the grand jury that it wasn't self-defense, that it wasn't in defense of you and Nicole?"

"That's in God's hands," she said, absolving herself in advance of anything that might ensue. "You've sinned against the Commandments. Adultery, killing, bearing false witness—"

"Didn't you hear Jerry Hobson saying he was going to kill Nicole? He said that right in front of you."

"He said he was going to get rid of a problem," she said, easily dismissing it. "That only meant send her away. Paul Plowright and Jerry Hobson are good people. They could not have done bad things."

"Gwen, think about this."

"I have prayed about it. I have His answers. I must give His testimony."

Here I sit, in the hallway, outside the room where the grand jury is meeting.

There are bailiffs here. There are two lights, a green one and a red one. If the green one comes on, I'm free. Free to get up and go wherever my feet want to take me. If the red one comes on, it means that the grand jury has decided that there is probable cause to charge me with a crime, probably felony murder or murder two. Then the bailiffs will hold me and wait a few moments until someone comes out and informs me of the charge on which I'm being arrested.

The DA didn't renege on his deal with Max. He just shrugged. With Jorge Guzman missing, probably somewhere in Mexico, and Plowright in a coma, there were three witnesses to the shooting. He'd put all three on, and let the grand jury decide what the grand jury wanted to decide.

I was, of course, not present to hear either Nicole's testimony or Gwen's.

Max had gone over Nicole's testimony with her, and we both presumed she remained solid and that her testimony supported mine.

I also presume that Gwen told the grand jury exactly what she told me she intended to tell them.

At least I knew what she was going to do. I was able to explain that even if my wife thought she was in God's hands and that His invisible shield protected her—and all of us—I had not been able to see that shield. I had no way to sense or otherwise perceive His protecting presence, and therefore I did what seemed sensible when an armed man was pointing his gun at me and at two unarmed women.

Here I sit, in the hallway.

Grand jury decisions only require a simple majority. In our state, the grand jury is usually made up of seventeen people. It doesn't have to be, it can be as few as thirteen or as many as twenty-three. The law only requires an odd number to avoid tie votes.

Today's magic number is nine. Nine out of seventeen to vote to indict or not to indict me.

We don't know, but the demographics suggest that thirteen or fourteen of the grand jurors are Christians, a category that includes Catholics and all Protestant denominations. Twelve or thirteen believe in miracles. Ten believe in the devil.

Gwen's testimony, however else she sees things, includes certain facts. Hobson had a gun. I had a gun. She, Nicole, and Plowright were unarmed. Even if she chooses not to credit it, we had, all of us, heard someone say, on video, that Hobson employed people who raped, tortured, and physically intimidated people. And that he intended to do at least something about Nicole.

It comes down to this. Will at least nine people think I should have stayed my actions because Gwen had informed us that we were safe, under His protection?

Or will at least nine people think that I was right to act on the facts as they appeared to me in this earthly, strictly secular reality? That whatever God thinks or wants, it's still up to us, each of us, to figure things out for ourselves.

That should be a simple question, right?

Lawyers are not permitted in the grand jury room. Max is sitting on the bench with me, to my right.

Then Manny sits down on my left. We look at each other. It bothers me that I still haven't gotten Ahmad Nazami out. "The good news," I say, to tell him something, "is I got the report from the lab this morning. The prints from that vial of pills are a match for the ones I got from MacLeod's computer. Plowright was there."

"You already told me that," Max says.

"You do good work," Manny says.

"I don't know what's gonna happen here," I say. "Do you?"

"It's gonna work out," Max says.

But he doesn't really know. None of us can know what's coming up around the next corner. So I look to Manny. If he isn't just a figment of my imagination, maybe he can access that kind of information.

"What that grand jury does in there," Manny says, "that's about them. Not about you."

"Yeah, right," I say.

"What? If they indict you, will that make you think you did the wrong thing?" Manny asks.

"No," I say.

Max says, "Take it easy. Relax."

I stand up to ease the tension and walk down the hall to stretch my legs. Max lets me go. Manny comes with me.

"We will get Ahmad out," I say to him.

"I know."

"He's pretty damn lucky to have had you, and now Max," I say.

"And you," Manny says. "How are you holding up?"

"Tell you the truth, not so good. Gwen and I aren't going to make it. That can't be good for Angie, so I screwed that up too. Here I am, wondering if I'm going to get indicted, then face a trial. We've been through a lot of trials together, you and I, and we do our professional thing and pretend that the client is just a client, a thing, someone in a role, but we know the kind of hell that puts you through. Worse if you're innocent."

I remember that to anyone else it will appear as if I am talking to myself. I look around to see if anyone is watching. We are down at the east end of the corridor, over by the stairs that go down to the holding cells. There is no one immediately nearby. Then I look down the long, long hall, with its high vaulted ceiling, shining marble walls, and bronze busts of heroes of the state and of justice set in niches in the walls. It seems to go forever. The old-time chandeliers no longer work, waiting for some time in the future when the legislature might vote the funds for renovation. In search of a discount solution, someone installed mercury vapor lamps. They produce a light that is jagged rather than smooth across the color spectrum, with phosphorescence and strange sodium yellows. Now it seems to shimmer and even shake.

I feel hot, then chilled, and I break out into a cold sweat. The floor seems to be crumbling in the distance, more and more of it falling away, the collapse moving slowly toward me. There is no sound. I know it is a hallucination of some kind. I don't doubt that. But I can't stop it either. There are figures down there, in the rubble. I can't make out their faces. Most of them are going about their own business, but some look up at us. The bronze busts seem to lean inward, as if they are trying to come alive and escape from the places where they've been fixed in time.

Stress. Exhaustion. Fear. It's all catching up with me. I've lost everything that I thought made order and meaning out of my life, and now I am watching the physical world crumble around me as well. I am staring into the abyss. I am seeing the chaos that's right out there, beneath and around everything. More figures are gathering down in the hole where the floor used to be, the legions of the lost and the mad. I feel dizzy. I am terrified that I'm losing my mind and think I might faint or fall to my knees in tears.

Then Manny puts his hand on my shoulder, like he used to do sometimes. I feel the weight and the warmth of it, just as if he were real. And it steadies me.

He stands there beside me, a figure from a distant legend told by Herodotus, the ghost of a comrade who's fallen in the battle that still clashes around me. The two of us together, standing at the edge of the abyss. As every one of us does.

We stand straight, eyes forward. We are fighting to hold back the chaos. To do it, we've brought what weapons we could, those special human ones, rationality, justice, a knowledge of right and wrong. Even those things that might be called vanities, a craving for honor and glory. He lets me know, wordlessly, through his presence and posture and the testimony of his life, that whether or not this particular battle is lost or won, there will be others, for the chaos always remains, and no matter how many battles we might win, the last one remains, the one in which we die. His steady hand and his set face tell me what he's come to say, that I must not despair in the face of it or accept false tales to deny it. I must know it and continue nonetheless because that is our glory. And our true salvation.

NOTE TO THE READER

Much of the material for the law-enforcement Bible study group depicted here is taken from "When a Christian Takes a Life" at biblestudysite.com.

One paragraph of Paul Plowright's speech on dominion is actually a quote from D. James Kennedy, pastor of Coral Ridge Ministries.

The article Plowright cites from the *Kuwait Times* appeared on July 21, 2007, written by Dr. Sami Alrabaa. It was about the curriculum in schools funded by Saudi Arabia. Though Plowright's dialog greatly condenses the article, it is accurate to the spirit of the original.

The poll Plowright refers to from ChristiaNet about addiction to pornography among Christians also exists. It's not particularly scientific; nor does it make comparisons with non-Christians. But it unquestionably refers to a pervasive reality.

The idea of taking a public university's endowment private and then shrouding its operations in secrecy, the managers free to do whatever they want with the money, is based on a real event at the University of Texas in 1996 when George W. Bush was governor of the state.

Their endowment was $16.5 billion.

Bush created UTIMCO (University of Texas Investment Management Company) and gave it to Thomas Hicks to run. The relationship was extremely lucrative for both of them.

Some years earlier, Bush had organized a group to buy the Texas Rangers baseball team. The same year that Hicks got hold of UTIMCO's billions, he bought the Rangers. Bush's original investment was $600,000. His share of the sale to Hicks was $13 million.

Hicks went on to become a "Pioneer," a big Bush fund-raiser, and was vice chairman of Clear Channel Communications, the largest owner of radio stations in the country and a big supporter of the Republican Right and George W. Bush in particular.

The point, in terms of the novel, is that the fictional scheme is not only plausible but has been done.

Would it be done with a religious group?

Of course. That's what "faith-based initiatives" do. They take money that used to go to secular organizations and give it to Christian organizations, thereby rewarding the people who put the administration in office and sustaining them so they will be able to help in future elections.

Some people think that's a great idea. Others do not.

Fiction makes its own demands.

Even a novel of ideas should only go on about those ideas long enough to show how they motivate the characters and generate the action.

Some readers may want less. Presumably they skim.

Other readers may want more, more detail, more explanation more support and justification.

When it comes to religion, I have found that almost everyone ha their own ideas, and many people want to express them.

We are fortunate to live in a time when the final page is not th end, and the dialogue can continue.

Readers who want more or who would like to share are invited t visit larrybeinhart.com

The website features a series of essays, the things that Professor MacLeod would have said had he been real and the things he would have written in *The Book of Nathaniel* had it been published. The site also includes a forum for an ongoing dialogue about religion, irreligion, faith, belief, and their intersections with politics, war, money, life, and death.

There are also videos, interviews, and reviews on the site.

Readers may e-mail the author at beinhart@larrybeinhart.com.

√9/0